BTU Alumni #4

PUCK PERFORMANCE

BTU Alumni Series Book #4

ALLEY CIZ

HOUSE OF CRAZY
PUBLISHING

Also by Alley Ciz

BTU Alumni Series

Power Play (Jake and Jordan)

Musical Mayhem (Sammy and Jamie) BTU Novella

Tap Out (Gage and Rocky)

Sweet Victory (Vince and Holly)

Puck Performance (Jase and Melody)

Writing Dirty (Maddey and Dex)

Scoring Beauty- BTU6 Preorder, Releasing September 2021

#UofJ Series

Cut Above The Rest (Prequel)- Freebie

Looking To Score

Game Changer

Playing For Keeps

Off The Bench- #UofJ4 Preorder, Releasing December 2021

The Royalty Crew (A #UofJ Spin-Off)

Savage Queen- Preorder, Releasing April 2021

Ruthless Noble- Preorder, Releasing June 2021

All's fair in love and potatoes

Melody Brightly
Broadway Star.
Pink hair.
A smile that hits me harder than a slap shot.
Terrible taste in hockey teams.
Full of secrets.
The one woman I fail to defend my heart against

Jase Donnelly
Defenseman.
Charming.
Sexy as puck.
Makes my hormones give a standing ovation.
The one guy I can never be with, but can't stay away from.

Our sexy as puck hero may have helped name The Coven but he's about to meet his match in PUCK PERFORMANCE—BTU Alumni #4. He might exaggerate so much he'll end up in the sin bin and there's a chance she'll burst into song, but they'll have you laughing and speaking in shouty capitals. No potatoes were harmed in this HEA-guaranteed interconnected stand-alone.

Puck Performance (BTU Alumni, Book 4)

Alley Ciz

Paperback ISBN: 978-1-950884-07-0

Ebook ISBN: 978-1-950884-06-3

Cover Designer: Julia Cabrera at Jersey Girl Designs

Editing: Jessica Snyder Edits, C. Marie

Proofreading: Gem's Precise Proofreads; Dawn Black

❀ Created with Vellum

For Sean Hanna,
You were one of my favorite people to watch on stage. I miss you
everyday.

Author Note

Dear Reader,
Puck Performance can be read as a stand-alone but it is
interconnected in the BTU Alumni world. You do not need to read
Power Play, Tap Out, or Sweet Victory *first but they might help*
you keep track of the crazy cast of characters as large as The Coven
and their guys.

For those of you coming into Puck Performance AKA BTU4 from
the BTU Alumni world, this book starts off at the same time as
Sweet Victory.

Either way I hope you enjoy Jase and Melody's story.
Crank up the show tunes and jump on in.
XOXO
Alley

Text Handles

Melody: BROADWAY BABY
 Zoey: DANCING QUEEN
 Ella: FIDDLER ON THE ROOF

The Coven
 Rocky: ALPHABET SOUP
 Jordan: MOTHER OF DRAGONS
 Skye: MAKES BOYS CRY
 Maddey: QUEEN OF SMUT
 Becky: YOU KNOW YOU WANNA
 Gemma: PROTEIN PRINCESS
 Beth: THE OG PITA
 Holly: SANTA'S COOKIE SUPPLIER

The Boys
 Jase: THE BIG HAMMER
 Cali: HOLLYWOOD
 Vince: DAUNTLESS SUPERMAN
 Lyle: MR. FABULOUS
 Jake: THE BRICK WALL
 Deck: BIG DECK

Ryan: CAPTAIN AMERICA
Nick: THE BOONDOCK SAINT
Damon: THE GREEN MONSTER
Justin: THE SEAL DEAL
Gage: THE KRAKEN
Wyatt: HUGE HOSE
Griff: THE FEROCIOUS TEDDY BEAR
Ray: JUST RAY
Tuck: WANNA TUCK
Jamie: ROCKSTAR MAN
Sammy: THE SPIN DOCTOR

IG Handles

Jase: EnforcedByJaseDonnelly13
Nate Bishop: BadAssBishop13
Jordan: TheMrsDonovan

Donnelly

| Ruth | Robert | | --sister-- | Eileen (aunt) |

Robert
|
Ryan | Jane (T) | Jordan (T) | Sean
Dog- Navy

Donovan

Jake Sr | Sarah
|
Jake | Carlee

McClain

Jack | Babs
|
Justin | Tyler | Connor | Maddey
Dog- Trident

Reese

Tracy
|
Becky

Samson

Lyle | Kyle

Hawke

Jamie | Sammy

Steele

Vicki | Vic | --brother-- | Mick | Hope
|
Vince | Rocky
Gemma

James

Gage | --cousin-- | Wyatt | Beth
|
baby

Storm

Peggy
|
Dex

Donovan/Donnelly

Jake | Jordan
|
Lacey (IT) | Lucy (IT) | Pregnant with baby Logan
Dog- Navy | Black Lab
Dog- Stanley Chocolate Lab

Roommates

Melody Brightly
Zoey
Ella

Fighters at The Steele Maker

Deck (Declan) Avery
Ray
Griff
Nick
Damon

Other Covenettes

Skye Masters
Holly Vanderbuilt

NY Storm Players

Chris 'Cali' Callahan
Chris Harrison
Edvin Ringquist

Other Hockey Players

Tucker Hayes- Chicago Fire
Chance Jenson- NJ Blizzards
Wade Tanner- LA Lions
Nate Bishop- Boston Bruisers
Anthony Fallon- Boston Bruisers/NY Storm

James/Steele

Gage | Rocky
|
Pregnant with baby Ronnie

Playlist

*

Gypsy: Rose's Turn
Lauren Hill: Doo Wop (That Thing)
Glee Cast: Broadway Baby
The Lonely Island: Dick In A Box
Mama Mia!: Mama Mia
Wicked: Defying Gravity
Hairspray: I Can Hear The Bells
Hamilton: The Reynolds Pamphlet
Gene Kelly: Singing' In The Rain
Rent: Light My Candle
Cinderella: In My Own Little Corner
One Direction: If I Could Fly
Wicked: No One Mourns The Wicked
Chicago: Razzle Dazzle
Spring Awakening: Totally Fucked
Hamilton: Say No To This
Chicago: When You're Good To Mama
Rent: Out Tonight
Hamilton: Satisfied
Billy Joel: Piano Man

SMASH Cast: That's Life
Queen: Bohemian Rhapsody
Christina Aguilera: Beautiful
Chicago: Cell Block Tango
Hairspray: You Can't Stop The Beat
West Side Story: The Rumble
Grease: Hopelessly Devoted To You
Hamilton: Ten Duel Commandments
Hailee Steinfeld: Love Myself
Beyonce: Best Thing I Never Had
Hamilton: My Shot
SMASH Cast: Let Me Be Your Star
Christina Aguilera: You Lost Me
SMASH Cast: Don't Forget Me
The Star Spangled Banner
The Sound of Music: I Have Confidence
Hairspray: Without Love
Queen: We Are The Champions
Available on Spotify

Prologue

Jase

Mid-November

The smell of the ice.

The scrape of skates.

The roar of eighteen thousand fans pushes at my back as I dig past the burn in my thighs and chase the puck into the corner, slamming my body against Fallon, a winger from Boston, for possession. With two periods of hockey almost over and the score still tied at zero, neither team wants to be the first to give up a goal. I'll be a monkey's uncle if it's us.

I hate losing. Sure, it's part of the game, but no athlete worth their salt *likes* to lose. On top of that, when we play Boston, it's my personal mission to make sure we end up with the higher number on the scoreboard at the end of the night.

I angle my body down, my shoulder digging into Fallon's armpit as our sticks slap for control of the vulcanized rubber.

Bam!

I'm slammed into the boards.

"Fuck you, Donnelly." Nate Bishop, my counterpart on the Bruisers, rams me again.

Rotating the carbon fiber stick in my gloves, I shift the blade nose down, hooking over the edge of the puck, and send it flying back to where Chris Callahan is waiting for my pass like I knew he would be.

With a final shove, I free myself from Fallon and Bishop, shooting a *fuck you right back* look at the latter, and haul ass down the ice to help create a scoring opportunity before the buzzer sounds.

Except for the goalies, the other ten of us on the ice are playing like we're back in Mighty Mite days. The electronic sound of the buzzer fills the Garden, calling an end to the second period without either team putting the biscuit in the basket.

My lungs heave and my legs feel like overcooked fettuccine—my boy Vince doesn't let us use that skinny-ass spaghetti in reference to our big man muscles—as my two dozen teammates and I trek across the rubber-matted floor to the locker room. We have seventeen minutes to regroup and shore up our energy reserves for the last twenty minutes of regulation play.

We may only be a month and a half into the season, but rivalry games have a way of making it feel like Game 7 of the Stanley Cup.

And yes, I know the New Jersey Blizzards are *technically* our rival, but beating the Boston Bruisers is a personal endeavor.

Fucking Nate Bishop!

"You good, man?" Callahan asks when I chuck my helmet into my locker.

"Yeah, Cali." I inhale deeply in an effort to rein in my emotions.

"Bishop?" There's zero judgment in his tone, only understanding.

"Bishop." I nod.

My archenemy, the Joker to my Batman, the Lex Luther to my Superman—and dammit, this is what happens when I spend too much time with Vince.

Bishop may be a top defender in the league, but I *detest* the guy. There are very few people I don't like in this world.

Actually…there are only two on my shit list: Tommy Bradford, my twin sister's violent douchecanoe of an ex-boyfriend, and UFC fighter Curtis 'The Cutter' Cutler, but that's a story for another time.

The important thing is, both asshats are extreme cases of douchebaggery. So how, you might ask, did Nate Bishop get himself added to the list of world's biggest twat waffles? The answer is long and complicated, but the CliffsNotes version is he crossed a line.

Hell, he didn't just cross it—he skated past it like he was running blue line drills.

And, shit, thinking of Bastard Bishop has me more tense than the suspension cables holding up the Brooklyn Bridge.

I pull my jersey and chest protector over my head, sending them the same way as my helmet, and reach inside my locker for my phone. Only the comic relief my people can provide will be enough to rid me of my negative thoughts.

DAUNTLESS SUPERMAN (Vince): Bro, looking a little slow out there. Did you not eat your Wheaties this morning? Gotta up your nutrition game.

THE BIG HAMMER (Me): Careful, Creed. I'll tell Gem you're insulting her food.

DAUNTLESS SUPERMAN: Shiiiiit. Don't do that, man. The Coven already owns my ass since I'm in training camp. I DO NOT need anything else to set them off.

I snort at the ridiculous but accurate statement from my best friend. The two of us came up with the nickname for our sisters and their closest female friends back in our BTU days. Even all these years after we graduated, the name still fits them to a T.

I swear, there aren't enough fingers and toes in this locker room to count the number of times I've let those ladies tell me what to do.

Speaking of the Covenettes, Vince wasn't the only one to text me.

MOTHER OF DRAGONS: Listen, I love you and all, and some days I even consider you my favorite brother, but could you maybe spend a little less time in the sin bin and a little more time out on the ice? I don't know if you know this or not, but you are one of the top scoring defensemen in the NHL. That said, you CAN'T light the lamp if you're sitting in timeout like your nieces. Now stop trying to LITERALLY kick some Bruiser ass and go win the game. Please and thank you.

I laugh out loud, causing the teammates near me to turn my way.

"Jordan?" Cali asks, well versed in the stuff my twin texts me during games.

"You know it."

THE BIG HAMMER: *GIF of Anna Kendrick saluting*

MOTHER OF DRAGONS: Idiot. Love you anyway though.

THE BIG HAMMER: Love you too, wombmate

MOTHER OF DRAGONS: *kissy face emoji* *fist emoji*

THE BIG HAMMER: *fist emoji*

She's done this all our lives, sensing when I'm spiraling—because yes the two of us share ESP and yes it is real and we love that it drives our older brother Ryan nuts—and knowing exactly what to say to reset me.

I screenshot our exchange and pull up my Instagram.

screenshot of text exchange with Jordan
EnforcedByJaseDonnelly13 Pep talks from your other half are the best. I'm coming for you @BadAssBishop13 #TheBestDefenseman #NYStorm #GoStorm #WeatherWarning #AStormIsBrewing #TakeNotes

I'm ready.
Ten minutes until the start of the third.
Let's do this.

♡

Melody

I sip my beer—probably not the best idea to be on my third of the night—as the sold-out crowd waits for the NY Storm and the Boston Bruisers to take the ice for the third period.

The beer—plus all the screaming I've been doing—will not have my throat thanking me when I have to perform tomorrow, but I *need* it if I'm going to survive this nail-biter of a game.

I'll probably have to go on vocal rest to have a voice for both my shows, but it's totally worth it. Other than getting to live my dream of singing and dancing across the Broadway stage, hockey is the thing I'm most passionate about, although I don't get to take in as many games as I would like.

Aside from Mondays when my current show is dark, most

of my evenings are booked. Performing eight shows a week leaves very little down time, but you won't hear a complaint from me. Broadway has been my dream since kindergarten, and I am blessed to be able to live it.

Tonight, instead of donning the waitress uniform of my character, I'm rocking the black and gold of my Bruisers jersey. Unlike my two Storm fan best friends, Ella and Zoey, I'm one of only a small cluster of people repping the colors of the home team's rival.

Thank god for my *ah-may-zing* agent and the stipulation she worked into my contract for me to have the night off whenever the Bruisers are in town.

Music booms through the arena, and both teams make their way out of the tunnels and onto the ice for warm-ups.

"Gah! He's just so damn dreamy," Ella gushes as Jase Donnelly shares a knuckle bump through the glass with two guys in front of us.

"He really is," Zoey agrees. "He's like a long-lost Hemsworth brother with that blond hair and chiseled jaw."

These two have not stopped drooling over hockey hunks all night. With our seats only a dozen rows from the ice, we are set up for prime viewing.

"Why's he knuckle-bumping Boston fans, though?" Ella asks when she notices they are also sporting black and gold jerseys.

"I think those are his old college teammates," I say without thinking.

"Oh *reeeaaallly*?" Zoey drags out the word in a sing-song tone.

Shit.

"*Somebody* knows more about the New York defenseman than they let on." Ella gives me a knowing look.

I take another deep swallow of beer, ignoring *both* sets of eyes turned my way. They may be the best friends a person could ask for, but a girl is entitled to her secrets.

Chapter One

O*ne week later*

The biggest perk of playing for a team only a short train ride away from where I grew up is how easily my people can come out to support me—though supportive might not *necessarily* be the right word to describe how my friends are when they come to my games.

As a proud Jersey boy, both my family and I have been rooted in the NJ Blizzards fandom for years. Combine that with the fact that both my brother Ryan and my brother-in-law Jake play for the team, and let's just say Mom is the only one I can count on to cheer me on without giving me shit.

Even JD—my sister, my biggest supporter, my *best*-best friend, my wombmate, my other half—is the biggest shit-talker. She may not be here at the moment, but each Covenette is like a pseudo-sister, and they are more than happy to pick up the slack.

"No way. That goal in the second was a gimme. Sean could have scored on Tampa's goalie he was so out of position, and he's nine," says Becky, resident ballbuster and troublemaker of the Covenettes, referencing my second goal from tonight.

"Bull." Griff comes to my defense. "The *only* reason he was out of position was because Jase's deke was a thing of beauty."

It really is a shame that in a group as large as ours, Griff is the only one who grew up a fan of the Storm. Most people wouldn't argue with a guy of his size—though in fact he's really a cuddly teddy bear—but The Coven is filled with women with bigger balls than us men.

"Of *course* you'd say that. You practically bleed gray and black for the Storm," says Skye, JD's oldest friend and subsequently mine.

"This is true, but it doesn't negate the fact that what I'm saying is true."

I finish off the last of my beer as I listen to my friends debate the merit of my on-ice performance. Most players only have the talking heads to critique their game, but *nooo*, my family puts the experts on SportsCenter to shame—and unlike the analysts on television, I can't turn them off.

"You know the phrase, 'With friends like you, who needs enemies?'" Cali drops down next to me in the booth, jerking his chin toward my *loved* ones.

"Nah man." I smile, turning my attention to my teammate. "It's all done with love."

"If I didn't *know* them, I think I would start to question if you'd taken one too many hits out on the ice." As my closest friend on the team, he has first-hand Covenette knowledge.

"Somebody has to make sure this one's head doesn't get too big without Jordan here." Skye pats my cheek a little harder than needed. She's been busting my balls since kindergarten.

My buddy and old college teammate, Nick, snorts his beer through his nose. "Yeah." He wipes away the last of the residue with the back of his hand. "Like you *all* aren't experts at that job."

This type of back-and-forth can go on for hours, days, *years*. Ain't nobody got time for that.

"Well…as *much* fun as this has been"—I nudge Cali to let me out of the booth—"I'm going to get myself another drink."

I make my way through the crush of people filling the team's preferred bar—aptly named The Sin Bin—in pursuit of another beer. The space may be full, but the beer is cold, the food is hot, and we can usually catch whatever game is still happening on the west coast.

"Freddie, my man." I reach across the oak bar to shake hands with the owner.

"Jase! What can I get my favorite D-man?"

There's no way to resist returning the smile peeking out from beneath Freddie's Santa-Clause-esque beard. I swear the guy's eyes even twinkle the way the man in red is known for, always so damn happy.

"I'll take another Stella please." I place my empty bottle on the bar.

I don't indulge much during the season, but one, it's early, and two, tomorrow is one of my rare days off. I'll sleep in then hit the gym later on.

"You got it." Freddie pulls the familiar green bottle from the cooler and pops the top with the opener he keeps in his back pocket. He may look like a skinny Santa, but homeboy slings drinks like Tom Cruise in *Cocktail*. "Hell of a game tonight. Three more points to your total—not bad."

Yes, two goals and an assist are pretty good stats in a game, especially for a defenseman.

"At least *someone* appreciates what I did on the ice." I chuckle and nod toward the area filled with my family.

"Ahhh." A knowing gleam enters his gaze. "That's what you get for consorting with the enemy."

A bark of laughter escapes at his unique description of my squad.

"That's one way to describe them."

"They give you too much shit, you send them my way, you hear? Unless it's that pretty sister of yours—then you're shit out of luck."

"She's not here." Freddie, like most people, has a soft spot for JD. "But anyone else? You got it. Thanks Freddie."

"Any time. And hey"—he waits until I turn back around —"keep up the good work out there. Who knows? If you do, you might even be able to challenge that brother of yours for the Art Ross Trophy."

The beer in my stomach sours at the mention of Ryan. Don't get me wrong, I love my brother. He's honestly one of the best people I know, but I've spent my entire life being compared to him.

Why else do you think I work my ass off the way I do?

It would be nice to be recognized for *my* accomplishments and not as Ryan Donnelly's younger brother. Even when our college team won our third NCAA National Championship in a row—that one after he graduated—he got credit. We were the team he built, after all.

I'll take the night to kick back then get back to the grind tomorrow. Nothing is going to stand in the way of me hoisting Lord Stanley's Cup over my head come June. Then maybe I'll get the respect I deserve.

Cheering from one of the sectioned-off back areas breaks me from wallowing in my first-world problems. I look over, my height making it easy to see over most of the patrons, and spot a group of ladies cheering for whatever game Freddie has on.

Even from a distance, I can tell they're all pretty, but it's the short one in the middle with light pink hair and a body that's curvy like a 50s pinup girl who has my feet moving of their own accord. Her ass is perfectly cupped in a pair of painted-on skinny jeans and draws me in like a beacon as it shimmies with her celebration dance.

I toss a quick look over my shoulder at my people, but none of them are paying me any attention.

Perfect.

I may not be a man-whore like my buddy Tuck—and no, I'm not judging him; the girls literally call him M-Dubs for short—but I do enjoy playing the field and have been going through one hell of a dry spell lately.

It's one of the friends who spots me first, and I can tell she recognizes me.

"Ladies." I make eye contact with each of them, saving the one I want for last.

"Holy shit, you're Jase Donnelly," says the one who spotted me. She's wearing a Storm shirt and is clearly excited to see me up close.

Flashing the smile that launched many an endorsement deal, I say, "That's what my jersey says. And you are?"

"I'm Zoey. This is Ella." She points to other girl wearing a Storm shirt. "And this is Melody." She nudges her pink-haired friend to get her attention.

She turns and I'm hit with the darkest eyes I've ever seen, the onyx color growing more prominent as they widen when they lock on me.

Fuck. She's even more gorgeous up close.

I catalog everything about her: pink hair, cute little freckle under her left eye, lips painted in the same shade as her hair and begging to be kissed.

The best part? I'm not the only one scoping out the situation.

But my smile drops when I catch sight of what's going on below the neck, and before you judge and call me an asshole for being a boobist, I'm not. I'm a proud supporter of members of the Itty Bitty Titty Committee.

It's not Melody's breasts—which are full, high, and

displaying just the right amount of cleavage to draw the eye, by the way—that have me frowning. What? I may support the IBT, but I'm still a guy. No, that honor goes to what is stretched across them.

A Bruisers shirt.

A fucking Bruisers shirt.

Really, universe? A Boston fan?

Chapter Two

Melody

I've been on cloud ten since this morning. Yes, I know the saying is cloud nine, but I'm so flipping stoked I needed to jump to the next cloud because it wasn't enough to contain my excitement.

Tony eligibility. The two words have been flashing through my brain like a marquee all day. *Freaking* Tony eligibility.

God! I've acted on Broadway more than half my life and have been blessed to play a few lead roles in major productions, including *Wicked* and *Hamilton*—but this?

Holy crap!

Move over, Rose, it's my turn. Sorry not sorry, Bernadette Peters.

Gypsy, what a fantastic musical—but not the point.

If I land this role, I'll be eligible for a *fucking* Tony! A Tony! The holy grail of all that is theater.

Yes, yes I know there is still a long way to go before the role is officially mine, but being requested to audition by the producers tells me my chances of getting cast are more than good.

And shit, the role couldn't be more perfect for me. Marilyn

Monroe. I cannot even begin to explain how much I love the OG bombshell.

Not even the fact that my parents didn't call or text me back when I told them the news is enough to burst my happiness bubble. Plus, my brother's surprise FaceTime call helped wipe away the sting of neglect.

Ella and Zoey insisted we go out and celebrate after tonight's performances—being in the business themselves, they both understand the potential of today—and I was so happy I didn't even balk when they picked The Sin Bin for drinks.

I'm well aware the bar is a favorite of the city's hockey team, and though my friends may not be puck bunnies, they dance along the line like one of Zoey's choreographed pieces. Still, the *last* thing I expected was to come face to face with one of them, least of all Jase Donnelly.

Yet...here he is, looking pucking sexy AF, and tall—so damn tall. I mean for reals, how is it possible that he seems bigger in person than out on the ice? A pair of skates easily adds six inches to a person's frame—*hello*, that's simple arithmetic.

I have to crane my neck back to practically a ninety-degree angle to be able to see all of him. My breath hitches when I meet his smizing hazel eyes—seriously, he could teach Tyra Banks a thing or two. Combine that with his boyish grin, and I know I'm in trouble.

Involuntarily I run my gaze down his body, taking in the way his broad shoulders stretch the black cotton of his t-shirt, pushing the seams to the limit.

Yes, a lot of my fellow thespians are ripped due to spending countless hours dancing across the stage, but none have the bulk of a hockey player, and like my best friends—though less enthusiastically—I have also gravitated to the bulkier build of puck heads most of my life.

Except...

Jase Donnelly is the last hockey player I should have my eye on. Hell, he is the only person on the entire island of Manhattan I should stay away from.

This is bad. So, *so* bad.

"Don't you know it's against the rules to wear that shirt in here?" He points to the Boston Bruisers V-neck I'm wearing.

Gah! Even his voice is sexy. Deep and husky, it washes over me, and I swear my girls audibly swoon.

"Last time I checked, there wasn't a dress code," I sass before taking a step back when the fresh scent of whatever soap he uses after a game hits me. *Soap and ice.*

"You're not wrong." His hand runs over his chiseled jaw, the faintest tint of yellow from a healing bruise decorating the left side. "But maybe you should take it off before Freddie sees. He's a die-hard Storm fan. I'm surprised he let you in here wearing it."

My damn hormones pirouette, saying, *Yes please*, wanting to do as he asks if only he returns the favor, because I know there is a washboard stomach underneath the cotton. Thank you to the four-story billboard in Times Square of him in all his shirtless glory for that piece of information.

"Freddie?" I cross my arms over my chest and don't miss the way his eyes drop down to my cleavage. *Boys.*

"The owner." He brings his gaze back to my face and hooks a thumb in the direction of the white-haired man behind the main bar.

"Oh, you mean Pops?" Zoey chimes in, a blush staining her cafe au lait skin, neither her Brazilian nor her Cuban heritage enough to hide the hockey-god effect. I should really pat her on the back for not going full-on fangirl. "Nah, no worries there. He loves us."

"You ladies come here a lot?" A knowing smirk plays at the edges of his lips. Full lips...kissable lips. *How would they feel pressed against me?* And sonofabitch, there go my hormones again. I swear those bitches are drunk, though I've only had one glass of champagne.

"Often enough." Ella shrugs, her almond-shaped eyes dancing with mirth. "Depending on our work schedules, we try to meet here once a week or so."

"And what is it you ladies do?"

"We work on Broadway."

Why are they engaging? They *know* nothing good could come from prolonged conversation with him.

"Well, as gorgeous as you three are, you must be actresses."

He's smooth, I'll give him that. Given his reputation, though, I shouldn't be surprised. From everything I've heard, he has a bevy of bunnies at his disposal.

My two traitors—err, friends—giggle and blush while I get into a slap fight with my hormones. *We are not attracted to him, you hear me?*

"Only Melody is an actress." Zoey cups my shoulder. "I'm a choreographer, and Ella plays violin in the orchestra."

"Ah, I see." Another rub of that jaw. "I wonder if you've been in anything I've seen, but I'm sure I would have remembered a face as beautiful as yours. And you know, the pink hair stands out."

I roll my eyes at the beautiful comment as it is *obviously* a line. "Theater buff, are you?" Skepticism bleeds into my words.

"Not a buff per se, but the women in my life are fans and have dragged me to my fair share of shows."

The women in his life—at least he admits to being a player.

"Why don't you give me your number so the next night I have off, I'll come check out your show and we can get a late dinner after."

"Yeah...I don't think so."

Twin gasps of shock come from either side of me. This

entire scenario is straight out of one of their fantasies—mine too, if I'm being honest—but I shut that shit down faster than a slap shot.

Going out with Jase could only bring about one thing: trouble.

"Why not?" The crestfallen look on his face almost has me accepting.

Don't be stupid, Mels.

Jase Donnelly is a no-go.

As if having read it in a script, I can see him gearing up to press his case, but a very pretty strawberry blonde approaches first, wrapping an arm around his waist. When he automatically drops his arm around her shoulders, I tell myself that pang in my chest is not jealousy.

"I'm heading out. I just wanted to say bye now in case I miss you in the morning. My flight to LA is at stupid o'clock," the redhead says once she has Jase's attention.

"Sounds good. You know the code to my place."

Nope. Not jealous at all.

And you call yourself an actress. You can't even lie to yourself convincingly. Damn that year I played Elphaba, because my subconscious is cackling at me like a pro.

"And you're sure you don't want me to go with you to JFK?" Jase asks her.

"Nope. You've already scheduled your driver for me. You sleep in." She pats him on the chest, and I have the overwhelming urge to rip the hand away.

Whoa. Down girl. No need to go all West Side Story *on the chick.*

A buzz of awareness fills the space. On either side of me, both my friends are smiling, like Jase wasn't just attempting to flirt with us—me—all while already having someone warming his bed. How can they look at him all moony-eyed while I'm standing here wanting to slap a bitch?

"Love you. Fly safe," Jase says.

My teeth snap together as I watch him bend to brush a kiss across her cheek.

"Love you too, you big lug." She sticks her tongue out as she starts walking backward.

He returns the gesture, a glint of sliver catching the light when he does.

Holy shit.

He has a tongue ring? *Lord give me strength.*

I've just witnessed him in the arms of another woman—discussing how said woman will be sleeping at his place, no less—and yet one glimpse of that naughty piercing makes me want to throw all common sense out the window.

What the hell is wrong with me?

Clearly I need to run my lines again, because the one that tells me Jase Donnelly is a no-go has not stuck.

Okay, time to go before I do something stupid.

Without a word, I exit stage left.

Chapter Three

From the Group Message Thread of The Coven

MAKES BOYS CRY (Skye): Jor, Rock, where you two at? I need to consult with my Jase experts IMMEDIATELY!

MOTHER OF DRAGONS (Jordan): *GIF of Woody from *Toy Story* strutting and saying, "I'm here."*

ALPHABET SOUP (Rocky): *GIF of Julie Andrews from *Victor Victoria* making a grand entrance*

YOU KNOW YOU WANNA (Becky): Ooo ooo.

YOU KNOW YOU WANNA: *GIF of girl clapping excitedly*

YOU KNOW YOU WANNA: I think I know what this is about.

PROTEIN PRINCESS (Gemma): Oh man. What did I miss by staying home?

THE OG PITA (Beth): You guys have all the fun. Have a kid, they said. It will be fun, they said. BOOOO. Mama wants to go out and have a cocktail, or you know, five.

ALPHABET SOUP: Yeah, because motherhood has slowed you down, B. You know if Wyatt wasn't on shift you would have been in the city.

THE OG PITA: You are correct. And Gem did mix me a mean cocktail, so…

THE OG PITA: *GIF of Betty White toasting with a gigantic wine glass*

PROTEIN PRINCESS: Plus, if you'd gone, you wouldn't have been able to see Holly when she got back from her date.

PROTEIN PRINCESS: *GIF of girl waggling eyebrows*

SANTA'S COOKIE SUPPLIER (Holly): I plead the fifth.

MAKES BOYS CRY: Yeah…like that's going to fly. But we'll get back to you. Jase first. Then his BFF.

MOTHER OF DRAGONS: Okay, so what do you want to know, Skye?

MAKES BOYS CRY: Has Jase been seeing anyone recently?

QUEEN OF SMUT (Maddey): Ooo ooo. Why? Are you finally turning into my second favorite trope?

SANTA'S COOKIE SUPPLIER: I thought you said Gemma and Chance were your favorite trope?

QUEEN OF SMUT: Oh those two? Abso-fucking-lutely. Enemies-to-lovers is my jam, but I'm also a sucker for best friend's brother/brother's best friend.

PROTEIN PRINCESS: THERE IS NOTHING GOING ON BETWEEN ME AND CHANCE JENSON. IT IS NEVER GOING TO HAPPEN.

PROTEIN PRINCESS: I REPEAT

PROTEIN PRINCESS: NEVER

PROTEIN PRINCESS: GOING

PROTEIN PRINCESS: TO

PROTEIN PRINCESS: HAPPEN

THE OG PITA: Oh, shouty capitals and texting like Beck. You must REALLY mean it.

ALPHABET SOUP: Okay, before this conversation can go fully off the rails—no, Jase hasn't been seeing anyone. Why?

MOTHER OF DRAGONS: Please tell me Maddey is right and I'm ACTUALLY going to get one of my besties as a SIL??

MAKES BOYS CRY: What? No. Eww. Geez. I literally think of Jase as a brother. Gross.

YOU KNOW YOU WANNA: What she means is we saw him talking to this *gorgeous* girl tonight.

YOU KNOW YOU WANNA: Fun fact.

YOU KNOW YOU WANNA: She totally blew him off.

MAKES BOYS CRY: Oh she did? *sad face emoji*

YOU KNOW YOU WANNA: Yup.

YOU KNOW YOU WANNA: *GIF of a baseball player striking out*

YOU KNOW YOU WANNA: But…

YOU KNOW YOU WANNA: He did get her number from her friends when she wasn't there.

MOTHER OF DRAGONS: Oh. This is going to be interesting.

ALPHABET SOUP: Yeah, yeah, yeah. Interesting…blah, blah, blah. Since my bestie CLEARLY has some explaining to do—what do we know?

THE OG PITA: Did you snap a pic?

YOU KNOW YOU WANNA: No *sad face emoji* She dipped out before I could.

YOU KNOW YOU WANNA: But…

YOU KNOW YOU WANNA: She's a Broadway actress.

MOTHER OF DRAGONS: What's her name?

MAKES BOYS CRY: *GIF of Felicity Smoak cracking her knuckles at her laptop*

MOTHER OF DRAGONS: You know I love a good internet stalk.

YOU KNOW YOU WANNA: Melody Brightly.

MOTHER OF DRAGONS: On it.

Chapter Four

Though I know I'll end up getting in at least a light workout later, the one luxury I allow myself when I don't have morning skate is to not set an alarm. By the time I emerge from my bedroom in a pair of faded BTU Titans lounge pants, Skye should be gone, but I'm not at all surprised to find Gemma in the kitchen prepping my meals for the week.

Our squad doesn't believe in a silly thing like boundaries, so naturally we all have access to each other's places.

"Hey there, Hemmy."

I snort at the ridiculous nickname but accept the fresh mug of coffee she holds out in offering. I blame Vince—her cousin, my best friend—for his superhero obsession rubbing off on everyone. I've lost count of the number of times I've been told I look more Hemsworth than Donnelly, but whatever. That's not a bad gene pool to be linked to.

"Hey, Gem." I drop a kiss on the top of her head then take a healthy swallow of the nectar of the gods. "Pecan?"

"Yup. Lyle ground the beans for you yesterday knowing it's your favorite."

Freshly ground specialty beans is one perk of having a coffee shop owner as a friend.

"What's on your agenda for the day?" I settle in at one of the barstools at the counter, thumbing through my texts and social media notifications.

DAUNTLESS SUPERMAN: Bro. There are days I wonder which one of us has the more savage sister. I screen-shotted this for you since I know JD has him hidden from your feed.

DAUNTLESS SUPERMAN: *screenshot of @BadAss-Bishop13 IG*

picture of Jase with Skye and Becky at The Sin Bin last night

BadAssBishop13 Maybe if @EnforcedByJaseDonnelly13 spent less time in bars with bunnies, he might be scoring hat tricks like @CaptainRyanDonnelly9

comment **TheMrsDonovan** Hey @BadAssBishop13, maybe if you spent more time focusing on your game and not my twin's, MAYBE you'd be in the running for the Art Ross *shrug emoji* #FoodForThought

My fingers curl around the phone, the protective case around it groaning from the force. Fucking Nate Bishop. For as long as I can remember, the guy has had an issue with me. I want to say it originated from us playing for rival teams in college, but we've been taking shots at each other since long before the BTU Titans beat out the Penn State Nittany Lions in the Frozen Four our senior year.

I'm not surprised JD broke her *do not engage on social media* rule to come to my defense. We've been together since conception, and a bond like that tends to lead to rule-breaking when warranted.

"Today is my Storm day. I finished with Harrison this morning, and once I'm done with you, I just have to head next door to Cali's." Gemma's voice breaks through the haze of anger I feel any time Bishop is involved.

She slides a plate across the counter, and it's filled with an omelet I know from experience is loaded with more vegetables than a supermarket produce section.

"Lunch after? I should be done downstairs by the time you're at Cali's."

She nods then says, "You do know today is *supposed* to be your day off, right?"

I nod and barely refrain from rolling my eyes. I swear the eight Covenettes have a Dory-like memory when it comes to remembering I already have a mom, and an awesome one at that.

"All this"—I flex my left arm, making the Olympic rings tattooed on the inside of my bicep dance—"doesn't happen on its own. It's hard work looking this good." I heave a sigh. "But it's my cross to bear."

A wet dish towel smacks me in the face.

"You, sir, are ridiculous."

I shoot her a wink and she rolls her eyes, one of the only Steeles immune to my charms.

"And what would Rock say to you not giving your body proper rest time, hmm?" She arches a brow at me and levels me with a knowing look.

Her cousin, my ex-girlfriend turned bestie—yes, I said bestie; it's not the first time, so deal with it—Rocky would *not* approve. As one of the best physical therapists I've ever had the privilege of having work on me, she would give me a lecture longer than one of Maddey's romance novels.

Still, I need to train if I'm going to have any hope of stepping out of my brother's shadow, as Bishop *so* helpfully pointed out.

"Nah." I wave the question off. "You know Balboa loves me. She'd be so impressed with my work ethic she would offer to name my future nephew after me, but to keep the peace, I would politely decline. Can't have Vince getting jealous because his sister loves me more."

"Oh my god." She buries her face in her hands, speaking into them. "I can't even with you. I swear, I don't know how my cousin ever dated you."

"Gem, Gem, Gem." I shake my head. "You love me just as much."

I get a snort in response, letting the subject drop as I polish off the rest of my breakfast, the sounds of Lauren Hill's "Doo Woop (That Thing)" filling the silence. Gemma has a thing for 90s R&B, something she has in common with our friend Lyle.

"I think Sammy and Jamie are home. Should I see if they want to get together tonight?" I ask, referring to two more of our friends. There are so many moving parts when it comes to our group, I sometimes feel like I need to borrow one of Rocky's numerous degrees to keep track of us all.

"As much as I'd love to, I can't stay the night." She continues to slice the pepper she's portioning out for me.

"Why not? You always stay when you come out to cook for us."

I have a four-bedroom apartment for just this sort of thing. I'm always down for letting my friends crash at my place.

"With Vince in training camp, I gotta be there to feed the beast." She places the prepped pepper in a container and gets to work on a cucumber. "Plus, I gotta make sure he's not cheating on his diet."

"You mean like sampling some of the treats your new roommate makes?"

My buddy recently started dating Gemma and Becky's

roommate Holly. She also happens to be the new kickass baker at Lyle's coffee shop Espresso Patronum.

"I told Vin he can eat Holly's cookie any time he wants as long as he stays away from her *actual* cookies until after the fight."

I have the misfortune of taking the last sip of my coffee at just the wrong moment, and I choke at Gemma's blunt statement. The Covenettes are no joke.

"You know…" She sets the knife down, resting her elbows on the counter, leaning in my direction to look me in the eye. "I heard Vin isn't the *only* one with his eye on a pretty thing."

Goddamn Coven.

Is nothing sacred? I'm not at all surprised to hear the girls have already been informed of last night's crash and burn. It's never good to be the subject of one of their Coven Conversations. Their group chat is the bane of our existence.

The one plus side is at least I managed to convince Melody's friends to give me her number. They even went as far as letting me plug mine into her phone too. I wish I could see her reaction when I text her later. Naturally I saved my contact with my usual text handle.

Knowing anything I say could and *would* be used against me, I mime zipping my lips shut, place my mug in the sink, and head to get ready for the gym.

I have a text message to compose.

Chapter Five

Melody

THE BIG HAMMER: So...when are we going on our date?

BROADWAY BABY: Um...I'm pretty sure you have the wrong number because I don't know WHO you are or HOW your number got stored in my phone. And while we're on the subject, who the HELL puts their contact name as THE BIG HAMMER??? Trying to overcompensate for something there are we???

THE BIG HAMMER: Don't worry, baby, you'll get to see just HOW WRONG that statement is. All in good time.

BROADWAY BABY: Baby??? Um how about not.

THE BIG HAMMER: What? *hands up in question emoji* It's in your text handle.

BROADWAY BABY: It's a song, but that's NOT the point.

THE BIG HAMMER: No?? Okay, I'll bite. What is the point, beautiful?

BROADWAY BABY: Oh, first baby, now beautiful. Why do I get the feeling I'm not the only one who doesn't know the name of the person they're texting?

THE BIG HAMMER: Oh...I know your name, Melody Brightly. A man doesn't forget these things, especially when the name is as beautiful as its owner.

BROADWAY BABY: Smooth. Real smooth.

THE BIG HAMMER: Thank you.

THE BIG HAMMER: *GIF of man taking a bow*

BROADWAY BABY: That WASN'T a compliment.

THE BIG HAMMER: Compliments are in the ear of the beholder.

BROADWAY BABY: The phrase is: Beauty is in the eye of the beholder.

THE BIG HAMMER: Potato, vodka.

BROADWAY BABY: I'm sorry? Did we switch over to some sort of word association game without my knowledge?

THE BIG HAMMER: No. It's like potato, po-tah-to. My buddy likes to use "Potato, vodka" instead since vodka comes from potatoes and all. I thought it was clever so I started to use it myself.

BROADWAY BABY: Thanks for the unprompted science lesson.

THE BIG HAMMER: Anytime, baby.

BROADWAY BABY: Ugh. Are we back to this again?

THE BIG HAMMER: When were we ever off of it?

BROADWAY BABY: You are THE MOST frustrating person EVER.

THE BIG HAMMER: I may have been told that a time or two.

BROADWAY BABY: Why do I feel like that's a low estimate?

THE BIG HAMMER: *laughing face emoji*

BROADWAY BABY: Okay, so seriously—are you gonna toll me your name?

THE BIG HAMMER: You know…I was going to, but I think it's more fun this way.

BROADWAY BABY: *GIF of person banging their head against the wall*

THE BIG HAMMER: You are funny, baby.

BROADWAY BABY: STOP calling me baby *angry face emoji*

THE BIG HAMMER: *GIF of Chris Kattan saying, "No can dosville babydoll."*

BROADWAY BABY: Did you just *How I Met Your Mother* GIF me?

THE BIG HAMMER: Yup. My sister and BIL are OBSESSED with that show.

BROADWAY BABY: Why won't you tell me who you are?

THE BIG HAMMER: Because.

BROADWAY BABY: Because why?

THE BIG HAMMER: Because I don't think it would be in my best interest to do so.

BROADWAY BABY: But why?

THE BIG HAMMER: Wow.

BROADWAY BABY: Wow what?

THE BIG HAMMER: Nothing.

BROADWAY BABY: Okay, you can't do that.

THE BIG HAMMER: It's really nothing.

BROADWAY BABY: If it was nothing you wouldn't have said anything.

THE BIG HAMMER: Okay, fine. Just remember you asked for it, so don't go getting offended.

BROADWAY BABY: Oh no. With a statement like that, I make no promises.

THE BIG HAMMER: You really are funny, baby, but okay, I give. That whole section of our conversation reminded me of ones I've had with my nieces.

THE BIG HAMMER: ...they are toddlers.

BROADWAY BABY: *GIF of girl putting her hand to her chest in mock offense with the word "GASP" at the bottom*

BROADWAY BABY: But in all seriousness, I'll give you a pass because that's actually kind of cute.

THE BIG HAMMER: Just like me.

BROADWAY BABY: THAT remains to be seen. You know...since I have no idea what you look like since you won't tell me WHO you are.

THE BIG HAMMER: All in good time.

BROADWAY BABY: Grrrr. For real?

THE BIG HAMMER: Ooo I like it when you growl at me, baby.

BROADWAY BABY: I'm hanging up now.

THE BIG HAMMER: We're texting. You can't "hang up."

BROADWAY BABY: Semantics. Now, for real, why won't you tell me who you are?

THE BIG HAMMER: I will. All in good time. Patience, grasshopper.

BROADWAY BABY: I don't understand what you are waiting for.

THE BIG HAMMER: Can I be serious for a moment?

BROADWAY BABY: Why do I find it hard to believe that is something you are actually capable of?

THE BIG HAMMER: You know me so well already, baby.

BROADWAY BABY: **rolls eyes**

THE BIG HAMMER: I don't want to tell you who I am yet because I'm afraid it will hurt my chances.

BROADWAY BABY: Chances of what?

THE BIG HAMMER: Getting you to fall in love with me.

I stare at my phone, waiting for the screen to light up with another text, but it never comes. When I answered the first ping, I was annoyed. However, the longer our conversation continues—though there was a better chance of Mimi *not* going out tonight than me admitting it—the more highly entertained I am.

No matter how much I rack my brain, I can't figure out who my mystery texter is. I should probably call my brother and see if it's one of his friends messing with me. It wouldn't be the first time.

Time to put it out of my mind and head to the theater for the first of my two performances of the day.

I'm slinging my messenger bag over my head when it hits

me. The number didn't come up as a number or even UNKNOWN like most new ones would. No, this person's info was saved in my phone. And seriously, who the hell calls themselves 'The Big Hammer'? What is he, fifteen? Then again, that's probably the mentality of most of Teddy's friends.

Still...*I* didn't save it, so...

Stepping out of my room, I look down the hall at my roommates' open doors—my wouldn't-know-how-to-mind-their-own-business-if-their-lives-depended-on-it roommates/best friends.

I scrunch my nose and press my lips together, making a face, having a pretty good idea who Mr. The Big Hammer is.

Nice try, buddy.

When my phone buzzes again, I almost don't check it, already resolved not to engage in more texting with *him*. I may be an actress, but I don't need that kind of drama in my life.

I risk a glance at the screen when it buzzes a second time and smile when I see it's my brother.

TEDDY: So??? Did we hear back yet?

TEDDY: Don't keep me in suspense over here, Care Bear.

I love that even though his schedule is crazy enough to rival my own, my older brother still manages to be involved in my acting career. Little things like this make me wonder how we can share the same genes as our parents. That is not a road I want to go down right now, though.

BROADWAY BABY: Not yet, but it should be today or tomorrow.

TEDDY: You better call me IMMEDIATELY!!!

BROADWAY BABY: Don't I always?

TEDDY: Truth. Okay, gotta go. Keep me posted.
Love you.

BROADWAY BABY: Love you too!

His text is completely unnecessary. He is *always* the first person I call when it comes to audition news, and—fingers crossed—he will be the first one I'll call if I ever do receive that Tony nom. He likes to stay informed every little step of the way. I'll wait until I know if the role is mine for sure before I reach out to my parents, though I don't expect much more than a text in response—if I even get that.

Don't dwell on things you can't change, Mels.

Following my own advice, I pop my earbuds in and head for the subway, arriving at the theater with more than enough time for my hair and makeup to be done before the two o'clock curtain time.

♡

"So…" I say around a swallow of wine.

"So?" Ella is the picture of innocence as she keeps her attention on the old episode of *Sons of Anarchy* we have playing on Netflix. I can't blame her—because Charlie Hunnam, duh.

One of my favorite parts of my day is when we're all back in our apartment, showered, dressed in pajamas, and curled up together on our couches in the living room. *SOA* is the most recent show we've been bingeing, and even though it's a rewatch, we don't complain. I mean, you saw I mentioned Charlie Hunnam, right?

And let me tell you, in the season we are currently on,

when the Sons are sent to jail, Mr. Hunnam is looking especially fine with his shorter hair. *Le sigh.*

He also kind of reminds me of a certain hockey player I shouldn't be thinking about, and oh yeah, I was trying to say something, wasn't I? Damn sexy badass bikers distracting me.

"When were you two going to tell me you gave Jase Donnelly my phone number?"

I'm not 100% certain he's my mystery texter, but the badly feigned expressions of shock staring back at me confirm my suspicions.

"Oh don't even try it." I point at them with my wine glass. "It's a good thing *I'm* the actress in our trio, because the two of you suck."

"You know what?" Zoey straightens, getting as serious as she can—which is not very. "I'm not even sorry we did it. You should have given that Greek-god-of-hockey-playing-perfection your number *as soon as* he asked for it."

"You're nuts, you know that?"

"Never claimed I wasn't." She shrugs.

"But for real, Mels," Ella cuts in, "you should've given him your digits yourself."

"Plus, you should know better than to leave your phone behind when you go to the bathroom."

I let out a puff of frustration, downing the rest of my wine in one swallow. Are best friends supposed to drive you to drink?

"You guys *know* why I didn't give him my number."

"Pfft." Ella waves me off. "That's a bullshit excuse and you know it."

"Really?" I arch a brow.

"Well…okay, no. It is a legitimate concern, but you're also an adult and can make your own decisions when it comes to your love life."

"One text conversation does not a love life make." I go for

another gulp of wine then remember I'm out and in need of a refill.

"He texted you?"

"*Already?*"

"He didn't wait three days?"

"Wait? A *conversation*? As in you sent multiple messages?"

Ella and Zoey's questions come at me like pucks flying at a net in shooting practice.

Picking up the Moscato from the counter, I long to forgo the glass and drink straight from the bottle. Unfortunately, Sundays are a matinee performance, and I'm not the type to show up hungover.

Meddlers One and Two lunge for my phone, already scrolling through my texts. I could stop them, but it would only pull the focus back to everything and make them think something will happen when in reality it's a dead end.

I retake my spot on the couch, tucking my legs underneath me, and focus my attention where it belongs—on a shirtless Mr. Hunnam.

Chapter Six

THE BIG HAMMER: *meme of potatoes saying, "It's amazing how potatoes give us chips, fries, and vodka. Get your shit together, every other vegetable.*

BROADWAY BABY: I see we are sticking with the theme from our first convo?

THE BIG HAMMER: Yup. Gotta be consistent.

BROADWAY BABY: If you were really worried about being consistent, you wouldn't have waited more than a week to text me again.

THE BIG HAMMER: Sorry. I had to travel for work and I'm the dumbass who forgot to grab his phone before he left *facepalm emoji*

BROADWAY BABY: Your bad luck must have followed you, seeing as you lost 2 of your 4 games.

THE BIG HAMMER: Can't win them all.

THE BIG HAMMER: Wait.

THE BIG HAMMER: Hold up.

THE BIG HAMMER: You know who I am?

BROADWAY BABY: Yup.

THE BIG HAMMER: Did you figure it out on your own or did your girls rat me out?

BROADWAY BABY: I figured it out but they confirmed it.

THE BIG HAMMER: Okay then. So…when are you going to let me take you out on a date?

BROADWAY BABY: How about the 2nd of never?

THE BIG HAMMER: *sad face emoji* Oh come on, baby, don't be like that.

BROADWAY BABY: **rolls eyes** Are we really back to the baby thing?

THE BIG HAMMER: You'll like it. I promise.

BROADWAY BABY: I wouldn't hold your breath.

BROADWAY BABY: Or maybe do. If you hold it long enough, I won't have to worry about you harassing me any longer.

THE BIG HAMMER: 1st off: ouch, that's harsh, baby. 2nd: My sister went to college on a swim scholarship, so I picked up a thing or two about lung stamina, and I'll have you know, my stamina is REAL good.

BROADWAY BABY: Are you trying to get me to sext you?

THE BIG HAMMER: No, I was just stating a fact. When we sext, you'll know. There won't even be a question.

BROADWAY BABY: There will NEVER be a "when."

THE BIG HAMMER: Never say never, baby.

BROADWAY BABY: You know, I want to say something about how cocky you are, but with your jockhole, playboy reputation, I'm really not all that surprised.

THE BIG HAMMER: Playboy reputation? I thought you said you knew who I was?

BROADWAY BABY: Oh I do, Jase Donnelly. That is why I should probably stop talking to you now. Nothing good can come from us keeping this line of communication open.

THE BIG HAMMER: Oh good, you DO know who I am. With you calling me a playboy, I was starting to think you had me confused with Tuck. Though the guy is one of my closest friends, he's really the only one from the squad who could be considered a "playboy", as you so eloquently put it.

BROADWAY BABY: Did you really just use the word eloquently?

THE BIG HAMMER: Yeah? So? Just because I'm a jock doesn't mean I'm dumb. I'll have you know I actually graduated from both high school and BTU with honors, thank you very much.

BROADWAY BABY: No. Sorry. That is not what I meant at all.

THE BIG HAMMER: It's okay. I forgive you. And you can make up for both it and calling me a playboy by joining me for dinner sometime this week.

BROADWAY BABY: Not so fast there, buddy. I apologize for the unintentional dig at your intelligence, but the jury is still out on the whole playboy thing.

THE BIG HAMMER: You know, you have me questioning my entire public profile. I think I need to have a serious discussion with my other half about this.

BROADWAY BABY: Your other half? See what I mean? PLAYBOY!

THE BIG HAMMER: Take a chill pill, babe. I'm talking about my sister. Since we're twins, I've always considered her my other half. We were wombmates, after all. But JD manages all my PR, so if it's out there that I'm some playboy, I must have done something to piss her off and cause her to spread fake news about me.

BROADWAY BABY: That is actually a little bit adorable.

THE BIG HAMMER: That's me, baby—adorable.

THE BIG HAMMER: *picture of Jase mugging it up for the camera*

BROADWAY BABY: Yeah, "adorable." Still doesn't change the fact that when you first asked me out, you had another woman sleeping at your apartment. It's things like that that SCREAM playboy.

BROADWAY BABY: You've gone suspiciously quiet over there.

THE BIG HAMMER: Sorry. I was just trying to figure out what you were talking about. Do you mean Skye?

BROADWAY BABY: She the gorgeous, tall redhead? Then yes.

THE BIG HAMMER: *GIF of Mike Tyson cracking up*

THE BIG HAMMER: Omg no. No, no, no. Gross. Skye is my sister's BFFL, and she's pretty much my adopted sister. So no, nope, no way.

♡

THE BIG HAMMER: *picture of Jase wearing a t-shirt that says, "I may look like a potato now, but one day I'll turn into fries and you'll want me then."*

BROADWAY BABY: Funny. *laughing emoji*

BROADWAY BABY: You're the sexiest potato I've ever seen. Why don't you take your shirt off and prove it.

THE BIG HAMMER: *picture of Jase shirtless, holding up

his left arm, flexing to show off his biceps and Olympic rings tattoo*

BROADWAY BABY: Um...why are you sending me pictures of you half naked? I told you multiple times in the last week I'm NOT sexting with you.

THE BIG HAMMER: You asked for it, baby.

BROADWAY BABY: I did not.

THE BIG HAMMER: Did too.

THE BIG HAMMER: *screenshot of the conversation proving this*

BROADWAY BABY: OMG. I'm going to murder Zoey. Word of advice: don't leave your phone unattended around your drunk friends. It could lead to homicide.

THE BIG HAMMER: Need help burying the body? We could turn it into a date. Instead of the boring dinner and a movie, we could do dig a shallow grave, grab a burger and fries. Good times.

BROADWAY BABY: There is something seriously wrong with you, you know that?

THE BIG HAMMER: So I've been told.

THE BIG HAMMER: Why are you guys drunk?

BROADWAY BABY: We're celebrating.

BROADWAY BABY: *picture of Melody, Ella, and Zoey glassy-eyed and cheesing holding champagne flutes*

THE BIG HAMMER: 1st: you are way too beautiful for words. You should ALWAYS smile like that. 2nd: I am impressed with the lack of typos going on in this conversation right now. And 3rd: You ladies sure seem to celebrate a lot. The night we met you were drinking champagne.

BROADWAY BABY: Ah. I had a big audition that day, and today I officially signed the contract for the role. And Zoey got the job as the choreographer. It's a win-win for us.

THE BIG HAMMER: Big part?

BROADWAY BABY: The biggest. It'll be the first time I'm eligible for a Tony.

THE BIG HAMMER: That's like your version of the Stanley Cup right?

BROADWAY BABY: Yup.

THE BIG HAMMER: What's the role?

BROADWAY BABY: *GIF of Marilyn Monroe in the iconic white dress being blown up*

THE BIG HAMMER: Holy fuck!

♡

THE BIG HAMMER: Merry Christmas *Santa emoji* *Christmas tree emoji*

BROADWAY BABY: Merry Christmas. Enjoying your short break?

THE BIG HAMMER: Mostly.

BROADWAY BABY: Too much family time? I thought you *loved* your family?

THE BIG HAMMER: Oh I do. It's like a college reunion at my sister's place every Christmas break. But I could do without getting my ass kicked in Mario Kart by a pair of 9-year-olds.

BROADWAY BABY: Mario Kart? Really? Aren't you a little old for video games?

THE BIG HAMMER: Gasp! Bite your tongue woman. Mario and his friends are sacred in our group.

BROADWAY BABY: Oh I'm so sorry. Please accept my humblest apologies.

THE BIG HAMMER: You are forgiven. It's okay, I have two cute blondes here to cheer me up.

BROADWAY BABY: Okay. I'm hanging up now.

THE BIG HAMMER: I thought we already established you can't hang up in a text convo. And geez woman, maybe I should have gotten you a bottle of chill pills for Christmas instead of the gift I did get you, because way to OVERreact.

THE BIG HAMMER: *picture of Jase sandwiched between two blonde toddlers*

BROADWAY BABY: OMG. They are the cutest!!! Are those your nieces?

THE BIG HAMMER: Yup. And thank you. It's good genetics.

BROADWAY BABY: You do know you don't get to take credit for it, right? They are your sister's kids, not yours.

THE BIG HAMMER: Twins, remember? Of course I get to take credit.

BROADWAY BABY: You're fraternal twins.

THE BIG HAMMER: Whatever. We have the same blond hair.

THE BIG HAMMER: *video clip of Jase asking the twins who their favorite person is, them answering with "Unk, Unk, Unk" and kissing him on each cheek*

BROADWAY BABY: Well shit. My ovaries just exploded.

THE BIG HAMMER: I can make you explode, baby.

BROADWAY BABY: And there he is.

BROADWAY BABY: Wait a second—did you say you got me a present?

THE BIG HAMMER: Of course I did. You think I'm the type of guy who doesn't buy his girl a Christmas gift?

BROADWAY BABY: I swear to god if you tell me you got

me a dick in a box I'm going to block your number in my phone.

THE BIG HAMMER: *GIF of Justin Timberlake and Andy Samberg for the *SNL* Dick in a Box skit*

BROADWAY BABY: OMG I can't even with you.

THE BIG HAMMER: Don't even start—you know you're already starting to fall in love with me.

BROADWAY BABY: **rolls eyes** Maybe you should have asked Santa to bring you some decent go-kart skills if you are losing to a pair of third graders.

THE BIG HAMMER: Nope. I only asked the big man for one thing this Christmas.

BROADWAY BABY: And that is?

THE BIG HAMMER: You.

Chapter Seven

Melody

J*anuary*

What the fuck am I doing?

I've asked myself that question more times than I can count since I agreed to this, because what in the actual fuck?

Damn you, Jase Donnelly, and damn your stupid-looking —okay, gorgeous—face. And your potato memes, and your cute pictures with toddlers, and…and…*gah!*

Sonofabitch I still can't believe I'm doing this.

Seriously, Mels. You are out of your mind here.

Oh, so now you want to put up a fight, hormones? But when he's standing in front of us you're all, "Take my panties! Take my panties!"

Shit—I can't believe I'm having an argument with my hormones. Thank god I didn't do it out loud.

It took a month and a half for the charming bastard to do the impossible, and I'm not talking about this date I've agreed to. No, he made me *like* him.

I worry the sleeve of the slouchy knit sweater peeking out from underneath my coat, my gut clenching, screaming at me that this can only end in disaster.

Thankfully I had the foresight to recommend doing something low-key and out of the public eye. First dates are nerve-racking enough; neither one of us needs the added pressure of the paparazzi.

I refuse to think about the other reason.

With every text that pings on my phone, the guilt inside me grows. Though I've faulted him at every turn, thinking the worst, assuming information I heard secondhand was credible, Jase has calmly answered and reassured me. He's being nothing but honest, and me? I do nothing but lie—even if it's only by omission. What's even worse? He's not the only one I'm lying to.

To Jase's credit, he seemed excited by my suggestion and offered to cook for us at his place. Unfortunately, it led to me being subjected to Zoey and Ella acting out all the naughty things they think will be happening tonight.

I really need to find new friends.

They were also zero help in the getting ready department when I was stressing over what to wear. Since we're staying in, I didn't want to be too fancy or too casual, so while Meddlers One and Two pretended to hump each other on my bed, I settled on a pair of dark wash skinny jeans, low-heeled beige booties, and my favorite tan chunky knit sweater.

When Zoey finally stopped gyrating on top of Ella, she took one look at me, cursed in Portugese, and complained I was wearing a "grandma" sweater. I promptly flipped her off and proceeded to show how, when tucked into the front of my jeans and paired with a white crochet bralette, it was the picture of a sexy-comfy vibe.

The numbers on the elevator continue to climb, and with each floor ticked off on the way to the penthouse, doubts continue to creep in.

Geez, girl. You act like you've never been on a date before.

You can do this, Mels.

It's just dinner.

I'm right. I can totally do this.

I'm an actress. I'm well versed in controlling my emotions, and if not actually controlling them, at least projecting what I want others to see. All I have to do is act like Jase doesn't affect me and it'll be fine. I'll be fine.

Ping!

I take a deep breath as the elevator doors slide open, telling myself once again, *I got this.*

And I do, until I step into the hallway and see Jase. *Mamma Mia!*

Leaning against the doorjamb to his open apartment, legs crossed at the ankles, arms folded over his massive chest, he's deceptively casual in his hotness.

"Hi," I squeak. I had to be announced by the doorman when I got here, but I didn't expect him to be *waiting* for me. Can't a girl get a minute to prepare herself?

"Hey, baby." The smirk that's been on his face this entire time is devilish, and the way he unabashedly scans me from head to toe conveys zero shame. He can't see much thanks to the heavy winter coat I'm wrapped in, but the way he watches me is downright carnal.

"Really?" I arch a brow. "You're starting with the *baby* stuff from the jump?"

"Come on, baby." He pushes from the wall, my gaze automatically falling to watch the way his muscles shift underneath his hunter green polo as he closes the distance between us with the same grace I've watched him exude on the ice. "By now you know me better than to ask that."

Arms slide around my waist, the scent of soap and ice invading my nostrils as he bends to place the gentlest of kisses on my cheek. The move is so unexpected—I was sure he would go for a kiss on the lips right away—my breath stalls in my lungs.

Straightening, he takes one of my hands in his, threading our fingers together, and leads me into his apartment.

"Cute." He taps the pink puff ball on my winter hat, helping me out of my coat and storing it inside a closet.

"Thanks. Keeps my ears warm." Anyone who lives in the city knows the way the wind whips through the skyscrapers is no joke. "Plus Ella made it."

"She did?" He links our hands again, the innocent move weighted by intimacy as he continues leading me into his place.

"Wow," I murmur, catching sight of the floor-to-ceiling windows in the room.

"Yeah." His free hand rises to run through his hair, the action the first to ever come off as self-conscious. "I know it's a little much, especially since I don't live here full-time, but I got a really good deal because a lot of the units were new."

It's clean. Leather couches, chrome and wood accents, a handful of muted throw pillows for good measure. There's artwork and pictures carefully scattered throughout the space.

"You only live here during the season?" I scan the tastefully done décor; it is nothing like the bachelor pad I assumed it would be.

"Yup. I spend most of my time at a place a few of us have down the shore during the offseason."

This is a whole different level of wealth.

"Something smells amazing," I say to change the subject.

He doesn't let go of my hand as I follow him into the kitchen area. The entire main space is one large open concept room, so I can see everything in a glance: kitchen, dining room, living room, and seating area by the wall of windows. I would never admit it to him—because lord knows he wouldn't let me live it down—but I like the way he stays in constant contact with me.

"Chicken pot pie and"—he spins, his arms looping around my hips again—"four different types of potatoes."

Why doesn't that surprise me?

"Went a little overboard on the potatoes, did we?" I have to tilt my head back to see him. Even in my heels, he has about nine inches on me.

"How could I not? Potatoes are totally our thing."

"Did you really just say *totally*?"

Held in the circle of his arms, I'm close enough to see the way the dark green of his polo brings out the green flecks in his hazel eyes.

"My life is ruled by women. Some of the Covenettes' words rub off on me and slip into my vocab from time to time."

"Covenettes?"

He brushes an errant curl from my face, the long fingers skimming the skin at my temple and down my face before finally tucking it in place behind my ear, his thumb staying out to caress the line of my jaw.

Sparks of electricity radiate from everywhere he touches, and even under the warm yarn of my sweater, I break out in goose bumps.

My lips part, tongue peeking out of its own accord, and his eyes flash, turning greener as they lock on my mouth.

This.

This right here is why I tried to keep my distance.

Everything about Jase Donnelly just...*consumes* me.

Chapter Eight

Meal done, empty plates pushed to the side, I'm still pinching myself, not at all certain any of the night has been real and not another elaborate daydream. To be fair, the ones involving Melody Brightly have tended to fall more into the NC-17 category than the PG territory the night has stayed in—so far.

Let me tell you what a feat it has been, too. Like, I deserve a medal—and I'm not talking about the one I won for the good ol' US of A in the Olympics—for the restraint I used in not mauling her the second she stepped off the elevator earlier looking like the physical manifestation of everything I've ever wanted and never knew I did.

She was all pale pink hair tumbling down her back in loose waves, matching pink lips, and dark doe eyes watching me, keeping her distance as if unsure if she should come in or run away. If she'd had any idea how badly I wanted to know what she looked like with her lip gloss smeared from my kisses and her hair mussed from holding on to it while driving myself deep, *deep* inside her, she just might have run.

Outside of Vince, I haven't said a word to anyone about

Melody. I'm not stupid enough to think they don't know about her. Hell, two Covenettes were in attendance the night we met. So what if I'm still letting them believe nothing came from my crash and burn? And yes, I am well aware of the fact that both JD and Rocky will want to skin my hide when they learn of me withholding information, but that's a battle for another day.

Plus, Vince is the only one who understands my pain without it becoming fodder for a Coven Conversation. He had a hell of a time convincing Holly to be his girlfriend but eventually won her over, making him the perfect sounding board. Sure, Holly's reluctance stemmed from some serious issues, but I had my best friend's back through each time he was shot down. It's time for him to return the favor.

"So..." I drop a hand to one of her knees. I made sure to sit perpendicular to her instead of across the table, keeping her within touching distance our entire meal. "How was your first week of rehearsals?"

Aside from seeing the occasional show, I know nothing about the ins and outs of producing a Broadway musical. To say I was shocked to hear her schedule was as crazy, if not crazier, than my own would be an understatement.

The smile that overtakes her face hits me like being checked into the boards. I really need to ask Maddey for a better word than beautiful, because holy crap this girl is something else.

As if forgetting all about how she's been trying to keep her distance all night—yes I did pick up on this and I *will* get to the bottom of it—she leans forward, resting an elbow on the table and propping her chin on her fist.

"It was amazing." There's a wistfulness to her tone. "It's my first time being part of a production start to finish as a lead."

"Is it different when you're a lead?"

"The bones are the same, but there are additional rehearsals needed when you have a part outside of the chorus. I've been a lead or a supporting lead a few times in my career, but I always stepped in after the production had been running for a while. Seeing how the musical goes from just words and bars of music on a page to what it will be is... just...*magical*."

Drawn by the passionate way she speaks, I mirror her posture, the hand on her knee skimming up her jean-clad thigh, hooking itself on her hip and dragging her a few inches closer. I don't miss the way her lips part from the move.

"How does it work? Do you just sing and dance all day?"

She laughs, the tinkling sound resonating deep inside me. My new mission in life is to hear that sound every day.

"Some days feel like that, but the first week is more technical than anything else. First we get introduced to anyone involved in creating the show: the director, the producers, the creative team."

My eyes wander to where her sweater slouches down her arm, exposing her collarbone. Two thin straps bisect her bare shoulder, and I want to slide my finger under them, follow the line, and push them the way of her sweater.

She pauses, noticing my distraction.

"Sorry." I bite back a grin, because I'm not sorry at all. The damn sweater has been playing peekaboo with her body all night. It's its own fault, really.

"We do the fun stuff like seeing all the sketches for the sets and costumes, but there's also the boring stuff like the advertising plan that we go over too."

"Oof. Don't tell my sister you think the advertising stuff is boring when you meet her. JD and Skye live for PR and marketing."

"You plan on me meeting your family?" She shifts away, surprised.

"Of course. Even if I didn't plan on it, it's inevitable. My people are a very codependent bunch."

"You and your family..." I watch her throat as she swallows. "You're close?" She looks away. Unable to see her eyes anymore, I'm not quite sure how to read the question, but if I'm not mistaken, I'm picking up an air of sadness.

"The closest." Absentmindedly, I continue to run my thumb over the jut of her hip bone. "Honestly, I don't know how my parents managed having three, then four, athletes for children, but we always had at least one of them there when we had a game or a meet."

Her inky black lashes fan as she peeks at me through them, not flirtatiously, more shy, as if embarrassed to be asking. "Do they still come to a lot of your games now that you play professionally?"

Do they ever.

"Not every game since Ryan and I are on different teams, but a good number of them. Sean is the only one whose games Mom sees every one of, but a youth hockey schedule isn't as insane as the NHL." I pause, a thought hitting me. "But both my parents *watch* every game, whether live or on replay."

Melody's jaw drops open as if shocked by the information. There are eighty-two games in a regular NHL hockey season. Multiply that by two sons, and...well, yeah. I'm pretty sure the cape JD wears comes from Ruth Donnelly—the OG Supermom.

"Wow." Again she looks away, her head bobbing like she's answering some unasked question. I spend enough time with the women in my life to get a sense there's more going on beneath the surface. The urge to pry is strong, but that's too heavy of a conversation for a first date.

A chuckle breaks free as a memory resurfaces. "Hell, the only reason I saw you the night we met was because I needed to get away from the shit-talking Skye and Becky were giving me."

"*Mmmhmm.*" Her lips twist.

I scoot my chair around, our knees intertwining like two Vs. "One of these days I'm going to find out how you developed this preconceived notion of me as some Lothario when I'm really not."

She worries the corner of her lip between her teeth, and I reach to free the pink flesh from the abuse. The urge to replace her teeth with my own is strong, but this topic is one I've tried and failed to get clarification on for six weeks.

I'll be damned if some misguided idea about my reputation will keep me from getting the girl. There's...*something* holding her back from giving us a real shot, and I need to figure it out so I can vanquish the demon and come out the victor.

"I'll have you know I had one girlfriend in high school and one for a few years in college."

"Why did you break up?"

"My high school girlfriend wasn't super serious. We split shortly after graduation, each of us going to college on opposite coasts."

"And the one in college?"

"You know..." My lips tip up thinking of how many times both Rocky and I have been asked this question through the years. You'd think by now one of us would have an actual answer. Alas, it seems to be as elusive as the Holy Grail. "I honestly couldn't tell you. One day we were a couple, and the next we kind of just reverted back to being friends."

"Really?" Skepticism drips from the word.

"Really." I use my thumb to trace circles over her hip through her jeans. "Rocky is still one of my best friends. It helps that she's a Covenette and besties with my sister too."

"I can't believe you just said bestie."

"I'm confident enough in my manhood to use it."

"I bet you are." She snorts. "I feel like I need to meet these Covenettes you talk so much about."

"You will, but not yet." I press deeper into her personal space, bringing my face to the curve where her neck meets her shoulder. I catch the faint scent of bubble gum as I inhale, my lips brushing her skin when I speak. "For now, I want to keep you to myself, because once you meet them, the girls will adopt you as one of their own. They like to collect friends like Ariel does trinkets for her hidden cave."

"First bestie, now a Disney reference."

"What can I say?" I continue to speak against her soft skin. "I'm a good time. They'll tell you that too." My teeth nip at her neck. "For now, I want to enjoy you being just mine for a little bit longer."

"I-I'm not yours though," she stutters as I drag the metal ball of my tongue ring up her neck. She can deny it all she wants, but there is no way for her to hide the way I affect her. Her skin flushes a delicate shade of pink, goose bumps are visible on the skin her sweater has exposed, and her breathing is as labored as mine after blue line drills.

"Oh, but…baby, you are." I press one last kiss to the soft spot behind her ear, straightening back in my seat before I can take things further.

I *will* find out if she tastes as good as she smells, but if I learned anything from book club, it's that chicks can't resist a slow burn. I'll take this so slow we'll burn like incense.

A minute—a full sixty seconds—of silence passes before she clears her throat, her onyx eyes blinking up at me from beneath thick black lashes. *Shiiit*, the hazy glaze in them makes me want to say fuck the slow burn and reach for the kerosene.

"You know…all night you've asked me about work, but we haven't talked about you being picked for the All-Star Game again."

Her question is a bucket of cold water on my raging libido.

Yes, I was selected to represent the Metropolitan Division at the All-Star Game for the second time in the four years I've been playing in the NHL.

And yes, one of the two years I didn't make the team was my rookie season, when it is statistically unlikely for a player to make it—Ryan notwithstanding—and the second time there was no game because of the Olympics, for which I was selected.

But, her poor taste in hockey teams aside, she has a good base in terms of hockey knowledge. I love my brother dearly, but I don't want him encroaching on my date. The last thing I want is for the subject of the Metro's captain to be brought up.

"I was picked—what else is there to say about it?"

"Are you kidding me?" Her eyes widen so there's a full circle of white around her dark irises. "It's a major accomplishment, and you should be proud."

Well, I'm an ass.

"I am." My thumb traces patterns on her thigh, the denim material heating more the longer I touch it. "The whole weekend is a good time. Most of my family will fly out, and it usually turns into a mini BTU Titan reunion even if we aren't all on the same team."

"But you get to play on the same team as your brother and brother-in-law. That's gotta be fun, right?"

Yes, I love teaming up with my brother. It isn't Ryan's fault people credit him with his team's success.

I may keep a grueling training program to prove I can stand on my own merits outside of the great Ryan Donnelly, but even I know what I feel has nothing on the pressure he must feel to live up to the hype surrounding him. It's the biggest reason why I've never said anything about my own insecurities.

"Of course I enjoy getting to play with my brother. He's

like *the* all-star—there was never any doubt he would get selected."

Her brows pucker and she looks at me like I just grew an extra head. "As a Boston fan, I will deny this if ever asked"—she holds her hands up in a pledge—"but you are the top defender in the league. Why *wouldn't* they pick you?"

My lips twitch at her unknowingly taking a dig at Bastard Bishop. "You mean to tell me you think I'm better than your boy Bishop?"

She stills, her eyes darting back and forth as if looking for an escape.

"The Olympics was my favorite, though." I throw her a bone with the quick subject change, knowing what it's like to be possessive about the teams you root for.

A shadow passes over her face so fast I'm not even sure it really happened. Not the reaction I was expecting.

One of her hands lifts to twirl a section of hair around her fingers. "Why?" The playfulness is back.

"About a third of the roster was made up of BTU alumni, with five of us from the same playing years."

"Who were the five?"

"Me." I point to myself, shooting her a wink, and I don't miss the blush it causes. Note to self: *Hey, self. Make sure you wink at her—a lot.* "Ryan, obvs, Jake, Tucker Hayes from Chicago, and Wade Tanner from L.A."

"I can't believe you just said obvs." She giggles. "I think that's worse than totally, bestie, and the Disney reference combined."

"Thinking I should turn in my man card, huh?"

"Maybe a little." She holds her pointer finger and thumb barely an inch apart.

"All right, smartass." I give her side a playful pinch. "Before you have me doing one-armed push-ups to prove how much of a man I really am, how about I give you your Christmas present?"

Her eyes light up like Times Square.

"You can do them with only one hand?"

I chuckle.

"Oh, baby." I squeeze her thigh, pulling her a fraction of an inch closer. "I can do *a lot* of things with only one hand."

Chapter Nine

Melody

You know that GIF where Charlie Sheen is pulling at his collar and steam comes out? Yeah, that's me right now.

The last hour and a half has been a crash course in teasing and sexual frustration. I don't think there's been a minute since I stepped inside the apartment that Jase hasn't been touching me in one way other another.

The way our knees knocked together under the table, how his hand would constantly reach out to touch me...and don't even get me started on what it felt like when he dragged his piercing down my neck.

He's tossing sexual innuendos out like Reese's Pieces to draw me to his side like Elliot did to E.T. And like the alien, I willingly follow him to the living room, letting him guide me to the large leather sectional, my hand once again held in his.

The callouses earned from years of shoving his hands into hockey gloves rub across my skin, and all I can think of is what they would feel like on the rest of me. He may have been touching me all night, but it's only been over my clothes.

"Shouldn't we clean up the dishes?" I ask, letting him pull me down to sit.

"I'll worry about them later." He angles his body to face mine, our knees once again touching, then reaches for a present on the coffee table I didn't notice earlier.

It's roughly the size of a shoebox, though slightly wider, and... "Are there elves playing hockey on this wrapping paper?"

"Gotta be festive."

Gah! When he does things like showing his playful side, I can't help but fall for him a little bit.

Falling for him is a mistake, Mels. Fucking hell. It would be *really* helpful if my subconscious could pick a side already.

His finger is back to tracing those maddening figure eights on my thigh, and I've officially lost count of how many times I've told myself not to sleep with him on the first date.

There have been a few close calls, like when he ran his tongue ring down the length of my neck. The cool metal was a direct contrast to his warm mouth, and I was stupid close to saying *Fuck it* and asking him to take me right there on the table.

Zoey and Ella would be proud if you did.

Shaking off those lustful thoughts before they can take root, I refocus my attention on the box in hand, letting out a startled laugh as the present comes into view.

"Did you really get me a Mr. Potato Head?"

"Yup, and I got myself a Mrs. Potato Head. This way we each have something close by to make us think of the other."

Swoon. Dammit.

"Did you push them together and make them kiss before you wrapped mine?"

"Duh."

"You speak like a fifteen-year-old girl."

"Guess I should blame JD for all the times she used to dress me up growing up."

My jaw hits the ground. "*Seriously?*"

He throws his head back, his blond hair flopping, catching

the light in golden waves, and he full-on belly laughs. It takes him a while to get himself back under control enough to speak, wiping a tear from the corner of his eye as he brings the now swirling green and gold irises back to me.

"You have *no idea* how badly I want to say yes, but no, JD did *not* dress me like a girl growing up."

"Well that's a little disappointing." I pout.

He lifts a hand to stroke a thumb across my protruding bottom lip, his other fingers hooking under my chin and holding me in place. His thick blond lashes grow heavy as his eyes lock onto my mouth.

He's going to kiss me.

It wouldn't be the first time his lips were on my body.

Cheek.

Temple.

Top of the head.

Across the knuckles.

Behind the ear.

And who could forget the neck? I sure as hell can't, not with the wetness in my panties.

Jase's head lowers.

My eyes drift shut.

The moment charges.

He shifts closer, the heat of his body radiating to mine more and more intensely the nearer he gets.

His lips are about to touch mine when the sound of three beeps sounds in the distance, followed by a door opening and closing. A gorgeous blonde walks into the room speaking on a phone.

A girl who has the code to the apartment.

Chapter Ten

I spent the night building to *this* moment.

Every touch, brush of my lips, and drag of my tongue was leading to finally discovering what Melody's lips taste like.

Slowly, so slow I'm practically a slow-motion replay, I lower my face, the scent of bubble gum intensifying the closer I get to the promised land.

I'm a hairbreadth away when I hear the three beeps of the front door's lock disengaging. Cali is a dead man for choosing now to drift across the hall. I turn to tell my meddlesome teammate to get the hell out, only to let out an audible curse when I see it's Maddey striding into the room.

"No way, Jor." Of course she's on the phone with my twin, because I've obviously done something to piss off the man upstairs. "I swear these boys will never le—" Her words and steps abruptly stop when she spots Melody and me on the couch.

I barely hold back a scowl when I see the green pallor of Melody's skin. She looks like she's going to be sick, and I'm sure my girl is drawing all sorts of incorrect conclusions. Every time she's been faced with or heard of another female, she's assumed I'm sleeping with them. My wombmate and I need to have a serious discussion about the rumors circulating about me.

"Um, Jor?" Maddey's wide blue eyes bounce between us. "I know I've been in my writing cave this week, but is there something you need to tell me about Jase?"

She's too far away for me to overhear my sister's response, but her excited squeal is hard to miss.

Without missing a beat, Maddey disconnects the call without a goodbye, striding over to pick up the remote on the coffee table to connect to the video chat system our entire squad has installed.

Within seconds, hazel eyes that match mine are blinking at me from my flat-screen television.

Well this should be interesting.

I cup one of Melody's knees in an effort to offer comfort, but her body has more tension in it than my hockey stick. Fucking one step forward, two steps back.

"Jason." JD levels me with one of her mom looks.

"Whoa, whoa, whoa. What's with the use of my legal name?" I hold the hand not on Melody up in surrender. I'm not giving up contact until she relaxes—and maybe not even then.

"I think it's warranted in this situation."

"Besides, it's not like she middle-named you or anything, Trip." Maddey perches on the arm of the couch closest to Melody, propping elbows on her bent knees and leaning forward, settling in for a good story.

"Trip?" Melody's voice is small as she asks, and I hate it. I don't ever want her to be scared to ask me something.

"It's short for Triplet," Maddey answers. "Since these two"—her finger bounces between me and where my sister is displayed on the screen in high-definition glory—"are twins, and Jordan and I"—now her finger bounces between herself and JD—"look like we could be twins ourselves, we like to say I'm their triplet who was separated at birth."

"Plus it drives Ryan batty," JD adds gleefully.

"Yes. An added benefit for sure," Maddey agrees, looking back at JD.

I shake my head at how ruthless these two can be when they want to be.

"So…" Maddey's attention once again comes back to us, and I swear it feels like my balls try to crawl back inside my body.

Better prepare yourself for epic embarrassment, Donnelly.

"Tell me *all* the things." Mischief I'm more than acquainted with dances in Maddey's icy eyes.

I swear, *tell me all the things* should be The Coven's mission statement.

"How are you being so cool about this?" Melody asks instead of answering. She moves to rise from the couch, but I tighten my hold on her, keeping her in place. *No running away, baby.*

"Cool about what?" Maddey tilts her head like her yellow lab, Trident, is known to do.

"Finding me in your boyfriend's apartment."

Sonofabitch I was right. I want to find every person who ever put these misconceptions in her pretty head and punch them in the face.

Maddey laughs so hard she falls off the couch, and when I look toward the TV, my twin is in a similar state, arms curled around her pregnant belly.

"Babe, you okay?" I can hear Jake call out before he, too, joins the call.

Perfect, another witness to the shit-show.

"Jase."

"Jake."

"What's up with these two?" he asks me instead of addressing the two hyenas.

"Ja—Ja—" Maddey struggles to speak through her laughter, clambering back onto the couch. "Jase's girlfriend thought I"—a hand flattens on her chest—"was his girlfriend."

"His girl—" Jake spots Melody amongst the chaos of the two blonde she-devils. "Oh. Hi."

She gives a half-hearted wave, confusion written all over her face and still fucking tense.

"I don't know if I should be offended or not by how *hysterical* you find the idea of me being your boyfriend to be," I grumble. "I'll have you know I make an *excellent* boyfriend."

Any girl would be *lucky* to have me as their boyfriend. I earn expert-level achievements when it comes to the whole significant other thing. *Not really the point here, Donnelly.*

"Oh yes, we know. Rocky *sings* your praises." Sarcasm practically pools on the floor Maddey's words are so heavy with it. "The idea of us being a couple is just even funnier to me since I almost married your brother."

"Yup." JD finally has her own laughter under control. "That's a *little* too incestuous, even for our group."

"Family," the girls say in unison as Jake says, "Coven."

"These are the Covenettes you talk about?" Melody asks as her eyes dart between me and everyone else in this ridiculous conversation.

"Two of the eight," I answer reluctantly.

"Okay, okay." My sister settles herself on her husband's lap. "Before you go off on one of the Coven tangents you and Vince love so much, how about you tell me why you kept the fact that you have a girlfriend from me, oh wombmate of mine?"

"I'm not his girlfriend," Melody says.

"We'll see about that." I give her knee a squeeze, trailing a finger down to rub inside the bend of it, a tremble finally breaking her rigidity. "And you." I bring my attention back to my twin. "Hi Pot, I'm Kettle, nice to meet you. Or did you conveniently forget you kept your relationship a secret from me when you two started dating?" I point to the couple on the screen.

For months, the two dated behind all our backs. It was the only time either of us had kept something from the other. There was a point I thought I was going crazy as the secret messed with our twin connection. It doesn't happen often, but I do enjoy when I get to use it against her.

What? Trust me, JD is the queen of revenge plots. I have suffered quite a bit at her hands.

"He's got a point, babe." Jake buries his face in the crook of JD's neck.

"Whatever. That was only because Tweedledee and Tweedledum made me promise not to date one of their teammates."

"And look how well that turned out." I smirk. I couldn't be happier for them, but I'm not going to sit here and take shit in front of the woman I'm trying to impress.

"Oh wait—is that a baby crying?" JD cups a hand over her ear as if trying to hear better. "Gotta go. Love you Jase." She jumps from Jake's lap and runs away like a coward.

"Love you too, JD," I call to her retreating back.

Conversation pauses as Jake turns to watch his wife walk away, and I bite back the urge to gag over him checking out her ass. He's lucky he loves her unconditionally, otherwise I'd be kicking *his* ass, especially with how blunt my sister tends to be about their sex life.

There are just some things a brother doesn't need to know.

"Well, seeing as you have your hands full there"—he gestures to us—"I'm going to go take advantage of my wife. Gotta stock up before the next road trip."

See what I mean? T-M-*fucking*-I.

"Oh, wait." Remote in hand, Jake pauses. "Bro code mandates I give you a heads-up."

I groan. "I don't need to hear about whatever new position you found that helps you do my pregnant sister, thank you very much."

Jake's emerald eyes flash with humor. This, this right here is the side of him that chose Tucker as a childhood friend. It's trouble. *Trouble*, I tells ya.

"As much fun as it is for me to watch you squirm when I do"—I want to take shots at him without his goalie gear for the grin he shoots me—"that wasn't what I was gonna say." He points to Maddey. "And don't you start with it being research."

She holds up her hands in surrender. We are all accustomed to seeing parts of our lives show up in her books.

"Pregnancy brain may have made her forget to say anything, but earlier Jordan was cursing you from here to LA for your Throwback Thursday post."

I shrug. Personally, I think my post was awesome. Who doesn't want to see an Olympic gold medal? So what if I tagged Bastard Bishop in it and went all Borat on him saying, "You'll never get this. You'll never get this."

"Look, bro, it doesn't matter to me either way. You piss her off, I get the perk of angry sex." *Gag me.* "But she was muttering stuff about changing your passwords so you can't ramp up the beef between you and Bishop before the All-Star Game."

Melody is still fucking tense under my hold and I fucking hate it.

"All right, I'm out for real. Deuces." With a two-finger salute, Jake ends the call.

With one half of the inquisition gone, I rearrange Melody, draping an arm over her shoulders, tucking her tight to my side, letting my thumb drift along the skin of her upper arm exposed by her slouchy sweater. She resists the embrace at first, but eventually she nuzzles in. *Right where she belongs.*

"Not that I'm not happy to see you or anything, Madz, but what are you doing here?"

"I'm doing a popup signing at an indie bookstore here tomorrow, and if I didn't get out of Jersey, there was a very real chance you would no longer have an older brother."

I bury my face in Melody's bubblegum hair at the laughable suggestion.

"What did Ry do now?"

"He's just being his typical overprotective self. I keep reminding him we are no longer a couple and he needs to stop worrying about me."

Over the last couple of months, she has received a handful of odd "gifts." Ryan isn't the only one concerned; he's just the most vocal about it.

"Madz, you and I both know that will *never* happen. It may not be in the romantic sense anymore, but he still loves you."

"I know." Like a deflating balloon, Maddey sags, running a hand through her hair and sending her long blonde curls tumbling in disarray. It's not discussed often, but even years later I can see how she still feels the weight of the three-carat diamond.

"And I love him too, but man...you alpha men are *exhausting*."

This time I laugh hard enough to shake Melody, who's watching us like a soap opera. At least the veil of mistrust seems to have lifted from her eyes.

Why, oh why, isn't Jordan my evil twin? All we need is that and one of us to end up with amnesia and we could make it official. Move over *Days of Our Lives*, the BTU Alumni are about to take your crown. Joey Tribbiani taught me a lot. I could totally be the next Dr. Drake Ramoray.

"You do love to write about us, so we can't be *all* bad."

"Yeah, well, keep annoying me and see how I write you guys into my next book."

It's pathetic how much that threat keeps us in line.

"It's not like Ry to act without cause. Did you get another gift?"

"I don't want to talk about it." Her tone turns sharp, and I hold my hands up in surrender.

Pissing Maddey off is not the objective of the night. Getting Melody to fall for me is. Time to turn this bad boy around.

Chapter Eleven

My mind flashes an alert that declares *Not enough storage space* as I try to process everything. I've heard countless stories of the harem of women Jase keeps, but at every turn, all he's ever done is disprove the rumors.

There was Skye, who I assumed was sleeping in his bed when I heard her talk about staying over. Wrong. She's his sister's best friend and stayed in the guest room here.

Then there were the twins he talked about when we texted. I thought he was bragging about bedding two girls at once, but, wrong again; they were his nieces.

And when Maddey showed up, I assumed she was his girlfriend because she had the code to his apartment.

Serves you right, Mels. You know what they say happens when you assume.

All the stories I heard about how Jase would spend the day with his girlfriend and hit on bunnies at night makes me wonder if the *girlfriend* was actually just one of his close friends. Plus, I never really understood *why* I was even told them in the first place. Who am I to judge when people need to vent?

I know better than to listen to what other people say. I guess it's a good thing I went with my gut and finally let Jase talk me into a date, because every day he's done something to prove he is not only a good guy, he's exceptional.

I haven't said much since our unexpected guest showed up, but I'm learning so much sitting here listening.

The tension has grown thick enough to cut with a knife. There's obviously something more going on with Maddey's arrival than what's being said, but it's not my place to pry. Instead, I ask, "You're an author?"

The dark expression lifts from her face. "Yup. I write romance."

As a lover of all things happily ever after, I indulge in the occasional romance novel.

"Ooo, I wonder if I've read anything you've written."

"You mean Trip hasn't told you about his career moon-lighting as one of my cover models?"

I whip around, the hand that was on my shoulder falling to my hip.

"You've been holding out on me, Donnelly?"

"I can't give away all my secrets at once, baby. Gotta keep giving you little breadcrumbs, leave you wanting more so you keep coming back to me."

Ba-bum. Ba-bum.

My damn heart is a traitor, tap-dancing for Jase.

Why's he got to go around saying things like that? How's a girl supposed to stay away?

That's the problem—I can't. Consequences be damned.

"I always knew you had hero inspiration potential, Jason Donnelly," Maddey declares.

"Geez, not you too with the legal name, *Madison.*"

Maddey sucks in a breath through her teeth. "Don't make me start calling you Jay."

"You don't like being called Jay?" Oh the possibilities.

"Don't get any ideas, baby."

But I am. So many ideas—ones that can never come to fruition.

"Jase has all my books on the top shelf." Maddey points to a glass and chrome bookcase near the windows.

I jump from my seat instantly, Jase chuckling behind me.

It's not just the top shelf—all of them are filled with neatly organized romance novels.

Warmth envelopes my back as Jase comes up behind me. All night he's been in contact with me, but this? This is him *surrounding* me. His legs along my calves, the bump of his knees above where mine bend, the backs of my thighs lined up with the fronts of his, the hard muscles of his stomach pressed against my back. All of him covers all of me.

He curls around my shoulders, and I watch the flex of his forearm as he reaches to pluck two books from the middle of the Belle Willis section.

"These are mine." One of his arms snakes around my middle, bringing me tighter against him, if that's even possible.

I look down, and holy shit these are total one-click-worthy covers. He really is too attractive for his own good.

Time loses all meaning as I get lost in being enveloped by all things Jase. Maddey's clap has me jumping like it's the loud noise in the deathly-silent scene of a horror movie.

"Oh-kay then." I look over the bulge of Jase's biceps to see her bending down to pick up her bag. "Since the only action I'm getting lately is the scenes I write, I'm going to get out of here before the pheromones coming off you two get me pregnant."

"Madz," Jase growls, and I bury my face in the hollow of his armpit. It's not my preferred place to stick my nose, but he's so damn tall it's how we fit together.

"Lighten up, Trip." She pauses as she passes the kitchen table cluttered with the remnants of our meal. "You had Gem's pot pie for dinner? So jelly."

I tilt my head back over his arm and look up to see an adorable blush staining his cheeks. "I thought you said *you* made dinner?"

He cups the back of his neck as the color of his cheeks darkens to magenta. "I made the potatoes."

"Oh, well"—I push up onto my toes, kissing the underside of his jaw—"seeing as that was the majority of the meal, I'll give you a pass."

"*Oooo*, busted." Maddey laughs evilly. "Can't wait for tonight's Coven Conversation. Night," she calls over her shoulder as she walks down the hall.

"Shit."

I hear the barely audible curse slip past those lips that were so close to touching mine before his head drops, his forehead resting on the crown of mine.

"Coven Conversations?"

"It's what we call the girls' group chat." He takes the books from me, returning them to the shelf. "*Nothing* good ever comes from them."

Damn, Mels—breathe. Don't jump to conclusions this time.

"And who's Gem?"

"Another Covenette and my part-time personal chef. And yes she made the pot pies we had for dinner."

I reach up to cup his warm cheeks. "You know..." My thumbs stroke across the thin layer of stubble he's sporting. "You're kinda cute when you're embarrassed."

"And you're just beautiful all the time."

Ba-bum. Ba-bum.

I'm so, *so* screwed.

What is it they say? It's better to ask for forgiveness?

"I should probably go." I don't want to, but I need to. If I stay here any longer, I'll end up acting out every one of Zoey and Ella's suggestions.

No sex on the first date, Mels.

I shore up my resolve while trying my hardest not to whine like a toddler throwing a tantrum.

"If you must." He sounds like the petulant child my subconscious is being.

"You do have a game tomorrow," I remind him.

"Do you and the girls want to come?"

With that much hope in his voice, there's no way I can say no. I have rehearsal during the day, and though my schedule is crazy, unlike when I have performances, it leaves most of my evenings free.

"Sure." His face brightens at my acceptance, and that alone is worth the potential blowback. "And though I have a feeling I'll live to regret it, Zoey can too."

This time, instead of linking our hands, he keeps me tucked against his side, walking us to the front closet he stored my coat in earlier.

"What about Ella?"

"She has a performance." I snap my fingers as if to say, *Oh, shucks.* Zoey is the worse of the two, but at least I won't be tag-teamed by M1 and M2.

He makes a noise of acceptance in the back of his throat, and the growly sound rumbles through my body, hitting my sternum, traveling down my belly, settling in my clit and fanning the flames of desire he'd been adding to all night like one of the giant accordion fans they use in cartoons.

Yup, definitely time to exit stage right.

Slipping into a pair of Vans as I retrieve my gift, he grabs my coat, takes my hand in his, and leads me out into the hall, pressing the button for the elevator.

He's quiet.

I'm quiet.

Does he want me to stay? What did he think of our date? Was it the best one he's ever been on like it was for me?

"Hold on a second," he says, my hand waving by my side as he drops it and turns back for his place.

He's back almost as quickly as he left, and my eyes narrow suspiciously on the black and gray fabric draped over his shoulder.

"What did you just do?" I ask warily.

"Well." He switches the material from his shoulder to mine. "Can't have you supporting the enemy now that you're my girl. And besides, we aren't playing Boston tomorrow."

Ba-bum. Ba-bum.

"Who said I'm your girl?" I challenge. Pushing his buttons is my new hobby.

"Oh, baby." He shakes his head as if to say the subject is not up for debate, but I hold his stare.

Ping!

The elevator arrives, neither one of us moving for the doors, still locked in our standoff.

I should make things easier on us and just give in. Hell, we all know I'm going to. Showing up tonight was just the first step.

With a roll of my eyes, I turn on my heel, pushing the button to recall the elevator that closed as we lingered, and step inside when it opens right away, having not left the floor.

"You don't give up, do you?" I look at him through the open doors.

"Not when it comes to something I want."

There's *zero* doubt to what that something is—me.

"Guess I have a lot to think about," I toss out with a smirk as the doors start to slide closed.

"Fuck it." I hear him say before an arm is thrown out, catching the doors before they can shut all the way.

My eyes are locked on the opening as he stalks—not walks, not strolls, *stalks* like I'm his prey—into the car, not stopping until my back hits the wall behind me and he pins me to it.

Hands tunnel their way into my hair, fingers tangling through the waves falling around my shoulders. The back of my head is cupped and he crashes into me, every smartass remark I was about to utter gone at the feel of Jase's lips on mine.

I knew we had chemistry; it boiled between us all night.

But this…this isn't a kiss. It's ruination.

There's no coming back from this.

His lips are soft pillows against mine, and I part them to allow our tongues to tangle, the metal of his piercing whirling inside my mouth, giving a whole new meaning to the term *tonsil hockey*.

My scalp burns where my hair is pulled, and I'm dragged closer to his hard body before he steps forward again, pinning me fully to the wall of the elevator, the cold metal on my back a direct contrast to the inferno in front of me.

I was born to be on stage; no way am I going to be a member of the audience now. My coat and the jersey fall to the floor, followed by the gift box as I push up on my toes, my own hands grasping the short strands of his hair as I circle my arms around his thick neck.

We squeeze, tug, and pull as if we can't get close enough.

The bottoming out of my stomach has nothing to do with the speed of the elevator's descent and everything to do with Jase. *Talk about defying gravity, Elphaba.*

He sucks my bottom lip between his teeth, and as if that weren't enough, he drags the cool metal of his tongue ring against it to soothe away the sting. How it manages to stay cold inside a mouth hot enough to set me on fire I'll never know, but fucking hell it's erotic.

Holy Tracy Turnblad, I can hear the bells.

"You do realize you live in the building and don't have to maul the poor girl in the elevator, right, Donnelly?" A laughing male voice breaks in.

Spell broken, I finally notice the elevator has stopped moving.

Jase's eyes, now a deep forest green, never leave mine as he speaks to whoever has interrupted us. "Fuck you, Cali."

Great, busted by one of his teammates. I don't know if I should send him a thank you card for stopping us before things took a turn for the naked, or if I should offer him a cigarette—it doesn't matter that I don't smoke—to recover from the contact orgasm he might have if he steps inside the car with us.

"Sorry, man. You may look like a Hemsworth, but you're not my type."

"You're a dick." Jase's laugh tells me he's not angry.

Horny, maybe, at least if the pressure on my stomach is any indication, but no, not mad.

"And yet I'm still one of your closest friends. What does that say about you?" Callahan asks the rhetorical question, his gaze moving from his teammate to me. "I take it the date went well based on the PornHub-worthy kiss you guys had going on?"

My cheeks heat and I once again bury my face in Jase's armpit. I need to remember to tell him how much I like his deodorant.

"Cali," Jase warns, his arms tightening around me.

"What? I meant it as a good thing. This keeps me from having to listen to you bitch about how Melody keeps turning you down. Glad to see you managed to nut up and do something about this."

"*Cali.*" Jase's voice turns scary, taking on a dark quality I've never heard before.

"Relax. Don't go all big bad enforcer on me, and also get out of the elevator so I can go home. We have an early skate in the morning and I need my beauty sleep."

"Asshole," Jase mutters, threading our fingers together and retrieving my dropped belongings. "I swear he's just as bad as my family." His complaint loses its edge to the grin curving his lips.

I focus on how I want those lips back on mine and not the surge of jealousy I feel at what an amazing family he has—both blood and extended. My parents can't even be bothered to take three hours out of their year to see me in a show, yet his spend *hundreds* making sure not to miss a shift he plays on the ice.

At the glass doors of the building, I'm pulled to a stop. My hat is pulled onto my head and over my ears with a flick of the pom-pom on top and a kiss on the tip of my nose.

Ba-bum. Ba-bum.

Next, I'm helped into my coat, both his hands grasping the lapels and pulling me to him again. I brace myself with my hands on his chest, the muscles of his pecs flexing under my fingertips.

"As much as it pains me to admit it, I'll probably have to thank the asshole for the interruption."

"Why's that?" I tease.

"Because if he hadn't…" He bends, his mouth at my ear. "I was seconds away from taking you right there."

Ba-bum. Ba-bum.

Ba-bum. Ba-bum.

Breathe, Mels.

I blink, sucking in air like I'm drowning, stunned into silence.

Ba-bum. Ba-bum.

"I can't wait until tomorrow night." He pulls back to usher me to the door.

"Why?" I'm operating down a few brain cells.

"Because"—he drapes the jersey back over my shoulder—"I finally get to see what you look like wearing *my* name like you're supposed to."

Ba-bum. Ba-bum.

"Good night, baby." He slaps my butt and leaves me standing next to the town car he arranged to take me home.

How do I process the last five minutes of my life?

Need a magic eight ball?

My subconscious has jokes, abandoning me when I need help figuring this mess out.

There is one thing that's clear.

I never stood a chance against Jase Donnelly.

Chapter Twelve

From the Group Message Thread of The Coven

QUEEN OF SMUT: OMG!!! Let me tell you guys, our boy Jase has some good taste.

QUEEN OF SMUT: Well, I mean...I guess we already knew that from him dating Rock for a few years...but whoa baby.

ALPHABET SOUP: *GIF of Shirley Temple saying, "OMG thanks!"*

ALPHABET SOUP: But what did my bestie do to deserve the praise?

ALPHABET SOUP: You know what, hold on.

DAUNTLESS SUPERMAN: Oooo. Who knew dating a Covenette would get me invited into the CCs more than being related to two of you.

YOU KNOW YOU WANNA: Behave or we'll kick your ass right back out, Vin.

DAUNTLESS SUPERMAN: Ruthless, Beck. 100% ruthless.

SANTA'S COOKIE SUPPLIER: Don't worry, I'll keep him in line.

THE OG PITA: You guys are kinky late at night.

ALPHABET SOUP: Gross, Beth *puking emoji* I don't need to be hearing about that.

PROTEIN PRINCESS: *GIF of guy pointing up saying, "THIS."*

MAKES BOYS CRY: Since when did we turn into such prudes?

ALPHABET SOUP: Don't start, Skye, or we'll start asking you about Tuck's latest attempt at talking you back into bed.

MAKES BOYS CRY: *GIF of Lucille Ball sticking her tongue out*

MOTHER OF DRAGONS: Geez, can we EVER stay on topic? *squirrel emoji* *Dory fish emoji*

DAUNTLESS SUPERMAN: So why am I here?

SANTA'S COOKIE SUPPLIER: I think they want you to give up the details you know about Melody.

MAKES BOYS CRY: Wait? Melody? Wasn't that the name of the girl who turned our boy down all those weeks ago?

PROTEIN PRINCESS: Wait...hold on...we'll get back to that in a minute, but how come you know about this, Holly, and the rest of us don't?

DAUNTLESS SUPERMAN: She sleeps with me. She gets ALL the INSIDE information *winky face emoji*

YOU KNOW YOU WANNA: Don't be gross, Vin.

THE OG PITA: Dude, your sister might be preggers, but I doubt that would stop her from coming down the hall and kicking your ass.

MOTHER OF DRAGONS: Guys, Jake here...I know you love to jump from topic to topic, but can you please get on with it already? I would really like to take advantage of my wife, and your little Coven Conversation is getting in the way of that. So, CAN you talk about the chick who was at Jase's apartment tonight before one of the twins wakes up and cockblocks me. Please and thank you.

DAUNTLESS SUPERMAN: I second this. I'm having a sudden craving for sweets.

ALPHABET SOUP: OMG! This is the LAST time I invite you into one of these. Also, side note, Jor, you might be down a twin after I get through with him for withholding information.

MAKES BOYS CRY: So Melody was at Jase's tonight? Pretty girl, pink hair?

MAKES BOYS CRY: And...hold on...how do you three know about it?

QUEEN OF SMUT: I kind of accidentally crashed their date tonight.

MOTHER OF DRAGONS: And of course she video-chatted me right away.

THE OG PITA: Tell us everything.

Chapter Thirteen

During the season, my life is boring—at least as boring as the crazies in my life allow it to be.

Whether it's a game day or not, each day has a routine to follow.

Silencing my alarm, I roll from my bed, running a hand over my rumpled hair, and bring an ear to each shoulder, cracking my neck and shaking off the cobwebs of sleep.

The happy haze I've been in since my date with Melody follows me through the morning portion of my routine.

When I round the corner into the kitchen to grab whatever pre-made meal Gemma left for breakfast, I'm surprised to find Maddey awake, typing away on her MacBook Pro.

"Hey, Madz."

The coffee pot is half full, telling me she's been up for a while.

"Hey, Trip," she says around a yawn.

"Wasn't sure if I'd see you before I left or not."

Leaning against the counter across from her, I blow on my piping hot coffee and take a sip. *Ah, that's the stuff. Thank you, Lyle.*

"It wasn't the original plan, but after a *highly entertaining*

Coven Conversation last night, I had a few characters who wouldn't shut up until I wrote some of their words."

I don't even bat an eye at the mention of the voices in her head, but there is nothing scarier than the phrase *Coven Conversation*. After the events of last night, there is only one thing—or in this case, person—who could have been the topic of conversation: me.

"I take it you and my other half didn't waste any time filling in the girls?"

She takes a sip of her own coffee before saying, "To be fair, I was the one to bring it up."

"Shit."

My mug hits the counter with a slam, and I wince at the loss of one of my favorites. Cracked porcelain is the least of my worries, though.

"Yup." Maddey pops the P all too proudly. "Rocky isn't *all* that happy with you for withholding vital information."

I *so* didn't need my suspicions confirmed.

"It's like you really are my triplet. You read my mind almost as much as JD does."

"What can I say?" She lifts a shoulder. "It's a gift."

No respect. Madz is over here laughing at my expense, not at all concerned I'm about to get my ass kicked. Maybe I can convince Gage his pregnant wife shouldn't be hitting people in her condition, but with my luck he'll just be enlisted in doling out my punishment. Hell hath no fury like a best friend kept in the dark.

Yoshi!

Speak of the devil. I'm pretty sure I know who that text is from.

I chuck the remnants of my broken mug in the trash, wipe down the mess, and walk around the counter to drop a kiss on Maddey's head. "Gotta go."

"Tell Cali I need to talk to him about something later," she calls out as I grab my gear bag.

Cali may not be my favorite person after last night, but now I'm looking forward to seeing him. I know exactly what Maddey wants him for.

Another one bites the dust.

"You coming to the game tonight?"

"Thinking about it."

With a wave, I exit my apartment to find Cali already waiting for me in the hall, twirling his keyring around his finger. Living in the same building, we switch off which one of us drives the forty minutes to the Storm practice facility in Tarrytown.

"Well if it isn't our resident Romeo. And *how* are we this fine morning? Balls a little blue maybe?"

I flip him the bird, to which he only chuckles.

Hitting the button for the building's private underground lot, I turn and say, "Oh, before I forget." It's my turn to chuckle, knowing I'm about to drop a bomb on the smartass. "Madz wanted me to tell you she needs to talk to you later." I let the threat—yes, threat—hang there for a moment then add, "So don't make any plans for after the game."

"*Shiiiit.* She wants me to get half naked for one of her covers, doesn't she?"

"Probably." Definitely.

I ignore him for a minute to check my phone and wince when I thumb open the message.

ALPHABET SOUP: *GIF of Ricky Ricardo saying, "Lucy, you got some 'splainin' to do!"*

THE BIG HAMMER: Shit. You need to stop hanging out with Sammy.

ALPHABET SOUP: And YOU have to STOP telling my brother things instead of me.

THE BIG HAMMER: I'm sorry. I promise I'll make it up to you.

ALPHABET SOUP: Yeah you will.

"Eh." Cali slips on a pair of aviators, pulling out from the underground garage, bringing my attention back to him. "I guess there are worse things than having a gorgeous woman hang all over me for pictures. Maybe I'll get lucky and it'll be your fine-ass sister as my partner."

"First off." I level him with my fiercest enforcer look, the one generally reserved for Nate Bishop. "Too far. JD is off limits."

"You know I joke." His hands lift from the steering wheel in surrender.

"It's the only thing keeping me from shoving a hockey stick up your ass right now."

He laughs, not intimidated at all.

My sister can take care of herself. Hell, there are very few people—male or female—more respected than her and Skye in the sports industry. That said, my sister is very beautiful—I mean, how could she not be when sharing genetics with me? —so her presence in the locker rooms naturally comes with talk. We've had each other's back since the womb, and those protective instincts are imprinted on my soul.

"I take it by the way you and Broadway were trying to check each other for strep the date went good?"

Why am I not surprised he's already given Mels a nickname?

I play back all the highlights from last night: the dinner, the easy conversation, the way my girl's dark eyes sparkled when she opened the Mr. Potato Head I got her, and of course, *the kiss.*

Why don't I have a diary? The details of it need to be recorded in full-on glitter pen glory. I wonder if Jake's younger sister Carlee has one. She's nine, so she might. Sure, it is probably filled with all sorts of stuff about my younger brother Sean, but I can ignore that while flipping through for a blank page to borrow. Girl loves me; I'm sure she wouldn't mind.

I've never been more grateful to be pulling onto the campus that houses our practice facility.

I have a feeling Cali's razzing is only the start of what I'll be facing today.

♡

Waking up from my pre-game nap—the best part of my job, if you ask me. I mean, who doesn't love naps?—I'm not at all surprised to find JD working on an iPad in one of the massage chairs in the living room, an episode of *How I Met Your Mother* on the TV, volume on low.

"Morning, sunshine." She doesn't even look up from her work.

"Hey, wombmate." I grab a protein shake and plop onto the couch adjacent to her. "I'd ask what you're doing here, but I honestly expected you to be here before my nap."

"I wanted to get the girls settled with Mom first."

"I take it you're coming to the game tonight?"

"Yup. Already worked out all the details with Madz and the others."

I choke, almost suffocating from my protein shake going down the wrong pipe. *Fuck my life.*

"So…" The smile that blooms on her face doesn't do anything to soothe my nerves, because it's not a smile—it's a warning, one I've learned to heed in my twenty-five years. "Do we get to meet your girlfriend tonight?"

"Nope." I look toward the TV to keep her from picking up on the lie.

There is not one person—not even my mother—who has

had my back like my twin. I call her my other half for a reason. But in the same breath, there isn't another soul more willing to slap me with reality when needed.

If I make a mistake during a game, she's not afraid to tell me how I fucked up. It's not in a mean way, but to help improve my play on the ice. Ryan and I may be the professional hockey players in the family, but JD has just as much ice in her veins, if not more.

It's why I don't want her anywhere near the woman I'm still desperately trying to impress. I need to keep Mels as far away from JD's crazy couch coaching as possible.

"Bullshit." The iPad makes a *slap* as it's tossed onto the extended footrest. Eyes flashing golden fire turn my way. "Don't you dare lie to me, Jason Richard."

"Ouch." I mime a hit to the chest. "Low blow, Jordan Danielle. Real low blow."

"Whatever." She waves me off. "Now tell me why I'm not meeting her. Scared?"

"Hell yeah I'm scared."

She laughs—in my face.

"Cute, Jase."

I narrow my eyes. "Don't patronize me."

"Who me?" A hand goes to her chest, a mocking look of offense on her face. "I would *never*."

"Smartass."

She shrugs.

"Look." I shift forward, resting my elbows on my knees, letting her read how serious this is. "This isn't like when Madz and Ry started dating. Melody doesn't just know hockey, she follows it. So, whereas most of your couch coaching comments went right over Maddey's head, they won't with her."

She goes silent, studying me, looking for what's not being said. Thank god my vulnerabilities are buried deep enough not even she, who is known for reading my mind, can pick up on them.

"If what you're saying is true, you shouldn't have anything to worry about. Hell, you've just made the All-Star Team for the second time."

"I know."

"You also have an Olympic *gold* medal"—her frown tells me Jake was right and she's pissed about my post taunting Bishop—"to your name. Not many guys can say that."

"Only the two dozen other guys from our team," I mumble.

She gives me her serious mom face as one of her hands caresses the volleyball-sized bump under her shirt.

"What's with the crisis of confidence? Does this chick have you tied up in knots that bad?"

"Like she learned them from the McClain boys," I deadpan.

Maddey comes from a Navy family, and sailors are known for their knot skills, after all.

"Well then…I guess it's a good thing the girls are coming in for tonight's game."

I groan, already knowing I'm not going to like the answer but needing to ask. "Why's that?"

"Because, my darling brother"—she pats my knee like I'm one of her dogs—"just like Vince, it looks like you're gonna need the help of your *precious* Coven to help you get the girl."

I hate, *hate* that she's probably right.

"Now stop wasting time. You have to leave for the Garden in an hour. Give me *all* the deets."

Chapter Fourteen

Melody

"**Y**our first week was good then?"

I let out a curse as I stab myself in the eye with the mascara wand. I'm already running late for the game, so the last thing I should be doing is video-chatting with my older brother, but I wouldn't miss an opportunity to see him—even if it is only through a screen—for the world.

"Care Bear?" The use of my childhood nickname reminds me he asked a question.

I squeeze the now irritated eye in hard blinks, moving from the makeup mirror to the open MacBook next to it.

"What? Oh…yeah, it was good. We did our first read-through, and I can already tell I have decent chemistry with the majority of the cast members. And what we heard of the score was pretty epic."

"Am I going to have to sit through watching you kiss some guy in this one?"

I snort—hard.

God love him.

Good ol' Mom and Dad supported us financially, but the buck stopped there, so to speak. Even though the two of us spend the majority of our time living in separate cities, we work hard at keeping our relationship close despite the distance. Just because our parents are absent from our lives doesn't mean we have to be.

"Teddy." I rest my cheek against my fist and lock eyes with him through the webcam. "I'm playing Marilyn Monroe…I'm kissing *lots* of guys in this one."

Another snort escapes when he mimes gagging.

"Don't worry, three of them are my husbands."

"It is scary how much research you do for your roles."

"To be fair"—I go back to putting the finishing touches on my mascara—"outside of being eligible for a Tony, Marilyn is a dream role for me."

"How could I forget? You had that huge painting of her in that gold dress from whatever movie hanging in your bedroom growing up."

"*Gentlemen Prefer Blondes.* One of my favorites."

"What?"

"That's the movie it's from." I use a Q-tip to clean up the mascara underneath my eye and lift the laptop. "And what do you mean by *had*?" I swivel the screen so he can see the three-foot-tall painting in its place of honor above my bed.

"How did I not notice that the last time I came to visit?"

"No idea."

"Mels! You almost ready?" Zoey shouts from down the hall.

"Be out in a minute."

I need to wrap this up before Zoey comes busting in here in full Storm apparel. I *so* don't want to answer any questions *that* would raise.

"Look." I sit on the edge of my bed, MacBook in my lap. "I better go before Zo loses it."

"Okay, Care. Have fun. Love you."

"Love you too."

The lid to the laptop closes with a *snick* and I blow out a calming breath. I didn't lie to my brother, but keeping things from him makes me feel like reaching for the Pepto-Bismol.

Jase Donnelly, though? Yup, that's information better left undisclosed. Finding out about him will be a bigger bomb than the Reynolds Pamphlet, and I'm not cool enough to rap.

Clusterfuck, party of three.

Oh well. Like Mr. Hamilton, I should say no to this, but I can't.

"Mels!" Zoey's voice spurs me into action.

Jumping from the bed, I grab the jersey from the hanger I hung it on last night and slip it over my head, scrutinizing my appearance in my mirrored closet doors. The white skinny jeans hug my legs, showing off the muscular thighs I've earned from the countless hours of dancing I've done through the years, and the knee-high black leather boots with four-inch heels make my short legs look longer.

My choice of footwear may not be the most appropriate selection for a hockey game, but thanks again to my many years in musical theater, I can do anything in heels.

The rest of my look is casual: high ponytail, ends curling naturally, simple makeup, and silver hoops through my ears.

Then there's the black, white, and gray jersey. Jase must have given me one of his game-worn ones because I'm swimming in the material.

"Mels, come on, you know I like to watch warm—" The sound of the door opening precedes Zoey's voice before the words abruptly cut off.

Looking over my shoulder, I see my friend gaping at me like a fish, mouth opening and closing as she struggles to find the words to say. Zoey speechless is as rare as a unicorn.

"ELLA!" she yells, breaking her silence.

"What?" Ella has a container of leftover risotto in her hands, scarfing down her dinner before she has to leave for the theater. "Holy shit. *You're* wearing a Storm jersey?" Shock drips from her words.

"It's not like they're playing the Bruisers or anything." I pop a shoulder.

"True." She nods. "Wait." She holds a hand up like a stop sign. "Where did you even get this? It's *huge* on you." She pinches the material between her fingers, stretching it out.

"Oh my god!" Zoey shouts from the doorway, her eyebrows disappearing into her hairline. "Is this one of *his?*" We are now at screech-level decibels.

"I think it might be."

"Oh—my—god." Zoey rushes me, inspecting every inch of the jersey. "This *is* his. Holy shit, Mels. This is *unreal*. You're lucky you're one of my best friends or I would totally hate you."

"Like *I* didn't hate you enough for getting to go to the game." Ella pulls on the sleeve of the jersey again. "Now there's this." Her eyes meet mine in the mirror. "I take it things are starting to get serious?"

I drop my gaze, unable to look either of my friends in the eye as guilt once again washes over me. I worry the bottom of the jersey, lifting it from where it hangs mid-thigh. Are things getting serious with Jase? And what the hell am I supposed to do if they are?

Chapter Fifteen

"**B**ring The Storm" by Birds of Prey blares through the locker room while I use a roll of rainbow tape—affectionately dubbed Sammycorn tape by the BTU Titans—to secure my uniform socks.

"Bro..." Cali backhands my bare shoulder. "Why don't you *ever* put that shit on silent?"

Yoshi!

Yoshi!

My phone is blowing up with text notifications like Marlo can't decide if he wants to stay on his dinosaur sidekick. And yes, my text alert tone is from Super Mario Bros. You already know how seriously we take our Mario Kart, and the little green dude is *always* my avatar when we play.

"Sorry." I flick it to silent and pull up my messages.

DAUNTLESS SUPERMAN: Bro...you are soooooo screwed.

THE KRAKEN (Gage): I thought we had an understanding. You DO NOT piss off pregnant women. You wanna risk your life and mess with your sister, go for it. But, for THE LOVE OF GOD, can you refrain from getting your *bestie* (and I hate you BTW for making me have to use the word *bestie*...add BTW to the list too) all pissy. She lives with me. I'M the one who takes the brunt of the **whispers** hormones.

THE BIG HAMMER: Vin, you are failing at this best friend game. Doesn't bro code dictate that you're supposed to help keep the girls off my back?

THE BIG HAMMER: And, Gage, man, what can I say? YOU were the one who asked Balboa to marry you. Her living with you kinda comes with the territory.

DAUNTLESS SUPERMAN: You mean the same way you kept them off my back when YOU told me I needed to bend the knee with The Coven?

THE KRAKEN: *middle finger emoji*

THE BIG HAMMER: Ummm...I'm pretty sure my advice is one of the main reasons your way-too-good-for-you girlfriend is ACTUALLY your girlfriend.

DAUNTLESS SUPERMAN: *see Gage's previous text*

DAUNTLESS SUPERMAN: Also...there's this.

DAUNTLESS SUPERMAN: *picture of all eight Covenettes huddled together*

"Shit."
Fuck me.
"They're *all* here?" Cali unabashedly looks over my shoul-

der, eavesdropping. Although, is it eavesdropping if it's a text?

"It would appear so."

"By your tone, I'm going to say this wasn't planned?"

"Nope."

"Harrison!" Cali bellows, summoning the third member of our standard trio.

"What's up, Cali?"

"Hope you didn't have plans tonight. Covenettes in the *hiz-ouse*."

I roll my eyes. It comes as no surprise that Cali with his over-the-top personality is one of my teammates I'm closest with.

"Which ones?" Harrison plops down on the bench next to me.

"All of them." The glee in Cali's voice has me rolling my eyes again.

"What did you *do*?" Harrison's eyes are wide as they look down at where I'm lacing up my skates.

"Nothing," I reply through clenched teeth.

"Bull." Harrison eyes me, having plenty of experience with The Coven himself. "You must have done *something* to warrant an unplanned gathering."

Cali snorts, and my elbow connects with his side, eliciting a grunt of pain. *Serves you right, asshole.*

"Come on, Donnelly. Fess up," Harrison prods.

"Who says it's unplanned?"

Now Harrison snorts. "The fact that the three of us"—he waves a finger between him, Cali, and me—"would have had *plans* for after the game."

Damn him for being right.

"I think it has to do with our boy here's girlfriend," Cali practically sings like he's Gene Kelly in the rain. Yes, I've been brushing up on my musical knowledge.

"Girlfriend? Since when do you have a gir—" Harrison

slaps his thighs, joining Cali's laughter as realization hits. "Holy shit. You finally made a move on the actress?"

"Making a move was never his problem. It was getting her to say yes that was the issue." Cali is all too happy to clarify.

Ignoring them, I pull my chest protector over my head, followed by my black and gray home jersey. I won't bother with my helmet until game time, so all that's left to do is slip on my good luck charm—one of JD's hair ties.

Don't judge me. We all have them.

Ooo, story time. **rubs hands together** I love story time.

There's the aforementioned Sammycorn tape, which became a thing after Ryan scored a hat trick wearing it after a lost bet to Sammy. Any of the Titans who have gone pro like us still use it because our college team went on a fifteen-game winning streak going into our second Frozen Four victory.

Even our two guys who switched to fighting after college tape a piece in their shorts when they have a match. We take it *very* seriously.

Tucker ties a pair of laces from when his high school team won State to his skates, and Jake always kisses my sister— and nieces since their birth—through the glass before a game.

If that's not enough proof I'm not the only one with a quirk, Vince always needs Rocky to be the one to wrap his hands before a fight. Dude almost completely lost his shit before his fight a few weeks ago, but that's a story for another time.

Back to me.

So yeah, my only thing is I wear a hair tie of my sister's on my wrist, have since we were twelve and I had the best game of my hockey career because she had asked me to grab her one and I forgot to give it to her.

But as I slip the black elastic over my hand, it snaps. *Shit.* Reaching into my bag for a different one, I come up empty.

Now what do I do?

Intellectually, I know it doesn't have an effect on how I

play—hockey players have their superstitions, but at least we aren't as bad as baseball players—but the last thing I need with Melody in attendance is a change to my routine.

Wombmate, you better have a hair tie on you.

Half an hour before puck drop, we clomp our way down the rubber pads to the rink for warm-ups.

Pre-game ritual first, new hair tie second.

After my lap around the rink, I skate over to the boards in front of my sister's seats, knocking on the plexiglass to get her attention.

A chorus of "Jase!" "Trip!" "Dude!" Bro!" "Bestie!" comes at me as everyone greets me at once.

"JD." I single her out. "I need your hair tie." I gesture to my head in case she has a hard time hearing me over the noise in the arena. Without a beat, she pulls the one from her hair and slingshots it over the glass. God love her.

Pinching my glove under my armpit, I slide the tie home. "Love you," I call out, skating backward.

I take a few shots on goal as I scan the typical section that houses family members of the Storm—there are too many of mine for them to sit there—until I find a particular shade of pink.

She came.

Her black eyes are locked on me, and unlike my *so-called* supporters behind me across the ice, she's wearing the jersey I gave her—my jersey. And damn if she doesn't look even better in it than I imagined.

Digging my blades into the ice, I glide across it until I'm directly in front of her. The things I could do if there weren't half an inch of plexiglass between us.

Her smile is sheepish as she gives a small wave.

I'm basking in the glow of how that makes me feel when I'm knocked into the boards, my chest protector pinging off the glass.

My two about-to-be-dead teammates are jostling for position to flirt with my girl when I shove them off me. Did I say dead? No, that's too easy. Torture sounds better.

Why the hell doesn't anyone know how to mind their own business?

Chapter Sixteen

Melody

"Eep, oh my god. These seats are *epic*." Zoey snaps a selfie with the rink behind her to send to Ella. She hasn't stopped gushing since we arrived at the Garden.

"Zo, you act like we usually sit in the nosebleeds or something."

Whenever we come together, we sit on the lower level. Sure, we've never sat *this* close, but our seats haven't been anything to sneeze at.

"Oh look, there's Loverboy." Her arm stretches to point Jase out on the ice. Real subtle—not.

"Don't call him that," I hiss through clenched teeth, pulling on her arm.

Drawn like a magnet, my gaze finds him taking warm-up shots at the empty net. *God he lights my candle.*

Zoey's brows pinch together the way they always do when she smells bullshit. "Oh, Mels, baby girl." She links our elbows. "You've got it *bad*. Stop trying to deny it."

"I don't want to talk about it."

Deny, deny, deny.

Act—keyword there—like he doesn't affect me.

I'm cool, so cool I could be the ice the Storm plays on.

I keep telling myself this until the breath stalls in my lungs when I see a pair of golden-green eyes locked on me.

"Oh my god," Zoey whisper-shouts when Jase skates toward us.

"*Shhh.*"

Could she *be* more embarrassing? *Yes, I said this in my best Chandler Bing voice*

I wave, my traitorous heart flipping inside my chest when he winks. *The boy gives a good wink.*

I jump—literally jump—when he's slammed into the boards by two of his own teammates, the sounds of their bodies reverberating causing all eyes in our section to turn our way.

Jase doesn't linger, effortlessly gliding backward once free, leaving his teammates behind. I don't need the jerseys to recognize Callahan and Harrison, the former wearing a grin similar to the one he sported last night when he caught Jase and me making out like teenagers.

"Hey, Broadway," Cali says, looking like the Cheshire cat, and Harrison jerks his chin in hello.

"Hey, Cali."

Can your eardrum rupture from someone shouting next to you? I should probably check for blood or something because Zoey's squeal reaches an octave usually reserved for dog whistles.

As if auditory damage isn't enough, she's also working on pulling my arm from its socket by yanking on it, all while texting with the other hand. Did I really think it was a good thing Ella couldn't come? Because Zoey is practically live-tweeting every second of our night to our missing friend.

"You have zero chill," I tell her, my tone wry.

"I'm sorry, but not all of us can be as blasé about hockey hunks as you are, Mels. Besides, *I'm*"—she covers her heart with a hand—"a Storm fan, and *you* just had not one, but *three* of their top players say hi to you. I'm allowed a fangirl moment, thank you very much."

"Careful, Zo, your inner puck bunny is showing."

Zoey shrugs, unconcerned, holding out her beer to cheers before letting me read the messages from Ella.

FIDDLER ON THE ROOF: OMG!!! Can those be our seats when I get to come too?

FIDDLER ON THE ROOF: WHAT?! I need to know where to mail my letter. I need to issue a formal complaint that the BOSTON fan of our trio is the one with a Storm player for a boyfriend.

FIDDLER ON THE ROOF: Can you hook a girl up? I'm not picky about which one. I'll even give Zoey first dibs. But come on?? Help a sister out.

Ella may be the quiet one, but her texts only prove why she and Zoey get along so well.

The next hour or so passes in a blur of the national anthem, hockey playing, and trash talk. Zoey may be more obsessed with what the players look like *under* their uniforms than I am, but we do share a passion for the game.

Thankfully, I'm able to keep her attention off of me and all swoony developments concerning a certain Storm defenseman by spending the entire first intermission discussing what we think the chances are of Ella making it into our show's orchestra.

Late in the second, we jump to our feet as Callahan flies down the ice on a breakaway thanks to a beautiful pass from Harrison. My heart races and my blood pumps as if I'm the one trying to beat out five other guys to the net.

With my breath held and cold beer spilling over my

fingers, we watch as one of the Dallas forwards glides up behind Callahan and crosschecks him from behind.

Everything after that happens in fast forward.

Callahan hits the ice—hard.

Zoey and I press our faces to the plexiglass.

Jase shoves Kruger, the Dallas player, for the illegal check.

Kruger rounds on Jase with a punch to the face.

My heart is firmly lodged in my throat as Jase's entire demeanor turns on a dime. Gone is the smirk and the guy who seemed like he was playing a pickup game with friends, a stone-cold warrior in his place.

He shakes off the punch as if it were a playful tap and not a powerful right hook. His gloves hit the ice with a flick of the wrists and Kruger's green and white jersey is clutched in his hands as he hauls him in close.

Jase is one of the bigger players in the NHL, one of the things that helps him be the revered enforcer that he is.

The arena goes silent, sucking in a collective breath, waiting to see what will happen next.

Jase leans in to say something we're too far away to hear. Then without any showboating, he pulls his arm back, snapping out and landing two solid jabs in quick succession.

I don't want to know what it says about me that I feel each of the blows in my clit. This right here is one of the things I love most about hockey—the rawness, the intensity.

Black, white, gray, and green swirl together as members from both teams swarm and Kruger is shoved to the ice. The referees push into the fray, moving to hold Jase back from any further attacks, except...he hasn't budged.

He stands on the outside, back ramrod straight, jaw and eyes hard as he silently warns Kruger against making another move.

Fights—no matter how the rules have evolved through the years—will always be an integral part of the game, but the way Jase played his role was like a work of art. The up-close-

and-personal experience of him in full-blown enforcer mode…was…hot.

"Holy shit," Zoey says breathlessly. "I think I need a new pair of panties after that show."

You're not the only one.

"*Eep!*" The back of her hand hits me in the boob. "Mels." The hits pick up speed. "Oh my god, look." Hit-hit-hit. "Look." Hit-hit. "Look." Hit-hit-hit. "*Look.*"

I wrap a hand around the abusing one. "Stop, Zo."

"But he's *looking* at *you.*"

He is?

Sure enough, sitting in the penalty box, Jase's attention—which should be on what is happening on the ice—is on me.

He winks.

Again.

Damn that wink. Sweet Mother of all things Bernadette Peters I'm in trouble.

My face heats and I drop my head so he can't see just how affected I am by him.

Gurrrrrl, you is in trouble.

And of course, Zoey snaps another picture. Thank god Ella is working now.

Late in the third period, Callahan scores the only goal of the game thanks to an assist from Jase, and the Garden erupts in cheers as every Storm fan sings along with the goal song played any time the Storm lights the lamp.

When the game is over and most of the seats around us are empty, we hang back to watch the announcement of the three stars of the game: Callahan, Ringquist (the goalie), and Jase.

We're gathering our things after the team disappears into the tunnel when my phone vibrates in my pocket.

THE BIG HAMMER: Wait for me? I won't be long, promise.

BROADWAY BABY: Why? Don't you have your family here?

THE BIG HAMMER: Yup. That's why I want you to wait.

BROADWAY BABY: Um…I still haven't recovered from the ones I met last night. Don't you think I should be eased into it?

THE BIG HAMMER: You would think so.

BROADWAY BABY: What does that mean?

BROADWAY BABY: ??

BROADWAY BABY: Jase??

My eyes stay locked on my phone, willing it to light up with an explanation, but it remains dark.

"Mels?"

What the hell does he *mean*?

"Mels?"

Why isn't he answering?

"*Mels?*"

I'm jostled from my stupor by Zoey grabbing my shoulder and literally shaking me. "Huh?"

"Guuurrrrl. Phew." She wipes her brow. "You zoned out on me."

"Sorry."

"Who were you texting?" She perks up in her seat. "Oh, was it Loverboy?"

Does she have to call him that?

"What did he say? Oh my god! Were you two just *sexting*?"

"What? No."

"Well that's disappointing." Her lips tip down in a frown, making me laugh. Just because she's a total hornball and would be sexting doesn't mean I am.

"Can we go?" My words came out rushed. Jase's continued silence has a sense of foreboding prickling at the back of my neck.

"Sure."

Purses in hand, we make to leave, but then Zoey's eyes shift, locking on something over my shoulder.

"Um...Mels..."

Why do I get the feeling I don't want to know what's behind me?

"Melody?" I recognize the voice of Jase's sister Jordan.

You can do this, Mels.

But can I? Meeting a person's family is kind of a big deal. It's one thing to talk on video chat; it's a whole new level of serious to interact in person.

I suck in a deep breath and turn around. It's a good thing I'm sitting down, because I'm damn near knocked on my ass by what I see.

There isn't just one person, or two—no, there are *eleven* of them, eight female and three male.

Can I hide in my own little corner?

I'm going to kill Jase.

"Uh...hi?"

Way to make it sound more like a question than a greeting.

"Oh, good, it is you. I figured as much. I mean how many people with pink hair and a Donnelly jersey could there be at the game?"

"Holy shit, that's his sister, isn't it?" Zoey whispers in my ear. I nod, my gaze bouncing over each person in front of us.

Without warning, arms circle my neck as Jordan bends for a hug, her belly bumping me in the process.

"Wow. You're even prettier in person." She holds me by my shoulders, looking me over. "My brother has good taste."

"I'll say," says a deep male voice, followed by an "Oof."

"Behave, Champ," a female voice scolds.

"Damn, Blue."

"Gage. Rocky." Jordan whips around. "Can you two behave? We're trying to *prevent* Melody from running for the hills."

"Sorry," they mumble.

"You're doing this all wrong, JD," says the man I recognize as Vince Steele, his long legs stepping over the seats into the row behind us. "Let the best friend handle this one."

"Um, Vin...*I'm* his best friend." Rocky points to her chest.

I appraise her, recalling she's Jase's ex-girlfriend. She's gorgeous: model tall, long blue-black hair that hangs to her waist, and *way* more athletic than I'll ever be no matter how much dancing I do. Not gonna lie, it's a little intimidating.

"No, Rock, you're his *bestie*. It's different." He leans forward to drop an arm around both Jordan and me. "Anyway, I'm Vince, Jase's *best*"—he shoots a look at Rocky—"friend, and let me tell you, I am so happy to finally meet the girl my boy has *not* shut up about."

He's not the first to mention Jase talking about me, but I still have a hard time believing it.

"Please, Vin, I distinctly remember *you* having to come to us for help to get Holly to agree to a date." Skye's comment causes the group to snicker.

I struggle to keep up as Jordan cuts the others off from interrupting further so she can make introductions. Thank god I'm adept at memorizing lines, otherwise I would have zero hope in remembering them all as she makes her way through the horde.

"This is Zoey." I introduce my one friend, feeling vastly outnumbered, even with her continued texting with Ella. "You're the fighter, right?" I ask, turning to Vince.

"One of them." He nods then jerks his chin toward Gage. "My brother-in-law is another."

"And I take it you all"—I circle a finger to include the ladies—"are the rest of The Coven?"

"Aww, he's told her about us," Beth gushes.

"Please—Vin and Jase never shut up about The Coven. I knew about The Coven from Vince *days* before I knew his name." Holly shoots him a look so full of heat it almost makes me blush.

"And he wonders why it took him so long to get you to go out with him?" Gemma rolls her eyes, and I need to remember to tell her how delicious her pot pies are. Oh, that sounds way dirtier than I meant it. *Don't say that out loud, Mels.* "You're a real Casanova, cuz."

I slump back, leaning against Zoey, mind spinning.

"And I thought we changed topics like squirrels," she whispers.

"They put us to shame."

"Seriously."

Chapter Seventeen

First order of business: find my girl.

Second: survive the inquisition from The Coven.

The first task should be easy enough. The second, not so much.

Vince texted letting me know they found Melody and are still at her seats. With Cali and Harrison as reinforcements, we make our way around the outside of the rink.

There's no way to miss our squad—we are loud, crazy, and huge. In the middle of it all, there she is. Damn, my baby looks so good in black and gray.

Like a puck flying to the five-hole, I eat up the distance separating us, ignoring everything—friends, family, greetings tossed my way, all of it. Not giving a flying puck that I'm interrupting whatever she's talking about with my sister, I take her hand and pull her from her seat, her dark eyes going wide at the abruptness.

Spinning her, I take in my name stretched across her shoulders. *Mine.* The jersey is ridiculously big on her, but fuck if she isn't the hottest thing I've ever seen.

Curling my body around hers, her back flush with my front, I bend, my mouth brushing the shell of her ear as I say,

"Fuck, baby. I knew you would look good in my jersey, but *damn*, it's even better than I thought it would be."

"Jase."

She shudders when I roll the ball of my tongue ring along her earlobe.

"There's only one thing that could make it better."

"Wh-What's that?" she stutters.

"If you were naked underneath it."

The vein in her neck pulses under my mouth, where I'm sucking on the spot and riding the edge of pressure that would leave a mark.

"*Jase*." My name falls from her lips, a broken plea.

"Damn…Madz, get out your phone and start taking notes," Becky says.

"Seriously," comes from Beth.

"Who knew our boy was hiding such a dirty alpha under his hockey sweater?" Skye adds.

"I did," Vince declares proudly.

I ignore every smartass comment from my family and focus solely on the woman trembling in my arms.

Legs nudging the backs of hers, I guide us a few precious feet away, spinning her around, pressing her against the boards of the rink. It's been almost twenty-four hours since I've had her mouth on mine, and I'm not about to wait another second.

Cupping the back of her head in both my hands, I tug on the end of her ponytail to adjust her to the perfect angle. Her dark eyes shine like wet stones, and a tempting blush spreads down her neck and under the collar of my jersey as I hold her stare. I want to slip a finger under to lift the material and find out how far the blush has traveled.

Her lashes flutter as her eyes go hooded. Still I hold back.

Even though we talk every day, I can't help but shake the feeling she's keeping me at a distance.

I stroke the line of her jaw with my thumb, the pressure enough to part her lips.

No more waiting.

I slam my mouth onto hers, our bodies crashing into the boards.

Her head is in the protective cradle of my hands, my fingers tunneling beneath the strands of her hair and destroying her ponytail.

A sigh.

A moan.

The heat level rising, the ice behind us is at risk of melting.

I could be happy kissing her for the rest of my life. Well, maybe not *just* kissing.

"*Damn*, it's a good thing I'm already pregnant." Rocky's voice is the first one to pierce the haze of lust surrounding us.

"For reals. I just had a contact orgasm," Becky adds.

"I think I might have dated the wrong Donnelly brother. Damn, Trip." I don't need to see her to know Maddey's fanning herself dramatically.

"And I thought the elevator was hot. Way to step up your game, Donnelly." Cali laughs.

"Fuck you, Cali."

"I told you last night, bro—not my type. Your sister, however..."

I should smother him in his sleep on our next road trip.

"Sorry, Cali. I'm a one-dick woman, and I'm *more* than satisfied with the one I have." I hear my sister pat his chest.

"Jesus, JD."

"Oh don't get your panties in a bunch, Jase. You should be happy for me."

I may be responding to those determined to see me in a straightjacket, but my eyes never leave Melody. She's a vision: flushed cheeks, the freckle under her eye standing out in contrast, lips swollen, hair crazy like she stuck a finger in an outlet.

Pink is officially my new favorite color.

"Come on, baby. Let's take this shit-show on the road."

Chapter Eighteen

THE BIG HAMMER: Quick, send me a selfie.

BROADWAY BABY: 1ˢᵗ, that's random. 2ⁿᵈ, why?

THE BIG HAMMER: Because I miss your pretty face.

BROADWAY BABY: Awww…that was actually kind of sweet.

THE BIG HAMMER: What can I say? I'm a regular Prince Charming.

THE BIG HAMMER: *GIF of Prince Charming*

BROADWAY BABY: Yeah, you're way more Flynn Rider than Prince Charming.

BROADWAY BABY: *GIF of Flynn Rider from *Tangled* saying, "Hi."*

THE BIG HAMMER: Well…he gets the princess in the

end, so I'll take it, but I don't want a GIF. I want a picture of you.

BROADWAY BABY: You're ridiculous, you know that?

THE BIG HAMMER: This may be true, but it doesn't change the fact that I need a picture of you.

BROADWAY BABY: It's only been 3 days since you saw me.

THE BIG HAMMER: Doesn't matter. Give it to me.

THE BIG HAMMER: *GIF of Chris Pratt pointing down and saying, "Right now."*

BROADWAY BABY: Oooo…Chris Pratt is hot.

THE BIG HAMMER: *angry face emoji*

BROADWAY BABY: Don't worry, big boy. Hemsworth is still her favorite of the Chris-es

THE BIG HAMMER: Hey Zoey!

BROADWAY BABY: Hey, handsome.

THE BIG HAMMER: Can you do me a favor before Mels realizes you stole her phone?

BROADWAY BABY: Sure! What do you need?

BROADWAY BABY: *GIF of Steve Carell leaning forward, waiting*

THE BIG HAMMER: You're my kind of people, Zo. Can you take a picture of my girl and send it to me? She's refusing to do it.

BROADWAY BABY: I got you.

♡

THE BIG HAMMER: How was your day, baby?

BROADWAY BABY: It was good. How about yours? Congrats on the win BTW.

THE BIG HAMMER: Awww, did you watch?

BROADWAY BABY: I might have caught a period or two.

THE BIG HAMMER: Hot damn! We'll make a Storm fan out of you yet.

BROADWAY BABY: Yeah…I wouldn't go that far.

THE BIG HAMMER: We'll see.

BROADWAY BABY: Your own twin doesn't root for your team…what makes you think you can convert me?

THE BIG HAMMER: *GIF of Stephan Colbert saying, "My heart actually hurts when you say that."*

BROADWAY BABY: I'm pretty sure I'M supposed be the drama queen in this relationship.

THE BIG HAMMER: OMG. Did you FINALLY admit we are ACTUALLY in a relationship?? Good job, baby.

BROADWAY BABY: Oh geez *facepalm emoji*

♡

THE BIG HAMMER: Daily check-in text with my girlfriend.

BROADWAY BABY: Who said I was your girlfriend?

THE BIG HAMMER: Um…that would be you. Remember?

BROADWAY BABY: Can't say I recall that.

THE BIG HAMMER: *gasp* And you're the one who memorizes lines for a living???

THE BIG HAMMER: That's okay, baby. I'll be that person who hides in the hole in the stage for when you forget. Here's some proof.

THE BIG HAMMER: *screenshot of past conversation*

BROADWAY BABY: Why doesn't this surprise me AT ALL?

THE BIG HAMMER: *kissy face emoji*

♡

THE BIG HAMMER: I'm SO ready to come home and sleep in my bed.

BROADWAY BABY: You act like you had away games all week. You have one road game and it's in Philly.

THE BIG HAMMER: I know, but it's been a week since I've gotten to see you in person and not just on a phone or computer screen. I miss you.

BROADWAY BABY: You know, Mr. Donnelly, you have these moments when you are surprisingly charming.

THE BIG HAMMER: Oh, baby. Can you call me Mr. Donnelly when I get back? That was hot.

BROADWAY BABY: Annnnnndddd…THERE'S the guy I've gotten to know.

THE BIG HAMMER: *boomerang of Jase winking*

BROADWAY BABY: Damn Zoey and Ella for telling you how I feel about your winking.

THE BIG HAMMER: Hey, I don't feel bad for you at all. You may have them, but I have the entire damn Coven.

BROADWAY BABY: What are you doing?

THE BIG HAMMER: Going on a mission for cheesesteaks and fries with Cali and Harrison.

BROADWAY BABY: Should you really be eating that on game day?

THE BIG HAMMER: When in Philly. *shrugging emoji* Plus, anything potato-related makes me think of my girl. What are you doing?

BROADWAY BABY: In Duane Reade.

BROADWAY BABY: *picture of Melody, Zoey, and Ella duck-facing while holding up a variety of ChapSticks*

THE BIG HAMMER: Damn my girl is hot *string of fire emojis*

BROADWAY BABY: *GIF of Justin Timberlake saying, "Oh stop it."*

THE BIG HAMMER: Make sure you stock up. I plan on spending A LOT of time kissing those lips when I get back.

BROADWAY BABY: I don't know about that, All-Star. I might need to put them on their own bye week after all the kissing I've been doing today.

THE BIG HAMMER: Excuse me??? Want to try that again? **wiggles finger in ear** I'm pretty sure I heard you wrong.

BROADWAY BABY: Lol. We're texting, not speaking. It would be your eyes you'd need to fix, not your ears.

THE BIG HAMMER: Now's not the time to be cute. Want to tell me again why you need ChapStick?

BROADWAY BABY: Because my lips are chapped.

BROADWAY BABY: *GIF of Michelle Tanner rolling her eyes and saying, "Duh."*

THE BIG HAMMER: And what, pray tell, are they chapped from?

BROADWAY BABY: Kissing.

THE BIG HAMMER: Like from kissing your hand, your pillow—hell, a poster or life-sized cardboard cutout of me because you miss me so much??

BROADWAY BABY: Ooo, do they sell life-sized cardboard cutouts of you?

THE BIG HAMMER: Answer the question, Mels.

BROADWAY BABY: Ooo, you called me Mels, not baby. You MUST be serious.

THE BIG HAMMER: ???

BROADWAY BABY: Oh no. Your use of question marks is increasing.

THE BIG HAMMER: Mels????

BROADWAY BABY: A Mels and 4 question marks. Okay, okay, before you run out of characters, although *thinking face emoji* can you run out of characters in a text message? Asking for a friend *crying laughing emoji*

THE BIG HAMMER: MELS?????

BROADWAY BABY: Oooo, shouty capitals. Fine, keep your pants on, Donnelly. I was kissing a man, obvi.

THE BIG HAMMER: Melody, I am THE ONLY person you should be kissing. WTF!

BROADWAY BABY: It's okay. I promise. Joe's a really good kisser.

THE BIG HAMMER: MELODY BRIGHTLY!!!!!!!!!

BROADWAY BABY: Oh, full-named. And look at all those pretty exclamation points.

THE BIG HAMMER: Don't make me rent a car and drive the 2 hours back to the city. I will gladly take the fine for being late to kick someone's ass. I DO NOT find this funny. Who the fuck is Joe??????

BROADWAY BABY: My husband. He made sure to make an honest woman out of me.

THE BIG HAMMER: WHAT THE ACTUAL FUCK!

BROADWAY BABY: Remove the hockey stick from your butt, Donnelly. I'm talking about Joe DiMaggio. You know, my second husband.

THE BIG HAMMER: OH MY GOD. You've been talking about the musical THIS ENTIRE TIME?

BROADWAY BABY: Maybe...

Chapter Nineteen

I collapse on the tile floor like a starfish, panting. This week has been brutal. We've been learning the choreography for all the big numbers of the show, and Zoey isn't holding anything back. Hell, she is straight-up kicking the entire ensemble's ass.

Man down.

No one mourns the wicked, Mels.

"You know…" There's a shit-eating grin on Zoey's face as she peers down at me, looking fresh as a daisy whereas I feel like a drowned rat. "For someone who left an active show, you're pathetically out of shape, boo."

"I don't even have the energy to flip you off," I grumble.

"Maybe if you were actually sleeping with your hockey hunk, your stamina wouldn't be shit right now."

"You make me sound like some type of high schooler with a purity ring."

She snorts, dropping down to mirror my position on the floor, so close our noses almost touch when I turn to look at her.

"Besides…we haven't gotten to see each other since the

night we went to the game two weeks ago. Between rehearsals and his game schedule, we are busy, busy, busy."

"Please tell me you two are at least having tons of phone sex with your nightly video chats?"

I shake my head.

"Sexting?"

Another shake.

"Not even a dick pic?" The incredulity in Zoey's voice has me chuckling before I have to wrap an arm around my sore core muscles. My best friend is a dance Nazi.

"Nope. The closest we've come to sharing *salacious* photos was when you busted in on me after my shower and sent him the pic of me in a towel. I still can't believe you did that, by the way."

"Sorry not sorry."

"Melody?" one of the production assistants calls out.

"Yes?" I crane my head back to look at the quintessential Brooklyn hipster.

"You have a visitor."

"*Shit!*" I slap both hands over my face. "What time is it?"

"Noon," he answers then calls to the room, "That's lunch everyone. See you all in an hour."

I groan.

Why did the day Jase and I agreed to meet for lunch have to be choreography day?

"Can you let him in?"

"You got it, Mels."

I should get up, wipe the sweat from my face, straighten my ponytail, *something*, but I can't move.

"Hey, baby." Jase's deep voice rumbles through me.

"Hey there, All-Star." I speak through the fingers spread across my face, trying to hide.

"Shavasana is one of my favorite poses in yoga, but I think I'd much rather see you in downward dog."

The dirty promise in his words sends tingles chasing down my spine. I didn't lie when I told Zoey we haven't sexted, but Jase has skated the line with the same precision he uses on the ice.

"*Ooooh*, dirty talk yoga-style. I like it," Zoey says, pulling out her phone, and I just know she's texting Ella.

"Hey, Zo."

"Loverboy."

Upside down, I watch one of his blond brows lift, the left side of his mouth hitching up into a lopsided smirk.

"Loverboy?"

"Ignore her. Lord knows I do." I side-eye my best friend.

Jase moves to stand over me, straddling me with one foot on either side of my hips. He's dressed casually in a pair of light-wash jeans, a black t-shirt that's molded to each one of his bulging muscles, a leather jacket, and a black Storm hat worn backward. His teeth flash as his smirk becomes a full-blown smile.

How is it he's able to look both the bad boy and the boy next door? *God he hits me with the razzle-dazzle.*

"Are we still going out to eat? Or did you just want to have a picnic right here?"

"We can go out. Help me up?" With great effort, I lift an arm to him.

Ignoring it, he bends, curling a hand around my hips then scooping me up and tossing me over his shoulder as if I weigh nothing.

I let out a squeal as the world goes topsy-turvy.

He smacks my ass, giving the cheek a squeeze.

"*Jase.*"

"Just giving my girl a hand. Now, what are you in the mood for?"

"Jase, put me down."

"Nope."

"Jase."
"Mels."
I harrumph.
He chuckles.

Chapter Twenty

P aco's Tacos is one of the city's hidden gems. It is small, only big enough for a handful of small pub tables, and looks like what I imagine a food truck would if it had inside seating. It isn't fancy, but the food is out of this fucking world.

"I don't think I've ever been here," my girl says as we take our seats across from each other after ordering, my arm easily spanning the wooden table to touch her.

"I picked well then. Paco makes the best fish tacos in the tri-state area." It's serendipitous her rehearsal space is only a few short blocks away.

"That's a bold claim to make, Mr. Donnelly."

"Oh, baby." I tuck the errant curl that escaped her ponytail behind her ear. "I told you what it does to me when you call me that."

"I know, but did you ever stop to think that I like it?"

"Minx."

"Minx? Really?"

I shrug and pull her in for a kiss. I missed her something fierce while I was gone.

"I pick these things up in book club," I say when I finally

release her.

She rests her chin on her fist, and the way her dark eyes sparkle while looking at me hits me in all the feels.

"Book club?" She arches a brow.

"Are you really surprised to learn this? I mean how could we not actually read the books with me on the cover?" I wave my hands down my upper body as if to say, *Look at all this.*

"You're ridiculous." I don't miss the way she follows my movements, checking me out. *I see you, baby.* "But tell me more about this book club."

"It originally started with us reading Maddey's books when she started out, but over the years it has evolved into a bi-weekly occurrence."

The rapt way she stares at me while I explain is everything. We're not discussing anything deep, but she makes it feel that way.

"How do you manage that with your schedules?"

"They usually do them when the Blizzards are home and the rest of us video-chat in."

Her expression changes, becoming almost wistful the longer she listens to stories about the antics we get up to. I'm happy she's starting to lose the doubt she seems to wear around her like armor, but I'm not sure I like what this new look could mean. It's not the first time I've seen it, either.

You gonna nut up and finally ask, Donnelly?

"Rehearsals going good?" I ask, needing to change the subject.

"Yeah. This week feels like it's been all choreography, all the time. I'm counting down the seconds until it's the weekend. Weekends off is the *one* perk to rehearsals."

"Need a break?"

We sit back as Paco drops off our plates loaded with the famous fish tacos, the smell of fried fish and cilantro making my mouth water. It's a good thing I don't have to be as strict with my diet as the fighters, because Gem would have my ass for the work I'm about to put in here.

"A break, an ice bath, a massage—you name it, I need it. Don't let Zoey fool you—she cracks that whip like no one else."

"Sounds kinky. Can I watch?"

A napkin hits me in the face, the paper opening up from the ball she crumpled it into.

"You're such a perv."

There's no missing the way she's biting her cheek to hold back a smile.

"You still like me, baby." I wink because I know how much she likes it; both Zoey and Ella told me so. They might have Covenette written all over them, but I'll use their proximity to my girl to my advantage. Besides, they are more than willing to give me all the dirty details—especially Zoey.

"Debatable," Mels says around a mouthful of food.

Her *mmm*s have my dick stirring in my pants, and I wonder if she'll make those sounds in bed.

"What if I told you I'd offer up my services and give you the massage you need?"

"Is that just a ploy to get me into bed?"

"Oh, baby." I wipe a stray streak of salsa from her lip, another one of those *mmm*s escaping at my touch. "I don't need a ploy to get you into bed. When the time comes, you'll be *begging* me to take you there."

Her eyes flare and she sucks in an audible breath.

I want you too.

The sexual tension crackles between us. It has been too many days since we saw each other in the flesh, and even then we weren't alone. My family—the ultimate cockblocks.

I need her, my mouth on hers, in a room—preferably with a lock on the door—and *hours* of uninterrupted alone time. Then maybe the beast inside will quiet down enough to be able to think of something that isn't Melody, though it's doubtful.

"Are you excited for this weekend?" She stacks her empty plate on top of mine like I want to be on her.

The All-Star Game.

I have a love-hate relationship with the entire weekend. Love because it's a good time and the skills competitions are a way to show off in a fun way. Hate because it's just another time I'm compared to Ryan.

It doesn't matter that we play different positions; the comparisons always come. He went offense, I went defense. Hell, my entire style of play was crafted around being able to help protect Ryan on the ice growing up. He's older, but I'm bigger. As a freaking prodigy on ice, there were always people gunning for him.

"It'll be a spectacle, that's for sure."

One of her dark brows lifts.

"Well…" I lean forward on my elbows. "You've met the infamous Coven. You think they were bad after a game? You have *no idea* how they are during these things."

"Tell me."

The tingles set off by the absentminded way she traces patterns on my forearm is distracting. What was it she asked?

Oh, yeah. The All-Star Game.

"Okay, let's see." Bubble gum invades my senses as I overtake the table with my size, getting as close to her as possible. "Whether it's all of us like this year or only one, everyone travels to the game. Siblings, parents, Covenettes, friends, babies—you name it, they are there. *God*, it was a miracle we didn't incite an international incident during the Olympics with the ridiculousness our family brings.

"I like to exaggerate—at least according to JD—but when I say there are like fifty people who make up our cheering section, it's a pretty close estimate."

"I can't even imagine." Another wistful expression falls over her beautiful face.

"What about your opening night? You're the lead, so won't the audience be packed with your family?"

Her gaze falls, my forearm her sole focus. "No, not really. My brother will come if he doesn't have work and *maybe* my aunt and uncle, but that's about it. And Ella if she's not a part of the orchestra."

"What about your parents?"

"Probably not. I think I was in high school the last time they saw me in anything."

Ah, that's *what I've been picking up on.*

My heart breaks.

Scrolling through my memory, I recall every time she tensed, looked away, lost the sparkle in her eye, or changed the subject if we were texting when she heard stories of my insane family.

I may have my hang-ups over not measuring up to Ryan, but they *do not* stem from my parents. That baggage is all my own. Ruth and Robert Donnelly couldn't be more supportive if they tried.

To hear that her parents can't bring themselves to show up for something as major as opening night as a lead in a Broadway musical has me feeling a little rage-y.

Broadway show or kindergarten production, your kid has a performance, you show up.

"I'm sorry, baby." I curl my fingers around the back of her neck, pulling her in and pressing a kiss to her forehead.

Silently I vow to always show up when it counts.

Chapter Twenty-One

Walking back to rehearsal after lunch, I thank god for every one of my acting chops. Without them, there would be no way to hide the riot of emotions I'm feeling.

The way his hazel eyes softened to a pale green when he asked about my parents told me he picked up on the hurt, but I shoved it down before he was able to see how deep it actually runs.

Intellectually, I know my parents care, but the only member of my immediate family who has ever showed it is my brother.

And what would he say about you dating Jase?

Ignoring the way my conscience taps its foot at me, I snuggle deeper into the arm wrapped around my shoulders and walk through the door to the rehearsal room.

"Which one of these guys is the one trying to move in on my woman?" He scowls at the room like the big, bad defenseman he is.

"You're ridiculous."

"Mels." Is it wrong that I like the way he growls my name? "Show me."

"Let's see." I tap my pursed lips. "Husband number one." I point to the actor playing James Dougherty. "Husband number *three*." Another point to the Arthur Miller actor. "But the one from the *infamous* ChapStick day is husband number two." Finally I point to Mr. Joe DiMaggio.

His hold tightens and I roll my lips to restrain a smile. Pushing onto my toes, lips to his ear, I whisper in my best breathy Marilyn voice, "And don't forget Mr. President."

I feel more than hear Jase's groan as I point out the JFK actor.

"Fuck this."

I'm hurled around and our mouths fuse together.

Holy hell. Where did he learn to kiss like this? Sure, I've spent more time kissing men on stage than in real life, but not once can I recall ever feeling this level of *passion*. It's just a freaking kiss, for cripes' sake.

But the way Jase Donnelly does it is so much more.

There are nips and sucks and don't even get me started on that tongue ring. How is it I always forget about the piercing until he uses it against me?

Whistles and applause echo in the room, but still, he doesn't let me go. My fingers curl in the cotton of his shirt, our bodies pressed together like Lego pieces.

With one last drag of the ball bearing across my bottom lip, he releases me, his thumb following the same path. *Well shit, Jonathan Groff, I'm totally fucked.*

"Mine." I don't miss how he says this loud enough for our captive audience to hear.

Oh my god. Are they giving us a standing ovation? Fucking Zoey.

"Come over tonight?"

I'm nodding before he even finishes asking.

"Zo," he calls out to my soon-to-be-dead ex-best friend.

"Yes, Loverboy?" she sing-songs. Is she filming us? I swear to god, if she's FaceTiming Ella…

"Don't go too hard on my girl."

"Why?" The arch of one of her eyebrows is not promising. "Because that's your job?"

I'm squeezed in a bear hug as Jase barks out a laugh.

"Damn, babe. No wonder The Coven didn't scare you. I think Zoey is a long-lost member."

Too bad she'll never get to accept membership because I'm going to murder her.

Chapter Twenty-Two

"Aww, come on, Donnelly. Don't be like that." Cali spins, trying to evade my attempts to push him out of the apartment.

"Fuck off, Cali. Mels will be here any minute, and we aren't a tricycle." I take advantage of being the largest member on the Storm roster and manually move him to the door.

"Man, I knew this would happen." He digs his heels in, pressing his shoulders harder against my grip.

"Knew what would happen?"

I *so* don't have time for this. My time with my girl is limited enough; I don't need any party-crashers interrupting.

"You'd go and get yourself wifed up and forget all about me."

I'm almost to the door. So close to being free.

Just…a…few…more…inches.

"Me, *me*, your OG brother husband."

The door is right there.

"Um…I think both Tuck and Vince would fight you on OG status there, bro."

Finally! The door.

I contort my body to stretch around my pain-in-the-ass teammate-turned-best-friend—even if the OG title is incorrect —to reach for the handle.

Just another inch.

I call on every ounce of yogi beaten into me by Rocky through the years.

Got it.

My fingertips skim the nickel handle.

I curl my hand over it and push down, yanking back as the lock releases and the door pulls open.

"*God.* Way to kick a man when he's down, Donnelly."

A shove.

A push.

A grunt, followed by a squeak.

Cali pulls up short, and without his counterweight, I continue my forward momentum until I'm flat on my back, in the hallway looking up at my I-am-so-smothering-you-with-a-pillow teammate and my startled-looking girlfriend.

"Oh my god, Jase. Are you okay?" Her eyes are wide, a hand covers her mouth as if to hide a smile, and the other is pressed against her heart.

"Fine," I grumble.

Through his laughter, Cali holds out a hand to help me up

"Hey there, Broadway." He slings an arm around Melody's shoulders for a side hug.

"Do I even wanna ask?" She finishes hugging Cali and immediately folds herself into my arms.

"No," I answer while Cali says, "Your boy over here is being mean to me. I think you should hold me instead." He opens his arms.

"Get your own woman," I threaten.

"But yours is so nice."

"*Cali*," I growl, not missing the shy smile coming from Mels.

"Okay, okay." He holds his hands up in surrender. "I'm

going. You guys go be all couple-ly while the rest of us are left alone…all by ourselves…with no one to talk to."

"Are you sure hockey is the right career choice for you?" Melody asks as Cali walks backward to his apartment.

"How is that even a question, Broadway?" His arms are out as if to say, *look at all this.*

"Because…you sure have a flare for the dramatics. I get the feeling you'd be just as at home on stage as you are on ice."

He perks up like an eager puppy, and I remind myself I'm an animal lover. "If it means I get to play your co-star and kiss you, sign me up."

He's one of your best friends. Don't hit him. Don't hit him. He's just trying to get under your skin.

"Cali, if you don't turn around and get your ass in your apartment in the next three seconds, I'm going to have Jake tie you between the pipes while Ryan and I take slap shots at you."

"Fine, fine, fine. Be a buzzkill, brother husband."

I release the breath I've been holding as he disappears behind the closed door. I love my friend—he really is like another brother to me—but *damn* does he push my buttons.

"Hey, baby." I lay a too-quick kiss on her and lead us into the safety of my apartment.

"Brother husband?" She has the cutest furrow between her brows.

"Don't ask." I pull her with me onto the couch.

My balls tingle at the groan she expels, shifting her around until she's settled under my arm.

"I take it Zoey didn't take it easy on you after I left?"

"Not even a little bit." A moan. "My best friend is a sadist."

I laugh. I have a few of those in my own life. "Well, my offer still stands."

"Which one would that be? The one where you offered to play massage therapist?"

"Oh, baby, I'm *all* about role-playing." She pops me on the chest. "But, for real, I'll rub all your aches and pains away."

"I know you're probably angling for a happy ending, but I'm sore enough not to care. Do your worst, All-Star."

I link my fingers together, cracking the knuckles.

Time to get to work.

Chapter Twenty-Three

I'm bone-tired and should be home sleeping, letting my body recover for what I'm sure is going to be yet another killer day of choreography tomorrow.

Zoey = The Devil.

But this close to Jase, his eyes darkening as they turn greener, a buzzing awareness replaces the exhaustion.

"Lose the shirt, baby." A finger runs along my collar, following it down where it hangs off my shoulder, his touch making every one of my hormones fight for center stage.

"Oh now I get it…you're using a massage as an excuse to get me naked."

"Baby." That finger follows the line of my arm, dragging the material of my shirt with it. "I don't need an excuse. If I wanted you naked, you'd be naked."

Holy shit.

"I should be telling myself to say no to this."

"Did you just use a *Hamilton* reference on me?" His deep chuckle hardens my nipples almost as much as his Broadway knowledge.

"I probably shouldn't tell you how hot I think it is that you picked up on it."

"Why not?" He's back to tracing my collar. Back and forth. Back and forth.

"I wouldn't want your ego to get so big it explodes."

"Oh, Mels." Almost everyone calls me Mels, but hearing it said in his deep voice hits me in the feels—and in the clit, but that is an issue for another time. "Don't you fret. The Coven would *never* allow that to happen."

He is the most ridiculous and charming man I've ever met. Still...he pulls me in like no other.

"But for reals." He pinches my top and tugs. "Lose the shirt. Let me help heal what ails ya."

I don't move.

Not a muscle.

Not even to breathe.

If I do this, it could be the catalyst for something I can't take back. I already feel like I may be in this too deep, but to cross the line into the physical would be an entirely different ball game. And yes, I know that's a baseball metaphor, but whatever. My brain cells are currently having a heated debate with my hormones about the situation; I deserve a pass.

"Let me level the playing field."

See? He did it too.

He reaches behind his head, pulling his t-shirt over it in that sexy one-handed way guys do that is the equivalent to us ladies removing our bra under our shirts. My brain cells lose the battle as my hormones give a standing ovation to the deserves-to-be-applauded perfection in front of me.

I gulp—audibly.

"Does this help?" He waves a hand down his body...his oh-my-god-I-need-to-check-my-chin-for-drool body.

No. No it does *not* help.

I know he did it so I wouldn't feel the pressure of being the only one shirtless. Unfortunately, now all I want to do is fuse myself to him like cling wrap.

"Forgot your line, baby?" He leans in, his lips brushing my ear, and says, "I'll be happy to tell you what to say here."

I suck in a stuttering breath. There is not one thing about him that doesn't overwhelm me.

"Why do I get the feeling if I left the dialogue up to you, it wouldn't be filled with *actual* words?"

"Oh...there would be words."

One of his blond brows is arched, and there's a devil-may-care smirk pulling up the right side of his mouth.

"There would be a *yes*, and an *Oh Jase, take me now,* and let's not forget the ever-important *Oh Jase, you are such a stud.*" His smirk transforms into a full-blown smile so bright it takes my breath away, the green and gold of his eyes practically dancing.

"You are *the* most over-the-top person I have ever met, and I spend my days with actors." I shake my head with a facepalm.

"You know you love it. Don't play. Now come on." He circles his finger. "Lose the shirt so I can introduce you to my magic fingers. Then maybe some other time you'll get to meet my MD."

"MD?" I'm almost afraid to ask.

"My magic dick."

Yup, I shouldn't have asked.

"Oh my god." I barely manage to get the words out I'm laughing so hard.

"You have the best laugh, baby."

Swoon.

Needing the relief a good back rub—the real kind, not the kind with quotation marks men like to use for code to get to sexy times—I give in and remove my shirt, folding it and placing it on the coffee table.

Now he's the one sucking in a breath with a hiss through his teeth. I peek at him through my lashes. His eyes turn a forest green, and he's rolling his tongue ring across his upper lip.

I can't recall ever seeing him do that. To be honest, unless he's using it on me, I almost forget he has the piercing —almost.

I'm in another bralette, this one a cute baby pink color similar to the hue of my hair with a scalloped design on the edges. Aside from my pretty underthings, I'm dressed for comfort in a pair of simple black leggings.

"*Fuck me*," he whisper-curses.

Yes please.

I'm quick to close the curtain on those thoughts, stupid hormones trying to take control again. *You will not fuck the hot hockey hunk tonight. Your legs will stay closed. This show is not doing previews.*

Easier said than done.

"Lie down." His voice sounds as rough as the ice after a full period of hockey.

I do as he asks, bending my elbows, resting my face on my folded hands, shivers racking my body. They have nothing to do with the cold leather on my bare stomach and everything to do with anticipation.

"Let me know if I'm too heavy," I hear him say before I feel him straddle the backs of my thighs. He doesn't actually sit, his ass barely resting on my legs, the weight not at all uncomfortable.

His large calloused hands mold around my shoulders, his thumbs pressing in just the right spot to have me moaning in equal parts pleasure and pain.

He works on my potato-sized knots—damn him for making me always have spuds on the brain—dancing his fingers down the length of my spine, each vertebrae cracking.

That's it—I'm quitting Broadway and Jase will have to leave the NHL because this is what I want to do for the rest of my life. His hands on me, all my aches and pains handled by his very accurately described magic fingers.

Up and down my back, he kneads away every knot that dares show itself in his presence.

When the long length of his fingers curve around the front of my ribcage, his thumbs smooth slow semicircles lower, occasionally dipping into the waistband of my leggings, brushing across the top of my thong, which is pink to match my bralette. I'm about to be literal putty in his hands.

The shifting of his weight is the only warning before his lips press a soft kiss between my now loose shoulder blades. The pressure of his lips is whisper-soft, only adding to the sensation.

The touch remains light as he follows the line of my spine.

Down to the band of my leggings.

Up to my shoulders.

The pressure finally increases on pass number two, but the lazy tempo does not.

All the while he continues to massage.

Pass number three is when he kicks it up a notch. That goddamn ring dances its way over each bump, my skin heating and goose bumps rising.

As he reaches the end of the line for the fourth time, his thumbs fully disappear beneath the band bisecting my back before hooking under the straps of my thong.

A fresh wave of desire hits, the heaviness of my breasts amplified as they push into the leather cushions.

As he makes his trek up my body, his thumbs remain locked on my underwear, pulling it along with him.

Fire flashes through my veins as the drenched lace tightens, trapping my engorged clit beneath it.

"Tell me to stop, baby." His voice is dark with promise.

"I—" I swallow a sob. "I can't."

Another tug.

He shifts, blanketing my body while simultaneously

holding himself above it. His chest burns my back, and the strength radiating from the thighs holding me in place is unparalleled.

"Jase," I cry with another tug, the pressure pulling and pushing on my clit too much and not enough. I need...that's it—I just need.

Another shift and he has the back of my thong in one hand, keeping a steady pressure, the lace setting off sparks as it drags against the rosebud of my ass, his free hand snaking around my hip and into the front of my pants.

I squirm, to run away or seek more, I'm not sure. Though he's pinned me with his upper body, his lower half is held off me, preventing me from rubbing against him and returning the torture—err, pleasure.

Slowly, so fucking slowly there isn't a doubt in my mind he knows *exactly* what he is doing to me, one—just one—of his fingers traces me from the top of my slit to the bottom, increasing the already maddening pressure tenfold.

Back and forth he traces.

Up, down.

Serpentining over my pleasure button.

"Jase."

"I know, baby." His breathing is labored in my ear, that damn ring whirling against my lobe.

"Jase."

I need him to go *beneath* my underwear.

"Jase."

I'm going to come.

Finally, *finally*, his finger stops toying with me, pressing down.

That's it.

In three, two, on—

Chapter Twenty-Four

Beep-beep-beep.

My head drops to the top of Melody's back when I hear the lock on my front door disengage.

"Shiiiiiiittt," Tucker drawls. "I thought Blondie was taking after her twin and making up stories."

Murder is wrong.

I thunk my head softly on her skin. Where's a wall when you need one?

This is *soooo* not how I wanted the evening to go. Cali was child's play compared to what has just invaded my apartment. Yes, invaded, like those aliens trying to take over the world.

As soon as Mels realizes we are no longer alone, her body coils tight underneath mine, and this time it has nothing to do with the orgasm that was at the tips of my fingers before we were so rudely interrupted.

Unfortunately, I'm well versed in what is about to go down.

Is it too late to be adopted into a different family?

Blindly, I search the floor for a shirt—mine, Melody's, it doesn't matter. No one gets to see her like this but me.

Another pass and I touch cotton. Sitting up, I use my body to block her from view and slip my shirt over her head. The two idiots have stopped before entering the living room—thanks to Ryan, no doubt. If it were up to Tuck, his ass would already be on the couch.

"Tuck." Ryan uses his captain voice. "Didn't we teach you to think before you speak?"

Yeah, there's no corralling Tucker Hayes. Once he realizes exactly what he interrupted, the razzing I'll get will be *endless*.

"Where's the fun in that, Cap?"

Ryan may not technically be our captain anymore, but we all still use the title.

With Mels covered, I help her sit up and tuck her tight to my side, not giving a damn that I'm still shirtless—it's not like they haven't seen more in the locker room.

"What are you puck heads doing here?" I readjust the hockey stick straining against my zipper.

"I'm pretty sure you're a puck head too, little brother." Ryan takes one of the massage chairs, while—surprise, surprise—Tucker plops himself next to Mels.

"Well *hellllloooo*. Who might you be, beautiful?" He lifts one of her hands to brush a kiss across the knuckles.

He's one of your best friends. You probably shouldn't hit him.

"Taken." She pulls her hand free and wipes it on her leggings. *That's my girl.*

"Bro." Ryan sucks in lungfuls of air, trying to get his laughter under control. "I totally see why JD likes her."

"You too with the teenage valley girl vocabulary?" Mels says to Ryan, reminding me of how much crap she gave me during our courtship.

Shit. If she heard the way I described the start of our relationship, she would give me so much shit.

"Our lives are run by women—we pick up certain things." Ryan shrugs.

"What are you guys doing here?"

It's not that I don't *want* to see them—cockblocking aside—I just hoped our relationship would've had the chance to grow some roots before it was exposed to the golden boy of the NHL.

I love my brother, really I do, but all my life I've never felt like I measure up. Since the teams were announced, Mels has taken to jokingly calling me All-Star. The question I ask myself is, would she still call me that after spending time with *the* All-Star?

"It's the All-Star break," Tuck answers, cutting Ryan off.

"I'm well aware," I deadpan.

"So…" Tucker gives me a look that screams, *You've got to be kidding me.* "We always hang out. But what do I find when I get home? Nothing."

"Hey." Ryan rears back.

"Sorry, Cap. What I meant was I get home, expecting to find three Donnellys"—he holds up three fingers—"only to find I'm missing one."

"Good job counting, bro," I tease.

"Fuck you, man." There's zero heat behind Tuck's words. "Who the hell do you think our nieces get their smarts from?"

"Me," Ryan and I say in unison.

"Whatever, not the point." Tucker waves us off. "What's important here is when I ask my little sis where her twin is, I have to hear you're ditching us because you went and got yourself a girlfriend."

"Little sis?" Melody directs the question to me.

"Back in our college days, Tuck here thought two older brothers wasn't enough for JD and declared himself big brother number three."

"BB3 for life." Tucker thumps his chest with a fist.

It's his unwavering loyalty that keeps him alive when he lives for pushing buttons.

"I have *so* many questions right now." Mels covers her mouth as if to hold in a laugh.

"Tuck has that effect on people," Ryan says wryly.

"Hate the game, not the player." Tucker mimes brushing off his shoulder.

"Do you even *hear* the things that come out of your mouth?" Ryan's brows furrow as if to say, *what the hell?*

"Listen...just because you two don't take advantage of the perks that come with your station—"

"Our *station*?" I snort.

"Why do we hang out with you?" Ryan facepalms.

"Jake," we say, again speaking in unison.

Melody's eyes are wide as they bounce between us. She wore a similar expression the night The Coven ambushed her. I give her a squeeze and drop a kiss on her temple.

"Your family..."

"Yeah?" I ask when she doesn't continue.

"It's not like anything I've ever experienced before." Her words are barely a whisper.

I feel a twinge in my chest. It made me so angry earlier having to hear about how, outside of her brother, her family is so absent.

Mine, on the other hand, takes *invested* to entirely different levels. Honestly, cockblocking like this is only the tip of the shit-show iceberg Tuck is usually the ringleader of.

"Tell us the truth." Tuck leans over, tapping his ear as if waiting for me to part with some big secret. "You didn't come home because you're hiding out from Blondie, right?"

"Why would I be hiding from JD?"

Mels is looking on like all she needs is a bowl of popcorn to really enjoy the show.

"Um..." He looks to Ryan then back to me. "Because even Jake ran away to Chance's earlier to hide from her ranting over your latest Insta post."

"It's true." Ryan nods. "I think Jake is looking to get a sign made that says *Don't piss off pregnant women* just so you'd have to wear it this weekend."

I snort. I wouldn't put it past Jake to do that. He did marry my sister, after all, and revenge is her middle name. Fine, it's Danielle, but it *could* be revenge.

Sure, JD warned me to cool it with the Bishop stuff, and I listened—mostly. She may not have changed my social passwords—something it sounds like she wishes she did as blocking Bishop from my feed isn't enough to keep the juicy stuff from me. Shoutout to Vince for sending me the goods.

I *had* to respond to Bishop's boast about how he beat me out for hardest shot last year. It was my duty.

The highlight reel I posted of all the times I've bested him through the years was a thing of beauty, if I do say so myself.

"Don't you think this feud has gone on long enough?" Ryan arches his brow, giving me the *I'm not mad, just disappointed* look our dad perfected when we were younger. "You guys have been sniping at each other since high school."

"Every hero needs a villain." I offer a shrug.

"Bullshit." The uncharacteristic roll of Ryan's eyes gives away just how annoyed he is. "Neither of you idiots are hero material, acting like children. You're antiheroes at best."

I'll take it. I love Deadpool.

"There's one thing I never understood." Tucker kicks off his shoes, making himself right at home.

"Only one?" Ryan counters.

"*Oooh,* Cap has jokes tonight." Never trust that gleam in Tuck's eyes.

"Spit it out already, bro," I prod.

"I always thought your *brodium* started after the Frozen Four."

Ryan and I share a look, silently asking, *you wanna take this or should I?*

With a heavy sigh, Ryan asks, "Brodium?"

"Like the opposite of bromance, because odium means a general hatred or disgust directed toward someone as a result of their actions."

"Do you always get a vocab lesson when he shows up?" Mels jerks her chin at Tuck. I squeeze her a bit tighter, adoring her for not being afraid to trash-talk, even if her voice sounds a bit forced.

"Oh I like this one." Tuck bounces a finger at Mels. "She reminds me of Blondie a little."

I like her too. A lot, actually.

"But stop trying to distract me from my point." He wags his finger at her as if to say, *Naughty girl.* "High school? Isn't he from Maine or something?"

"Massachusetts," the resident Bruisers fan corrects.

"Same diff."

"*What?*" Mels' easy smile is back as she tries to hide it in the curve of my arm.

"Still in New England, so it counts."

"Oh my god." She shakes with laughter. "How you can go from giving definitions of advanced vocabulary words to mucking up geography is beyond me."

"*Covenette,*" Ryan coughs under his breath, and I'm full-on cat-who-ate-the-canary grinning. That right there is the highest honor.

Dragging up my history with Bishop isn't my favorite way to spend a weeknight, but if I don't offer some kind of explanation, we could be at this all night. Information and females—two things Tucker goes after like a dog with a bone.

"We met at the hockey camp in Lake Placid."

One of the most prestigious summer hockey programs is run out of the upstate city. It's invite only, as in they only offer spots to the most promising-looking players under eighteen. Naturally, Ryan was invited multiple years. Unfortunately, so was Bishop.

The summer before my senior year, I was finally offered one of those coveted spots, and Bishop and I didn't get along from the moment I stepped inside the dorms.

"The one year I was invited, we butted heads the whole

time. Hell…" I scoff in the back of my throat. "I knew who he was from visiting Ry with JD through the years, but the asshole was on my case every chance he got."

I rarely—hell, *never*—talk about that summer. I don't need Ryan internalizing the shit Bishop spewed, but I know I gotta give them something.

I hold my girl a little bit tighter.

"He loved to tell me I was only given a spot because the camp recruited Ry"—I gesture to my brother—"to help coach."

Mels stiffens beside me, and Ryan curses under his breath.

"Normally I can shake shit like that off." Lies. "But I always suspected there was a vein of truth to the statement, and thus the *brodium*"—Tuck smirks at my use of his word—"was born."

"That's *crap*." Mels whirls on me, cheeks flushed in anger. Ah, that's why she stiffened. My baby was offended on my behalf. "*Hel-lo*." She pokes me in the forehead with each syllable. "All." Another poke. "Star." Poke.

Snatching her hand before it can make contact a fifth time, I nip the tip of her finger, her eyes flaring with banked heat, and place a swift kiss on her parted lips.

"So…" Tucker breaks into our moment. He waits, looking to me, then Mels, then Ryan, and finally back to me. "Has she passed the test yet?"

"Why do I feel like, knowing your friends, he's talking about a literal test?" Melody's eyes open further, a full circle of white now around the irises.

"Because, baby." I wink and she blushes, just as I knew she would. "You already know us so well."

Tucker snorts. "God, Cap. I thought you and Jake were cheesy with this love stuff. But, *damn*, Jase…you're like a giant wheel of gouda."

I need to start taking applications for new friends.

"Tuck," Ryan warns. I may not have the same connection

with Ryan that I do with JD, but anyone can pick up on my frustration. It's palpable—well, unless your name is Tucker Hayes, apparently. "You wanna clue us common folk in on what test you're referring to?"

I'm glad Ryan asked, because I'm almost too afraid to.

"How are her driving skills?"

"Um…I live in the city. I take public transportation everywhere," Melody answers.

"Ah, I get it." Ryan leans back, the leather creaking under his weight. "But it's not much of a test without Madz here."

"Well, seeing as your bestie is avoiding you, I don't think we have much of a chance getting our ringer here."

"Tuck." It's my turn to issue a warning. We are all well aware of the strain on Ryan and Maddey's relationship lately.

"Sorry." Tuck holds his hands up in surrender. "But how 'bout it? You up for a little MK?"

"MK?" Mels looks to me.

"Mario Kart," I explain. "We're the reason the younger generation plays. It's a staple of the squad."

"Really?" Her black eyes sparkle with interest. Like with The Coven, she doesn't back down, and I adore it.

"You up for the challenge, baby?"

"Bring it on, All-Star."

Chapter Twenty-Five

THE BIG HAMMER: Would you believe me if I told you Tuck almost got strip-searched by TSA this morning?

BROADWAY BABY: After meeting him? Abso-fucking-lutely.

THE BIG HAMMER: OMG. You really are the perfect woman.

BROADWAY BABY: *GIF of Selena Gomez saying, "Tell me something I don't know."*

THE BIG HAMMER: Did you really just hit me with a GIF from *Another Cinderella Story*?

BROADWAY BABY: Did YOU really just catch THAT movie reference?

THE BIG HAMMER: The Coven, baby. I'm also surprisingly well versed in Hallmark Christmas movies.

BROADWAY BABY: Nope, not even a little bit surprised by this information.

THE BIG HAMMER: What are you doing?

BROADWAY BABY: Just got to rehearsal. You?

THE BIG HAMMER: *picture of Jase, Ryan, Tucker, Jake, and Jordan in different rows in first class*

BROADWAY BABY: Safe travels. Text me when you land?

THE BIG HAMMER: You got it, baby. Try not to miss me too much while I'm gone.

♡

After twenty-five years, one would think I would know better than to underestimate JD. But as Jake and Ryan unfold a ping-pong table in one of the hotel's empty banquet rooms, I realize that's exactly what I did.

"When did we get so old that busting out the ping-pong balls isn't for beer pong?" Wade Tanner, All-Star from the LA Lions and fellow BTU alum, drags over a chair to watch the show.

"I don't know who you're calling old, Grandpa, but I'm still a young stallion."

"Grandpa?"

"If the shoe fits." I pop a shoulder.

"Cara, baby," Wade calls to his college sweetheart. "Jase is calling us old."

"No." I shake a finger. "I called *you*"—I point to Wade—"old. Not your wife."

"She's older than me." His words have a screech to them.

"Bro," Ryan jumps in. "Don't throw your woman under the bus."

"Yeah, man. Talk about bad form." Jake pulls JD into his side, resting a hand on her baby bump.

I cup my hands around my mouth to shout over the noise. "Balboa, I need some protection over here."

"Oh, is the big bad enforcer not tough enough to handle his friends on his own?" Rocky takes the open chair next to me.

"No? Hold me." I throw my legs over hers. If she wasn't also pregnant, I would have jumped in her lap.

"Donnelly." Gage's tone is a warning. "Don't you have your own woman now? Get your hands off mine."

"Champ, play nice." Only Rocky could get away with admonishing the six-foot-seven heavyweight giant.

"Only for you, Blue."

The room continues to fill with our squad and family members. A lot of the other players are out, living up the nightlife, but our group is simple and prefers laidback gatherings like this.

"So." I turn to see Rocky with the smirk all the Covenettes have whenever they are being all *Coven-y*. "I heard you were Tuckered the other night."

"Did you really just use his name as a verb?"

"Uh-huh."

"Geez." I rub the back of my neck. My balls are still blue no matter how many times I've taken care of myself. "Don't let him hear you. You know it would go straight to his head."

"Oh yeah…I can see it now." She holds her hands in the air as if putting the next words up on a screen. *"You've been Tuckered* would be a hashtag. Skye and Jordan would have that bad boy trending faster than your slap shot."

"Lord help us if that happens."

"Unk, Unk." My nieces—JD and Jake's almost-two-year-old twins—Lucy and Lacey toddle-run into the room.

"How are my favorite girls?" I scoop them into my arms before anyone else can claim them. Blood or not, every male in this room is considered their uncle. It's a fight to love up on them.

"Don't bogart the cuteness." Vince swoops in as the girls cry, "Bin, Bin," still not mastering the V in his name.

See what I mean? I've had them for like two seconds. Luckily for Vince, my phone vibrates in my pocket, so I let him have them.

Freeing my phone, I see the screen flash with a selfie of Mels kissing her Mr. Potato Head, and I swipe to accept the FaceTime call.

"Hey, baby."

"Hey, All-Star."

My pulse picks up seeing her happy face. My girlfriend is too damn beautiful for words.

"Is that Broadway?" Cali calls out, butting in, of course.

"You mean my new best friend?" Tuck asks while Jake says, "Hey!"

"Relax, Brick. You'll always be number one in my heart." Tucker thumps his chest twice with a fist then points to Jake.

"What are you up to?" Melody's voice brings my attention back to the phone.

"About to watch my wombmate kick my brother-in-law's ass in ping-pong."

"Ping-pong?"

Before I can say anything, my hand is batted and my phone is snatched away.

"Hey there, best friend." Tucker plasters on his charm-the-ladies-out-of-their-panties grin as he looks into the camera of my stolen phone.

"Hi, Tuck."

"She was my friend first." Cali shoves Tucker to the side, taking his turn.

"What are you guys, five years old?" Rocky plucks the phone from Dumbass #1 and Dumbass #2. "Jase rarely gets to see Mels. Let the man speak to his own girlfriend."

See why she's my bestie?

"I'd listen to her. I taught her everything she knows." Gage tucks his wife into his side.

"Fake news," Vince shouts.

"Listen, baby," I say once she's back in my hand, "can I call you back later after I ditch the crazies?"

"Yup. Besides, I have my own crazies to keep me entertained in the meantime."

Could she be more perfect for me?

I hang up and pocket the phone before anyone else gets any ideas.

"Things are going good there?" Rocky turns, giving me her full attention.

"Yeah. I mean we don't get to see each other as much as I'd like, but we're making it work."

"You seem…" She tilts her head, studying me. "Different."

"Different?"

"Yeah, different. I can't quite put my finger on it, but you seem…I don't know…more settled."

I pause, taking stock. Am I?

Yes, yes I am. Melody silences all the noise, the bullshit, and helps me see past my own insecurities to who I *could* be.

"Can I ask you a serious question?"

"Here?" She gestures to the craziness around us.

"When you and your octopus—"

"Kraken." Her tone says, *Be nice.*

"Sorry, couldn't help myself." I mime waving a white flag. "But in all seriousness—"

"*Can* you do that? Be serious, I mean?"

"Oh, Balboa." I chuckle. "And you call yourself my best friend? It's like you don't even know me."

"Oh no, Jase." She ticks a finger in a *no-no* gesture. "It's *because* I know you that I say that."

Years of friendship is all she needs for proof.

"Fair enough. Can I ask my question now?"

"Yes, you big baby."

"Why are we friends?"

"*That's* your question?" She arches a brow.

Oh my god, this is karma getting me back for all the shit I've given her through the years. But doesn't me helping her get together with her husband count for anything?

"No." I suck in a deep breath. "When...when you and Gage started dating...I know...I know you told him all the stuff about the gym and your...*feelings*." I shudder like feelings are something contagious.

"You mean like how I felt pigeonholed into the job and how I felt like I needed to work twice as hard to feel like I deserved it?" Her gray eyes soften in understanding.

"Yeah...that."

Please, please tell me. I'm lost here and I need guidance. Be my sherpa, Balboa.

"It's not really something I can quantify." Her hand goes to her belly, rubbing circles on the baby bump poking out. "Why?"

My insecurities over being the *less than* Donnelly brother are not something I've discussed with *anyone*, not even Rocky when we dated.

I may have been the one to broach the subject, but I chicken out, not ready to delve deeper into this particular area of self-doubt, shoving it into the penalty box in my mind. Time for a redirection.

"I don't know." A lie. "I guess being with Mels, getting to know her made me wonder why the subject never came up with us."

Liar, liar, pants on fire.

"Well, to be fair...I wasn't a full-time employee when we were together. My issues came *after* graduation."

"You know I'm always here for you right, Rock?"

"I do." She places a reassuring hand on my forearm. "You're my best friend outside of the girls for a reason—even when you tell my brother about having a girlfriend before you tell me." Guess she hasn't fully forgiven me for that. "You're a good man, Jason Donnelly. Don't let my crap ever make you doubt that."

"Love you, Rock."

"Love you too, Jase." A growl comes from behind her. "Oh hush, you. I may love him, but I'm *in* love with you." She kisses her husband on the cheek.

Is this a sign? Does my best friend's ability to get over her crap mean I can get over mine?

You do when you're with Mels.

Sure, it may not be *all* the time, but my subconscious is right. When I'm with my baby, my baggage feels lighter.

"Now." Done with their little love-fest, the James-es turn their attention to me. "How about you tell me *all* the things while we watch Brick actually lose at ping-pong for once."

That's a plan I can get on board with.

Chapter Twenty-Six

I burrow under the covers, sinking into my pillow-top mattress. My entire body is wrecked, from the top of my messy bun to the tips of my beat-up toes.

I've seen every production Zoey has choreographed throughout her career so I know how talented she is, but witnessing it firsthand is magical. If only muscle memory would take over so I could stop feeling like I've been hit by bus. That would be great.

One more day and I'll have the weekend to recuperate. I do love that particular perk of rehearsals. If only I could spend it with Jase.

Did I really just think that?

Shit. I'm in deeper than I thought.

Speaking of the hockey hunk…

"Hey there, All-Star," I say after accepting the video chat request.

"Hey, baby." There's that wink.

"Back in your room?" I take in the tufted headboard behind him.

"Yup. I left all the crazies downstairs so I could talk to my girl without anyone jumping into our conversation like earlier."

Yeah, that was entertaining.

I prop myself up on an elbow to see him better. "Taking advantage of being roommate-free?"

"Hell yeah." He runs a hand through his hair, the muscles of his arm popping with the movement. "In college I was always the one forced to room with Ryan for away games."

"Why do I have a hard time believing your brother is a bad roommate?"

"He's not." He chuckles. "He's a model roommate...well, except..."

"Except?"

Another chuckle, another tousle of hair.

"Dude snores louder than a herd of elephants."

"He does not." I choke on a snort.

"He does. I think I've lost count of the number of times JD has tried to murder him in his sleep with a pair of socks."

"Socks?"

"She would shove them in his mouth to shut him up."

I drop my phone, not having expected that at all.

"What?" I scramble to pick it back up.

"You okay over there, baby?"

"Yup. Fine. Just dropped my phone." I circle a hand in the air. "Details please."

He's ridiculous 99% of the time. I'm never sure how much I can believe, but I'm highly entertained as we share stories of our time in school—him in college, me from the arts high school I attended with Ella and Zoey.

Every day he does something, no matter how minor, to prove he is nothing like the playboy I believed him to be. Yes, he is cocky, alpha, exaggerates like a boss, and can turn anything into a sexual innuendo, but he is also sweet, kind, and loyal.

"So..." He shifts the pillows behind him and leans back.

"So…"

"Is there a limit on the number of people who can come to opening night of your show?"

"Well…yeah. There are only so many seats in the theater."

"You're cute when you act clueless." He shakes his head. "What I mean is, are you limited in the number of people *you* can reserve tickets for?"

"I don't think so." I mull it over. "I think the most I've ever needed to reserve was three or four, but getting an extra one or two shouldn't be an issue."

Acquiring the tickets won't be an issue; the problem will lie with if *all* the tickets—or one in particular—are used.

C-O-M-P-L-I-C-A-T-E-D.

Don't you think it's time to tell them, Mels? The longer you continue to lie, the worse it's going to be. You know the truth always comes out.

"Yeah, no, baby. I'm talking we need like two dozen or so."

What?

I blink. There are no words. Where's a script when you need one?

"Did you really think we weren't coming to your show?" There is a hint of amusement lacing his words.

"Well…I mean…you guys…" Words. Seriously, I need words. "You all have your own packed schedules. I don't expect you to worry about making it."

"First off." He sits up, getting serious. "It's not a worry. And second, we *want* to be there."

I'm not gonna cry. I'm an actress. I have impeccable control over my emotions, can cry on demand, go from angry to happy in the blink of an eye if the scene calls for it—but holding back tears? Talk about a challenge.

"Baby." Jase's tone gentles when he sees the one tear I couldn't prevent leaking out and trailing down my cheek.

"I'm fine." I wipe it away.

"Yeah…no. You've met the women in my life. If The Coven has taught me *anything*, it's that when a girl says she's fine, she's anything but." He levels me with a look. "Talk to me, baby. Tell Big Daddy what's wrong."

"Big Daddy?" I slap a hand over my face.

"What? Doesn't work?"

I shake my head.

"Challenge accepted."

I roll my eyes. I see what he's doing, though. He's using humor to let me off the hook—for now at least.

Do you think he has enough of a funny bone to let you off the ultimate hook, Mels?

"Tell me this." His words cut into my self-flagellation. "Am I in bed with you?"

I pan the camera to show my duvet then back up.

"No, no, no. I know you're on the phone with me in bed, but am I in there with you?"

"Why do I feel like you're talking in riddles?"

"Mr. Potato Head—is he sharing your pillow with you?"

Another pan of the camera, this time to show Mr. Potato Head in all his glory on my nightstand—not in bed.

"You wound me, baby." He mimes being stabbed in the heart.

"I feel like I need to change your text handle to *I can't even*, because I swear I think that about you *multiple* times a day."

He looks to the heavens as if searching for an answer. "Just goes to show I like you more than you like me."

"What? It's not like *I'm* in bed with you."

"Au contraire." It's his turn for a camera shift, and there on the pillow next to him is Mrs. Potato Head.

I should have known better.

"You're something else, Jase Donnelly."

"So I'm told." He punctuates the statement with one of his winks. "Now tell me this."

"I feel like we're playing twenty questions with all the *so tell me this* you're hitting me with tonight."

"We can if you want, but what I have in mind might be just a *little bit*"—he holds his thumb and forefinger an inch a part—"more fun."

"Oh yeah?" I arch a brow. "What did you have in mind?"

"You and me, baby." His expression turns salacious. "We have some unfinished business."

"We do?"

He nods. "I believe someone was denied an orgasm the other night. I think it's time to rectify that."

My entire body flushes with the memory.

"What?" I have to swallow down the lump that's formed in my throat. "What did you have in mind?"

The green of his eyes takes over the gold as he looks at me through the five-inch screen.

Why do I think I'm going to really, *really* like what he has in mind?

"So tell me this."

I groan. "Again with that. I think you need to go find Maddey and have her teach you a new way to phrase that."

"I thought I was the jokester in this relationship?"

I shrug, one of the straps of my tank top falling down my arm, and I don't miss the way he tracks the movement or how his eyes turn even greener.

"I do live with Zoey, meaning I'm force-fed sarcasm with my morning coffee. Some of it was bound to stick."

No matter how much I pick up from my best friend, my sarcasm game is in the minors compared to Jase's.

"I feel like I should send her a thank you gift."

See what I mean?

"Why's that, All-Star?"

"Well, my little sweet potato—"

"No." I shake my head so hard my messy bun tilts to the side. "Just…no."

"You don't like it?"

"I *never* thought I'd say this, but I prefer baby to sweet potato."

"I don't know…" I get distracted by the way his muscles pop and flex as he shrugs. "I think I like it. Potatoes are our thing. That's it—now and forevermore, you will be Sweet Potato."

"No words." Happiness blooms inside me.

"We're getting off topic here."

"Oh, I'm *sorry*." Yeah, even I wouldn't believe me with how sarcastic that sounded.

"Okay, smartass."

"Did I hurt your feelings?" I pout.

"You did. Why don't you take your top off to make it up to me?"

"*What?*"

"You heard me, Sweet Potato." I narrow my eyes, making his lips twitch. "Take your top off. I think it's about time I see those gorgeous tits of yours."

Oh my god. Is he trying to do what I think he's trying to do?

"Jase."

"Come on, baby. Let's have some fun. Let me show you how good I am."

"How *good* you are?" Is it wrong that I'm intrigued?

"Yup." He pops the P. "I'm so good, baby, I can make you come all the way from St. Louis."

My breath hitches and I'm sure I'm blushing everywhere —not because I'm embarrassed, but because I believe him.

"Are you trying to get me to have phone sex with you, Jason Donnelly?"

His eyes brighten and he straightens.

"Oooo, I don't know what to address first…how hot 'phone sex' sounds rolling off your tongue like it's something forbidden…or that you used my full name…or that I think I liked it."

Am I actually considering this?

He's quiet, waiting for my answer.

Yes or no, Mels?

Before I can change my mind and chicken out, I run across my bedroom to lock the door. As soon as the lock clicks into place, I jump back in bed, landing with a bounce.

I'm really doing this, aren't I?

Yes. Yes I am.

"Where'd you go?" Jase asks when I get back.

"Seeing as we seem to attract interruptions like magnets, I wasn't taking any chances."

"Ah…Zoey?"

"And Ella." I nod.

Now what?

"Time to lose the shirt, Sweet Potato."

People are going to start to think I have an eye condition with how often I roll my eyes at him. "You're really sticking with this Sweet Potato thing?"

"Without a doubt. Now strip."

Now or never, Mels.

I grip the bottom of my tank, pulling it over my head and tossing it over the side of the bed.

Jase sucks through his teeth, the sound whistling through my phone's speaker.

"Fuck, baby."

"What? No more Sweet Potato?" I can't help but tease.

"Not the time, baby. Not the time." He shakes his head, his eyes not once leaving my chest. Did I forget to mention I wasn't wearing a bra?

His eyes continue to change, turning greener and greener until almost none of the gold is left.

"*Damn* you have no idea how badly I want to forget about

all the people it would piss off and hop on a plane to be there with you right now."

Me too.

"Now—now what?" I choke out.

"Grab my buddy Mr. Potato Head."

"What?" I frown. "Not a chance. I'm not masturbating with a children's toy."

"What kind of animal do you take me for, Sweet Potato?" He feigns offense.

I level him with a look that screams, *Really?*

"Point taken," he concedes. "Still…grab my replacement."

"Why?"

"I want you to use him to prop up your phone. You're gonna need two hands for what I have in mind."

Oh, boy.

I grab Mr. Potato Head from my nightstand, but before I put him on the pillow, I remove his eyes in an effort to spare his virtue.

"Very good," Jase says after I have the toy arranged as a makeshift phone stand. "Lie back and let me put all the things I've learned from being a romance junkie to work."

Swallowing down my nerves, I do as I'm told. Goose bumps cover my skin, at odds with the lust burning through my veins.

"Place your hands on your shoulders."

That is *not* where I thought he would start, but I follow his directions.

"Skim the tips of your fingers down the length of your body, *slowly*." I begin to do as instructed, but he stops me. "Lighter. Keep your touch so it's like you're barely making contact with your skin."

The new featherlight pressure only heightens every sensation.

"Much better. Keep going."

My eyes flutter closed as I travel over the swell of my

breasts, down the slope of my stomach, stopping once I hit the cotton of my sleep pants then reversing the path.

"Using the same light touch, draw circles around your breasts, starting on the outside, making the circles smaller and smaller until you hit your areolas."

Circle, circle.

"Brush your nipples with your thumbs and cup your tits, hold them up to the camera."

I twist to the side, the weight of my breasts filling my palms.

"God, you have the prettiest tits I've ever seen," he growls. "They'd be in my mouth if I were there."

Oh that filthy mouth of his—a filthy mouth with a tongue ring.

"Pinch your nipples."

My thumbs and forefingers close around my nipples and pleasure shoots straight to my clit.

"Now twist."

"Jase," I cry.

"That's it, baby. Flatten your hands over them and squeeze."

Pinch.

Twist.

Squeeze.

"Shit, baby. I've never been jealous of a pair of hands before."

"Ja—Jase, touch yourself."

"Oh, baby. Your wish is my command."

I force my eyes open, not wanting to miss my chance to watch.

The ink on his inner biceps winks at me as his fingers splay over each pack of his abdominals. Is it wrong to want to lick him? Because I really, *really* want to lick him.

Unlike me, there's *zero* hesitation in his actions.

His hands slip under the band of his sweatpants, pushing them down and pulling himself out.

He's hard. And big—*really* big. Like *how does he expect it to fit* big.

I swallow at the sight.

The mushroom tip is practically purple, glistening with arousal.

His hand moves on his shaft.

Up then down.

"Touch yourself, baby."

"I—I am."

"No." The veins in his neck strain, his head moving side to side. "Put your hand inside your panties."

Another swallow and my hand is on the move again.

One finger breaches the band on my pants, then a second. Soon enough my hand is slipping beneath the lace of my panties, the wetness obvious as the fabric lifts.

"What do you feel?"

"*What?*"

"Tell me what you feel. Are you hot? Swollen? Wet? Is your clit pulsing under your finger?"

Yes, yes, yes, and all of the above.

"I'm right, aren't I? I can see it on your face. You're flushed, and the prettiest pink is traveling down your neck and over your breasts."

What is he doing to me?

"Use your forefinger and middle finger and alternate them."

Forefinger. Middle finger.

Forefinger. Middle finger.

"That's it, baby. Back and forth. Back and forth. Keep the rhythm steady."

I'm embarrassingly close to coming.

"No, baby. Eyes on me," he instructs when my eyes start to close again.

Thank god I listened because his hand is on the move again.

Up. Down.

In smooth, sure strokes, he works his length.

"Lower your hand and slip those fingers inside."

"Jase."

"Don't be embarrassed, baby. If I can't be there with you, I need you to fill the space for me. Do it. Let your wetness ease your entry."

I do.

"Oh god."

"Yeah, that's it. It's nice, right? God I bet you're tight."

"Jason."

"Pump your fingers in and out. Don't stop until you come."

The cliff is right there, waiting for me to fall.

"Jase."

"I know, baby. I'm right there with you."

If the speed of his strokes are anything to go by, he is.

Our movements sync.

Up and down for him. In and out for me.

Up.

Down.

In.

Out.

"Jas—"

I bury my face in my pillow to muffle my cries as I hear him roar.

I have no idea how long I lie there, hand in my pants, lungs heaving as I try to recover.

If he can make me come like this over the phone, how the hell am I going to survive him in person?

Chapter Twenty-Seven

THE BIG HAMMER: *picture of Mrs. Potato Head with a hand over her face.*

THE BIG HAMMER: I think we may have scared Mrs. PH last night.

BROADWAY BABY: I told you they are children's toys. Just because the box says suitable for children ages 2 and up doesn't mean they should be hanging out with people in their 20s. At least not the way we used them.

THE BIG HAMMER: I don't know. I think our way of using them was way more imaginative than anything I came up with as a kid.

BROADWAY BABY: WHEN you were a kid? I know LEGALLY you're an adult, but mentally...

THE BIG HAMMER: Ouch, Sweet Potato *knife emoji*

BROADWAY BABY: *GIF of chimp playing the piano with the caption "DRAMATIC MUSIC!"*

THE BIG HAMMER: I miss you.

BROADWAY BABY: Miss you too *kissing emoji*

♡

I reach for the pitcher of beer Zoey placed on the table to refill my cup. Ella took the night off and we decided to make the most of it watching the NHL All-Star Skills Competition at The Sin Bin. Much to their disappointment, I'm *not* wearing a Storm shirt like them.

I may have given in and worn Jase's jersey to the game, but my heart belongs to the Bruisers. Still, in an effort to be a supportive girlfriend, I am wearing the shirt Jase gave me the other night and sent him a picture.

I'll give you three guesses what's on it.

Figured it out?

No?

Okay, I'll tell you. Mr. Ridiculous got me a shirt with—yes, you guessed it, even if you didn't—potatoes on it. This one is two potatoes high-fiving, and underneath them it says 'Best Spuddies.' He's such a dork, but he's my dork.

Also…it should come as no surprise that he got himself the same shirt.

So far the BTU Alumni are two for two, with Tucker Hayes taking home the title for fastest skater and Jase's brother Ryan decimating the competition in the puck control challenge.

We're seven goalies in on the save streak challenge, with Jake Donovan being the last to step between the pipes. Normally a goalie faces one player from each team in a selected division, but with so many players coming from

BTU, they switched it up and he's only facing those who used to be Titans—plus Cali.

Jake's already edged out San Jose's goalie, Hall, by one goal, and now the guys are huddled at center ice. After all the stories I heard last night, I can only imagine what they are all plotting.

They break and Tucker heads for his shot, but instead of taking a breakaway for the net, he starts twirling like an ice dancer, using his stick as his dance partner.

"What in the world?" Ella exclaims next to me.

I'm pretty sure things are about to take an entertaining turn.

Tucker misses, unsurprisingly.

I scoot forward, literally on the edge of my seat as I see Jase take the puck. He gets into position and then Cali is jumping on his back, and the two jokesters of the NY Storm try their hand at the man nicknamed The Brick Wall.

After Jake blocks the shot, he holds out his arms as if to ask, *That's all you got?*

Wade Tanner skates out, but instead of going to center ice, he goes behind the opposite goal, the audience in the arena and inside the bar silent, all of us waiting with bated breath for what is going to happen next.

He holds an arm in the air, and the four others hustle to join him.

"Oh my god." I laugh as the five of them skate out in a V shape, passing the puck between them as they head for Jake. "He just called for the flying V."

"Well, they messed that up then because it's the captain who is supposed to call for it," Zoey states in a display of her own knowledge of *The Mighty Ducks*.

"The only thing that surprises me is they didn't have the jerseys ready to go."

"You better text Loverboy and tell him how disappointed we are about that oversight." Zoey puts on a good front of being serious, but it cracks the instant she looks my way.

On the TV we hear the announcers say, "Should have gone with the knuckle puck," as Jake makes a glove save.

"Can we *please* watch the trilogy this weekend?" Ella asks.

"Oh, but I always cry when Hans dies in the third one." Zoey pouts.

"Yeah, but the guy from *The Sandlot* is so hot in it." Ella says this like she's a lawyer who just rested her case.

"He's in two"—I hold up my fingers in a peace sign—"of the Mighty Duck movies. Don't you think you should know his character's name?" I take another sip of my beer.

"Nope." Ella shakes her head, her ponytail whipping her in the face, snagging on the long lashes framing her almond-shaped eyes. "He will always be Benny the Jet to me." A hand goes over her heart. "All I'm saying is the guy did some good growing up."

My beer sprays the table at her comment.

Using a napkin to clean up both the table and my face, I focus back on the TV where Cali is about to take his turn. He gets into position, bending over, one hand at the top of his stick, the other halfway down, but then he straightens and looks toward the team benches. He waves to someone, gesturing for whoever it is to come out.

Every eye in the bar is riveted to the screen. Freddie even turned the volume up to hear the announcers. "Looks like even the youngest Donnelly is getting in on the fun."

Sean Donnelly and Cali huddle together, and the way their bodies are hunched over, it's hard to make out what they are doing. A few seconds later, Sean reaches underneath his Blizzards jersey and pulls out one of those mini souvenir hockey sticks you see in gift shops.

"Callahan isn't actually going to use that, is he?" The disbelief in Ella's voice is clear.

"I think so," I say as, sure enough, Cali retakes his position. Looking like the Hunchback of Notre Dame, he skates for his shot and misses.

"This is the best thing *ever*." Zoey throws her arms in the air, doing a little dance in her seat. "It's just like when they used to do the breakaway challenge a few years ago."

She's right. Through the years, the challenges have evolved or are switched out for others, but the couple of years the NHL did the breakaway challenge were some of the most fun to watch. It was a lot like the slam dunk contest the NBA does during their skills competitions.

None of us are really basketball fans, but we love to watch the crazy ideas the players come up with to dunk the ball. We even make sure to set our DVR for all the sports' all-star-type challenges if we are working during them.

The camera pans to the benches again, and I see Jordan hand a hockey stick to Ryan before he skates out for his attempt. He hands the stick to Sean when he gets to center ice, and I can tell it must be his because it's the proper size for a nine-year-old.

Sean takes the puck and positions himself at about a forty-five degree angle from his oldest brother, scooping the puck on the blade of his stick and tossing it to Ryan, who catches it on his own blade, something that is extremely hard to do.

Ryan juggles the puck with his stick, tossing and catching it over and over then circling the stick this way and that, never letting it drop, once again proving he's one of the best puck handlers in the league, if not *the* best.

"How long do you think they'll keep this up?" Ella asks when Ryan misses.

"No idea." I could honestly watch this all night.

Again all five convene in a huddle before pulling in Sean to join them. The youngest Donnelly is so much smaller than the others that when he gets folded into the group, he disappears like a kid playing in racks of clothes.

This huddle takes longer than the first, and when they

finally break, it's Sean who has the puck. He stands there, shifting his feet back and forth on the ice, waiting. For what, I'm not sure.

The announcers are speculating amongst themselves until Jake's little sister—in her own Jake Donovan Blizzards jersey —skates out to pass off a pair of black hockey gloves.

Jase told me all about how close Sean and Carlee are, and I snort when he gives her a kiss on the cheek as he accepts the gloves. Looks like charm runs in the family.

I don't know if it's because he's the only one taking the shot seriously, or if Jake gave him a gimme—I suspect the latter—but Sean's shot finds the upper corner of the net, finally bringing an end to the competition.

I drain my beer and immediately reach to refill it. I gotta be prepared because the next two challenges are what Jase is known for.

I can't wait to see what happens.

Chapter Twenty-Eight

The Skills Competition is my favorite day of the All-Star Weekend. Through the years, the challenges have varied, but this year there are six: premier passer, fastest skater, save streak, puck control, hardest shot, and accuracy shooting.

I'm trying my best to stay out of my head and enjoy the day for the good time it's meant to be. JD is already gushing over the clickbait we turned the save streak challenge into, and she seems to have forgiven me for my post against Bishop. Why can't I shake off the anxiety of being compared to Ryan?

Outside of us both taking part as shooters in the save streak challenge, we don't even directly compete against each other.

A part of me wishes I could get away with calling Mels, because she always has a way of making everything—winning the Cup, the pressure I feel about trying to prove myself outside of being Ryan Donnelly's bother, all the bull-shit—fade away.

Even now, as I lean against the boards in front of one of the team benches, I can't help but think of my girl.

JD has Jake's Optimus Prime goalie mask propped on top of her head like a hat while the two of them canoodle over the half wall, my sister staying safely off the ice.

The two of them have been hashtag couple goals since college, and with Mels I finally feel like I've found my shot at it.

Ryan and Wade are hanging with the lovebirds while Tucker and Cali—an honorary member of the BTU Alumni contingent—are joking around with Sean and Carlee about my little brother's goal. The two youngins have been among the family members allowed on the ice since Ryan's first All-Star appearance his rookie season.

"I still can't believe you weren't the one to score on Jake, Tuck." Carlee lives for taunting her brother's best friend.

"I was taking it easy on him, Car." Tucker holds out a fist to bump. The way my fuckboy of a friend completely melts for the kids has always been one of my favorite things to witness.

"Don't let him lie to you, babe. None of them bring it like me." Sean thumps his chest twice then throws out his arms.

"How does Mom put up with your ego?" Ryan pulls Sean into a headlock and ruffles his hair.

"She was well practiced after dealing with yours for years."

"Burn!" Tucker cries, stretching out his arm for another fist bump, the two of them blowing it up at the end.

"You ever worry about what he'll be like once he surpasses all of us in his career?" Jake asks me as he leans around Cali.

"Honestly"—I look over to where Sean and Carlee are laughing together—"if Carlee wasn't in his life, I'd be afraid he'd turn out like Tuck."

"Hey!" Tuck shoves me to the side.

"What?" I hold my hands up in surrender. "I'm just saying that kid has every ounce of game and swagger we have—as much as all of us put together. Combine that with how promising of a hockey player he's proving to be, and homeboy will slay it with the girls."

"Truth." Tucker agrees. "He will be crushing pussy."

"Tucker!" JD yells, and Jake reaches out to slap him upside the head.

"Sorry, Blondie."

"You better be, BB3."

"He totally will though." Cali's whisper isn't as quiet as he thinks, and now he's the one being smacked.

"I swear the twins are more mature than all of you." JD pulls out her phone to take some behind-the-scenes footage to use on our social media accounts.

Tuck has been in rare form after winning the day's first event—fastest skater. I'm waiting for premier passer, my first event.

The Zamboni has already finished resurfacing the ice, and we're just waiting for coordinators to finish setting up.

There are three parts to the challenge. First, I get ten pucks to successfully pass from behind the net to three plastic hockey player cutouts in front of it.

Next, I have to get a puck in four different mini nets. The size of the net isn't the challenging part; it's having to bounce the puck over a plastic barrier in front of it that's tough.

Finally, I have to hit four of the five targets set up at the opposite end of the rink when they are lit, with the targets changing every three seconds. The player who completes all three in the least amount of time is the winner.

I've won this event both times I've competed in it, and I'm not looking to have that change. The title I would like to get back is hardest shot. Fucking Nate Bishop stole it from me last year.

The lights inside the arena dim, and everyone not competing in the premier passer challenge exits the ice to sit on the team benches. They announce all the players in the order they will compete, my teeth snapping together when I hear them call Bishop's name right before mine as the last competitor.

The tension in my jaw only intensifies when Bishop is the only one who manages to come close to my time from last year of one minute ten seconds.

"Sure you can handle this, Donnelly? Or are you going to need your little brother to come out and take care of this one for you too?" Bishop says as we pass each other on the ice.

I deserve a medal for not engaging with him.

"Or maybe we should have your sister try. I'd even be willing to teach her the proper way to handle a stick."

Sonofabitch.

I go from Bruce Banner to the Hulk in zero seconds flat. My stick clatters on the ice and my gloves bounce in opposite directions as I toss them down with a flick of my wrist. I surge forward, grab him by the front of his sweater, and haul him inches from my face.

I'm seething, full-on raging at this asshole.

"I *dare* you to say something else about JD." I move in even closer, our noses brushing.

Hatred burns in his eyes as he glares at me. *Well, join the club, motherfucker. The feeling is more than mutual.*

I couldn't tell you why I never mentioned anything about the shit he's spewed through the years. Maybe it's because she's my twin and I feel like it's my responsibility, or maybe I'm just trying to keep the peace and keep everyone out of jail. Who knows.

I release my grip, shoving him away hard enough that we both glide backward.

"Buckle up, buttercup, and watch what an Olympic-level player can do."

I give him a wink as I take my own dig.

I may have my hang-ups about being compared to Ryan, but I sure as shit know I'm better than Nate Bishop.

Time to fucking prove it.

Chapter Twenty-Nine

THE BIG HAMMER: *picture of sweet potato fries*

BROADWAY BABY: Do I even want to ask?

THE BIG HAMMER: They're sweet potato fries.

BROADWAY BABY: Yes, I can see that, All-Star. But why are you sending me a picture of them?

THE BIG HAMMER: I wanted you to know I miss you and I'm thinking about you, my little sweet potato.

BROADWAY BABY: *GIF of girl rolling her eyes*

THE BIG HAMMER: *boomerang of Jase winking*

BROADWAY BABY: Dammit!

THE BIG HAMMER: Hehe.

BROADWAY BABY: OMG. Did you really just type hehe?

THE BIG HAMMER: Don't hate.

BROADWAY BABY: *facepalm emoji* I really do need to change your contact name to 'I can't even.'

THE BIG HAMMER: You know *thinking face emoji* I'm a little disappointed you haven't asked me the most important question of all.

BROADWAY BABY: Why don't you share with the class?

THE BIG HAMMER: You asked me why I sent you the picture but not WHY I'm eating them.

BROADWAY BABY: Um…because you're hungry and I'm sure Gemma would rather you eat them than regular French fries?

THE BIG HAMMER: While I'm sure that's true and all, no, that's not why I'm eating them…but if Gem asks, yes that's why.

BROADWAY BABY: Okay, I'll bite. What's the real reason?

THE BIG HAMMER: I figured I'd get some practice in before our date this weekend.

BROADWAY BABY: Practice?

THE BIG HAMMER: Eating sweet potatoes.

BROADWAY BABY: Did you take a puck to the head last night and I missed it? Because you're not making any sense.

THE BIG HAMMER: You're so cute when you act clueless.

BROADWAY BABY: …

THE BIG HAMMER: You're sleeping at my place after our date, right?

BROADWAY BABY: Maybe.

THE BIG HAMMER: What is this maybe stuff you speak of?

BROADWAY BABY: Well, if you'd asked me prior to this conversation, my answer would have been yes, but since you're dancing around the question, I might be reconsidering.

THE BIG HAMMER: *GIF of Zach, Screech, and AC Slater dancing in their underwear saying, "Slumber party!"*

BROADWAY BABY: Oh I love *Saved by the Bell*.

BROADWAY BABY: Still not an answer though.

THE BIG HAMMER: Okay. Let me know if this is clear enough for you.

THE BIG HAMMER: After I blow your mind with the EPIC date I have planned, I am going to spend the rest of the night eating YOU, Sweet Potato.

BROADWAY BABY: Well played, Loverboy. I think you just broke Mels.

BROADWAY BABY: Also…HOT DAMN!

THE BIG HAMMER: Thanks Zo.

Chapter Thirty

F*ebruary*

"You're a hot mess." Zoey rehangs yet another shirt I toss her way.

I shoot a glare over my shoulder at Captain Obvious sitting on my bed. I wish Ella were here; she would actually help, unlike Miss Ballbuster here.

"Not. Helping." I go back to searching my closet again, praying the right outfit will jump up and shout, *Wear me!*

"I don't see what the big deal is. It's not like it's your first date or anything."

I bury my face in the rack of clothes in front of me. Technically what Zoey says is true. In the month or so since I had dinner at Jase's, we've gone on a handful of dates, but tonight is our first *big* one. I couldn't tell you why, but it feels more official than the others.

It also doesn't help that Jase has refused to tell me what we are doing. And holy crap don't even get me started on how he ended our text convo a few days ago.

"Oh my god, I can't watch this anymore." Zoey pushes the pile of discarded clothes out of the way and rises from my bed, taking me by the shoulders and reversing our positions. "You sit here and let Mama take care of you."

"Because when you're good to Mama…"

"Mama's good to you." She finishes the lyric to one of our favorite songs from *Chicago*. "There's my little thespian. Now let's find you something that will get your hockey hunk so worked up he'll be dying to get at your sin bin."

"Oh my god, Zo." I hide my flaming cheeks in my hands. "You did *not* just say that."

"You're damn right I did. It's high time you jump on that hockey stick and take it for a spin."

I scrunch my face. "Not really sure that's correct."

"Fine. I'll speak to you in my language." She tosses a pair of dark wash skinny jeans, a white V-neck, and a long merlot-colored buttoned sweater at me. "You two need to finally stop dancing around each other and get to the horizontal mambo already." I'm smacked in the face with a matching set of white lace lingerie.

"That was so easy it was almost a cop-out."

"Whatever. It works." A pair of suede camel-colored thigh-high boots land by the bed, and she folds her arms over her chest. "Wear that. Go, have fun with your boyfriend, and for god's sake, put his finely-honed athletic prowess to the test."

She may be a nut job, but I wouldn't trade her in for the world.

"Besides…when a man says he wants to spend a night dining algina, you don't turn that down."

Don't ask. Don't do it. It's best not to engage.

I can't help myself. "Algina?"

Zoey stops in the open doorway of my room. "You know…" She makes a rolling motion with her finger. "Like alfresco but for your vagina."

I knew I shouldn't have asked.

"Plus, hockey players really know how to work their hips." She calls the parting shot over her shoulder as she leaves me alone in my room.

I need to shake off these nerves so I can enjoy the night. Humming "Out Tonight" from *Rent*, I pull on the outfit Zoey selected. She is a pain in the ass, but she sure as hell knows what she's doing when it comes to outfit selection.

The jeans and boots show off my legs to perfection, and the t-shirt is casual yet tight enough to be sexy. I leave the buttons open on the sweater, letting it hang to the middle of my thighs.

A peek at the time tells me I need to hustle if I'm going to be ready before Jase arrives. It's a risk having him pick me up here, but he didn't want to worry about if the Storm's plane was late and having me wait for him.

I'm wrapping a tan tartan scarf around my neck when the knock comes.

It's just a date, Mels. No big deal. He likes you, you like him. Don't worry about anything else.

I take a deep breath, only to expel it in a rush when I open the door.

Holy hell does Jase Donnelly clean up nice.

His blond hair is styled, his black sweater has to be cashmere and molds to his chest like it was made for him, and don't even get me started on the way the dark jeans hug his massive thighs before tapering to a pair of classic black and white Chucks.

Would it be wrong to give him a standing ovation? Probably, but damn he's hot with a capital H-O-T.

"Hey, Sweet Potato." Mischief sparkles in the golden-green of his eyes.

I'm in trouble.

"Hey, All-Star."

"Are you two going out, or are you just going to stand there eye-fucking each other all night?"

I'm going to kill Zoey.

"Hey, Zo." A knowing smirk plays on Jase's lips.

"Hey there, Loverboy." Zoey wiggles her fingers in greeting.

Yup, I'm definitely going to murder her. It's a good thing I have a second best friend.

"Good*bye*, Zo." I grab my coat and push Jase out the door before she can say anything else.

"Night. Oh, and Mels," Zoey calls out as the door shuts, "go forth and have all the crazy monkey sex you want tonight. There's no rehearsal tomorrow. It's not like you have to worry about being sore."

Why? Why am I friends with her?

A muscular arm wraps around my middle, pulling me against a hard chest. All embarrassment fades at the sense of home the embrace brings.

"Though I'm fully on board with that suggestion"—Jase runs his nose along the shell of my ear—"we should probably limit the amount of time she spends with Becky and Skye."

We should probably limit the amount of time she spends outside of a padded room. I keep that thought to myself.

"Why?"

"I don't know if the world can handle the trouble the three of them could create together."

And just like that, all the awkwardness fades.

$\heartsuit$

When the town car parks in front of a nondescript door twenty minutes later, I still have no idea what we are doing. No matter how much I pried, Jase remained all mum's the word. My only clue is the small lit metal sign above the door: *The Duel*.

Ever the gentleman, Jase holds the door for me to step through, lacing our fingers and guiding us down a long, narrow hallway.

We come to a stop at another door, this one with a bell. A few seconds later, it clicks open and a bear of a man steps out, a deep scowl on his face.

Where the hell did Jase bring us?

I shift so Jase's bulk is blocking me but stop when I see the man break out into a grin upon spotting my boyfriend.

"Donnelly. It's been a minute," he says in a deep bass.

"I know, Tiny." Jase reaches out to share a complicated handshake while I stand there mouthing, *Tiny?* "You know how it is when the season kicks into high gear."

"Hell yeah. You boys are looking good this year. You going to bring home the Cup for us?"

"That's the plan."

Dark eyes crinkle at the corners and white teeth flash against dark skin when Tiny turns my way. "And who is this beauty?"

Jase gives my fingers a squeeze, pulling me forward to his side. The affection I see in his gaze when he looks down at me causes my heart to tap-dance inside my chest. "This is my girlfriend Melody Brightly. Mels, this is Tiny."

I love ironic nicknames.

"It's nice to meet you." Tiny greets me warmly before saying to Jase, "No Cali? You're taking on the rock-star contingent by yourself?"

"Nah." An arm drops around my shoulders. "My girl here is a Broadway star. She's my ringer."

The two of them share a look I can't decipher then Tiny thrusts an arm behind him.

"Can't wait for it all to go down. You know the drill. Drop your phones and head on in. Your fanboy already has a whole section for you guys. Guess I should have figured you'd be showing up tonight."

"Your *fanboy*?" There's no stopping my chuckle at the blush overtaking Jase's cheeks.

"You'll see," is all he says.

Tiny clicks the door shut behind us, and I follow Jase to a room where we check our coats and phones.

"Our phones?" I ask.

"You'll see," he repeats, not saying anything else on the subject.

Excitement bubbles and a buzz hums beneath my skin as he weaves us through the tables and chairs.

I take in the place, trying to figure out what it is. It reminds me of a speakeasy, all dark paneled walls and black tufted-leather booths. The only light in the space comes from Edison bulbs strung across the ceiling and wrought iron sconces intermittently placed throughout.

There is a huge oak bar taking up the entirety of one wall, but what really captures my attention is the curved stage, complete with velvet curtains tied back on the sides and two grand pianos—one black, one white—polished to a high shine in the center.

"Did you bring me to a piano bar?"

"A *dueling* piano bar, Sweet Potato." The smirk on his face is the same 100% pure cocky male one he had the night we met.

I should say something biting, knock him down a peg or two.

That's not what I do, though.

Instead I launch myself at him, wrapping my arms around his neck and sealing my mouth to his.

This date is...so...me. How else did you think I would react?

Who cares that we are in a public place, or that we stand amongst the tables, probably preventing patrons and servers from getting through.

All that matters is this kiss.

I catch a hint of mint with each stroke of his tongue, and a shiver chases down my spine when the metal of his ring whirls inside my mouth.

No one kisses like Jase Donnelly.

He may have a gold medal for hockey, but he deserves *all* the medals for kissing. The Schuyler Sisters would never have to worry about not being satisfied if they kissed Jase.

We kiss.

And kiss some more.

Applause rings out when the pianos stop playing, but when the catcalls and wolf whistles continue, I realize they are for us, not the musicians.

He keeps me close, resting his forehead on mine. "I'm going to apologize in advance for this evening."

"Why?"

Now I'm really confused. Everything about this place is so perfectly me, so I can't imagine there's anything he would need to apologize for.

"Because." He lifts his head, casting a look over mine with a grimace. "This is going to make me sound so high school… but this place is more fun when you come with a group." He cups the back of his neck. "I mentioned I was thinking of bringing you here, and it kinda snowballed from there."

"You mean The Coven is crashing our date?" I tease.

"*God* no." He shudders. It's adorable how someone who is a beast on the ice is intimidated by a group of women. Except…Jase's contradictions are some of things I find most endearing.

"There's only one…well one and a half of them here. It's bad enough I feel like a teenager who needs a chaperone for a date—there wasn't a *chance* I'd have them *all* here." He strokes the line of my jaw with his thumb, and I lean into the touch. "I want you to *still* be my girlfriend when the night is over."

"One and a half?"

"You'll see." He relinks our hands, this time not stopping until we arrive at a section of booths and tables in the corner by the stage. I love how he's always in constant contact when we're together. Not in a possessive, controlling way, just…touching.

"About time you showed up, Donnelly."

"Yeah…this whole thing was *your* idea."

"We were starting to think you didn't love us anymore."

"Leave my boy alone."

"Ah, Pete—the ever-loyal Storm fan."

My jaw goes slack as I stand there gawking while the five members of Birds of Prey discuss Jase like they do it every day. Sure, he's a professional athlete—one who comes from an impressive bloodline—but BoP is on an entirely different level. They are rock gods.

"Um…Jase." I pinch the washboard under his sweater.

"Yeah, baby?"

"Don't you think maybe you should have told me we would be hanging out with *rock stars*?" I hiss through my teeth.

"Relax, Sweet Potato."

Easy for him to say.

Chapter Thirty-One

Hours and countless songs later, I'm patting myself on the back for a job well done.

For days I warred with myself, debating if this was the best idea. Group dates aren't really something people in their twenties do on the reg, but The Duel is always more fun when you come with one.

It has been one of our favorite haunts in the city since BoP stumbled upon it years ago. Who doesn't love a good piano bar? Good music, cold beer, fun times, and the added bonus of none of it ending up on social media because part of The Duel's draw is its anonymity.

Plus, unlike our first date, the people with us were actually invited to be here.

"Your move, Broadway Baby," Jamie says, retaking his seat with a smug grin after he and Pete finish their rendition of Billy Joel's "Piano Man."

After my girl got over being starstruck—an entertaining thing to witness given how she gave zero fucks when she first met me—she's been going toe to toe with Jamie for the title of bar champion.

"You've added her to the Coven Conversations?" I whine, turning to Holly.

"Nope, but thanks for pointing out that oversight." Holly reaches for a cocktail napkin and asks Mels for her number. Vince gives me a look that screams, *You're in for it now.*

"How do you know her text handle then?" This time I direct my question to Jamie.

"It's a song, dude."

Oh yeah. I remember Mels telling me this.

"Well…" Mels taps her chin in thought. Her lips purse, moving side to side, and I can't resist their tempting draw. She may be thinking of her next song, but I'm thinking of all the things I will be doing to her when I get us home later.

"Holly? Do you know the words to 'That's Life'?" Mels looks around me to see her better.

"Oh, I love that song." Holly claps her hands in front of her. "That's a good duet, too."

"Wow, you wanna do a song that's not a Christmas carol?" Vince teases.

"You know Christmas music has not been on my playlist since New Year's. Behave, Muffin."

"But you like it so much better when I don't, Cupcake." Holly blushes until she's the same shade as Melody's hair.

"Is this why you call me Sweet Potato?" Mels nods to the two eye-fucking each other next to us. "You needed something that falls in the food category?"

"No, baby." I drag my palm down her leg. "You know potatoes are our thing."

Her black eyes sparkle as she sticks a finger in my face. "I'm telling you this right now, All-Star: I'm not down for food in the bedroom."

I nip the tip of finger, causing her to suck in a sharp breath. She has no idea what I'm capable of doing to her in the bedroom. I don't need food to help.

"I wouldn't be so quick to rule out frosting. Right, Cupcake?" Vince's comment earns him a smack to the chest.

The ladies get up for their song before my best friend can dig himself into a deeper hole with his girlfriend.

I lean back in my seat as I watch them standing next to the stage. The beaming smile on my girl's face and the easy way she laughs with Holly like they've known each other all their lives warms my heart. Fitting in with our squad can seem like a daunting task. Hell, Gage the six-seven giant was even intimidated when he met us, but Mels just rolls with every dysfunctional punch.

"Oh you have it bad, man." Sammy grins at me over his beer.

"What makes you say that?" I hedge.

"Don't even try it," he scoffs. "You forget, I lived with your other half. I'm well versed in how to read a Donnelly twin."

Damn him for being right.

"Well, looks like we have a ninth Convenette." Vince toasts his beer in their direction.

As the last notes of "Friends In Low Places" finishes, the ladies take their places on the large stage. I may have joked with Tiny earlier that I brought Mels to be my ringer, but even I wasn't prepared for the amount of talent she has.

Each time she's taken the stage tonight, she's owned it. She doesn't just sing the song; she acts it, feels it, becomes it.

If this is how she is during glorified karaoke, I have zero doubt in my mind she will win that Tony. Opening night for her show can't get here soon enough.

I just hope my family will be enough of a support system to have her forgetting about the lack of her own.

The opening strains of the song begin with Mels and Holly sitting with their respective pianist. Mels starts, singing the first section before Holly takes over.

As the song builds and they sing about all the things

they've been in life, they rise from the benches, circling the pianos to the front of the stage, each placing their microphones in the stand on their side.

Earlier in the night, Holly was intimidated to sing with Mels since she's a professional, but she holds her own, and you can see how Mels encourages her.

On the second round of the chorus, they lift their mics again, meeting in between the pianos, getting lost in the song and playing off each other.

Mels has a hand to her chest, eyes closed as her knees bend to bounce.

Back and forth they sing. The audience is enthralled, cheering them on, and as Mels sucks in a final breath and belts out the longest, strongest note to end the song, the entire bar is on their feet.

"Well shit." I hear Jamie curse as the applause dies down.

"Sorry to say this, Jam"—Sammy puts a comforting arm around his husband's shoulders in a rare display of PDA—"but I think you lost."

"I ain't mad about it."

"Well, damn." Tiny takes the stage, the lights shining off his bald head, keeping the girls up there. "When our resident hockey player said he was bringing a ringer tonight, I wasn't sure what to expect."

He waits as a fresh wave of applause ripples through the packed audience.

"For those of you who have had the honor of being at The Duel on a night the famed Birds of Prey battle it out against the Storm contingent, you know we are at the point in the evening where we need to determine a winner."

Around me, every member of BoP vamps it up for the crowd, and Tiny's deep chuckle can be heard through the speakers.

"If you think BoP wins the night, let's hear it." Tiny cups a hand around his ear and leans forward.

Clapping and hollering ring out for a few moments. As it dies down, Tiny corrals the ladies to his side. "And if you think these two fine ladies"—he waves a hand over their heads—"showed the rock stars how it's really done…"

He doesn't even finish the sentence before people are on their feet, cheering and whooping in an overwhelming show of support.

"Yeah, I'd go with the beautiful women too." Tiny winks, and I bite the inside of my cheek to keep from laughing. "Like we end any night here at The Duel when these nutsos grace us with their presence"—he shoots a glance at our table—"it's time to give my guys a break while we enjoy a little 'Bohemian Rhapsody'."

Mels gives me a curious look as we all join them on stage. "Um…"

I wrap an arm around her waist and bend to place a kiss on her neck, breathing in her sweet bubblegum scent. "You'll see, Sweet Potato." My hand skims down her arm then I link our fingers. "Sit with me."

I lead her to the bench of the white piano, crack my knuckles, and stretch my fingers over the keys. Across from us, Andy and Ian take the bench at the black piano.

"Jase?" Mels looks at me like I have two heads.

"Hope you know your Queen, baby."

"Of course I do." Her gaze drops to my hands then back to my face. "You…you play the piano?"

"Oh, baby." I lean in, my lips brushing the shell of her ear as I speak. "I have all *sorts* of hidden talents." I pull back and meet her hazy eyes. "Don't worry—I'll show you a bunch of them when we get home." I emphasize my declaration with a wink.

That blush I adore makes an appearance.

Our time at the bar might be coming to an end, but the night is far from over.

Chapter Thirty-Two

"Did you have fun tonight?" Jase trails kisses along my neck, helping me out of my coat.

I'm buzzing. This night has already been more than anything I've ever experienced.

"I did. I can't believe I've never heard of it before."

"The Duel is one of the city's best kept secrets."

It's not the only one with a secret. You can't avoid it forever, Mels. You'll end up with just your parents.

I shake off those negative thoughts. This night has been storybook perfect, and I don't want anything to taint it.

I wrap my arms around his neck and push up onto the tips of my toes to kiss him for all I'm worth.

"I'm not taking *any* chances," he says when I break our kiss at the sound of the lock clicking. I don't think I've ever seen him use the deadbolt before. "We've had more than our fair share of interruptions. Not today, Satan."

I drop my head to his shoulder, giggling. He's so ridiculous.

Suddenly I'm in his arms, my legs automatically hooking around his waist, and we're on the move. I have no idea how we make it to his room without wiping out.

He continues to carry me until we stop next to the massive bed facing floor-to-ceiling windows that match those in the living room. I slide down, rubbing against every one of his delicious muscles along the way.

He groans, rocking his hips into me.

"Now…" His hands slip under my sweater, cupping my shoulders, and he nudges it to fall until it pools at my feet. "I want nothing more than to spend the rest of the night burying myself inside you, but I need to know if you're ready to take this step."

I press onto my toes again, circling my arms around his neck and threading my fingers into the hair at the back of his head. "I think the *real* question is are *you* ready? You talked a big game while you were away this week—are you sure you can live up to the expectations you've set?"

His smile turns wolfish, and the flutter in my belly makes me wonder if maybe I've bitten off more than I can chew.

"Oh, baby." His eyes darken to that familiar green. "I'm gonna rock your world."

Projecting more confidence than I feel, I nip at the underside of his jaw and whisper, "Prove it."

I expect to be thrown on the bed and ravished, but—like he's consistently been doing—he surprises me.

As if he has all the time in the world, he slowly circles me, curling his body around me from behind. One of his feet taps against one of mine until I spread them and widen my stance. He cups a hand over my hip, pulling me tighter into him, the hard length of him pressing into me.

I feel him *everywhere*.

Even through our clothes, I can make out the bumps and ridges of his abdominals as he holds me so tight. I breathe in the familiar scent of soap and ice as my hair is brushed to the side, his lips finding the sensitive spot revealed on the back of my neck.

An electric current zaps down my spine and I instinctively

arch my back, my ass rubbing against the erection I want inside me.

Jase groans, his teeth nipping at my back almost in warning, but as he continues to trail kisses, I can't stop the pop of my lower body. The contrast between his soft lips and the scruff of his five o'clock shadow is too much.

He licks across my pulse point, my heart rate pounding beneath the drag of his tongue.

"Jase," I plead—for what, I'm not sure.

"I'm just getting started, baby." An arm drapes over my shoulder and his hand disappears inside the V-neck of my shirt. With zero hesitation, he pushes the lace cup of my bra down, cupping my breast in his hand. My nipple pebbles beneath his fingers as he thumbs it to life before repeating the same maddening process on the other one until both breasts are free from the lace but supported by the underwire.

The hand on my hip tightens its grip to the point of bruising.

The fingers of the hand inside my shirt stretch until he has both my nipples in his maddening caress.

I guess it's a good thing Jase calls me baby, because with the way I can't stop the arch of my back and the movement of my ass, I'm pretty much dirty dancing on his dick.

I try to spin in his arms, but he stops me.

"Jase." I let out a frustrated growl.

"It's still my turn." He chuckles into my neck when I growl again, the vibration of the sound making my clit beg for the attention it's not getting.

"How is that fair?"

I don't even care that I sound like a toddler throwing a tantrum. Though our phone sex was hot, I hated that I couldn't touch him. Being denied now is the worst form of torture.

"I never said anything about playing fair, baby." He

removes his hand from my shirt to peel it from my body. "But I *will* go tit for tat with you."

The pile of clothes on the floor continues to grow as his sweater is added.

"That's better," he says on a sigh, the bare skin of his torso burning mine with each brush of my heaving chest.

The cold air of the room makes my already hard nipples tighten further.

"*God*, these are even more perfect in person." He cups a breast in each hand, lifting them as if testing the weight.

I moan, my head falling back on his chest. He hasn't even touched me below the belt and I'm close to coming.

The ball bearing of his piercing drags down my neck as he moves his hands. Instead of going for the clasp of my bra, he gets to work on my jeans.

The button opens with a flick of his fingers, and I can't hear the hiss of the zipper over the pounding of the blood in my ears.

Then he stops.

He leaves my jeans on.

He. Leaves. Them. On.

"Jase."

He chuckles again, and if I didn't want to use it so bad, I would totally punch him in the junk.

Finally, *finally* I feel pressure at the top of my slit, but like the night I didn't get my happy ending, he maddeningly keeps his touch *over* my underwear.

He pushes, the lips of my pussy parting around the tip of his finger as the lace of my panties abrades the freed hardened nub.

He reaches my entrance, circling over my underwear then retracing his path.

Up.

Down.

I latch onto his hard thighs as he uses his other hand to pull on the back of my thong, tightening the front until I feel my lips part around the lace the same way they did around his finger.

I'm burning up.

Goose bumps break out over every inch of my skin.

I'm on the verge of tears, but he continues to lazily drag his finger over me.

Up.

Down.

Figure eights dance along my clit and the flutters inside begin.

At my entrance again, he presses inside, and I hear the delicate fabric rip as he takes it with him.

I explode, my orgasm crashing through me.

"Fuck, baby." He bites my shoulder as I grind against him with his finger still inside me.

"Jase."

"I got you, baby."

My legs buckle, but before I can collapse on the floor in a pleasure-filled heap, he scoops me into his arms and lays me out on his bed.

He looms over me, and I'm finally able to get my hands on his magnificent body.

He groans as I drag them down his torso, thumbing his nipples the way he did mine.

I push up to capture his lips, pinching his piercing between my teeth when it whirls inside my mouth.

There is zero hint of gold in his eyes when we pull apart.

"Jase…I need you inside me."

"I know." He presses back, his biceps flexing as he lowers himself. "But not yet."

"Jason," I warn.

"Full-name me all you want, baby." He pulls one boot

then the other from my feet. "My MD isn't going anywhere near your sweet, sweet pussy until I complete my hat trick first."

Chapter Thirty-Three

I may be a defender on the ice, but in bed I'm 100% offense.

As much as I enjoyed how Melody's legs looked in her painted-on jeans all night, it's time for them to go.

My own jeans are a painful restriction, doing their best to choke the life from my dick, but if I'm going to succeed in my hat trick goals without blowing like I'm back in high school, they need to stay on.

Kneeling between Melody's legs, I take a moment to appreciate the vision spread out before me.

That blush I love so much covers her down to her navel, and as much as my dick would protest, I could spend the rest of the night just looking at her.

I *could*, but I'm not going to. I skim my hands up her calves, cup her behind the knees, and hook her legs around my hips. My control comes close to snapping when she uses the strength in those dancer legs of hers to pull me closer.

I place one more hard kiss on her mouth before setting out on my mission.

I nip and suck down the strap of her bra, letting it finally fall from her shoulder. I kiss and lick over the curve of her breast then take her nipple into my mouth.

She moans and arches up off the bed as I roll my tongue ring over the peak then trap it between the ball bearing and my tongue.

Her hands clutch at my hair, and I couldn't care less if I lose any of it as I move to her other breast.

Her core writhes under me, trying to find relief against the blatantly obvious bulge in my pants. "Nice try, baby." I widen my stance just enough to keep her lower body suspended away from mine. "You'll come from *me* riding *you*, not the other way around."

"Jason."

I can't help but grin at the use of my full name. Usually I hate it, but knowing she's using it because she's out of control makes it hot.

My scalp burns as I travel down the length of her body.

Nip.

Suck.

Bite.

A drag of my piercing.

Over and over I continue my slow torment.

"You have the prettiest pussy." I hover over it, taking in the way the bare lips frame the white lace I've pulled between them.

"How would you know?"

"I'm looking right at it, baby." I lick a line from her entrance to the top of her slit. I spread a hand over her belly, easily spanning it, to hold her in place.

"Yeah, but—" Her nails scratch my shoulders, looking for purchase. "You can't really *see* it since you refuse to take off my underwear."

Looks like my little sweet potato is spicy.

Ignoring the taunt, I latch my mouth onto her pussy—lace

panties and all—and don't remove it until she's coming for the second time.

Without giving her the chance to come down, I tug the fabric until it rips, finally removing them like she wants.

My tongue, teeth, and lips continue to work her. Without giving her a reprieve, I add two fingers to the mix, the walls of her pussy still fluttering from her orgasm, and push her back to the edge for number three.

"Jase. Jase. Jase," Melody chants, and I pump my fingers inside her.

"Jase."

Pump.

"Jase."

Pump.

"Jase."

I pull her clit between my teeth and roll the ball bearing over it, and it's time for hats to rain down around us as I complete my hat trick.

I start to slow my movements to help bring her down, but she tugs on my hair again and this time I know I've lost a few strands.

"If you don't fuck me *right* now, I'm going across the hall to see if Cali is up for the job," she threatens.

I growl and haul her to me. "That's not the *least* bit funny, Mel-o-dy."

She laughs, not intimidated by me at all. "Then stop teasing me and make me yours already."

I shift back to stand, removing my jeans and retrieving a condom from my wallet, the bedside drawer too far away.

I grind my molars to keep from spilling inside the rubber. Protection in place, I blanket her body with mine, hooking a leg over my hips and wrapping my arms under her back, sliding home in one push she's so wet.

"Oh, baby." I pull back and push in again. "You've been

mine since the night we met." Pull back. Push in. "This only binds you to me more."

From the glint in her dark eyes, nothing else needs to be said.

We move together in sync like it's the hundredth time we've come together this way and not the first. As I fill the condom, semen isn't the only thing I've lost to this pink-haired beauty. I'm pretty sure my heart has followed like a BOGO special.

Chapter Thirty-Four

The sound of voices filters into my consciousness and I stretch my sore muscles. Man, I thought Zoey and her choreography were tough on my body, but they have *nothing* on Jase Donnelly in the bedroom.

If I'm this wrecked after sleeping in, I can't imagine how he's surviving his morning skate.

Morning skate. Shit!

I shoot up, lifting the sheets to cover my naked chest. I grab my phone, and sure enough, Jase shouldn't be back from the Storm's practice facility yet—so why do I hear voices from inside the apartment? Did I really have to date a guy who gives out the code to his place like it's a Playbill?

Spotting my overnight bag on the dresser, I remind myself to give my boyfriend an extra kiss for the thoughtful gesture.

I quickly get dressed in a pair of leggings, a sports bra, and my loose-fitting long-sleeved 'There WILL be drama (and singing and dancing and music and jazz hands…)' shirt. What? I'm a theater nerd.

Teeth brushed and hair tamed in a messy bun, I take a deep breath and brace myself for who I might find on the other side of the door.

It's probably one of the Covenettes.

Yeah, that's it. No big deal.

I can hear multiple voices as I make my way down the hallway, and it also sounds like someone turned on the television.

See? They make themselves at home. You don't have to do anything. Easy peasy.

"Sean, take your shoes off if you're going to sit on the couch like that. Treat your brother's place with respect," says a female voice.

"Sorry, Mom," a younger-sounding voice answers.

I stop in my tracks, feet glued to the floor like it's turned to fly paper.

Oh my god! His mom is here?

My hands automatically rise to smooth my hair and fidget with my clothes.

Listen, universe, I know I've met almost everyone else in Jase's family by them just showing up here, but don't you think it's going a little overboard having me meet his parents this way? **wags finger with hand on hip** And don't even start with me about this being karma.

Sure, I've never done the whole *meet a guy's parents thing* before, but is it really too much to ask for it not to happen after having spent the night screwing said guy's brains out all night?

"Oh!" Jase's mom says when she notices me, her hand covering her chest in surprise.

Her exclamation draws the attention of the other two occupants of the room.

"Mels is here." Sean jumps up on the couch, earning another reprimand from his mother.

"Hi." I offer the most awkward wave known to man.

Without warning, I'm pulled into a hug and squeezed inside a cloud of lavender. At first I stand stiffly within the embrace, unsure how to deal with maternal affection, but eventually I bring my arms around to return it.

"I am so happy to meet you, dear," she says, holding me by the shoulders and looking me over. I do my best not to cringe when thinking about what she sees. *Totally should have showered.*

"Same here?" The words come out as more of a question than intended. *Why didn't Jase tell me his* mother *was coming?*

Luckily she doesn't take offense, chuckling softly before linking her arm with mine and leading us to the open section of couch opposite the kids.

"Oh, sweetheart." She pats my arm, giving it an affectionate squeeze. "I'm sorry if you're feeling ambushed. I should have called first. The kids just wanted to see Jase before the game, and it didn't even occur to me that you might be here."

"Actually…it pretty much falls in line with how I've met every other member of your family."

I go on to tell her all about the video chat when Maddey showed up during our first date and how Ryan and Tucker dropped by unannounced. Ruth—as she insists I call her—apologizes for her children and blames their father for their bad manners.

Carlee informs me I got off relatively easily where Tucker was concerned then spends a considerable amount of time gushing over my pink hair before she and Sean get involved in a heated Mario Kart battle.

"You know…" There's a familiar twinkle in Ruth's eyes as she curls a leg underneath her and gives me her full attention. "I've seen you perform, and you are very good, my dear."

I'm caught off guard by the revelation.

She has?

I couldn't even tell you the last role my parents came to see me play. They probably wouldn't even be able to name them if asked. I want to say it doesn't bother me and I've grown used to it, but I can't. What child doesn't want their parents to show an interest in their life?

"You have?"

"Oh yes. After my son told me about you, I asked him which shows you've been in. The girls and I try to see a few throughout the year, and I save all my Playbills as mementos. I went back and checked the ones I knew you had a role in, and there were several that included you."

"Wow...what are the odds?"

"You've played some big roles in quite a few highly rated productions. I would say chances were pretty good."

I'm not sure what to say.

"I'm really looking forward to opening night. It was one thing to think you were amazing as just an actor on stage—I can only imagine how much more special it will be knowing you."

Tears prick the backs of my eyes, but I blink them away.

God. I never stood a chance when it came to Jase Donnelly. How could I when this is the type of stock he comes from? I have a feeling he's not the only Donnelly I'm at risk of losing my heart to.

Please forgive me.

"Now...tell me all about how you got started on Broadway. From what I remember in your Playbill bio, you've been doing this for many years. I want to know all the things."

I can't help but laugh at how much she reminds me of Jordan.

I go on to explain how I fell in love with acting when my kindergarten class did a production of *Peter Cottontail* and I played one of his sisters. I tell her how I would stay with my aunt and uncle who live in the city and they would take me to auditions.

I lose count of the number of questions she asks. The sense

of pride I feel coming from her when I tell her how I've been a member of the Actors' Equity Association—the union that represents stage performers—since I was eight years old finally has me losing the battle with my tears.

It's when I'm once again wrapped in one of her hugs that Jase arrives, and the look on his face is priceless.

Chapter Thirty-Five

I say goodbye to Cali as we step off the elevator onto our floor. Foregoing sleep in favor of making love to my girlfriend all night may not have been the best thing to do the night before a game, but hell if I was going to feel sorry about it.

Am I bone-tired? Sure.

Does that mean I made a mistake? Not in the least.

Besides, the best part of my job is the built-in time for a nap. Plus, with tonight's game being a rivalry game against the Blizzards, I actually get an extra hour for my nap as the puck won't be dropping until eight o'clock instead of at the usual seven.

That being said, I am hoping my girl is still naked in my bed and I can just slide in next to her before I slide back into her, if you know what I'm saying.

I'm not really sure what to do when I find her wiping tears away while she hugs my mother.

"Mom?"

"Hi, sweetheart." She comes around, holding out her arms for a hug, and like any good mama's boy, I automatically go to her. I may have outgrown her by a foot, but no one bear-hugs like Ruth Donnelly.

Leaning over the back of the couch, I plant a kiss on my girl's lips. Cupping her cheek in my hand, I thumb away another tear and hold her watery gaze. "You okay?"

Melody nods.

"You sure?"

"Yeah." She reaches up, her small hand wrapping itself around my wrist, stroking the sensitive skin on the inside as she leans into my touch. "You have the *best* mom."

My heart gives a pang. Here I am worried she would feel uncomfortable meeting Mom without me when really it's the stuff it could bring up for her, witnessing how crazy involved my parents are in my life when hers can't be bothered to show up when it counts.

I need to remember to give her brother a hug or something on opening night for always making my girl feel like a priority to him at least.

"Dude, you better not be logged in on my account and messing up my score." I drop down on the couch next to Sean.

"Jason." My mom scolds me like I'm nine years old and not twenty-five.

"Puh-lease." Sean waves the wheel-shaped controller in my face. "I would *boost* your stats if I played for you."

"Yeah right." Carlee snickers. "He would only get a boost if *I* were playing, Donnelly."

Carlee is the only one who can put Sean in his place—forget the fact that the rest of us are almost three times their age.

I bite my knuckle, trying not to laugh, and bury my face in Melody's neck when I fail. Being ambushed—for the third time, I might add—by my family must have prevented her from showering, because I'm hit with the most intoxicating scent. I didn't think I would find anything better than the sweet bubblegum one I've come to associate with Mels, but it mixed with mine and sex now tops the list.

Mels trembles, and I feel a pinch at my side from her clutching the bottom of my shirt as I drag my nose down the length of her neck. Her responsiveness is a major turn-on, and I will myself back before I have an embarrassing situation on my hands.

Sporting a boner the size of the Empire State Building in front of my mom is not an achievement I need unlocked in the game of life.

"Hungry?" I ask Mels, getting up to head to the kitchen. Normally on game days I'll grab lunch with my teammates, but I forwent that part of my usual routine to spend more time with her.

"What's Gemma have prepped?"

Yeah, I haven't lived down the pot pie incident.

"There's a chicken stir fry we can share?" Gathering the appropriate dishes, I portion out the meal and call over my shoulder, "Are you two hellions hungry at all?"

"I resent that classification." Carlee shoots me a look her older brother has given me a time or two.

"Look, Car." I lean across the island on my elbows. "Your best friend is my younger brother. Comes with the territory."

"Sean Patrick!" Mom scolds when he flips me off. "Oh, don't you start, Jason Richard." She turns on me when I snort. "You think I don't know where he gets it?"

"It wasn't me." I'm the picture of innocence.

"Oh really?" Mom folds her arms over her chest, and I have the overwhelming urge to gird my loins when I'm hit with the full force of her mom look. Shit, no wonder JD is so good at it. She learned from the best. "Refresh my memory then..."

I clamp my mouth shut, refusing to take the bait of her incomplete sentence.

"Which one of my children was the one to teach my darling granddaughters to say *asshole*?"

Do not laugh. Do not laugh.

No matter how much I tell myself this, when I hear Mels say, "Oh my god," and fall over laughing, I lose the battle. What? Hearing a pair of one-and-half-year-olds volleying *asshole* back and forth between them was funny as hell.

"But to answer your earlier question, no, they don't need food. We're meeting up with Sammy and Jamie soon. I know how important your pregame nap is, and I would never want to interrupt that."

Can you tell she's raised three hockey players?

Food heated, I retake my spot on the couch, pulling Melody's feet into my lap as we settle in to eat. I don't miss the knowing looks Mom shoots my way while she talks to Mels about her rehearsals.

It takes lots of hugging and kissing as well as a promise that Mels will join them in their box at the Garden tonight before we are alone once again.

She lets out a shriek when I scoop her into my arms and sprint for my bedroom.

After locking the door, I toss her onto the bed. "Strip," I command, removing my own shirt and carelessly tossing it to the ground.

"What?"

"You heard me, baby." My thumbs hook in the band of my joggers, and I rid myself of them and my boxer briefs in one go. The sight of her in my bed already has me at half-mast, and the way her dark gaze automatically homes in on my MD has my sails waving proudly.

"What about your nap?"

"What better sleep aid is there than an orgasm?" Kneeling on the bed, I peel her shirt off her since she still hasn't made any moves to do it herself.

"I thought athletes weren't supposed to have sex before a

game…something about weak legs and stuff." Her arms rise in an effort to help me remove her sports bra.

"I guess we'll find out, won't we?" She lies back as I roll down her leggings. "Personally, I think the memory of how it felt to have your sweet pussy milking my cock will put a pep in my step. Live and learn, I suppose."

"Oh god." She moans, whether from my words or the feel of my dick sliding through her folds when I cover her body to kiss her, I don't know, nor do I care.

Her nails scour my back as I drag the head of my dick back and forth over her clit.

I would love to spend hours drawing out our pleasure, making her come over and over, but she's right—I do need to nap.

One of her arms flings out to the side, the sheets making slapping sounds as she flops it around.

"Looking for something, Sweet Potato?"

Her neck arches when I bite her pulse point.

"Condom," she rasps as I make another pass over her clit.

Unlike her shorter arms, my wingspan is enough to reach the bedside drawer. I make quick work of sheathing myself and get into position at her entrance.

"Fuck, you're so wet already, baby." Liquid fire covers the head, the heat so pronounced I can barely tell there's a layer of latex between us.

"I am. Now stop fucking teasing me and fuck me."

"Demanding, woman."

I yelp when she pinches my side.

Circling my hips, I work myself inside her with small thrusts, giving her body a chance to adjust to my size.

"More." Her ankles lock at the small of my back, her hips rocking up to meet mine thrust for thrust.

"Harder."

I snap back and surge forward.

"Jase."

"Mels."

I hiss at her nails digging in hard enough to know I'll have some interesting marks I'll have to explain in the locker room later.

"Jase."

I don't know what's better, the way my name sounds falling off her tongue breathily or her tight heat surrounding me.

"Jase."

I snake my hands around her lower back, cupping her ass and tilting it for a deeper angle, driving into her until we explode together.

When we finally catch our breath, we each take our turn in the bathroom. Mels attempts to pull on a shirt, but I drag her back into bed before she can, telling her I'll sleep better pressed against her skin to skin.

We settle under the covers, my big spoon to her little, just like last night.

I was kidding earlier when I made the sleeping pill comment, but joke's on me.

Normally when we play the Blizzards, my mind spins with what I need to do, the plays I'll need to make, what I can do to make sure I stop them—but mostly Ryan—from scoring. The worry about being compared to my brother always increases by ten when our teams play.

Yet today, as my eyelids slide closed, sweet bubble gum filling my nose, the warm body of the woman I'm falling for snuggled in my arms, everything fades away and I drift off to sleep.

Chapter Thirty-Six

Melody

I've been to a lot, and I mean *a lot* of hockey games in my life, but none of them have compared to what I experienced tonight.

Unlike the first time I came to watch Jase play—you know, when I wore his jersey—I didn't watch this one from his seats. No, this time I watched from a suite with Jase's family. I have the feeling they aren't the sort to let a little thing like fire code get in the way of a good time because there were *way* more people in the suite than I'm sure is allowed, which is kind of ironic seeing as one of his friends is a fireman.

I also couldn't believe the number of parents I was introduced to. Zoey has been teasing me mercilessly all night, but I also haven't missed the knowing looks she's cast in my direction.

Both my brother and I have managed to be very successful in our chosen careers, yet witnessing what it's like to have not only involved parents but a complete support system makes me wonder what could have been if we had others cheering us on.

Forget cheering us on; I'd be happy with them responding to my messages. I don't care how they choose to do so: phone call, text, email, snail mail, carrier pigeon—hell, I'd be okay with smoke signals at this point.

According to my message and call logs, it's been a month since we had any two-way conversation.

"Aren't you worried someone will snap a pic of you and Jase and post it?" Ella leans across our table to be heard over the noise inside The Sin Bin and to not be overheard by any nearby Covenettes.

Ella, Zoey, and I were part of the first wave to arrive at the bar, and Pops—or Freddie to everyone else—had reserved the entire back room for us.

"No way," Zoey answers for me. "I mean look at her"— she flicks the brim of the Storm ball cap I'm wearing—"she has on her fancy-shmancy disguise."

I swat her hand away and roll my eyes. Mock all she wants, but it's effective enough. All the guys of BoP have them on. If it helps rock stars keep some anonymity, why can't it work for me?

"Okay," Becky says as she and Gemma drop down on the open bench next to Ella. It's been nice getting to know the person responsible for all the delicious food I've had whenever I'm at Jase's, but I have a feeling I might want to keep Becky away from Zoey. If those two team up, they will be doing the cell block tango.

"I apologize in advance," Gemma says, her thoughts obviously mirroring my own.

"Don't ruin my fun, Gem." Becky pouts.

"I wouldn't *dream* of it." Gemma holds up her hands, the gesture coming off as sarcastic as her words.

"I'm going to pretend you actually mean that and focus on what's important here." Emerald eyes turn our way, and I feel Zoey perk up beside me. *Lord help us. You can't stop the beat.*

"Beck, you realize you speak like you text, right?"

"What?" Becky's brows pinch together.

"You can never just get to the point. I swear you drag

things out just to torture us." Gemma levels her with a look I myself have used on Zoey countless times.

They continue to banter, but the words themselves no longer register as my sole focus turns to the sexy-as-puck hockey player stalking in my direction.

My heart skips a beat, and like a spotlight shining, I'm hit with the startling realization that I love him.

This man I thought was a playboy and wouldn't know what loyalty was if it bit him on the ass has turned out to be the exact opposite of everything I believed.

I need to channel my inner Maria, take a page out of the *West Side Story* script—but without all the death—and not care what anyone else thinks. Jase Donnelly is too good to let go.

"This is a cute look on you, Sweet Potato." He taps the brim and angles his face under it to place a searing kiss on my lips.

"Hope you don't mind I borrowed it." I wipe a streak of lip gloss from the corner of his mouth.

"Not even a little bit. You look good in black and gray." He winks and I melt, like always. "I like seeing you in my things, letting the whole world know you're mine with my name on your back."

"Does that mean the other thousand or so people rocking Donnelly Storm jerseys are yours too, Hemmy?" Jase drops his head with a groan at Becky's taunt.

"Beck, why do you always start trouble?"

"It is my middle name," she states proudly, and Zoey says, "Me too." Now I'm the one groaning.

"It's not, but it should be. It suits you better than Danielle, that's for sure."

"Look at you, remembering middle names." Becky reaches out to pat his cheek patronizingly. "But to answer your question, Gem and I are here on a recruiting mission."

"Balboa!" I jump at Jase's sudden shout.

"What's up, bestie?" Rocky asks after she and Gage make it to our table.

"Can you please remove your other best friend from the vicinity?" A muscular arm wraps around my back, but I feel him wince as I snuggle into his side. He took a nasty hit in the second period, and it must have left a bruise.

"Is she picking on you for the loss? You can't win them all, Jase. Plus, it's not our fault you play for the wrong team."

"Funny, Rock, but no. She's over here trying to add to your ranks. I'm pretty sure Becky approving membership to The Coven is one of the signs of the apocalypse."

"I swear your picture should be next to the word exaggerator in the dictionary," Rocky says but motions for Becky to get up.

"We could always ask Maddey to check to see if it is." The unexpected comment from Gage has everyone laughing.

"My man." Jase holds out a fist for him to bump. "We're finally starting to rub off on you."

"*Oooh*, now *that's* a visual," Zoey says, and I shoo her out of the booth as well.

"I sure hope you let your trainers check out those ribs earlier. You know I'm not afraid to make a call if I have to," Rocky calls over her shoulder as she takes the troublemakers away.

It might not be the best decision to let Zoey and Becky go off together, but I prefer to enjoy the night with my boyfriend without having to fend off innuendos the whole time.

"Damn Coven," Jase curses. If he was trying to hide the fact that he's injured, he isn't doing a good job of it. Plus, he's told me multiple entertaining stories of how Rocky has caught all of them attempting to play off being hurt and failing at one point or another.

When he pulls me in again, I'm more conscious of hurting him and place a hand on his chest. He's solid muscle, and I absentmindedly run a finger along the buttons of his pinstriped shirt.

"I'm almost afraid to ask." Jase snakes a hand under the wide sleeve of my jersey, tracing patterns down to my elbow and back.

"Afraid to ask what?" It takes a moment to focus on his words and not the tingles his touch makes me feel.

"If you still want to be my girlfriend after tonight."

Used to his exaggerating nature, I can't help but tease him a little. "You mean because you lost to your brother?" I feign a disappointed pout.

A veil falls over his hazel eyes, but it disappears so quickly I can't tell if it was real or a trick of the light. Teasing him over a loss is a staple of our banter—hello, proud Boston fan, remember?—so I don't know why this would be any different.

I think maybe my guilty conscience is starting to play tricks on me.

"No." His lips quirk, and there's my cocky boyfriend. "I just want to make sure you weren't scared away by my crazy family."

I cast a quick glance at Gemma across the table, but she and Ella are lost in their own conversation.

"No way. I love them." His eyes flash at the words, and it takes considerable effort not to tell him they aren't the only ones I love. It's not fair to say it before revealing my secret.

I tell him all about my time in the suite, from Sean and Carlee's antics to how absolutely adorable his nieces are. He playfully shudders when Gemma chimes in to say they officially made me a member of The Coven, but the look of pride reflected on his face is unmistakable.

This weekend has been a fairytale. Too bad my secret feels like the Evil Queen's poison apple.

Chapter Thirty-Seven

BROADWAY BABY: Question.

THE BIG HAMMER: You forgot your question mark.

BROADWAY BABY: Funny. But for reals. I need to know…how committed are you to me?

THE BIG HAMMER: I feel like this is a trick question, Sweet Potato.

BROADWAY BABY: I promise it's not.

THE BIG HAMMER: If you're asking if I'm seeing anyone else, the answer is a big HELL NO.

THE BIG HAMMER: And if this your roundabout way of asking me if I'm okay with you seeing other people, the answer would be an even bigger HELL FUCKING NO.

BROADWAY BABY: Relax there, All-Star. You're the only guy for me.

BROADWAY BABY: Well...

BROADWAY BABY: At least...

BROADWAY BABY: Until...

THE BIG HAMMER: I knew you getting added to the Coven Conversations wasn't going to be good for me. You're over here texting me like Becky about a topic that is ruining my Tim Hortons experience, baby.

BROADWAY BABY: Sorry, babe. Ooo, now I want a donut *donut emoji*

THE BIG HAMMER: Mels...

BROADWAY BABY: Sorry. Okay, so I'm not trying to jump the gun at all and assume things.

BROADWAY BABY: And I don't want you to feel pressured at all or think I've turned into some stage-5 clinger or anything.

BROADWAY BABY: I'm just curious, and...

THE BIG HAMMER: Wow. I didn't think it was possible to ramble in text form, but look at you totally pulling it off.

BROADWAY BABY: Sorry again. Okay, so say we are together for a while, like for years...

THE BIG HAMMER: Okay, this is more along the lines of what I like to hear. Keep going.

BROADWAY BABY: Well, okay good. So say we are

together for years—would it make you mad if I left you in, say, about 9 years?

THE BIG HAMMER: Excuse me? **rubs eyes** Hold on. I HAD to have heard that wrong.

BROADWAY BABY: Read, All-Star. Remember you can't hear a text.

THE BIG HAMMER: Mels…

BROADWAY BABY: Oh wow, this is so much more fun than I thought.

THE BIG HAMMER: You are in so much trouble when we get back from this road trip. I'm going to spank your ass for torturing me.

BROADWAY BABY: Ooo, Loverboy, that's hot.

THE BIG HAMMER: Hey, Zoey.

BROADWAY BABY: Hey there, hot stuff.

THE BIG HAMMER: Normally I wouldn't like you cutting in on my time talking to my girl, but since she's not really telling me anything, do you think you could tell me why Mels would say she wants to commit to being with me for years only to break up?

BROADWAY BABY: Oh. That's easy. She wants your brother.

THE BIG HAMMER: Come again?

BROADWAY BABY: Now, now. Save the dirty talk for when I haven't stolen your girlfriend's phone. I'm just saying your bro has hella game.

THE BIG HAMMER: If that's really the case, why wait 9 years? Ryan is single and clearly the better of the two of us.

BROADWAY BABY: Ryan?

THE BIG HAMMER: Yeah, Ryan. You know, my older brother, plays for the Blizzards? Mr. Captain America himself.

THE BIG HAMMER: *GIF of Marvel's Captain America pulling apart firewood with his hands*

BROADWAY BABY: *GIF of woman spitting out water*

BROADWAY BABY: She doesn't want Ryan.

THE BIG HAMMER: Okay, now I'm really confused. And I room with Cali, so that's saying something.

BROADWAY BABY: She has to wait 9 years until it's legal. Then she and Sean are going to ride off into the sunset together.

THE BIG HAMMER: I'm officially done with this conversation.

♡

THE BIG HAMMER: How's the forbidden romance going?

BROADWAY BABY: ??

THE BIG HAMMER: Sean.

BROADWAY BABY: Oh! There's nothing forbidden about our relationship. I'm not pursuing him for another 9 years.

THE BIG HAMMER: So what do you call all the screenshots he's been sending me of your conversations?

BROADWAY BABY: Oh. That.

THE BIG HAMMER: Yeah. That.

BROADWAY BABY: We call that laying the foundation.

THE BIG HAMMER: No wonder Maddey has us reading an age-gap romance for book club, even though I guess technically yours is a reverse age gap.

BROADWAY BABY: LJ Shen's *Scandalous* is one of my favorite books. I love the Hotholes. They are amazing. Why else do you think Madz was okay with doing a reread for book club?

THE BIG HAMMER: I knew you were the influence in this week's pick.

THE BIG HAMMER: I'm starting to think Sammy has the right idea.

BROADWAY BABY: Um…what?

THE BIG HAMMER: Marrying a dude. Chicks are crazy.

BROADWAY BABY: Whatever. You love me anyway.

THE BIG HAMMER: That's a bold claim coming from someone telling me they want my brother, who is still in elementary school.

BROADWAY BABY: *GIF of Elmo shrugging*

THE BIG HAMMER: You talk this big game about leaving me for my younger brother, but I don't have to worry.

BROADWAY BABY: Oh yeah? And why's that?

THE BIG HAMMER: One word.

THE BIG HAMMER: Carlee.

♡

BROADWAY BABY: You in a better mood now?

THE BIG HAMMER: When was I in a bad mood?

BROADWAY BABY: When you were texting me during my lunch. You were a little off. Did Cali do something?

THE BIG HAMMER: I can't tell you how much I adore how you jump right to that conclusion.

BROADWAY BABY: *shrugging emoji* I do live with the female equivalent of him.

THE BIG HAMMER: This is true.

BROADWAY BABY: So…you wanna tell me what had you in a bad mood?

THE BIG HAMMER: *GIF of dancing potatoes saying, "Taters gonna tate."*

BROADWAY BABY: I was wondering when you were gonna hit me with a potato reference. It's been a minute.

THE BIG HAMMER: Can't go too long without it. It's our thing, Sweet Potato.

BROADWAY BABY: It really makes me question what type of people it makes us that potatoes are our thing.

THE BIG HAMMER: Awesome. It makes us awesome.

BROADWAY BABY: I'm more than okay with this. Now tell me who the hater is?

THE BIG HAMMER: It's stupid.

BROADWAY BABY: If it's bugging you, it's not stupid. Spill.

THE BIG HAMMER: It's nothing I haven't experienced before. I'll get over it and it'll blow over.

BROADWAY BABY: Don't make me call in rein-forcements.

BROADWAY BABY: *GIF of Coven members walking*

THE BIG HAMMER: **groans** You are an evil woman, baby.

BROADWAY BABY: It's a gift. Now tell me.

THE BIG HAMMER: Fine, but only to get it out of the way so we can get to the good stuff.

BROADWAY BABY: The good stuff?

THE BIG HAMMER: Sexting of course. What are you wearing?

BROADWAY BABY: No, no. There will be none of that until you tell me what I want to know first.

THE BIG HAMMER: Fine, but only because it means I get to see your pretty face after.

BROADWAY BABY: Awww.

THE BIG HAMMER: And your boobs.

BROADWAY BABY: Yeah that sounds more like you.

THE BIG HAMMER: JD officially put me on social media timeout.

BROADWAY BABY: That's why you're in a bad mood? Because you can't Snap or Tweet?

THE BIG HAMMER: No. I couldn't care less about that.

BROADWAY BABY: ??

THE BIG HAMMER: Nate Bishop is trying to start a Twitter war posting memes of me skating on Ryan's coat-tails and stuff.

BROADWAY BABY: *picture of Melody in only a hot pink bra*

THE BIG HAMMER: Bad mood gone.

Chapter Thirty-Eight

M*arch*

Yoshi!

I finish buttoning the last button on my white Oxford shirt before reaching into my locker for my phone. I'm dog-ass tired, but the high from today's win will be enough to get me through the rest of the day.

BROADWAY BABY: Guess where I am?

BROADWAY BABY: *picture of Melody in front of the Storm mural in the tunnels of the Garden*

"Oh, man. I know that look." Cali chuckles, clapping me on the back.

"What look?" I shrug him off to slip into my suit jacket.

"You get this lovey-dovey look on your face any time you text with your girl."

I want to say I'm a man and we don't do the whole lovey-dovey thing he's accusing me of, but deep down I know he's right. I'm ass over head in love with Melody—if only I could find my balls and actually say the words.

For weeks Mels and I have been dancing around our feelings. Any time one of us has made an offhand comment about love, it's either been ignored or the subject is changed.

Who knows though? Maybe today everything will change.

"Guess that means you're not coming out for beers?" Cali prods.

I give him a *what do you think?* look.

Spending time with a bunch of hockey players or taking advantage of the rare opportunity to spend time with my girl? Yeah, no contest.

Mels and I have been squeezing in time together whenever we can. It's not easy, but we do our best to make it work. As we enter our final full month before the playoffs and she inches closer to opening night, free time is hard to come by.

Taking advantage of a rare afternoon game for me and her being out of rehearsals early? Sign me the fuck up.

"I wouldn't think a guy with a harem would know how to do *lovey-dovey*." I grit my teeth at the dig from the new winger the Storm acquired from Boston before the trade deadline.

After losing one of our own top wingers to a season-ending injury, the trade for Fallon was a crucial move if we wanted to continue our push for the Cup, but of *all* the players the front office could have selected, he's one of the worst.

It isn't that he came from Boston—players get traded or move to rival teams on their own; it's the nature of the business. No, he sucks as the pick because he's best friends with Nate Bishop, and if his comment wasn't proof enough for you, I'll tell you he is just as much of a twat waffle.

"I see you get your information from the same fake news sources as your boy Bishop." It takes everything inside me not to get in his face. "But for the sake of the team and all, how about you just keep my name out of your mouth and we'll be okay."

"Aww, Donnelly, don't like hearing about your man-whore ways?" I want nothing more than to knock the smarmy smile off his face. "From what I hear, being easy runs in your family. Must be a twin thing."

That was a mistake. A big *fucking* mistake.

Every good intention I have is gone and I'm across the locker room in a flash. No one, *no one* gets to talk about my family, *especially* not my other half.

I get one solid shove in before arms wrap around my middle. Callahan, Harrison, and Ringquist hold me back, my rage so strong they barely manage.

I bite out each word. "Jordan—is—off—*fucking*—limits."

Ringquist moves so I'll have to go through him if I want to get at Fallon again. Taking on our veteran goalie is not in my top ten of things I ever want to do.

"Look, we get it. Bishop is your boy. No one"—he turns to level me with a look—"is going to hold that against you."

Fallon scoffs, but Ringquist continues as if he didn't.

"But the *only* way Jordan Donnelly-Donovan is talked about in this locker room is with respect."

"I didn't know your sister hyphenated?" Cali asks.

"She didn't," I answer, nostrils flaring, fists still clenched and wanting to strike.

"*Not* the time, Cali," Ringquist growls, eyes never leaving Fallon.

The big Swede is tenser than I can recall ever seeing him. It makes sense; he's one of the players on the team who has known my sister the longest. JD may have only been in the PR business for four years, but she's worked with the Storm through the Garden of Dreams Foundation since our college days.

"Unless you want not only your new team but half the

NHL looking to kick your ass, I'd suggest you learn that fast."
Ringquist's threat is clear.

"Whatever." Fallon shrugs off the players holding him
back, smoothing the lapels of his suit jacket. "You guys are so
touchy."

Fucker.

Whatever. I don't need this shit. I have a girlfriend to see.

Grabbing my gear bag, I push through the locker room
doors and there she is. With adrenaline from what just went
down still pumping through my veins, it only takes three
steps and I'm in front of her. Another two and I have her
backed up to the wall, hands cupping her face, fingers
tangled in pink waves, mouth on hers.

There is nothing sweet about this kiss. It is primal and
fierce. I want to lose myself inside her, forget about trades,
dickhead teammates, playoff pressure, all of it.

She doesn't shy away from my intensity, instead meeting
me stroke for stroke, her tongue licking over the ball of my
piercing.

I groan.

She sighs.

It's a miracle I'm not dragging her into the locker room.

"You know, with the number of times I've walked in on
you two making out, I feel like I'm a part of this relationship."
I drop my head to the wall at the sound of Cali's voice. "Does
that make us a throuple?"

"What the fuck is a throuple?" Why is this even a question
that needs asking?

I lower Mels to the ground but keep her tucked
against me.

"*You know.*" Cali waggles his eyebrows. "It's a couple, but
with three people."

"Why do I feel like you've been spending too much time
with Maddey?" Melody asks, and I could kiss her again.

"Aww, Mels," Cali says. I shove off the arm he drops around her shoulders. "You really are becoming a Covenette."

"You say that like it's a bad thing."

The idea should scare me, but it doesn't. The girls "inducting" her into The Coven only proves she's mine for keeps.

"No way. You Covenettes love me. Jase, on the other hand—"

"Mels?" The absolute *last* person I want saying my baby's name calls it out from behind me.

Like the throuple Cali thinks we are, the three of us turn to face the locker room. The urge to introduce my fist to his fugly face is strong.

It only gets worse when Mels says, "Fallon?"

Chapter Thirty-Nine

I blink rapidly.

Clearly my eyes are playing tricks on me.

No.

No, no.

Nope. Just nope. There is *no way* Fallon is here. He's supposed to be in Boston.

"What are you doing here?" he asks, taking the words right out of my mouth.

"I was just about to ask you the same thing."

This is bad. Really, *really* bad. How am I going to explain this? Jase is going to flip.

"I was traded."

Shit! Why didn't I pay attention to the trades? I knew the deadline passed and that the Storm had a big hole to fill to stay in contention for the Cup. But damn, how was I supposed to know of *all* the teams they could make a trade with, it would be Boston?

"You were?" There's a squeak to my voice belying the panic churning inside.

"Yup."

I grip Jase's hand so hard it makes *mine* hurt. He hasn't said a word since Fallon made his appearance.

"Teddy didn't tell me."

I talked to him yesterday. Why didn't he mention Fallon would be living in my city?

Fallon's gaze drops to where my hand has a death grip on Jase's, holding on as if he will float away like a rogue Macy's Thanksgiving Day balloon if I let go. Given what is about to go down, it's a very real possibility. "Looks like he's not the only Bishop keeping secrets."

Shit!

"Bishop?" Jase looks at me, confusion written all over his handsome face.

This is my worst nightmare come to life. The only thing missing is me being naked. I know it is long past when I should have told Jase the truth about my identity, but him finding out like this is the *absolute* worst possible way it could have played out.

"Hold up." Fallon chuckles. The sparkle in his eye does not look promising. "*She's* your *girlfriend*?"

No, no, no, no, no, no.

"What's it to you, Fallon?" Jase's voice is hard.

Another chuckle. "Oh this is fucking perfect. I feel like I should have Nate on speaker for this."

"Fal," I warn, plead—hell, I don't really know what I'm doing right now.

I tug on the hand in mine, spinning around to beg Cali to intervene. If I can get Jase away *before* Fallon drops the bomb, I might just be able to save our relationship.

"Babe?" There's a tick in Jase's jaw. "How do you two know each other?" He bounces a finger between Fallon and me.

"Yeah, Mels—how *do* we know each other?"

Who is this person? Why is he being so…so…mean?

I've always stayed out of the rivalry between Jase and

Nate. Seeing this side of Fallon is a different experience, one I don't much care for.

I don't speak.

I don't move.

I don't even think I'm breathing.

How is this happening? Why is this happening?

No, no, no.

"Forget your line, Mels?"

"Fuck you, Anthony." His taunt snaps me out of my stupor.

"Ahhh, there's the drama from our little actress."

"Fuck off, asshole. She's mine, not *ours,* and sure as fuck not yours, Fallon."

The growly way Jase claims me gives me hope. Unfortunately, like I have the script, I know what's about to happen in the next scene.

"Oh she's *yours,* is she?" Fallon crosses his arms. "If that's true, what's Melody's last name?"

The satisfied smirk on his face makes me wonder what I ever did to him to make him act so hateful. This isn't the guy who would crash my video chats with my brother, who sat in the front row for my shows, who was just as much a brother to me as my Teddy Bear.

No, this version of Anthony Fallon is a stranger.

"Let me give you a hint, Donnelly: Brightly is a stage name."

"*Ooo,* Melody has a stage name. *What a crime.*" Cali says the last sentence with so much sarcasm it practically pools on the floor. If Jase wasn't already vibrating with anger next to me, I could kiss him for it.

"No, you're right, *Callahan.* Having a stage name is not newsworthy. The part that makes this particular revelation fun for me is—"

"Fal...don't," I implore.

Please don't do this.

"No. The fun part is"—he looks at me then turns his full attention on Jase—"her legal last name is…"

He pauses, and I brace for the hit I know is coming.

"Bishop."

Time freezes.

The curtains close.

The lights turn off.

Everything around me turns to static. With one word, the trajectory of my life is thrown off course.

"Bishop?" Jase asks.

"Yup." God, how can Fallon get so much glee into one little word?

"As in…"

Don't say it. Don't say it.

"Nate Bishop."

Fuck!

"Jase," I try to cut in, but they continue.

"You've been dating the younger sister of the guy *everyone* knows you hate."

Golden-green eyes stare at me like I'm a stranger. My hand sways he drops it so fast.

"Jase?"

He takes a step back, and my heart cracks.

"Jase, I was goi—"

A shake of his head, another step back.

"Jase, *please.*"

My heart splits in two at the look of betrayal swimming in his hazel eyes.

"Jas—"

He turns on his heel.

No. What are you doing, Jase?

He takes a step, then another.

No, no. Jase, stop.

Another step.

No.

I reach for him, but he avoids my touch.

Four more steps and he's halfway down the hall.

Please don't walk away.

He keeps walking, my silent pleas going unanswered.

He hits the metal door at the end of the corridor with so much force the sound echoes like a gong.

He…

He…

He…left me.

Chapter Forty

Melody

BROADWAY BABY: Jase please talk to me.

BROADWAY BABY: Please answer the phone.

BROADWAY BABY: I'm sorry.

BROADWAY BABY: I wanted to tell you.

BROADWAY BABY: I was going to tell you.

BROADWAY BABY: Please let me explain.

BROADWAY BABY: I'm sorry. So, so sorry.

BROADWAY BABY: Jase.

BROADWAY BABY: Jase, please.

BROADWAY BABY: *GIF of crying potato*

No matter how many texts I send, he doesn't answer.

Chapter Forty-One

THE BIG HAMMER: ~~Why didn't you tell me?~~

THE BIG HAMMER: ~~How could you *not* tell me?~~

THE BIG HAMMER: ~~Was this all a big joke?~~

THE BIG HAMMER: ~~Did you two have a good laugh about it behind my back?~~

THE BIG HAMMER: ~~I hate the way I don't hate you. Not even close, not even a little bit, not even at all.~~

THE BIG HAMMER: ~~And shit, I hate that you have me quoting *10 Things I Hate About You.*~~

THE BIG HAMMER: ~~FUCK!~~

THE BIG HAMMER: ~~I love you.~~

No matter how many texts I compose, I delete them all without hitting send.

Chapter Forty-Two

Melody

Tears.

Wine.

Send texts that only get ignored.

More tears.

Rehearsal.

Tears with wine.

Rehearsal.

And—you guessed it—tears.

Chapter Forty-Three

E at.
   Sleep.
   Hockey.
   Type out text messages to Melody but delete them before sending.
   Repeat.

Chapter Forty-Four

Melody

BROADWAY BABY: Are you ever going to talk to me again?

I swear I've sent more texts that have gone unanswered in the past two weeks than I have in my entire life.

TEDDY: Jase Donnelly, Mels?

Shit! It's never good if he's calling me Mels. *At least he responded.* This is true, but not much has come from the few times Nate has actually done so. Most of the time he quickly shuts down and shuts me out.

Just like Mom and Dad.

BROADWAY BABY: I'm sorry. I don't know how many more times you need me to say it before you forgive me, but I am. It's not like I planned for it to happen.

My fingers fly across the screen, desperation bleeding into each tap.

BROADWAY BABY: Please don't shut me out. You're the only family I really have. I need you, Nate.

TEDDY BEAR: If that were true, you wouldn't have been with HIM.

Tears prick the backs of my eyes. I've already lost the man I love; I can't lose my brother too.

BROADWAY BABY: I'm sorry. Please, please, please can we talk?

"How's the fit?" the show's costume designer asks after she secures the zipper on the dress, the question finally pulling my attention away from the lack of dancing dots on my phone. Fucking Nate has gone back to ignoring me.

"It's perfect." I force myself to respond as I lift my gaze to the full-length mirror in front of me. Not even the sight of me in the iconic white dress synonymous with my character is enough to cheer me up.

For the last two weeks, I've merely been existing, my heartbreak over losing Jase so acute all the joy has been sapped from the world.

I've never been more grateful for the start of tech rehearsals. The tedious task of nailing down the timing for all the set and costume changes along with the other million things necessary for a successful production are what I need to survive.

The days are long and grueling, and the only reason I haven't cried myself to sleep the last few nights is because I've been too exhausted from tech to do so.

The cherry on top is that my brother—the only person in my family who has been there for me unconditionally—is still barely speaking to me. I can only hope when the show goes to Boston for a week of touring previews, we'll be able to mend the rift I caused, because texting and calling are obviously not working.

"Mels?"

I turn to face the door of my dressing room and see the stage director. "Yes?"

"You have a visitor."

Jase? My heart leaps, hoping against hope he's here.

"Should I bring her back?" he asks. I realize I haven't responded to his statement.

Her? With one pronoun, that hope dies like a burned-out spotlight.

Who could be here?

I get my answer a few moments later when Jordan Donovan steps into the room. It's not that I'm not happy to see her, but she isn't the Donnelly twin I long to see.

Talk about being hopelessly devoted.

"Um…" My words trail off. What does one say when her ex's sister shows up at her job?

"I didn't mean to ambush you or anything." Jordan shrugs. "Okay, maybe I did a little, but really I just wanted to see how you're doing."

How am I doing?

I'm a mess. A disaster.

I lost my boyfriend. My brother isn't speaking to me. Outside of Zoey and Ella, my entire support system has been stripped away.

Thank god I'm an actress and am good at pretending, because I'm in full-on fake-it-till-you-make-it mode.

"I'm okay."

"No you're not." Jordan levels me with a look so much like her twin's it's painful.

"You're right." I step off the stand the costume designer used during my adjustments, silently thanking her when she leaves the room to give us privacy. "But whatcha gonna do?"

"You mean besides kick my wombmate's dumb ass for walking away from *the* girl because of who she is related to?"

I can't help it—a chuckle escapes. From most people, that would be an idle threat. From Jordan, not so much.

"Why aren't you mad at me?"

Aren't twins supposed to stick together?

"For what?" Jordan gets the same crinkle in her brow as Jase when confused.

"For lying?"

"*Pfft.*" She waves me off like I'm ridiculous. "Nope. No matter how hard Jase pursued you in the beginning, if you had told him you were related to Bishop, he would have dropped you like a hot potato." She smirks at her use of a potato reference.

"Can I ask you something?"

"Anything." Jordan rubs circles on her very large belly. *Homegirl looks ready to give birth right here. Shit—that was a total Jase thing to think.*

"Do you know *why* our brothers hate each other so much?"

It's the one thing I can't figure out. I know their history from the camp in Lake Placid. Nate would tell me all about his time there during our weekly chats, and that was when I heard the first stories of Jase being a playboy. Sure, I didn't know *who* it was my brother was bitching about, but hearing about how there was a guy who came to visit the camp with his girlfriend only to hit on bunnies stuck with me through the years.

Still…

It doesn't explain the *loathing* they have for each other.

If anyone would know, I'd think it'd be Jordan.

"Honestly? I have no idea. I've been trying to figure it out since you first started dating."

Wait. What?

"You knew I was related to Nate"—I swallow down the sudden lump of emotion—"*before*?"

"Yup." The circles continue on her belly. "Unlike my twin, I'm an expert in internet *research*."

I pull a face. "You mean stalking?"

"Potato, vodka."

I groan. "Not you too."

"Sorry." Jordan's expression says she's anything but. "Jase spends a lot of time with Vince, and I spend a lot of time with Jase. Some of the ridiculous stuff manages to stick."

This is true. I haven't even been able to look at a French fry without thinking of Jase. The jerk ruined one of my favorite foods for me.

Thank god pizza wasn't our running joke, otherwise I would have been forced to move. A person can't live in the city with the best pizza—and yes, New York has better pizza than Chicago, no matter what Tucker likes to say—without being able to eat it.

"But yeah…social media is a big part of my job. I pay attention more than your aver—" Her eyes go as wide as spotlights.

"Jordan?"

There's a beat of silence. Then, "My fucking water just broke."

"Say what now?"

I am *so* not equipped to handle this. And won't her doctor be in Jersey?

"Dammit, Logan. I told you this morning you needed to wait until later to come. I'm trying to get you an aunt here."

Um…

What?

Then it hits me—Jordan's talking to the baby, not me.

Wait…did she say aunt?

It's too much.

"Please tell me you drove into the city today and didn't

take a train?" I plead, not sure how one handles one's ex-boyfriend's twin sister going into labor.

"I did." She pulls her phone from her purse. "But my contractions are too close together. I would never make it to Jersey before this sucker is born."

"Your water *just* broke."

Does birth happen that fast?

"I know, but I've been having contractions all morning."

"WHAT?!" Probably shouldn't shout at pregnant women, but *hello!*

Who does this?

"They weren't that close together." She waves me off like it's normal for people to cross state lines when in the beginning stages of labor. "I was more annoyed dealing with Jase and his moping than anything else."

"You're insane. You do know that, right?"

Another brushoff and she pulls out her phone. "Hey, babe."

Good, she called Jake.

"So, um…" Guilty eyes turn my way. "Looks like your son doesn't want to wait and is coming before the puck drop." A wince. "Yeaaaah…about that." A grimace. "I'm in the city."

Jake's shout is so loud I hear it across the room.

"Yes I know. I'm sorry, okay. I'll make it up to you in six weeks when I can have sex again, but can we focus on what's important here?"

I look around the room. For what, I'm not sure. All I know right now is if Jordan is *this* nuts, it can't bode well for the person she shared a womb with for nine months. Or for me, for that matter, because I'm the idiot who's still in love with him. Who cares that I never told him?

"I know, babe. Look…New York Presbyterian isn't super far from here." Jordan looks my way again as she listens to whatever her husband is saying. I can only imagine what it is.

"No, I'm not alone. Mels is with me. You just worry about getting here as fast as possible."

Wait? Does she think I'm...

"I don't know. Call Justin—see if he can bring you in a cruiser. He can put the lights on."

Can we maybe go back to the part where she said she's with me and discuss what that means, please?

"He'll totally do it, and just to be sure, I'll text Madz. The girls and dogs are already with your mom. All you have to do is grab the hospital bag and make it to me before I push your impatient son out of Tuckahoe Fun Land."

"Um...?" I bite my nail, not sure how to articulate what I'm trying to ask as Jordan disconnects the call.

"Jake and I bonded over our love for *How I Met Your Mother* when we first got together. I figured a little HIMYM humor was needed at the moment," Jordan explains, reading my mind.

"So when you said *Mels is with me*, you meant..."

"That you would be the one holding my hand until Jake can get here." She holds up a hand before I can ask my next question. "And by 'hold my hand'"—she puts air quotes around the words—"I mean I'll squeeze yours painfully tight until the drugs are in my system and I'm feeling no pain. Joys of childbirth my ass. Give me all the drugs."

I focus on gathering my things and not the tears that are threatening to spill.

This might be the most ridiculous, crazy, couldn't-make-it-up-if-I-tried situation ever, but it only drives home the fact that Jase isn't the only one I lost.

Chapter Forty-Five

All our lives, JD and I have always been able to sense when something is wrong with the other.

Broke my arm playing roller hockey in third grade—JD brought Mom to the outdoor rink before anyone could call her.

When JD's appendix was close to bursting in seventh grade, I was the one who convinced Dad she should probably go to the hospital.

When Ryan and I snuck out for the hockey team's prank night freshman year of high school and were almost caught by the cops? Yup, you guessed it, JD was there to create a distraction so we could get out before that happened.

And when JD had nightmares after her douchemonkey ex-boyfriend, Tommy, went after her, I woke up no matter how late and called her.

So when I spend the end of practice with a rock in my gut, the first thing I do when I get back to the locker room is call her. I shoot her a text when she doesn't answer.

THE BIG HAMMER: Checking in? You okay?

MOTHER OF DRAGONS: What makes you ask?

THE BIG HAMMER: Well you are in your 22nd month of pregnancy and all *pregnant emoji*

MOTHER OF DRAGONS: *middle finger emoji* I'm 9 months pregnant, you dick. I'm not an elephant—even if I feel like one most days.

THE BIG HAMMER: *GIF of an elephant rolling in mud*

MOTHER OF DRAGONS: OMG I hate you so much.

THE BIG HAMMER: No way! I'm your favorite brother.

MOTHER OF DRAGONS: That's debatable.

THE BIG HAMMER: But for real. Is everything good? I've felt off for a while.

MOTHER OF DRAGONS: Well, knowing this is going to drive Ryan nuts *laughing face emoji* It's funny that you ask…

THE BIG HAMMER: *voice memo of Jase saying, "Jordan."*

MOTHER OF DRAGONS: Ooo a voice memo and my real name.

MOTHER OF DRAGONS: *GIF of the Joker asking, "Why so serious?"*

THE BIG HAMMER: And you wonder why I can't ever be serious?

MOTHER OF DRAGONS: *memoji of Jordan shrugging*

MOTHER OF DRAGONS: Also…I totally love these things ^^

THE BIG HAMMER: Jordan Danielle Donovan used to be Donnelly, don't make me come to Jersey.

MOTHER OF DRAGONS: Yeah…about that. Funny thing…

THE BIG HAMMER: ??

MOTHER OF DRAGONS: I'm kinda…

MOTHER OF DRAGONS: Sorta…

THE BIG HAMMER: OMG STOP texting like Becky.

MOTHER OF DRAGONS: I'm in the city. At New York Presbyterian, to be exact.

THE BIG HAMMER: WHAT?!

MOTHER OF DRAGONS: Calm your shouty capitals. I'm fine. I'm just in labor. That's all.

THE BIG HAMMER: THAT'S ALL?!

MOTHER OF DRAGONS: What did I say about your shouty capitals?

"Um…bro?" Cali asks as we store our stuff in his Maserati.

I pull my focus from my phone and the overwhelming

urge to commit sororicide. "What?" There's a little more bark to my tone than Cali deserves. Whatever—I blame JD and her cavalier attitude.

"Wanna tell me what's up with this?" He holds out his phone so I can see the text thread on the screen.

MOTHER OF DRAGONS: Hey Cali, can you pull the hockey stick out of my wombmate's ass and drop him off at NY Pres on your way home from practice?

"She's in labor. And before you ask what she's doing in the city and why she's not at home, I have no idea."

Cali shrugs and climbs into the sports car. "Okay then. Let's go meet our nephew."

Chapter Forty-Six

From the Group Message Thread of The Coven

MOTHER OF DRAGONS: Is it wrong that I pretty much forced Melody to accompany me to the hospital?

MAKES BOYS CRY: What exactly do you mean by "forced?"

YOU KNOW YOU WANNA: Like you dragged her in by her hair?

YOU KNOW YOU WANNA: Or was it more like *Look Who's Talking*-style where Kirstie Alley made John Travolta be there for her?

PROTEIN PRINCESS: To be fair...in *LWT* John Travolta kinda got suckered into being there for Kirstie Alley because the hospital staff assumed he was the father.

ALPHABET SOUP: OMG how cool would it be if we

could hear our babies' internal monologues like in that movie?

ALPHABET SOUP: *GIF of baby Mikey in *Look Who's Talking* laughing*

QUEEN OF SMUT: *GIF of girl smiling and clapping excitedly*

QUEEN OF SMUT: But it would have to be Bruce Willis who did it, just like in *LWT* because, hello, he was a McClane (I'll forgive the spelling).

THE OG PITA: Anyone else feeling like we need to have a *Look Who's Talking* double feature movie night?

MAKES BOYS CRY: I'm in

QUEEN OF SMUT: *hand raised emoji*

ALPHABET SOUP: Me too. And Jor, remember: get the drugs.

MOTHER OF DRAGONS: Yeah, there's not a CHANCE I'd be forgetting that.

SANTA'S COOKIE SUPPLIER: Um...am I the only one wondering what you're doing texting us while you're in labor?

MAKES BOYS CRY: Madz may be our Queen of Smut, but we all know Jor's other text handle could be Multi-tasking Queen.

ALPHABET SOUP: Preach *praise hands emoji*

MOTHER OF DRAGONS: Plus some things are too important to let the future murder of my vagina get in the way of.

ALPHABET SOUP: *GIF of woman spitting out water*

ALPHABET SOUP: ^^you just made me do this.

YOU KNOW YOU WANNA: Yeah, and thanks for that.

YOU KNOW YOU WANNA: Now Gem is bitching about water being all over the dash of her car.

THE OG PITA: It was funny at least.

YOU KNOW YOU WANNA: Except now she's giving us major side-eye since her car is reading her texts for her as she drives.

QUEEN OF SMUT: Jor, I hope you know I heard your husband say maybe he should call the hospital and tell them NOT to give you the drugs for being in the city in the first place.

MAKES BOYS CRY: Oooo, someone is trying to land himself in the dog house.

SANTA'S COOKIE SUPPLIER: You would think they would know by now we text each other everything. I mean I've only been a part of the group for a few months and I do.

ALPHABET SOUP: Oh, those be fighting words. Don't worry, Jor. Next time he comes to me to fix him in the offseason, I'll remind him of this by showing him the screenshot I just took of Maddey's text.

MOTHER OF DRAGONS: I love you.

ALPHABET SOUP: *GIF of girl thumping her chest saying, "I got you."*

THE OG PITA: Anyone else still wondering why Jordan has "forced" Jase's ex-girlfriend to play midwife?

MOTHER OF DRAGONS: Oh, yeah. That's right. Thanks for reminding me why I texted to begin with.

MOTHER OF DRAGONS: Long story short...I was sick of Jase moping around and waiting for him to pull his head out of his ass and fix his mistake. I thought it was time for a twin-tervention.

MAKES BOYS CRY: You were watching HIMYM last night, weren't you?

MOTHER OF DRAGONS: You know it. But so yeah, Melody is here and Jase is on his way. I just hope you guys get here before he shows up because I'm going to need some help getting them together so they can talk. Since you know...I'll be stuck in a hospital bed and all.

YOU KNOW YOU WANNA: *GIF of witches laughing around a caldron*

Chapter Forty-Seven

J ordan has been acting cagey since we got to the hospital, but I chalk it up to her being in labor. It can't be comfortable having a tiny human trying to make its way out of your body.

Aside from Jake, she hasn't called anyone else, but the amount of time she has spent texting has a chorus line of nerves dancing in my stomach.

The last thing I need is to be here when Jase shows up. There's no doubt in my mind that he will be here at some point. Jordan is his sister, his twin—where else would he be when she is about to give birth to his nephew?

I *want* to see him.

My heart yearns, aches for the briefest glimpse of him.

But...

I don't think I could *handle* seeing him.

There's a very real chance I would break down and start begging on sight. Ain't nobody got time for that.

I've lost count of the number of text messages I've sent him, and every single one has been ignored.

The nights I can't sleep—which is most of them—I've

stared at the open message thread, all blue bubbles of my words and none of the gray of his.

Those three little dots that tell me he's typing have made an appearance multiple times—hope soaring every time they do—but nothing ever comes from it.

What was he going to say?

Why doesn't he say it?

Is it wrong that I'm taking solace in the fact that he at least hasn't blocked me?

My head pounds and I feel nauseous. Jordan's the one getting ready to push a watermelon out of a hole not meant for something so large and yet I'm the one who's shaking like I've been volunteered as tribute.

Distraction. Yes, I need a distraction.

"Can I…" My words trail off, not really sure what to ask or if I even should.

Hazel eyes I'm well acquainted with turn my way. The strain that was around them has eased now that the epidural has taken effect. "You want to know how and when I figured out Nate Bishop was your brother?"

It is really freaky how she is able to read my mind.

"Yes please." My voice is small, none of the strength I've trained all my life to cultivate to be heard in the back of a theater present.

"You have a pretty distinctive hair color." Her gaze flits to my hairline, and only now do I realize I'm still wearing my Marilyn wig. Reaching up, I slide it off my head, worrying the platinum blonde curls in my hands.

"It was easy to recognize you in the posts your brother has of the two of you."

Both Nate and I try to keep our private lives off of social media, with one notable exception. Even before Facebook and Instagram were a thing, we had a tradition. Every time I was in a show—whether in the chorus or as a lead—Nate and I took two pictures together the first time he came to see it: one with me in full costume beforehand and another afterward in street clothes.

There's another pang in my chest. Will our tradition still continue?

"I've blocked all of Nate's social media accounts from Jase to keep the drama down as much as possible. Except for the things that trickle in from others, Jase doesn't see any of your brother's daily posts."

"I wish I'd paid more attention to their rivalry these last couple of years. If I had, I might *know* what the real issue is, but I've always stayed on the outside, not wanting to get involved."

Jordan sighs, shifting around on the bed, probably seeking a comfortable position. "I'm not sure how much that would have helped. If your brother is anything like mine—"

"A tight-lipped, immature asshole at times?"

"Exactly." She chuckles.

Why are boys so dumb? This isn't high school. We're too old for this kind of petty drama—and that's coming from a *drama* major.

"I've tried to get Jase to give me the details, but he straight-up *refuses* to talk about it. Do you think you could get it out of Nate?"

I shake my head. "Doubtful. Right now he's not even taking my calls. He'll only text, and that's rare too." I blink back the tears building behind my eyes. This is not the time for a pity party. As soon as Jake shows up, I have to get back to rehearsal. I can wallow in all my bad choices later.

The door to the hospital room is pushed open and I'm ready to fall to my knees in gratitude, but when *he* steps into the room, I almost go down for an entirely different reason.

The rails on either side of the hospital bed are meant to keep the patient safe, but as my hands wrap around the hard plastic, I pray they can do the same for me.

"I swear, if you weren't about to give birth to my nephew, I'd kick your ass. You don't text that sort of infor—"

Jase's words cut off and his eyes flare—flashing gold with anger and not green with love—when he spots me standing next to his sister's beside.

A kaleidoscope of emotions flashes across his features before he pulls on the same mask I've seen him use on the ice. Gone is the man I fell in love with; in his place is the hardened enforcer feared throughout the NHL.

The lyrics to "Ten Duel Commandments" play through my mind as we stand off against each other, only his laboring sister between us.

I wish things could be like the musicals I've made my life's work, because I really wish I could break out in song right now. Everything is better when said in song. And with jazz hands. Can't forget the jazz hands.

"Broadway!" Cali cries, rushing around his friend, who is frozen in place, and rounding the end of the hospital bed to hug me. My eyes flutter shut as I fall into his embrace to attempt to rid myself of the chill Jase's dead stare gave.

"Hey, Cali." I hold on just a little longer.

"Well shit, Jordan." Cali's hands curve around my shoulders, holding me out for his inspection as he speaks to her. "You should have told us there was a dress code for this thing." Again he scans the white dress I have on. "I feel supremely underdressed."

Trust Cali to break the tension. It really is no surprise he and Jase are such good friends. They are both ridiculous, yet so damn genuine.

And you threw it all away with a lie.

Clearly, I'm my own worst enemy.

I don't have to look to know Jase is still glaring at me; I can practically feel the tips of the daggers he shoots my way slicing into my skin.

"Why are you here?" Jase's hard voice cuts deep.

"Um…" I drop my gaze to Jordan, who shoots me a sympathetic look.

"You shouldn't be here, *Bishop*."

Ouch.

Not Sweet Potato.

Not baby.

Not Mels.

Not even Brightly.

I'm Bishop now.

"Jase," Jordan scolds since I've forgotten how to speak.

My eyes blink back tears.

His continue to shoot daggers.

"I'm…I'm sorry." The words come out more sob than speech.

"You're *sorry*?" Jase retorts incredulously.

Faltering under his harsh glare, I can only manage a nod.

"Liars aren't welcome here."

"Jase!" Jordan shouts, but he ignores her. He's radiating animosity.

"I never meant to hurt you."

Every time I heard him mention the feud with Nate, each insult I had to hear and sit through…it was like a knife in the back not to come to my brother's defense. The guilt that ate away daily over lying to the two men I loved the most in this world…

None of it could have prepared me for what I feel under his hateful gaze.

"Even your *brother*"—he spits the word—"who hates my guts, has always had the balls to at least tell me the truth."

"Bro." This time it's Cali who jumps in.

"No wonder your parents don't come around." If he physically flayed me open it, wouldn't be as painful as this. "But I get it." He shrugs like his vile words are nothing more than a passing thought. "If you're anything like your brother, I wouldn't want to be around you either."

"*Jason!*" Jordan bellows.

"Whoa, not cool, bro," Cali adds.

All the air is sucked from the room and I can't breathe, crushed under the weight of my broken heart.

I—

I need to get out of here before I completely lose my shit.

Shrugging out of Cali's hold, I turn on my heel and flee.

I barely register Jordan's protest or Cali's shout of surprise as I run down the hallway of the hospital, the *stomp-stomp-stomp* of my heels marking my progress to the elevator.

My hands slap the wall as I crash a palm against the button to call the elevator, hitting it repeatedly in my haste. Intellectually, I know pressing it doesn't make it arrive faster, but intellect has left the building, replaced by pure emotion.

Come on, come on, come on, I beg.

Press-press-press.

Ding!

A sob breaks free and I rush into the thankfully empty car, collapsing against the wall.

The doors close, the car begins its descent, and finally I lose the battle, the tears falling freely.

Chapter Forty-Eight

"**W**hat in the *ever-loving* fuck is wrong with you?!"
I drop my gaze to where JD is glowering at me from the adjustable bed. Blue and white hospital gown on, IV inserted in her left arm, actively in labor —none of it takes away from the *you are a fucking idiot* glare she hurls at me.

I see it, but at the same time I don't. Nothing's really registering since coming face to face with Melody for the first time in weeks.

And, holy fuck, what a sight she was. Marilyn Monroe may have been *the* sex symbol of an era, but the bombshell has *nothing* on my girl in that white dress.

Shit! She's not your girl anymore, asshole. You walked away from her—literally.

It's true. I can't deny it or, hell, even justify the way I left her standing in the tunnels under the Garden without a word. Can I even consider us broken up since I technically never said the words?

Seriously, who does that?

I'm an idiot.

No—you, sir, are an asshole. Wombmate's got it right. What the fuck did you just do? What you just said might be the most vile *stuff to come out of your mouth—ever.*

"Jason." *What the fuck?!* screams JD's look as she thrusts an arm toward the door behind me. "Why are you just standing there?"

I blink, slowly swiveling my head around to see the once-again-shut door.

"Go. After. Her."

I want to. I *really* do.

But I can't.

I won't.

Just like I haven't been able to send any of the hundreds of text messages I've composed, only to delete them.

I've been a mess, a complete shut-in outside of hockey.

Honestly, I can't believe my door hasn't been knocked down by my family demanding answers.

I know they know we broke up.

I know they know why we broke up.

I love her. I know for a fact I do. Yes, I mean in the present tense.

But...

I don't deserve her. I let her go before she figured it out for herself.

What is it they say? Better to have loved and lost than never to have loved at all.

If walking away then ignoring her didn't make me lose her, the shit I just said will.

"Jesus Christ, Jason." I wince; that's the third time JD's used my full name. "I don't understand."

Join the club.

"I thought you giving up was bad, but *that*?" She again thrusts an arm at the door, wincing when the IV pulls from the aggressiveness of the action. "What you just did here..."

I want to tell her. I want to be able to lay out all my fears, my insecurities, let her take them away and make me feel whole the way only she can because she's my other half and always has been. When one of us falls, the other is there to lift them up.

It's our motto, an unspoken oath since we shared a womb.

How am I supposed to tell her I broke our vow to each other by keeping this from her?

And if I can't tell Jordan, how the fuck do I explain it to Mels?

I can't.

So I don't.

Instead, I run, and when that doesn't work, I push.

"This isn't you, Jason." Another use of the full name. "You're a fighter, a protector. It's who you *are*. Why else do you think you became a defender?"

Because I would never be good enough to compete with Ryan on offense.

The thought is ugly and not what I need right now.

"You push, and you prod, and you make sure everyone else goes after what makes them happy, and yet you do *nothing* when it comes to your own happiness."

My gaze slides to the floor, studying the scuff marks on the linoleum. I may not have told Mels about my hang-ups, but I sure as shit knew hers—the information about Nate notwithstanding. After maliciously using them against her, I know it will be a while before I can look at myself in the mirror. And JD? Our eyes are the same, and whatever I might see in them would be a million times worse than any reflection.

My phone is out of my pocket and in my hands without me even realizing I reached for it. My thumbs fly across the screen, typing out a message, begging Mels to come back.

I hover over the send button, the blue arrow mocking me, daring me to tap it.

I shift an inch, and like the thousand or so that came before this one, I keep my finger on the delete button until this message is gone, just like its predecessors.

I made my bed. Time for me to lie in the emptiness of it.

Chapter Forty-Nine

 pril

Dropping my bag to the floor with a thud, I fall back on the bed, spread out like a starfish. There's a sense of relief that comes with being out of the city, away from the island that is home to both my heartbreak and my heartbreaker.

I keep waiting for the day when it won't hurt so much. Don't they say time heals all wounds? Well, whoever *they* are can go fuck themselves, because they are full of shit. The breakup happened a month ago—it's been two weeks since the smackdown in the hospital—and the cracks in my heart have not gotten any smaller. No, those bitches are as deep as the Grand Canyon.

The worst part? I can't even blame Jase for the mean things he said to me. I lied. For *months*.

I could have told the truth—should have told the truth.

My phone sits on the nightstand, mocking me with its silence.

Zero texts from Jase. Not that I've sent any since *that* day.

No response from my parents about going to dinner now that we are in the same city.

Silence, silence, silence.

Like the creeper I've become, I grab my phone, pulling up Jase's Instagram and scrolling through his posts.

Hockey.

Hockey.

More hockey.

Baby Logan.

Hockey again.

Mario Kart meme.

Hockey.

Hockey.

Not a potato reference in sight.

The other thing lacking from his feed? A single taunt to Nate.

When I come to about the dozenth post about hockey, I toss my phone to the bed, wincing when it bounces off the mattress and hits the floor with a smack.

I don't have time to wallow in self-pity. I need to be at the theater in half an hour for our final rehearsal before tomorrow night's previews begin. It's the final push before opening night, the last opportunity to test out material before we debut the show back in New York.

Seven days.

Nine performances.

One potentially awkward, needs-to-happen conversation with my older brother.

Good times, Boston. Real good times.

Rolling from the bed, I hoist my bag up to start unpacking. I hate living out of a suitcase, so this is always the first thing I do.

The alarm on my phone dings, telling me it's time to go or I'll be late.

There's only one thing left to unpack.

Unwrapping it from the hoodie I used to protect it during transport, I pull out Mr. Potato Head and set him on the bedside table.

Yes, I brought him with me. Yes, I know it makes me pathetic, but whatever. At least I've stopped texting him.

Once all his pieces are back in place, I kiss the spud on the top of his little plastic hat and leave.

The show must go on, after all.

♡

Honey, honey, honey. Where the hell did I put the honey?

I scan the counter in my dressing room for the little plastic bear filled with golden nectar.

Preview number five is in the books, and my throat needs the relief only a giant cup of hot chamomile tea with honey can offer. I've had to cut the wine out of my diet completely for the sake of my vocal cords—something my heart is still picketing in protest.

There you are. I spot the sucker peeking out from underneath my brown Norma Jean wig from act one.

I place it on top of the mannequin head I'm supposed to store my wigs on.

A check of the time confirms what I already knew—Nate is late.

Or he's not coming.

I do my best to ignore how much the idea of that particular scenario hurts and instead focus on preparing my tea.

My thumbnail traces over the tragedy and comedy masks engraved on the wooden tea box Jamie gifted me when he learned we like the same tea to soothe the throat.

Unfortunately, all it does is make me think of Jase—again.

Jase who is gone.

Jase who hates me.

Jase who I still love.

The friends I can no longer contact because it hurts too much to have a connection to the one who broke my heart and not have *him* in my life.

The same friends who had planned on coming to my show to support me because that's what they do and my own family—except Nate—can't be bothered.

Nate who *always* comes.

Except…

Nate's not here.

Chapter Fifty

I flip my phone in my hand.
  Screen up.
  Push with my thumb.
 Screen down.
 Another roll of my thumb.

Over and over it rotates, screen side up then screen side down. Each time the screen faces me, it lights up with the picture of Melody kissing her Mr. Potato Head and a fresh arrow of pain hits my heart.

I'm an idiot.

A moron of epic proportions.

Seriously, what the fuck is wrong with me?

Who the hell cares who her brother is?

I did—but not anymore.

The entire month of March is a blur, the only memory not hazy being the utter devastation on Melody's beautiful face in JD's hospital room weeks ago.

Fuck.

I know all about how crappy of a family tree my girl has, and what did I do? I beat her with the branches of it.

I am in love with Melody Brightly (Bishop)—whatever.

The name part isn't important; the fact that I will never stop loving her is.

I *need* to fix this, but even I know it will take more than a simple apology.

It's grand gesture time, and it's a good thing I have an entire orchard of support behind me.

My issues with Nate Bishop are exactly that—mine. They should have no bearing on Mels and me. I'll have to figure out a way to bury the hatchet—and not in his back like I would prefer—if I want to have a shot at my happily ever after.

It's time to come clean about the underlying issues the rivalry fed off of once and for all. Owning my shit will fix half the problem.

The other half? Well…Nate and I will have to learn how to deal with it like men and not the immature boys we've been acting like.

Before I lose my nerve or throw up—both options equally likely—I click one of the favorites saved in my contacts.

I shuffle my feet, unable to stay still, the ringing on the other end of the line like nails on a chalkboard as I wait for the call to connect.

"Hey, bro." Ryan's standard greeting eases the storm brewing inside me.

"Hey, Ry."

"What's wrong?" Leave it to him to pick up on my distress immediately.

I swallow down the hockey puck in my throat and remind myself this is Ryan, my big brother, my closet confidant outside of the person I shared a womb with. I can tell him anything without him taking offense.

"You busy?" I ask instead of answering.

"Not really. I was gonna head over to Chance's to watch the Fire game, but that's not as important as whatever is going on with you right now."

I'm tight with most of the guys on the Storm, but the Blizzards are a cohesive family under Ryan's leadership. The things that make him a great captain are all the things that make him the best big brother.

"You're home?"

"Yup."

"Video chat?" I'm already stepping into my living room and grabbing the remote.

"Sure." There's a click and the call disconnects. A couple of seconds later a goofy picture of Ryan with glittery makeup courtesy of Carlee fills my television.

"All right, little brother. Tell me what ails you."

I swear, being a smartass *has* to be in our DNA.

Where do I start?

How do I start?

How do I tell my older brother, one of my biggest supporters, the guy who would lay down his life for those he loves that I've felt inadequate *because* he's my brother?

"I take it this is about Melody?" he asks after I've been silent for a minute.

"She's part of it."

"And the other part?"

"Um…" I shift forward, resting my elbows on my knees, and drop my head into my hands, raking them through my hair.

"Look." I lift my head to see Ryan has shifted to mirror my stance, blue eyes locked on the camera. "I understand you feel betrayed by her not telling you Bishop is her brother—a topic we can discuss at another time—but if you love her, you can't let her go."

"I know."

"Take it from someone who lost the love of his life for good—it sucks. There's nothing I can do about my situation, but *you* can."

I fill my lungs fully before letting the breath out of my mouth in a steady stream of air.

"I already decided that before I called. I even have an idea for how I can win her back, but none of it will matter if I can't make peace with Bishop first."

Ryan nods, looking so much like our dad when we did something to make him proud it's scary.

"Melody's family is nothing like ours. Her parents don't even go see her shows. They just don't go. Like who does that?"

I jump up from the couch, unable to sit still any longer.

"Not all text threads have to turn into Coven Conversations, but *damn*...how does a parent not text their child back? Or return their phone calls?"

Left, right. Left, right.

Reach the end of the couch, spin on my heel.

Left, right. Left, right.

Other end, turn around.

"You know she told me she can go months at a time without hearing from them?" I keep pacing and look toward the TV to see a deep frown on Ryan's face.

Any time I think of the craptastic things my girl had to—and still does—deal with, I feel all rage-y like the Hulk. Children need more from their parents than bankrolling. There has not been one major event in my life or my siblings' lives that at least one of my parents hasn't been there for, and they have sons playing on *two* different NHL teams.

"Nate..." His name comes out a little growly. Sorry, but it does. Rome wasn't built in a day, people. "He is the only member of her family who has made a point of seeing her in every single production she's been a part of. I can't be the wedge that comes between them."

Ryan's eyes bounce between mine and I know he's taking his time, figuring out what to ask, and how.

"What is your beef with the guy anyway? It's gone on too

long for it to be about what happened at hockey camp. Hell, even the Olympics were more than two years ago—it can't *still* be about any of that."

"Ummm…" I drop my gaze again, ashamed to admit this part of the saga. "I may have led him to believe I hooked up with his girlfriend after we beat his team in the Frozen Four."

"You were dating Rocky then."

"I don't think he realized I had a girlfriend, or…I don't know. Maybe he thought I didn't care if I did." I shrug. "It doesn't matter. I didn't *actually* hook up with his girlfriend—I just let him *think* I did."

"Does Rocky know this?"

"Are you fucking kidding me?" I can't keep the disbelief out of my voice. I like being alive. It doesn't matter that nothing happened; she would have killed me on principle alone.

"So why the hell would you do something like that?"

Now for the hard part.

I can do this.

I *will* do this.

It's for Mels, for my Sweet Potato.

"It was my way of getting back at him for all the digs he made."

"Well, he needs to find a hobby or something because that's exactly what he spews—crap. He really should hire ATS to handle his social media so he stops posting bullshit about you and keeps his feed relevant to himself. Nothing he's ever said is true."

"Isn't it though?" My voice breaks on the last word. I'm *petrified* of Ryan saying yes.

"The fuck?" Incredulous blue eyes blaze like the hottest part of a flame. I guess I should be grateful we are doing this on video chat and not in person. The back of my head tingles as if it, too, knows it would have been smacked if Ryan were here.

I turn around, unable to survive seeing pity on his face when I say what I'm going to next.

"You're pretty much the reason I'm in the NHL."

"Again…what the fuck are you talking about?"

"You *did* get me a spot at that camp."

Ryan's nostrils flare. "The only way that is true is that I aged out and my slot was available."

I don't say anything. Fuck, this is harder than I could have imagined. I feel like I should be drawn and quartered for having such treacherous thoughts.

"Jase, look at me."

Craning my neck to look over my shoulder at the television, I only spin around when I see he's nearing Jordan-level mad.

"Now, you listen and you listen good." He punctuates the demand with a serious finger point. "That is the biggest load of bullshit I have ever heard in my life." It's his turn to yank a few strands of hair from his head.

"Is it really?"

"Fucking hell, Jason." All the cursing tells me just how pissed he is. Whether it's directed at me or on my behalf is yet to be seen. "Please, *please* tell me how you can even entertain that notion?"

"Are you trying to say the scouts didn't come sniffing because you were on the team? Hell"—I smack my thighs— "the NHL wanted you when you were still in *high school*. You turned down a multi-million-dollar contract to play in college, all so BTU had a reason to keep sniffing around."

"Not true."

I ignore him. Now that I've started, I can't stop.

"BTU wanted me because *you* wanted me on the team."

"I have half a mind to call our sister right now and have her smack some sense into you." I pray that's an empty threat. "Fine." He huffs out a breath. "I can't deny that may have factored into their decision, but the Titans would *never* have offered you a full ride if they didn't think you could deliver." He holds up a hand when I go to cut in. "*You* would never have been drafted by the Storm if not for your talent. No one, not even me, works harder than you do."

He collapses back against the couch, his shoulders sinking. This, *this* right here is what I didn't want. I don't need the words to know he's internalizing his guilt about the situation. He's not doing it to be a martyr or anything; it's just how he's wired.

"I'm sorry, brother. It was never my intention to make you feel this way."

It's a good thing I have all this baggage, because I'm about to go on one hell of a guilt trip.

"Don't, Ry. *None* of this is on you. It's my issues. I alone own them. I wish I could tell you why it hit me harder any time it came from Nate, but I can't. I love you. There is not one person in this world who is a better brother than you."

"I love you too, bro." He holds a fist out in front of him and I do the same, virtually bumping it.

Chest lighter now that the elephant in the room is off of it, I jump over the back of the couch and retake my seat. I'm not quite sure how he's gonna react when I tell him this part of why Nate Bishop sucks at life. I may be the hothead of the two of us, but Ryan wrote the book on how to be an overprotective big brother.

Maybe I should be the bigger guy and reach out to Nate to suggest he up his life insurance policy.

Chapter Fifty-One

MOTHER OF DRAGONS: So you finally decided to nut up and do something about getting your girl back?

THE BIG HAMMER: How the fuck did you know?

MOTHER OF DRAGONS: *GIF of Michelle Tanner rolling her eyes and saying, "Duh."*

THE BIG HAMMER: Shit. I was JUST on the phone with Ryan. Please let me be the one to tell him about this. You know how jealous he gets of our—in his words—"freaking twin ESP crap"

MOTHER OF DRAGONS: *GIF of Michelle Tanner saying, "You got it dude."*

THE BIG HAMMER: What's with all the *Full House* GIFs?

MOTHER OF DRAGONS: Sorry. I've been binge-watching it during midnight feedings. Your nephew is no joke.

MOTHER OF DRAGONS: *picture of baby Logan passed out milk drunk*

THE BIG HAMMER: Man I love that little dude. But for reals, I need help. BIG help.

MOTHER OF DRAGONS: Are you saying *gasp* you need The Coven?

THE BIG HAMMER: *the biggest of sighs* Yes.

MOTHER OF DRAGONS: On it.

From the Group Message Thread of The Coven

MOTHER OF DRAGONS: Okay ladies. Another one bites the dust.

MAKES BOYS CRY: Oh, oh…this is my FAVORITE.

YOU KNOW YOU WANNA: Please

YOU KNOW YOU WANNA: Please

YOU KNOW YOU WANNA: Please tell me it's Jase?

ALPHABET SOUP: Oh, did my bestie finally come to his senses?

QUEEN OF SMUT: About damn time, Trip.

SANTA'S COOKIE SUPPLIER: Vince said, "Bro, took you long enough to bend the knee."

THE OG PITA: Oh, I love the drama.

PROTEIN PRINCESS: Seems fitting. He IS trying to win back an actress, so…

THE BIG HAMMER: Are you guys done yet?

ALPHABET SOUP: Seriously?

QUEEN OF SMUT: Are you really asking us that right now?

MAKES BOYS CRY: It's like you don't even know us.

YOU KNOW YOU WANNA: *GIF of woman putting hand to chest and gasping*

THE OG PITA: *GIF of woman fainting*

PROTEIN PRINCESS: *GIF of Sutton Foster asking, "Really?"*

PROTEIN PRINCESS: ^^See what I did there? She's a big Broadway actress.

SANTA'S COOKIE SUPPLIER: Oh that's a good one.

SANTA'S COOKIE SUPPLIER: *GIF of Audra McDonald saying, "Really?"*

YOU KNOW YOU WANNA: *GIF of Idina Menzel saying, "Really?"*

THE BIG HAMMER: JD, can you rein in your squirrels, please?

ALPHABET SOUP: *string of squirrel emojis*

MOTHER OF DRAGONS: Okay, okay. What did you have in mind?

THE BIG HAMMER: First, I need to apologize.

MOTHER OF DRAGONS: YEAH you do.

THE BIG HAMMER: Really feeling the love right now.

MOTHER OF DRAGONS: Whatever. You deserve it. You were a dick. But please…proceed.

THE BIG HAMMER: *big sigh* So Mels has mentioned her family—outside of her douchebag brother—doesn't come to her opening nights.

ALPHABET SOUP: Um…you're trying to win her back. Word of advice: don't call her brother a d-bag.

SANTA'S COOKIE SUPPLIER: *GIF of girl pointing up saying, "This."*

QUEEN OF SMUT: Do you need me to give you notes on How to Grovel 101?

THE BIG HAMMER: You guys are the WORST!!

MAKES BOYS CRY: And yet you still come to us for help *emoji of person shrugging*

THE BIG HAMMER: *GIF of person banging their head against the wall*

MOTHER OF DRAGONS: Okay, before we break my twin, let's at least hear him out.

THE OG PITA: Unless he's sending a voice memo, we aren't ACTUALLY hearing him.

YOU KNOW YOU WANNA: Beth, have I told you lately how much I LOVE that you are a part of our squad?

THE OG PITA: *GIF of Melissa McCarthy making a heart with her hands*

THE BIG HAMMER: OMG. I can't even. I give up. I'm out.

Chapter Fifty-Two

From the Group Message Thread of the Boys—AKA Counterfeit Coven Conversations

THE BIG HAMMER: OMG. Why? Why did I do this to myself?

HOLLYWOOD (Cali)**:** Do I even want to know?

CAPTAIN AMERICA (Ryan)**:** Haha, I think I know.

THE BRICK WALL (Jake)**:** Yup. There's only one thing capable of bringing on a reaction like this.

DAUNTLESS SUPERMAN: **whispers** The Coven

WANNA TUCK (Tucker)**:** What are you whispering for, bro? They are like Beetlejuice—you have to say it three times to summon them.

WANNA TUCK: *GIF of Beetlejuice*

THE KRAKEN: There are days I legitimately wonder why I am friends with you guys.

THE BOONDOCK SAINT (Nick): Bro, you aren't friends with us. You're family.

THE GREEN MONSTER (Damon): True story.

BIG DECK (Deck): Have we taught you nothing?

THE SPIN DOCTOR (Sammy): You should know by now, you don't just marry one person when you marry a Covenette.

ROCKSTAR MAN (Jamie): This is also true. As an outsider, I can speak from experience.

THE SEAL DEAL (Justin): God, I miss the days when Madz didn't really have female friends. They are scary.

JUST RAY (Ray): Are we going to help our boy out or what?

THE FEROCIOUS TEDDY BEAR (Griff): If you were reaching out to The Coven, I assume this has to be about Melody?

HUGE HOSE (Wyatt): Um…anyone want to tell me why my wife looks like someone offered her a lifetime supply of calorie-free ice cream?

THE BIG HAMMER: *facepalm emoji*

DAUNTLESS SUPERMAN: Bro, you know the

Covenettes have ZERO chill. You seeking them out for help is like throwing chum in the water.

CAPTAIN AMERICA: Can we maybe get around to ACTUALLY helping Jase?

THE BRICK WALL: ^^I second this.

THE SPIN DOCTOR: You guys like to give the girls shit, but damn this conversation is just as scatterbrained as one of theirs.

WANNA TUCK: Ouch.

BIG DECK: Oh, burn man.

THE BIG HAMMER: OMG. I give up.

Chapter Fifty-Three

Melody

Opening night.

When my alarm goes off, I almost feel like I'm tempting the theater gods by not being more excited. Like I might as well walk through the doors and yell, "Macbeth."

Our short tour of previews received rave reviews, and already our production scale is being talked about in the same way as many of the greats.

Tony eligibility is there, and if the nominating committee likes me, I might finally have a shot at accomplishing the only dream I've ever had.

Well, at least the only one I had until I went and fell in love with Jase Donnelly, only to flop.

Thank god for routines to keep me sane.

Performance days all follow the same itinerary, with a few variations on the days of dual performances, but opening night has a few special and time-honored traditions.

If I'm going to have any chance of making it to curtain call without crying, I need to focus on my routine and not anything else. Which means not texting my brother—again— because if he ignores me—*again*—I don't think I'll recover. I haven't heard a word from him since before I left for Boston. This is the longest we've gone without communicating, and it's killing me as much as not being with Jase is.

I get out of bed and do a few stretches to loosen up.

Breakfast is a simple affair of fruit and yogurt before I spend twenty minutes with my steamer to help open up my vocal cords. I scroll through social media to pass the time, and no I do not check Jase's (total lie).

In the shower, I warm up with a few songs from the show, my favorite of late being the ballad I sing after Marilyn and Arthur Miller break up. It is gut-wrenching and heartbreaking. Pretty much it speaks to how I've felt the last month and a half.

As luck would have it, the Bruisers clinched the first round of playoffs two nights ago, and Nate will be free until the outcome of the Columbus / Tampa bracket is determined. The question is—will he come?

Our already frosty relationship has deteriorated to the point that I don't even recognize it. He's mad at me for dating Jase, and I'm hurt he flaked on our plans when the show was in Boston. It is a passive-aggressive cycle I'm completely over.

To be honest, I almost wish the Bruisers hadn't won in five games so at least I could say he wasn't in the audience because of work.

One of the last things I do before leaving for the theater is pack my performance bag:

Water bottle.

Jase won't be there.

Hand sanitizer.

What is Jase doing tonight?

Body spray.

Is he dating someone new?

Baggie of bobby pins (because you can never have enough of them).

Should I try texting him again?

Lip balm.

Why hasn't Nate at least sent a "Break a leg" text?

Hairbrush.

It's fine. Ella will be in the audience.

A picture of Zoey, Ella, and me from high school.

They are your family, Mels.

A picture of Nate and me after the last show I was in.

Will we ever take another one of these again?

My makeup and hair supplies are in a separate kit, which I leave in my dressing room instead of lugging it back and forth.

In an effort to drown out the toxic thoughts my mind insists on torturing me with, I pop in my earphones, crank up "My Shot" from *Hamilton*, and rap along with Lin-Manuel Miranda. I need to remember this *is* my shot and I'm not going to lose it because of a broken heart.

Nope. Time to take every ounce of anguish I've felt and pour it into tonight's performance.

Zoey is suspiciously quiet on our trip to the theater, but I don't inquire.

It isn't until I'm braiding my hair to fit under my wigs and applying my stage makeup that I'm able to relegate everything that isn't the show to the back of my mind.

Dressed in my first costume, I head to the stage for the passing of the Legacy Robe, one of Broadway's oldest traditions.

With it only being a couple of weeks away from the cutoff for Tony eligibility, we will be one of the last shows to get the robe this season.

Arms linked, Zoey and I join the circle of our castmates. In the center stands last year's recipient with the white robe draped over his arms.

The representative from the Actors' Equity Association goes through each custom we observe. First, he introduces each cast member making his or her Broadway debut tonight.

I may have been seven when I made mine, but I'll never forget the excitement, the nerves, and the joy. We applaud and cheer for them, our way of formally inducting them into the Broadway family.

Other formalities include introducing the production's Equity chorus counselors, naming anyone else who has had the honor of receiving the robe, and finally a reading of a scripted history of the robe.

Then the fun begins. Our production's recipient—the chorus member with the largest number of Broadway chorus credits—dons the robe, which is decorated with patches from all the other shows from the season.

Falling in line with various other weird theater traditions and superstitions, he must circle the stage counterclockwise three times, making sure to touch everyone for good luck.

A memento from our show will be added to the robe under the recipient's supervision, and during intermission, the rest of the cast will sign near it.

"Mels." Zoey grabs my hand as I move to exit the stage.

She's worrying her lip hard enough I'm afraid she might chew a hole in it. "Zo?"

"So...ummm..." Her chest rises and falls with a deep inhalation.

"Spit it out, Zo."

She curses in Portuguese, looks over her shoulder, down to the stage, at the curtain before finally bringing her gaze back to me. "I wasn't sure if I should say anything or not..."

"Do you think you can tell me before curtain maybe?"

"Fuck it," she says, more to herself than me. "Come here." She takes my hand again and pulls me with her deep into the wing of the stage.

We edge around the heavy red velvet fabric of the closed curtains, keeping to the shadows to avoid being seen by those in the audience.

"Look just off center in the orchestra." She keeps her hand close as she points.

What?

Is Nate here?

We have two minutes until curtain so I do as she says, scanning over ushers and people finding their seats. It's a packed house tonight, which only adds to the adrenaline.

What does she want me to see?

I keep scanning, only to double back.

Holy shit!

Jase is here.

Jase and what looks like most of his family and friends are here. It's hard to miss a group of men their size; they tend to stand out even seated.

What is he doing here?

Why did he come?

What does this *mean*?

My heart is pounding like I just finished the dance number at the end of scene three, and if I don't start breathing, I'm at serious risk of passing out.

My fake lashes brush my eyebrows as my eyes go wide, trying to make sense of what they're seeing, but it's impossible.

Does he forgive me?

Does he regret what he said?

Is he only here because of some sense of obligation?

"Zoey," I plead. For what, I'm not sure.

"He didn't want me to say anything to you."

"You *talked* to him?" I squeak.

What the fuck? He can text my best friend but not me?

"Yes. I helped him get the tickets for tonight."

The look I give says we are not done with this conversation, but with the shout from the stage director calling for places, there's no time to get into it.

"You know where he is. Go show him what you're made of." Zoey smacks my ass, because why wouldn't she?

One more glance at the audience then I roll my shoulders back, resolved to put on the performance of my life. Marilyn Monroe was a natural seductress, a force of nature, a *goddamn* icon even decades after her death.

Time to channel the bombshell for more than the show. We have a man to get back.

"Break a leg, Mels." Zoey wishes me good luck, but I don't need it. Jase sitting in the audience is all the luck I need.

Showtime.

.

Chapter Fifty-Four

This is it.

Showtime—no pun intended.

The groundwork has been laid. The Zamboni has laid down a fresh sheet of ice, if you will.

I've gone Macy's Thanksgiving Day Parade big for tonight's grand gesture.

Fingers crossed it's enough to get my girl back.

"You think this will work?" Cali's question echoes my thoughts.

"I sure as shit hope so." I keep my gaze locked on the red velvet curtain covering the stage.

"It'll work," JD says from my left.

"We got your back." Rocky rubs my shoulder from her seat behind me.

"Always, bro," Vince tacks on.

"I feel like a proud mama." Turning in my seat, I see Maddey has her hands clasped in front of her chest, a dreamy expression on her face.

"This can't be good," Justin mutters under his breath. If her own brother is concerned, it can't bode well for me.

"I'm almost afraid to ask." Ryan shifts in his seat next to hers. "But why?"

"It's like I helped write how this would play out. I mean it's tailor-made for Melody." Maddey waves an arm around the theater filling with people. "It's like I've taught you *all* the things, and my baby bird is ready to fly the nest."

"And to think…" I don't need to see Skye to know she's smirking. "He figured it out all on his own, unlike numb-nuts over here." She hooks a thumb at Vince.

"True…too bad he can't figure out how to actually get Holls to accept his proposals." Becky snorts.

Jake leans across JD. "Ignore them."

"Easier said than done." I rake a hand through my hair.

I'm still not all that confident this will work. Sure, Maddey is *all* about how this is my grand gesture and yes, that is my intention, but we aren't doing anything major.

Zoey and Ella proved themselves to be surprisingly willing allies, helping to arrange the more than two dozen tickets needed for our group. If my baby's family can't be bothered to show up and support her, mine sure as hell will.

I had to alter my original plans slightly to accommodate the traditions and superstitions of the theater, but as a lifelong hockey player, I understand.

My nerves are starting to take over, and listening to my people is not helping. The heels of my palms dig into the muscles of my thighs when I wipe the sweat on them off on my suit pants. My pulse is racing, and if I were wearing a tie, I'd be loosening it.

The lights of the theater flash, signaling that the show will be starting in a few minutes.

My surroundings fade, the lights turn down, and I focus on the stage. I shift, balancing on the edge of my seat. The orchestra starts to play. My breath catches in my throat as the curtains lift.

There she is.

My baby stands center stage, under a lone spotlight, curves fully on display in a tight skirt stopping midcalf. I drink her in, missing her pink hair, which is currently hidden underneath her brown wig.

The music eases down and Melody starts to sing, her voice sure and strong. I thought hearing her sing at The Duel was something, but holy shit, homegirl was holding out on me.

I'm enthralled from the first note.

Scene by scene, song by song, I don't know if I even blink as I watch her disappear, Marilyn Monroe taking her place. She owns the role so wholly the sight of her kissing other men doesn't have my hands clenching like I suspected it would.

Intermission comes, but my ass remains rooted in my seat.

Close by, Lyle is gushing over the glitz and glamour of the show, and the girls are talking about god knows what.

Me? I'm running through my plans like plays in the Storm's playbook, going over every angle, all the potential pitfalls, what I need to do in case I need to go for a rebound shot if the first fails.

Halfway through the second act, Mels has a solo number where Marilyn is singing about the loss of yet another husband. The heartbreak she portrays is visceral and hits me like a punch in the gut.

Her dark eyes find mine, and though I doubt she can see me with the bright lights—or, you know, due to the fact that she doesn't even know I'm here—none of it takes away from the feeling that she's singing *to* me.

Is she pulling from experience for her performance? Did she feel this way when I walked away? Was what I said too much for her to forgive?

She tells the story of how we—she and Arthur Miller, not she and I we—had magic but now things are tragic and we are left as shells. Fuck if that isn't precisely how I've felt all these weeks.

I let my issues ruin the best thing that had ever happened

to me, but I own my shit. Finally talking to Ryan was only the first step. The biggest will be extending the olive branch to Nate.

When Marilyn commits suicide, tears fall from my eyes, and I want to rush the stage and scoop her into my arms.

The stage goes dark, and the next scene is set, the show going on until we finally get to the last number of the show.

And as Vince would say, Holy Bombshell Batman is Mels something else in a sequined gold gown. She sparkles and shines, and I want to kiss the red lipstick off her face.

The somber mood in the theater from the death of an icon disappears as she sings about all the reasons the world shouldn't forget about her.

Melody isn't the only Marilyn on stage for the final number. In the stage's adaptation of a movie montage, spotlights around her turn on and off, depicting Ms. Monroe in her most recognizable roles.

She belts out the last note, holding it far longer than should be humanly possible.

The curtains close and the entire audience is on their feet giving a standing ovation, none clapping harder or cheering louder than me.

The red velvet rises for the cast's curtain call, starting with different groupings of the chorus and trickling down to the leads. Melody is the last to take her bow, and the noise level inside the theater could rival that of any Storm game.

With everyone on their feet, it's easy for me to scoop up my package and make my way out of the row, headed for the stage.

I'm coming for you, baby.

Chapter Fifty-Five

Melody

Without a doubt, that was the best performance of my career. I don't know if it was because Marilyn was a role I was born to play or the fact that I knew Jase was in the audience. Either way, I left everything out there on the stage, purging every chaotic emotion I've felt since the night we first met.

Rhythmic chanting of "Mel-o-dy! Mel-o-dy! Mel-o-dy!" filters through the applause, and there is no way to miss Jase's family. Thank god my face is caked in thick stage makeup because the heat in my cheeks has nothing to do with the hot lights shining on me and everything to do with them acting the same way they did when I was at the hockey game with them.

"Mel-o-dy! Mel-o-dy!"

"Whooo!"

"We know her!"

"Crushed it."

I shouldn't be able to hear them, but they are *that* loud.

There are a few waves when they notice I've spotted them. Scanning the group, I double back but don't see the one I want.

Where'd he go?

Did he leave?

Why would he leave?

Zoey rushes the stage, throwing her arms around me, and I let her distract me from my worries.

The opening night pomp and circumstance continues with flowers presented to those essential in creating our master-piece. Zoey for choreography, the director, the book writer, and the composer all get bouquets.

I expect Zoey to pass one off to me as well, but when I turn in her direction, all I get is a grin. She misses the questioning look I send her way, because she's not looking at me but at something over my shoulder.

Spinning around, the beads of my dress clack together in a swirl of fabric. I search, cursing her taller stature when it takes me precious seconds to find what—or in this case, who—put that expression on her face.

Waiting in the shadows, looking too good for my sanity in a dark gray suit and white collared shirt, sans tie, is Jase. He winks, and my insides turn to goo.

My mind whirls. *What does this mean? Is he here for me? Who else would he be here for? Does he forgive me? If he can forgive me, I can certainly forgive him.*

He stalks across the stage, his long legs eating up the distance between us with ease. Canting my head back, I notice his shirt isn't plain white; there are skinny green pinstripes in the weave, enhancing the color of his hazel eyes.

I eat him up with my gaze, starting at his carefully styled blond hair, moving down to those color-changing eyes, ghosting over the healing yellow bruise on his jaw I know he got from a fight in the first round, scanning the short scruff of playoff beard, only stopping once I get to those tempting lips that are tilting up in a smirk.

His tongue sneaks out to lick across his bottom lip, and the glint of his piercing has me digging the heels of my stilettos into the wood beneath them to keep from launching my body at him.

I remind myself we're in public, and if I touch him, there is zero chance of keeping things PG.

"Hey there, Sweet Potato." His deep voice rumbles through me; my nipples tighten and my panties flood. I've missed this man something fierce.

"All-Star." My voice cracks. "Wh-What are you doing here?"

His smirk turns downright devilish, and he pulls the hand I hadn't noticed was hidden behind his back free. "I heard it's tradition to give the lead actress flowers on opening night *after* the performance." He lifts his arm, a small mason jar cradled in his hands.

My eyes bounce between his handsome face and the orange flowers held out to me before accepting the offering. The jar is heavier than I thought it would be, and I almost drop it. Bringing them to my nose to sniff, my brow furrows. Upon closer inspection, I see these aren't actually roses. They're—

"Sweet potatoes," Jase says, completing my thought. "Gemma made them, and Skye did all the crafty shit to make it pretty."

In the audience, I can see Gemma and Skye holding hands, watching us like we're a part of the musical.

His large hands cup my elbows, his calloused fingers setting off their usual tingles. My body, having been starved for his touch for months, practically liquefies as he trails his fingers up the backs of my arms to my upper back, spanning it completely and tugging me a step closer.

Warm from the wall of heat in front of me, my eyes flutter closed as his thumbs trace circles on my bare skin.

"I'm sorry, baby." He bends, whispering in my ear. "I should have *never* said what I did. I regretted it the second the words left my mouth."

"I know," I whisper. Jase is an inherently good person.

He inhales against my skin, the air brushing my neck, the stubble of his beard following in the wake. It's like I'm an exposed nerve, my fingers doing their best to dig into the glass jar in my hands.

"I'm also sorry I walked away."

"Why did you?" I turn to bury my nose in the open collar of his shirt, taking in the familiar scent of soap and ice.

"Because I'm an idiot."

I giggle. Can't really argue with that. Then again, I wasn't the brightest bulb in the box either.

"I let my own shit get in the way, and…I found you guilty by association. But I realized none of it matters anymore." His nose runs along the vein I'm sure is pulsing visibly.

"No?" I sway forward.

"No." The word rings with conviction.

"Then what does?"

On stage, with the musical's full company surrounding us and a literal audience in front of us isn't necessarily the best place for this conversation, but beggars can't be choosers.

"You." He kisses the soft spot behind my ear. "*You* are what matters."

I roll my lips in to hold back a sob. Only three words could sound better than that.

He pulls back, staying bent to rest his forehead to mine. His hands are on the move again, rising to cup the back of my neck, his fingers threading together while his thumbs stroke the underside of my jaw. Eyes locked on mine, unblinking, he tells me, "I love you, baby."

All the hurt, every tear that fell, all the unanswered texts dissolve from existence with those words. Yes, we will need to talk about what happened, but not here.

I get why he told me now, but I'm not returning the sentiment yet. Those words are meant for him and no one else.

"Come with me." I jerk my head back, and he nods in understanding.

Adjusting my "flowers," I link my hand with his, luxuriating in the simple intimacy I missed more than I realized, weaving through the crowd, not stopping until we're inside my dressing room. The moment Jase's large frame steps over the threshold, I collapse against the door, shutting out the rest of the world.

The room isn't all that large, only made smaller by the new piece of furniture I added to it, AKA Jase Donnelly. Seriously, the man is *huge*. I wouldn't be all that surprised if his wingspan reaches wall to wall.

He's standing between the small loveseat crammed in the corner and the makeup vanity, and the glow from the large bulb lights surrounding the mirror bounces off his golden hair as he takes in my new home away from home.

A rack holding my costumes from earlier in the show is tucked against the only free wall to the right of the door. There's a shelf above the couch that's home to a Marilyn Monroe Funko Pop! doll and a couple of frames from past shows. I see his eyes widen when he spots Mr. Potato Head tucked into the back corner.

Of course he's here. Is he really surprised?

At least I refrained from having a picture of us in the room. I would have, but it was too hard to see his face. Creeping on his social media was enough torture.

"You…" He trails off, reaching for the famous potato.

"I wanted to keep you close, even if you didn't want me."

The toy looks barely bigger than the spud it portrays inside his bear paws. His thumbs smooth over the smiling face reverently.

The rough wood of the door scrapes my back as I push off of it and add the jar to the shelf.

"It was never a question of *wanting* you." His eyes remain locked on the toy as he speaks. "Was I blindsided by the information? Yes. Could I have handled how I reacted better? Absolutely."

There's so much sorrow in his voice, and I automatically step into him, anchoring myself with my hands on his hips. Finally, he lifts his gaze to mine, returning Mr. Potato Head to his place of honor and mirroring my stance.

"You didn't hold my family against me. It's not fair for me to hold yours against you."

"Um…your family is awesome."

"They're fucking crazy." His chest expands with a deep breath. "But they're mine and I wouldn't trade them in for the world." His grip on me tightens. "Just like you."

I swallow, wishing the words would come. Why the hell am I so nervous?

Chickening out, I ask, "Why do you and my brother hate each other?"

His eyes flare, flashing gold. "He didn't tell you?"

I shake my head. "He's barely spoken to me since Fallon told him we were a couple."

"Oh, baby." The corners of his eyes soften and his lips tip down. He pulls me in more, the sequins of my gown catching on the buttons of his shirt.

"I know part of it was about the Olympics, but I know there's more. Will you tell me?" I plead.

He nods. "So much has played into it. You're right—the whole debacle over me getting the spot on the Olympic team over him is only the most recent one. There was also when BTU beat his team in the Frozen Four, and you heard the gist of the Lake Placid stuff."

"That doesn't seem like enough to fuel the rivalry you have, though."

"It is when you combine it with how his *attacks*"—he puts air quotes around the word—"hit too close to home."

"Explain?" My arms loop all the way around his waist.

"All my life I've struggled with being Ryan Donnelly's

brother and being compared to him. I've had moments where I didn't feel like I truly earned my place in hockey."

"That's the biggest crock of shit I've ever heard. I love Nate, and yes, he's a great hockey player"—I squeeze Jase—"but I knew your stats long before we met."

That cocky grin makes a reappearance. "Are you saying you were my puck bunny?"

I pinch his ass and he yelps. "Keep saying stupid shit like that and see what happens."

"Sorry, baby. Please continue telling me all about how you pined for me from afar."

I roll my eyes and he laughs.

Dipping my head to make eye contact, I wait until he's focused on me, needing him to see as well as hear the sincerity of my words. "You are one of the best defenders in the league. Comparing you to Ryan is like comparing apples to oranges."

"That's pretty much what he said to me." Again he drops his forehead to mine. "God I'm such an idiot."

"But you're *my* idiot." I bite my bottom lip to hold back a smile.

"*Really* feeling the love, Sweet Potato," he grumbles.

"Well you should, because I do." He pulls back suddenly at my words. "I love you, Jase Donnelly."

His eyes flare then his mouth crashes to mine, and I'm lost—in the press of his lips, the feel of his tongue stroking mine, that familiar cold metal whirling inside my mouth.

Teeth nip.

There's sucking.

Groaning. Moaning. Sighs.

Hands move, his and mine. My face is cupped, his hair is pulled.

On and on we kiss. If we were in a car and not a virtual closet, the windows would be steamed to all hell.

The boy shorts I have on under my dress are completely destroyed; I'm so wet it's like they're nonexistent.

"Fuck." He curses against my lips, not fully breaking the kiss. "I've missed this."

I yank on his hair harder, grinding against the erection pressing into my belly. "Same."

Kiss. Kiss.

Stroke. Stroke.

His tongue retreats, and I capture his ring in my teeth and suck. With a pained groan, I'm moved until I feel the edge of the vanity table digging into my ass.

I'm spun, my back pulled against his solid front. I'm pushed, bent slightly over the table, forcing me to brace myself on my hands to avoid getting a face full of reflective glass.

It's his turn to grind into me, the hard length of his cock riding over the curve of ass.

The change of position is swift, but his actions are lazy.

In the mirror I watch him bend to nuzzle my neck before he drives me mad by dragging his piercing down the length of it.

His hands snake up my arms, starting at my wrists and swirling along my forearms, over my straightened elbows, up the ticklish skin of my triceps. Slipping underneath the spaghetti straps of my gown, he gives them a flick and they fall down. The material is weighted by sequins and beads, automatically sliding to my waist.

"What the hell is going on here?" He cups a breast in each hand, my head tipping back to his chest when he thumbs over where my straining nipples are hidden.

"Boob tape."

His reflection gawks at me like I'm a calculus problem, only instead of solving for x, he's trying to work out why I have no nipples.

"It adds a layer of support for the girls underneath costumes and help prevent them from giving me a black eye."

He barks out a laugh. "Fuck, baby, I've missed you."

Spinning in his arms, I loop my own around his neck, tugging him down for another intoxicating kiss. "I missed you too." Another kiss. "So much."

In a blink, my ass is on the vanity, the thigh-high slit of my gown allowing for my knees to fall open to accommodate his width. Hands cup the backs of my thighs, and my legs wrap around his waist, my ankles hooking at his back, the points of my stilettos digging into that delicious bubble butt of his, urging him closer.

Higher and higher his hands travel, the material of my dress converging at my waist like it's a cape tied around my middle. Simultaneous groans echo in the room when I roll my hips against the hockey stick straining against his zipper.

"Jase." I'm already reaching for his belt, pulling the leather free.

"Mels."

I'll have bruises on my ass from his grip, but who cares about a few battle wounds when the spoils are Jase inside me?

Metal clangs, belt hanging free. My thumb slips under the metal tab securing his pants, the button popping free followed by the hiss of a zipper.

I reach inside, teeth biting into my shoulder as I palm his hot length.

"Mels," he warns when I drag my thumbnail over the mushroom cap head leaking precum. "Keep doing that and this will be over before it starts."

"What happened to that stamina you used to boast about?"

"It's been over two months since I've been inside you. *Months*, baby."

He pinches my ass when I snicker. How can I help it when

he makes it sound more like two decades? Even when he's not trying to, he emanates exaggeration.

"Condom," he growls, fumbling inside his jacket.

I slap his hands away, retrieving the thin leather wallet and liberating the foil packet from it. He's sheathed, hooking my underwear to the side and moving into me quicker than the slap shot that won him hardest shot at the skills comp.

Though we exchanged the ultimate words of love earlier, there is nothing romantic about our coupling. This is raw, quick, down and dirty fucking at its finest. The slow, sweet love will have to happen when we have time and not when people could come knocking at any moment.

His hips pump and mine roll in a back-and-forth dance to orgasm. I cry his name only seconds before he roars mine.

"I love you." I clutch him to me.

"I love you too, baby."

God the way those words make me feel has me beaming brighter than any Broadway marquee.

"Though I gotta say, I feel like I cheated on you with the blonde wig and all." He tugs on one of the curls hanging in my face. I wince, the glue securing it to my scalp pulling my skin, and he curses. "Sorry."

"It's okay. Transforming back into myself is sometimes a painful process."

He slips out, tying off the condom and readjusting his clothes before helping me with mine. His hands linger on my shoulders, toying with the straps he's just fixed, and we stare at each other dopily.

I still have so many questions about his beef with Nate.

Two quick knocks sound on the door, and it opens before we can respond.

"Surprise."

Chapter Fifty-Six

The sight of Nate fucking Bishop is like a bucket of cold water to the face.

Really?

Fucking really? Homeboy had to show up *now*?

Can't a guy get five minutes to bask in the afterglow of a brain-melting orgasm before being faced with the bane of his existence? Hell, my dick is barely dry after fucking his sister. Yes I'm mentally fist-pumping over that.

I've come to terms—sorta—with being the bigger man and leading the charge in us kissing and making up. Well, not literally. The only Bishop I'll be kissing is the one with her legs currently wrapped around me.

To think, at one point I thought he deserved a hug from me—not fucking likely.

"Teddy!"

It soothes my ruffled feathers that Melody legitimately calls him this and it wasn't a way for her to hide his true identity from me.

"Care Bear." The disapproval in his tone has my teeth snapping together. I feel like I should offer him some prune juice, because the scowl he's sporting makes him look constipated.

"You came." Mels taps me to move so she can get down. It's the last thing I want to do, especially with Judgey McJudgerson looking at us like we just made a human sacrifice. The only thing murdered in this room was Melody's pussy when I took us to Poundtown. My lips quirk imagining the reaction I would get if I offered up that tidbit.

"Of course I did." Nate pulls Mels into a hug, throwing so much shade in my direction I need a full snowsuit to survive it. "Unless I have a game, you know I always come to opening night."

"I wasn't sure since you blew me off in Boston."

My hands clench into fists at how sad my baby sounds. Yes I know I walked away from her, but he's her brother. No matter how mad I get at JD—and let's be honest, that's bound to happen with how headstrong she is—I will *always* be there for her. You show up when it counts. It's what family does.

"I was still processing."

Mels frowns, and I can tell she's biting back a retort.

"I thought you two broke up." His words come out like an accusation.

"We did. We just got back together," Mels admits.

"Were you not watching us on stage?" I ask sarcastically.

I didn't think it was possible, but his scowl deepens.

"You're doing this to fuck with me, aren't you?" Nate asks me.

"The fuck?"

Is this asshole for real?

"Was this all a game? Hoping hearing about you screwing my sister would mess up my concentration and give you an edge when we play?"

"You *can't* be serious. Is that a legit question? Because if it is, you're completely fucked in the head." I cross my arms, hoping to keep from throwing a punch.

"What?" He shrugs, feigning innocence. "I wouldn't put it past someone with your reputation."

"You're fucking kidding me, right?" Incredulity bleeds into my words. This fucker. This guy who would taunt me by spewing vile slurs about my twin and the other important women in my life to get under my skin is going to stand here and accuse me of using *his* sister.

Like hell I'll stand for this shit. I purposely held back this particular issue I had with the older Bishop, but if he wants to throw stones, I'm going to launch some fucking boulders.

"You don't want to do this with me, Bishop," I warn. Like the fuckwad he is, he preens like a motherfucking peacock.

Shit. My temper is definitely flaring with this confrontation, because the amount of F-bombs I'm dropping increases tenfold.

"I'll do whatever I have to do to keep my baby sister away from a subpar-playing playboy like you."

With each word spoken, Melody's eyes narrow fractionally, and if that wasn't enough to broadcast her displeasure with him, the flaring of her nostrils is.

"Teddy!" Melody rounds on Nate. "What the fuck?"

"It's fine, baby." It's not, but I can suck it up and be the bigger man for my girl. It's not like I didn't say worse to *her*.

"No. It's not."

"Insult me all you want." *Asshole*, I think, but I keep that part to myself. "The stats speak for themselves. But tell me this: what kind of asshole ignores his sister over her choice of boyfriend?"

Okay, I guess I couldn't hold back the asshole line like I thought I could. But for reals, when JD told me she knew about Nate being Melody's brother before the whole Fallon incident, I didn't stop speaking to her over it. I gave her shit, she raised hell over me not telling her about my feelings of inadequacy, we hugged it out, and we moved on. You don't hold grudges when it comes to family.

"Care Bear," Nate cajoles.

"Don't, Nate." She places a hand on his arm. "You both love me." He scoffs at that. "Can't you put aside your differences for me?"

"It's because I love you that I can't allow this to happen."

Oh, wrong thing to say, buddy.

"*Allow*? You can't *allow* it?"

Discreetly, I knuckle my eardrum. She's reaching decibels not meant for human ears.

"Mels," he tries again.

"Nate," she deadpans.

"I'll never be okay with this." He gestures between Mels and me.

Who the fuck does he think he is?

"That's not up for you to decide, Nathan."

Does a part of me love how she's sticking up for herself? For us? Yes.

Do I enjoy seeing her fight with the only family who—until recently—has been there for her? Not even a little bit.

"I'm sorry, Mels." He sounds anything but. "I love you too much to sit back and let this asshat take advantage of you."

I'll show you who's the asshat, fuckwad.

"What are you saying?" Melody eyes him warily.

"If you want me in your life"—he points an aggressive finger at me—"then he can't be in it."

"*What?*" she sobs, falling back a few paces.

"I can't support this, and I won't sit by and watch it blow up."

Holy shit I wish I were live-streaming this for The Coven. They would tear him apart so bad there wouldn't be enough left of him to bury—metaphorically speaking, of course.

Two more steps and my baby is at my side, pressing herself against me. My arm automatically wraps around her middle, hugging her in tight.

"I'm serious, Mels." He watches us with disdain.

Another choked sob escapes the woman I love, and it feels like my insides are being sliced open with a skate. Walking away from her was the biggest mistake of my life, yet I'm about to do it for a second time.

I refuse to be the catalyst for my baby to lose the last vestige of family she has, even if it will be like reaching inside my chest and leaving my heart behind in the process.

"Fine." I bring Mels around to face me, keeping her back to her traitorous brother. Cupping her beautiful face in my hands, I press my thumbs underneath her chin to tilt it up toward me. The tears streaking down her cheeks have me once again fighting the urge to bash Nate's face in for daring to make her cry.

"Jase."

"I know, baby." I do. I really, *really* do. "I promised myself I would never walk away from you again, but I'm going to have to break that promise." I reach up to wipe away another tear. "You know how I feel about family. I can't be the cause of you losing yours."

The tears fall freely now, and when she starts to weep, I nearly cave. I can't though.

I may not have known she was talking about Nate when she told me the stories, but there was no missing how much they mean to each other. A broken heart is a small price to pay to ensure she doesn't lose more than she bargained for.

"I'm sorry." My body revolts as I bend to her ear so only she can hear me. My next words are for us and only us. "You'll always be my Sweet Potato." I press a kiss behind her ear, her nails digging into my sides as she clutches me to her tighter. "I love you."

With one last kiss to her neck, I straighten and somehow manage to walk out of the room.

Chapter Fifty-Seven

After watching the man I love walk away from me for the second time in as many months, I shift my attention to my brother, not really sure how to process everything.

There was the performance of my life.

One hell of a grand gesture.

Declarations of love.

Sex so hot if I were to text the girls about it, I would use all the fire emojis.

Then my brother showing up. My heart tripped over itself when I realized he *did* come, but then he had to go and lay out an ultimatum like he's the boss of me.

Sorry to tell you this, big brother, but you are not.

"Can you get out so I can change for the cast party?" I gesture to the door behind Nate.

"What about our picture?"

Is he for real right now? I'm standing here crying, because of *him*, and he thinks I want to take a *picture*? Men!

"This isn't really a Kodak moment." My voice is flat, emotionless despite the sarcastic comment.

"But it's tradition, Care Bear."

Nice try, buddy.

"Well...seeing as you just broke my heart, I think it's okay for me to break our tradition." I move around him and pull the door open. "Get. Out."

I can't even look at him when he finally does as I ask. He was supposed to be the man in my life to protect me—because let's be honest, our dad certainly doesn't care enough to fill the role—and instead he hurt me the most.

Jase may love me enough to walk away from us to protect the relationship I have with my brother, but if he thinks I'm letting him go without a fight, he has another thing coming.

Chapter Fifty-Eight

BROADWAY BABY: HOLY SHIT! HOLY SHIT! HOLY SHIT!

THE BIG HAMMER: What's wrong? Are you okay?

BROADWAY BABY: I'M NOMINATED FOR A TONY!!!!!!!!

THE BIG HAMMER: Holy shit that's amazing!

BROADWAY BABY: I can't believe it.

THE BIG HAMMER: I can. You were AH-MAY-ZING

BROADWAY BABY: Lol, I can't believe you just said ah-may-zing.

THE BIG HAMMER: *GIF of Rebel Wilson in *Pitch Perfect* saying, "Aca-believe it!"*

BROADWAY BABY: You know what this means?

THE BIG HAMMER: ??

BROADWAY BABY: I'm going to need a date.

THE BIG HAMMER: …

♡

BROADWAY BABY: Woooo!!!! Look who's going to the Conference Finals!!! I hope Jake and Ryan aren't too sad you guys beat them.

THE BIG HAMMER: Yeah, that was pretty nice.

BROADWAY BABY: Pretty nice? Um…I'm pretty sure Cali's picture of you two gloating over the two of them went viral.

THE BIG HAMMER: It did. Still not sure if JD and Skye are happy or mad about it.

BROADWAY BABY: It was hilarious. They should be happy.

THE BIG HAMMER: You know what this means though?

BROADWAY BABY: What?

THE BIG HAMMER: We have to play your team to make it to the Cup.

BROADWAY BABY: *GIF of Will Smith shrugging*

♡

BROADWAY BABY: I miss you.

THE BIG HAMMER: I miss you too, baby.

BROADWAY BABY: Then why the FUCK aren't we together?

THE BIG HAMMER: Because I refuse to be the reason you lose your brother.

BROADWAY BABY: That's stupid.

THE BIG HAMMER: I know, but it doesn't make it any less true.

BROADWAY BABY: No, it doesn't. If anyone is the reason for it, it's Nate himself.

THE BIG HAMMER: Whoa, you called him Nate.

BROADWAY BABY: Yeah, well, when you start tossing out ultimatums like you're a petulant child and not a 25-year-old man, you lose the right to your childhood nickname.

THE BIG HAMMER: Harsh.

BROADWAY BABY: And don't you forget it.

THE BIG HAMMER: Maddey would totally approve of your use of the word petulant.

BROADWAY BABY: Oh I know. She already praised me for it.

THE BIG HAMMER: You still talk to The Coven?

BROADWAY BABY: *GIF of Michelle Tanner rolling her eyes saying, "Duh."*

THE BIG HAMMER: Yup, you are def still talking to my sister. I can't believe she's still watching *Full House*. I would have thought she'd be done all these weeks later.

BROADWAY BABY: Oh she is. She's on to *Saved By The Bell* now, thanks to my recommendation.

THE BIG HAMMER: I'm surprised you're still talking to them.

BROADWAY BABY: Why?

THE BIG HAMMER: Because...

BROADWAY BABY: Listen...

THE BIG HAMMER: I thought I couldn't "listen" to a text.

BROADWAY BABY: God you're lucky you're cute. But just because you have some misguided notion that we need to be broken up, that doesn't mean I accept it.

THE BIG HAMMER: ...

♡

BROADWAY BABY: That's one hell of a right hook you have.

THE BIG HAMMER: Yeah...well...I gotta protect my boys. I'm not gonna let a dirty hit slide, even if the refs miss it.

THE BIG HAMMER: What about the goal or the assist I had tonight?

BROADWAY BABY: Oh those were nice too, but the right hook was the highlight of Game 4 for me.

THE BIG HAMMER: You do realize I used that right hook on your brother, right?

BROADWAY BABY: That was my favorite part *smiley face emoji*

THE BIG HAMMER: …

BROADWAY BABY: What? *shrugging emoji* Maybe you'll knock some sense into him and he'll butt out of our relationship.

THE BIG HAMMER: …

♡

BROADWAY BABY: *picture of Mr. Potato Head with Jase Donnelly and Chris Callahan bobbleheads*

BROADWAY BABY: Kick butt tonight. You bring this series back home for Game 7.

THE BIG HAMMER: Where did you get those?

THE BIG HAMMER: And I thought you were a Bruisers fan?

BROADWAY BABY: Ebay.

BROADWAY BABY: And seeing as the reason I am a Bruisers fan is the reason you refuse to be my boyfriend anymore and will only text me (at least you text me back this time around), a part of me can root for you.

THE BIG HAMMER: Why?

BROADWAY BABY: Because Mr. PH was getting lonely. He wanted to hang with his daddy.

BROADWAY BABY: Wait…

BROADWAY BABY: If he's supposed to represent you, does that make you his daddy? Doesn't it make him you? Did I just create a doppelgänger situation?

THE BIG HAMMER: There is so much wrong with your last text I feel like we need to stop texting.

THE BIG HAMMER: Actually…we should probably stop anyway.

BROADWAY BABY: Why the hell would we do something like that?

THE BIG HAMMER: I'm sure Nate would flip if he knew you were texting me.

BROADWAY BABY: *angry face emoji* *cursing emoji*

BROADWAY BABY: NATE

BROADWAY BABY: DOES

BROADWAY BABY: NOT

BROADWAY BABY: TELL

BROADWAY BABY: ME

BROADWAY BABY: WHO

BROADWAY BABY: TO

BROADWAY BABY: DATE

THE BIG HAMMER: Chill. Stop channeling your inner Becky. But for reals—I told you I cannot come between you.

BROADWAY BABY: You're gonna make me throw my phone.

Chapter Fifty-Nine

Melody

E*nd of May*

The last month has been filled with so many ups and downs I feel like I'm on a damn rollercoaster.

The show opened to rave reviews, culminating in twelve Tony nominations, including one for yours truly for Best Performance by a Leading Actress in a Musical and one for Zoey for Best Choreography.

I think I might have permanent hearing loss from how loud Zoey, Ella, and I screamed the morning they were announced. Unlike how I always imagined, the first person I reached out to wasn't Nate; it was Jase.

I still can't believe after one of the most romantic gestures *ever*, he gave us up so I wouldn't lose my close connection to Nate. Well, that backfired in spectacular fashion. I'm so fucking angry with my big brother over his Romeo-and-Juliet-esque decree I can barely manage a civil conversation with him.

How *dare* he try to dictate who I date.

At least this time around Jase isn't ignoring my texts. Sure, our conversations are more one-sided and any time I try to broach the subject of us he either deflects or stops answering altogether, but I refuse to give up.

He loved me enough to walk away. Well, I love him enough to not let him. No more games.

My usual stipulation of being off for when the Bruisers are in town doesn't kick in until the show is a few months old. I had to practically offer up my firstborn, but I was able to work out missing both of today's performances to handle my business.

Striding through the lobby of the Huntington Hotel not far from Madison Square Garden, I head straight for the elevator bank. I got Nate's room information from one of his team-mates earlier and don't care if I cut into his nap time. This conversation has been put off long enough.

Knock-knock.

The door swings open and I meet a pair of startled dark eyes. Yup, I am interrupting nap time if the rumpled hair, bare chest, and athletic shorts are anything to go by.

"Care Bear?"

"Nate." He winces at my use of his real name. *Yeah, well, you lost that right, buddy.*

Not waiting for an invitation, I push past him and into the room.

"Don't you have a show right now?" He runs a hand over his hair, shooting a look at his roommate and dropping into one of the armchairs in the room.

Stokes already knew I was coming—he was the one who gave up their room number—and he heads out to give us some privacy.

"I took the day off." I pace the space in front of the beds, too keyed up to sit. "You and I need to talk."

"About?"

Massaging the ridge of my brow, I wonder if he's always been this dense or if he's purposely being obtuse.

"About Jase." I hold up a hand when he goes to cut in. "Specifically *me* and Jase."

"I thought there *wasn't* a you and Jase?"

Don't smack him, Mels. He's your brother.

"Yeah," I huff. "*That's* the problem."

He looks at me like I just broke out into song. Well, no, that's not the best description, because I do have a tendency to do that.

"I love him, you big idiot." I slap my thighs in frustration. "I love him and he loves me so much he refuses to *be* with me because he's afraid it will affect our"—I wave a hand between us—"relationship."

"Oh, Mels," he says so patronizingly I really do almost punch him. "Don't be so *naive*."

"*Excuse me?*" I squeak.

"That guy has more bunnies than the entire Bruisers roster."

I slip my hands into my pockets, because with each word out of his mouth, the urge to punch him increases.

"I don't trust him. I told you how when he would visit Ryan, he would come with his girlfriend and hit on the bunnies when she wasn't around. You think that's the type of guy I want dating my baby sister?"

I never actually understood why he told me that. Back then, I figured he needed to vent and I was his sounding board, but the Jase Donnelly I've come to know, the man I love…would *never* do that.

Something prickles at the back of my memory. "Was his girlfriend a strawberry blonde?"

Nate's brow scrunches in confusion.

"Red hair," I clarify, and he nods. "That wasn't his girlfriend."

He scoffs. "Donnelly is pictured with more women on his Insta in a week than most people are in a year."

"*God*! I thought Jase exaggerated," I say, more to myself than him, but I do see a flare of hurt in my brother's eyes. "Nine times out of ten, those *women*"—I use air quotes—"are his friends."

"Friends," Nate scoffs. "More like fuck buddies."

Oh my god, who is this person in front of me? I thread my fingers into my hair, resting my hands on my head to keep from ripping it out.

"Look...I have no idea what your issue is with the Covenettes—"

"Covenettes?"

I wave him off. "It's their nickname—regardless, that's not what's important." I pull in a calming breath. "I've met them all and they are amazing. From the moment they met Zoey, Ella, and me, they treated us like one of their own. Do you have *any* idea how rare that is to find with girls, especially a group as large as them?"

"Bunnies stick together I guess."

"OH MY GOD!" Great, now I'm yelling at my brother. I didn't expect this to go over like we were having a tea party, but damn, this so wasn't the subject I thought would have us fighting. "They *aren't* bunnies. For Christ's sake, one is his sister, who's married. One is his best friend, also married. Another is his other best friend's girlfriend, and another almost married his brother. There's also his personal chef and friends from college rounding out the group." I tick off each person on my fingers. "They might not all *technically* be related, but they are *family*."

Nate's dark eyes soften at the mention of family, and I finally drop into the chair across from his and take one of his hands in mine.

"Do you know when I met his mom, she asked me more about my acting in one *hour* than Mom has in my *entire* life?"

"Mels…"

"By asking me to give him up, you're not just breaking my heart—which you are, by the way—you're asking me to give up the type of support system you and I dreamed about growing up." I squeeze his hand in both of mine.

"Care Bear—"

I continue like he didn't speak. "All our lives we've been each other's greatest champions. I was the only person in the cast who had an entire hockey team cheering them on from the front rows, and there are very few theater geeks who can recite hockey stats like lines from a script."

I reach so I'm grasping both his hands and dip my head to meet his eyes.

"You and I have always been an island unto ourselves when Mom and Dad couldn't be bothered to care longer than it took to sign the checks. We're Care Bear and Teddy Bear." This earns me a chuckle, and my spirits lift. "Why let some stupid grudge keep us from finding a family?"

Nate collapses against the back of the chair. "Fuck." He scrubs a hand over his face. "He didn't tell you about our"— he pauses, tilting his head side to side as if trying to find the right word—"rivalry?"

"Not really." Sure, most of the details are a bit fuzzy, but this makes me think I'm missing a few pieces of the puzzle.

"Shit. He might be a better guy than I've given him credit for."

Finally!

"Of course he is. I don't like people who don't deserve it— current company and their recent behavior excluded." I give him a look that dares him to test me on this. He's smart enough not to.

I'm confident things will get back to normal with us and that he and Jase will be able to work their shit out. Plus, if they don't, I'll just enlist my fellow Covenettes to help knock some sense into them.

"Still." He shakes his head. "I can't trust him."

"You're not the one who is dating him—I am. So guess what, big brother? It doesn't matter if you don't, because I do."

"Well you shouldn't," he snaps. "Because usually when a guy is okay with hooking up with a girl who has a boyfriend, they tend not to care if they themselves have one."

"What the hell are you talking about?" I tilt my head. He's not making any sense.

"After we lost to BTU in the Frozen Four…" Nate swallows and rubs at his ear. It's his tell when he's angry, so I wait him out. "I caught him hooking up with Dana."

"Dana?" I sit up straight. "As in your ex-girlfriend?"

"Yeah. I caught them looking very cozy by the bathrooms."

Math may not have been my favorite subject, but even I can tell something doesn't add up.

"So you're saying Jase knew Dana was your girlfriend and targeted her to get back at you from your beef from Lake Placid?"

"Yes. No. I don't know." Nate rests his elbows on his knees, threading his fingers in his hair and massaging his temples.

"Oh my god. I can't believe that bitch was almost responsible for me missing out on the best relationship I've ever had."

I blow out a breath, trying to get my emotions in check.

"It *killed* me not to tell you about dating Jase. I felt so guilty there were times it made me sick. I'd talk to you and keep this whole new part of my life from you, and I'd be with him hearing things about you and not be able to defend you. It sucked."

"Care—"

"And all because of a bitch who was the *literal* manifestation of a puck bunny."

"What?"

"Oh Teddy." I place a hand on his knee. "I love you, but the only thing Dana saw in you was potential dollar signs. Yes, you were projected to go high in the draft, but so was Jase." I hold up a finger, already knowing what he's gonna ask. "All you had was yourself in earning potential, but Jase was considered pedigreed. His older brother was the current Rookie of the Year in the NHL. Even though they weren't engaged at the time, everyone knew he was about to have a brother-in-law in the league too, not to mention all his former teammates and the fact that their family is connected to Rick Schelios. Dana probably saw Jase as a way to get *more*."

Then I remember something else—something important.

"Did you see them *actually* hooking up?"

"No."

"So why did you assume they did?"

"Dana had her hands on his chest and he winked when I confronted them."

Fucking Jase. Men really are morons.

"Yeah...nothing happened between Jase and Dana."

"How do you know?"

"Jase had a girlfriend back then, one he happens to be best friends with now. There's no way they would still be close if he cheated. I'm pretty sure he just wanted you to *think* they hooked up to fuck with you."

"Well shit." Nate collapses back against his chair. "Well fucking played, Donnelly."

I put a hand over my mouth to smother a laugh. If these two idiots could stop acting like teenage girls, I think they would actually get along.

Nate stays silent while he processes everything. Both of us were wrong, him with his ultimatum, me for lying about my relationship with Jase. As far as I'm concerned, we're even. We'll only have an issue if he tries playing dictator again. For now, I have places to be.

"Good talk." I double-tap his knee and rise from my seat. "Glad we cleared this up."

He rises with me, a befuddled expression on his face. "Where are you going?"

I walk to the door before I answer. "You have a nap to take, and I have a song to practice."

His brows scrunch in confusion. "I thought you said you took the day off."

"I did, and you'll see." I tap my temple. "Just remember to keep this conversation in mind. Love you, Teddy."

I hear, "Love you too, Care Bear," before the door shuts behind me.

That's one hockey player taken care of. Time for number two.

Chapter Sixty

The locker room is buzzing as we dress for the start of Game 7 of the Conference Finals. This is the second time we've gone all seven games—the first being our previous series against the Blizzards in the second round—and yes, our bodies are tired, but if we win this game, we're only four wins away from hoisting the Cup over our heads. It's so close I can practically taste the silver and nickel alloy.

I'm not saying the locker room is ever the most glamorous place to be—no matter how luxurious the facility—but at the end of May and into June, things take a turn. The extra bruises and all the facial hair from playoff beards isn't a good look on anybody. Well, except me. I pull off the scruffy look as well as any Avenger.

That being said, I can't wait to shave this shit off. It's itchy as hell.

Yoshi!

Yoshi!

Yoshi!

"Dude." Cali throws his hands in the air.

I flip him the bird, not giving a shit. I'm surprised he even heard my phone over the sound of Birds of Prey.

I thumb open my texts, wondering briefly if it's another one from Mels. I've been doing my best to distance myself from her, but like I told her, I promised I wouldn't walk away again. I may not be able to *be* with her, but texting has been our thing since long before we became a couple.

I miss her like crazy, though. She doesn't know it, but I've squeezed in seeing her show another half a dozen times in the month since opening night. It only gets better each time.

I'm supposed to be keeping my distance, a feat made harder the last ten days since our series against her brother's team started. Creeping from the audience to see her may not *technically* be keeping my distance, but what they don't know won't hurt them.

Have I been taking advantage of working out my frustrations with Nate when we play? Maybe. To be fair, whenever we've played the Bruisers in the past, I've ended up in the sin bin at least once. So what if that number has tripled for the last six games?

Looking down, I see I do have a message from her.

BROADWAY BABY: *picture of Mr. Potato Head with a Funko Pop! doll of Jase and one of Nate*

BROADWAY BABY: Why can't I get you two to get along IRL like you do as dolls?

I laugh. My baby is something else.
Shit. Not your baby anymore, Donnelly.

THE BIG HAMMER: *shrugging emoji*

Thumbing back, I go through the other texts that came through.

> **ALPHABET SOUP:** Only because the Blizzards are out.

> **ALPHABET SOUP:** *picture of Rocky wearing a Jase Donnelly Storm jersey*

> **THE FEROCIOUS TEDDY BEAR:** Do you see these posers?

> **THE FEROCIOUS TEDDY BEAR:** *picture of all the Covenettes wearing Jase Donnelly Storm jerseys*

> **MOTHER OF DRAGONS:** If anyone asks, I'm telling them this was for Halloween.

> **MOTHER OF DRAGONS:** *picture of Lucy, Lacey, and baby Logan in mini Jase Donnelly Storm jerseys*

> **DAUNTLESS SUPERMAN:** You need me to come back there and show you some moves so you can really lay Bishop out?

I have to be on the ice for warm-ups in less than five minutes. I make quick work of responding so I can finish dressing.

To Rocky:
> **THE BIG HAMMER:** Surrrrre. Wait until AFTER we break up and you marry someone else to FINALLY wear the CORRECT jersey.

> **ALPHABET SOUP:** To be fair...you didn't ACTUALLY play for the Storm when we dated *shrugging emoji*

Such a smartass.

> To Griff:
> **THE BIG HAMMER:** Yeah…they are totally closet Storm fans.

> **THE FEROCIOUS TEDDY BEAR:** True story lol.

> To JD:
> **THE BIG HAMMER:** FINALLY! You're raising them right. But it loses a little something with the Yeti headphones.

> **MOTHER OF DRAGONS:** Yeah, I'm not buying a new set of noise-canceling headphones. Sorry not sorry.

> To Vince:
> **THE BIG HAMMER:** Please. I taught you everything you know.

> **DAUNTLESS SUPERMAN:** In your dreams, puck head.

Tossing my phone in my locker, I slip one of JD's hair ties on my wrist and finish suiting up.

The sound of the opening ceremony and accompanying hype video echo in the tunnel as we wait to step onto the ice.

We charge out as a team, and I complete my full skate of the rink then look toward the suite level, finding my crazy-ass family waving down at me.

Across the ice, I spot Bishop, but the death glare I'm used to seeing isn't there. *Huh?* He looks almost…cordial.

Our starting line is announced as we finish warm-ups, lining up on the blue line opposite Boston's starters while the rest of our teams filter in and make their way to the benches.

"*And now, ladies and gentlemen, please rise and remove your caps to join our special guest tonight, Broadway's own Melody Brightly, to sing the national anthem.*"

Pinching my glove between my elbow and side, I remove it to knuckle my ear. With the flashing lights, booming music, and roaring crowd, my ears *must* be playing tricks on me. There's no way I heard what I think I just heard. Right?

It's Wednesday. Mels has two shows on Wednesdays. She should have just taken the stage for her second performance of the day, not be here about to walk out on the silver carpet laid on the ice.

So why am I trying to see past the Bruisers for a familiar flash of pink?

Chapter Sixty-One

The butterflies I experienced on opening night have nothing on the fire-breathing dragons currently taking up residence in my gut.

Though muted by the concrete surrounding me, the music and voiceover from the hype video the Storm plays before their playoff games thunders through my ears.

Just a few more minutes.

Breathe in through the nose. Exhale out the mouth.

Over and over I repeat the deep breathing exercises, quelling the urge to toss my cookies.

I feel like a complete rookie I'm such a basket case.

The national anthem is arguably the hardest song to sing live, and I'm about to do it in front of almost eighteen thousand in the arena and about another eight million watching from home.

Sure, it makes sense to be nervous when you consider all that, but none of that is what has me as skittish as a long-tailed cat in a room full of rocking chairs.

I ball my hands inside the long sleeves of my Jase Donnelly jersey, bunching the fabric inside them.

What if he's mad?

What if he doesn't understand what I mean by this?
What if he still refuses to be with me?

All these thoughts play on repeat in my mind until a touch on my elbow breaks me from my trance.

Turning my head, I see the representative from the Storm looking at me expectantly. "You ready?"

When I concocted this brilliant—albeit drunken—scheme to get my man back, the first person I contacted to help was Jordan. Of all the stories I heard from Jase about how The Coven gets shit done, including tracking down Holly when no one else could, I knew who to call—and it *wasn't* the Ghostbusters. Gotta love the irony of enlisting their help to get him to come to his senses.

Now, though? I could really go for the bottle of wine that got me into this mess.

You can do this, Mels.
You perform for people eight times a week.
You're nominated for a freaking Tony.

I keep my gaze trained straight ahead, and I don't know if it's a good thing or a bad thing that the Boston starting line—AKA my brother's line—is the one closest to me and not the Storm. I'll say good because I'm not sure I'd be able to go through with this seeing Jase's reaction.

It's different when I'm on stage. The lights are so bright, and the audience is one big shadow. Here? Not so much.

First things first: not forgetting the words and ending up in the top ten of national anthem flops next to Christina Aguilera at the Super Bowl.

"O'er the land of the *freeeee*," I sing, crushing the high note like every true Broadway performer is trained to do. The deafening sound of cheering as I continue to hold the note makes it impossible to even hear myself.

One more lungful of air for the final line, my eyes falling shut of their own accord. "And the *hooooome* of the *braaaaaaaaave*."

Opening my eyes, I see the massive American flag making its way around the arena over the heads of the screaming and whistling fans, popping against the backdrop of thousands of circling gray towels.

Hockey has always been my favorite sport to watch live, and playoffs and the subsequent Stanley Cup carry an electricity with them you can't find anywhere else.

I finally chance looking at the players on the ice. Nate is wiping underneath his eye, but all thoughts of bringing my brother to tears with my performance fall to the wayside as a blur of black and gray rounds the line of Boston players.

Snow sprays over my boots as Jase breaks at the edge of the carpet unfurled on the ice.

It takes me a moment to work up the nerve to lift my gaze from his skates, but I remind myself like Maria when she leaves the convent in *The Sound of Music*: I have confidence in me. Because if I learned anything from the cast of *Hairspray*, it's that life is surely lacking without love.

Chapter Sixty-Two

C ali's gloved hand hooks around my elbow the moment Melody steps out to sing the national anthem, keeping me in place.

What is she doing here?

I shift on my skates to get a better look, but I can't see much thanks to her short stature and the towering men in skates in front of me.

I must have fallen and hit my head on the ice because *surely* I'm hallucinating. How can she be here when she's supposed to be on stage thirteen blocks uptown?

The melodic sound of her voice filling the arena is all the confirmation I need that it really is her—I would know her voice anywhere.

It doesn't matter that the people filling the seats are rowdy hockey fans, most I'm sure already well on their way to being drunk; she has them as enthralled as the sold-out audiences who see her do her thing on stage.

It's the longest two and a half minutes of my life, and I curse every pause the overwhelming applause causes.

Shrugging Cali off the second Melody finishes the last note, I don't give a fuck that I'm about to delay the start of the game. I need answers, and there's a better chance of the Storm forfeiting the game than me waiting until it's over to get them.

Stopping in front of her with a spray of snow from my skates, I eat her up with my gaze. I need her eyes on mine immediately.

Committing a cardinal sin, I toss my stick to the ice, barely registering the clatter, and shuck my gloves off after it.

On instinct, I reach for my baby, and the screech of feedback from the mic hitting the ice when she drops it fills the area. I ignore it, cupping the back of her neck in both my hands and tilting her face to mine with a press of my thumbs under her jaw. Worried eyes blink at me, and she visibly swallows.

I tried to stay away, to keep my distance, not wanting to be a wedge between her and the assface behind me. There's the thought that Nate might try to put a stop to our reunion, but it's so fleeting it might as well have not existed.

Not a word is said as we stare at each other, my gaze eating up every detail about her like a starved man at a buffet. That's exactly what I am—*starved*. The closest I've come to seeing her in over a month has been twenty rows away, and all those times she was Marilyn, not my Mels, my Sweet Potato.

Now she's all long pink waves instead of platinum blonde, that freckle under her left eye I love to kiss isn't covered by stage makeup, and there's no drawn-on beauty mark to the left of her delectable mouth, which is painted with pale pink gloss instead of fire engine red.

As if I don't think she's breathtaking enough, when I get a glimpse of what's happening below the neck, I almost wipe out on the ice like a rookie. She's rocking a Storm jersey, and not just *any* Storm jersey either.

Mine. My girl is wearing *my* jersey, in front of me, the

sold-out crowd of over eighteen thousand, millions more at home, and—most importantly—her brother.

This is her claiming me as hers, and I'm done not doing the same.

My hold on her tightens, her hair tangling in my fingers as she's forced to take a couple of steps forward, closer to me.

"So you *do* know how to follow the rules." I nod at the jersey.

Her lips tip up at the corners. "Well...I wasn't given a dress code to follow or anything." My own lips lift, remembering how she tossed the same sentiment out the night we met. "But I didn't think my usual black and gold would help me get what I want."

"Oh yeah? And what's that?"

"You," she says with zero hesitation, and damn if that isn't my new favorite pronoun.

"Mels—"

"No." She shakes her head, cutting off any other objections. "You made your grand gesture, which you more than succeeded in. Now it's my turn."

I nod. Who am I to stop her?

"You love me." Her hands come up, clutching the collar of my jersey, pulling me until the edges of my skates glide onto the carpet. "And despite you acting like a *gigantic* idiot *more* than once..." She levels me with a look that dares me to argue. I don't take the bait. Yes, I may be an idiot, but even I have enough sense of self-preservation to not be *that* stupid. "I love you."

Pressing onto her tiptoes, she shifts to look around me at Nate. "He may be my brother, and yes I love him too, but I *refuse* to give *you* up. If he doesn't like it, that's his problem."

She moves back, using her grip on my jersey to tug me down until we are nose to nose. Our size difference has always made this position awkward AF and my skates aren't doing us any favors, but none of that matters when having her close makes everything right.

"Will you kiss me and call me yours already? You have a hockey game to play, after all."

Cheeky woman.

Instead of slamming my mouth on hers like every caveman instinct inside screams at me to do, I maintain my hold on her, keeping her in place with my thumbs underneath her jaw, and mold my lips to hers.

It's slow and consuming, the kind of kiss that, if this were a movie, would make viewers be like, "Now that's a kiss."

Her tongue is the first to press against the seam of my lips. As soon as I grant her access, she wraps it around the barbell piercing my tongue.

On and on we kiss, little moans of pleasure escaping her throat as we do. If it weren't for the cup protecting my junk, every person inside the Garden would see just how badly I want my girl.

"I'm all for happy endings and shit," Cali's voice breaks in as he skates up to us, "but maybe you should cool it before this turns into a not-safe-for-work scenario."

We do as he suggests, albeit reluctantly. Mels circles her arms around me, smooshing her face against my chest as she looks at my pain-in-the-ass friend. I drop my own arms, keeping her close with a hand spread over the large number thirteen on her back.

"Hey, Cali," she says, speaking way more politely than I think he deserves.

"Hey, Broadway."

I don't have to see her face to know she's smiling.

Around us, the arena sucks in a collective breath, and Cali stiffens beside us. A glance over my shoulder shows Nate skating toward us. The anticipation of what will happen when the two of us known rivals square off is palpable. Our shared connection has not been public knowledge, and my grip on Mels tightens.

Again, I can't read the expression on his face, but a part of me wonders if we're about to have our first fight before the puck even drops.

Mels straightens but keeps her hands anchored at my hips. I've never been more grateful than I am in this moment to not be one of those players who wears a shirt under his jersey. The feel of her fingers stroking the bare skin above my uniform pants is everything. It doesn't help that I've been denied her touch—yes, that's my own fault, I know—for over a month, and even *that* time in her dressing room wasn't enough thanks to her buttinsky brother.

"I take it this was the song you needed to practice, Care Bear?" All the tension drains from Mels body at Nate's easy tone. I'll wait to see how this plays out before I relax my stance.

"Yup. Like I told you earlier, you either get on board with this or find a new train."

I roll my lips in to stop a smile. I doubt gloating will do me any favors, but the struggle is real.

"All I want is for you to be happy." Bishop reaches for her to hug. "As long as I reserve the right to kick his ass if he breaks your heart, I'm good."

Yeah, never gonna happen, buddy.

The only reason I even walked away the second time was because of some misguided martyrdom. The only walking I'll be doing now is down an aisle to wait for Mels.

Our little pow-wow is broken up by one of the refs. Nate and I share a nod of understanding as he and Cali skate off, but before I can do the same, Mels grabs my hand in both of hers.

"Wait."

"Baby…as much as I want to stay, this is *kinda* my job." My smartass comment gets me a pop to the chest.

"No shit, Sherlock, but I have to give you something *before* it."

"Those type of things aren't suitable for primetime TV, Sweet Potato."

She rolls her eyes. "Stop being a perv." My hand gets pulled under the too-long sleeve covering her own, and a few seconds later, something slides over mine and onto my wrist.

The grip on my fingers squeezes, and she blinks up at me expectantly. On my wrist, next to JD's hair tie, is a new one, this one knotted at the end, and printed on the wide elastic are mini Mrs. Potato Heads.

I snort. We've obviously taken this potato thing to obscene levels. Her playing along, though? Just one more thing that proves she's perfect for me.

Risking the wrath of my coach, the officials, and probably all sorts of fines, I scoop her into my arms, her legs automatically going around me, and we kiss again.

Cheers and the occasional fog horn sound as we kiss, creating all sorts of Pinterest inspiration with our very public display of affection.

Keeping her in my arms, I skate us over to the opening she entered from, not lowering her until we get there. I place one last kiss on her lips after I set her down.

"Hope you bought extra." I hold up my arm, letting the material of my jersey fall away to reveal the elastics on my wrist. "Because I just got myself a new superstition, and you know how us hockey players are about our superstitions."

"Don't worry, I bought in bulk, All-Star."

"I love you, Sweet Potato." I shoot her a wink, skating backward.

"I love you too. Now go win."

Like that was ever in doubt. After what just went down, I'm about to have the best damn puck performance of my life.

Epilogue 1

July

The Fourth of July has always been one of my favorite holidays, and our squad tends to do it up big.

The majority of the offseason is typically spent down the shore. Maddey lives here year-round, my sister and Jake have a huge house a few away from hers, Sammy and Jamie are around, Cage used some of his winnings to get a house for his family, and I share another with a bunch of the guys. This year I've been splitting my time here and in the city since Mels needs to be there for the show. Not today though.

We arrived late last night, driving straight here after Mels was done with her performance. With her show dark every Monday and Broadway doing the same for the holiday, she took the Sunday between off to spend the next three nights here before we need to return.

Usually the festivities are held at Jake and JD's, but this year we will be starting off at my place because today is my "Cup Day." As is tradition, after a team wins the Stanley Cup —yes, the Storm won, and not gonna lie, I'm a little offended you doubted it—each player gets to have the Cup with them for a day.

JD and Skye have been bouncing off the walls—more so than usual—over the social media gold they will be able to capture. The video of the Cup being used to baptize my nieces during Jake's day with the Cup when the Blizzards won is still one of the most watched Cup Day videos on YouTube.

For a trophy that can only be handled by people wearing white gloves until it is presented to the winning team, it is almost appalling the treatment it goes through after.

Beer has been drunk from it, cereal has been eaten out of it, dogs have dined from it, and it has gone swimming and to strip clubs. One of the craziest stories from when the Storm won the Cup back in the 40s was that they burned the mortgage from the Garden in it after paying it off. The resulting extinguishing of the fire by the players peeing on it has been attributed to the fifty-three-year gap until our franchise's next win. It's also probably why Lord Stanley's Cup travels with a chaperone.

I haven't figured out what I want to do yet, but I'll worry about that later. For now, I'm going to focus on the naked woman draped over my chest like I'm her personal body pillow.

Breathing in the familiar scent of bubble gum, I run my fingers through the pink locks fanned across my arm, content to lie here. My season may have ended, but our schedules haven't gotten any less hectic. The press and publicity that's followed winning the Stanley Cup for me and a Tony Award for Mels has been insane.

"*Mmm*, that feels nice." Mels stirs in my arms, her body rubbing deliciously along mine as she stretches.

"Yeah it does." I roll so she's on her back with me hovering over her. Her dark eyes are still a little hazy from sleep as I smooth a thumb over that freckle I love so much.

"Do we have to get up?" She nuzzles into my touch, following the movement of my hand.

The muscles in my stomach jump at the feel of her fingertips tracing the grooves outlining them.

"We have about an hour before the Cup is due to arrive." I place a gentle kiss on her forehead, cupping the back of her head.

"*Mmm*," she moans again as I start to massage the back of her skull, the sound traveling straight to my already-hard-from-morning-wood dick. "*Whatever* will we do to pass the time?" Her teeth nip at the bump of my collarbone.

Hooking one of her legs over my hip, I settle myself between her lush thighs and grind against her with a mutual groan. She's already wet, the heat from her center pulling me in like a beacon.

"I could probably come up with a thing or two if I had to." I tease her with both my words and by running my tongue up her neck to her ear, letting the ball of my piercing drag along her skin in the way she's admitted drives her wild.

"Jase." Her hips thrust against me and I slide through her wetness, the lips of her pussy wrapping around my sensitive head as it bumps over her swollen clit. "Don't tease me."

Like that's gonna happen.

Rolling my hips, I do exactly that. Up and down, I have to grind my teeth each time the crown of my cock flicks over her. She's panting and I'm leaking precum like a spout.

"Jason," she growls. I smile into her neck at the use of my full name. It's cute how she does it any time she wants me to know she means business.

"*Fine*, ruin all my fun." I pull back with a pout.

"If you think this"—she grinds against me with a squeeze of her strong dancer legs—"isn't fun, you're doing it wrong, All-Star."

Really? I had to go and fall in love with a woman who was

meant to be a Covenette—AKA a total smartass. *Hello, Pot. Nice to meet you. I'm Kettle.*

"You should know better than to challenge me, baby." I curl my hands around her ribs, my palms leaving a trail of goose bumps down her belly as my fingers press into her back, skimming down it. Her skin is like the softest silk, and a part of me feels bad for abrading it with the rough calluses on my fingers.

"Why?" Her neck arches with another deep inhalation of bubble gum.

The tips of my fingers overlap as I anchor myself on her hips, tilting them ever so slightly, allowing me to push inside her with my next thrust.

With Mels on the pill, we've ditched the condoms, which only heightens every sensation—the heat, the wet velvet covering me like a glove, each ripple set off from my groin brushing her swollen nub.

"Hope you don't embarrass easily." Another pump and I'm seated to the hilt.

Her ankles lock at the small of my back. "I live with Zoey and Ella." *Not for long,* I think. "Embarrassment was conditioned out of me years ago."

"Good." I dig my fingers into the plump curves of her ass, holding her lower half off the bed. "Because I'm about to make you scream the house down."

All thoughts of the people I share the house with—including both our brothers, at the moment—vanish as we get lost in each other. I may be on top, but my baby gives as good as she gets.

Nails scrape my back, and anyone who isn't around to catch the soundtrack of what is happening behind the *locked* door to my bedroom will know how we spent our morning.

Air puffs against my neck with every breathy moan she exhales.

I want so badly to latch onto the pulse point on her neck

and mark her. If the tongue-lashing I received over the beard burn my playoff beard left on her is any indication, I doubt a hickey would be well received.

Ask me if I give a fuck.

I don't.

"Jase."

Sparks go off with the burn of my scalp from her hands clutching at my hair.

"Mels," I groan.

Though my pumps are lazy, sweat trickles down my spine.

"Jase."

"Mels."

My baby may be underneath me, but she doesn't let that stop her from meeting me thrust for thrust.

Legs squeeze.

Hands clutch.

Nails scratch.

Teeth bite.

My balls draw up tight, the tingle at the base of my spine begins, and I'm not going to last much longer.

Swiveling my hips, the new angle hits that sweet spot inside her. I'm not stopping until she's wailing my name like one of those high notes she's famous for.

Collapsing to the bed, I roll us so she's on top again and not crushed beneath my weight, tracing unidentifiable patterns in the perspiration coating the pearls of her spine.

She expels the most contented sigh, and already my magic dick is readying for the second period of play.

I couldn't tell you how long we stay in a tangled mess of sheets and naked limbs before reality rears its ugly head with a pounding on the door.

"Yo, lovebirds," Cali shouts. "The Cup is here."

"Yeah, so put some pants on and let's do this thing," Tucker adds.

Mels buries her face in my side at the sound of someone gagging, and it only intensifies when we hear Nate complain, "*Really*? We may not hate each other anymore, but I don't need to be hearing this shit about my sister."

The day of the Tonys, Nate and I had a come-to-Jesus moment, getting all the shit between us out on the table. In the month since, our rivalry is almost unrecognizable.

I'm torn between wanting to stay in bed with my girl— hello! She's *naked*—and rushing from the room. I feel like Sean and Carlee on Christmas morning with how excited I am.

The slap of skin rings out when Mels tap-taps my chest. "Come on, All-Star."

"Hmm?" I hug her to me.

"You're practically vibrating right now. Get up. Put some pants on like Tuck suggested and let's go get the Cup." She extracts herself from my hold, slipping into one of my Storm t-shirts and a pair of cutoffs. "I already know the first thing you can do with it." She kneels on the edge of the bed, leaning over me.

Glittering onyx eyes look at me with so much love my own heart swells. She doesn't have on a stitch of makeup and her pink hair is a wild tangle of sex waves, but she's never looked more beautiful to me. I love this woman so damn much I can barely stand it at times.

Pushing one of her errant waves behind her ear, I ask, "Really, Sweet Potato? And what's that?"

She places a kiss on the tip of my nose, pulling back with a smirk. "Brush your teeth with it on the counter."

"Are you saying I have morning breath?" I feign offense.

"*Sooo* bad."

She squeals when I grab her, flipping her under me again and laying a kiss on her so hot neither one of us is able to give a damn about morning breath.

The Cup can wait a few more minutes. The woman in my arms is all the trophy I'll ever need.

Melody

Epilogue 2

I'm all for a good improv prompt, but even I don't know how to respond when my boyfriend's sister and surrogate sister smother me in hugs for going viral all before my morning coffee.

The fact that I managed such a feat without being properly caffeinated was a stroke of luck. I mean, how was I supposed to resist snapping a bathroom mirror selfie of a shirtless Jase brushing his teeth, me doing the same next to him in his Storm t-shirt, the Cup in a place of honor on the bathroom counter. The whole scene *screamed* Instagram.

Since then it's been a flurry of other Cup Day photos. It started with Lyle filling it with Jase's favorite coffee from his shop and putting the Storm's logo in the foam on top. Yes he used a stencil for the letters, but he freehanded the crossing hockey sticks behind it and the thundercloud on top, as well as the lightning bolt trailing off the R.

"It's so pretty," I gush.

"Thanks, doll." Lyle wraps an arm around my shoulders and I snuggle into his side. I took an instant liking to the flamboyant barista. The way he unabashedly flirts with all the guys makes for great entertainment.

Jordan and Skye are snapping dozens of pics while they can.

"It's almost a shame for you to drink it," I pout.

"I made an entire pot, so you might want to share or you could end up vibrating," Lyle advises.

"If you start to vibrate, just hold yourself against Mels," Becky calls out from the living room.

"Oh yeah, we ladies do love us a good vibration," Zoey adds, proving once again how dangerous it is for the two of them to be in the same room together.

"*Pfft.*" Vince bro-nudges Jase. "My boy doesn't need vibrations to get his girl off."

"That's what the piercing is for." I shoot Cali the side-eye for the boast, but he only wiggles his tongue at me, making me blush. A quick glance at Jase only gets me a wink, and I heat for an entirely different reason.

"Oh *yeah*. It's all about a good piercing," Tucker brags. The testosterone in the house is creeping toward a gag-inducing level.

"How would you know, Tuck? You don't have your tongue pierced." Ella peers over as if looking for confirmation.

"Not the type of piercing I'm talking about." He shoots a wink at Skye. "Right, Bubble?"

Skye doesn't deem his comment worthy of a response, but the pinking of her fair skin gives her away.

"All right, assholes." Jase claps his hands to get everyone's attention, but before he can continue, two squeaky voices start volleying "*Asshole!*" back and forth. Jordan smacks him upside the head for her cursing two-year-olds.

"I can't even." She facepalms.

"You know I told your brother once I was going to change his text handle to that," I say in a show of solidarity.

"Oh, that would have been a *good* one."

"No-no." Jase wiggles a finger between me and his twin.

"There will be no teaming up of my other half and my better half."

Jordan and I shrug.

"Anyway." The look he gives me promises all sorts of dirty things. "Grab a straw and line up to help me finish this. This Cup has things to do and pictures to take. It can't be doing any of that filled with coffee."

With eight guys drinking, the coffee is gone in no time, and the Cup is promptly washed and dried for the next task.

There are poses of Jase holding it over his head and Nate feigning sadness. The bromance that has formed between my brother and my boyfriend would disturb me if it didn't make my life easier.

Unless they decide to use their newfound love of each other against me, I'm keeping my mouth shut.

Jase and Cali eat spaghetti à la *Lady and the Tramp* to show their Storm solidarity, and then Jase pretends to play tug of war with the Cup against Jake, Ryan, and Tucker.

Before the Cup is used to hold Jase's hotdogs in their—I kid you not—hotdog eating contest, one of the last pictures is Mr. and Mrs. Potato Head lounging on a mini hockey puck float in the "pool" they created inside the Cup, and in between the toys meant to represent us is my Tony Award.

When I think we're done, Jase rushes from the room, his footsteps pounding on the stairs on the way to our bedroom. He's back as quickly as he left and tosses a white t-shirt at me. The move catches me off guard, the material hitting my chest then falling to the ground.

By the time I've scooped it up, he's already changed into his, and I snort when I read the words 'She's my Sweet Potato' written in black lettering. Unfolding mine, I snort again seeing mine reads 'I Yam.'

Grinning like the corny fools we are, we stand behind the Cup, posing with it and our Playskool counterparts.

Jordan suggests us doing one holding them, and when Jase hands me Mrs. Potato Head, she rattles.

I give her a shake, trying to suss out what could be making the noise but failing. I would say it's her extra pieces, but neither of us store them inside the toys.

Flipping open the hatch in the back, I turn her over, leaving my palm open underneath to catch the last thing I expected to find inside.

"Shit! I didn't bring a notebook." I hear Maddey curse but tune out her and all my fellow Covenettes watching us like we're the latest episode of *The Bachelor*.

I look from my hand to my boyfriend and back again, trying to make sense of what I'm seeing.

"Jase?"

He reaches out, taking the metal object from my hand with a wink.

"Mels, baby." Arms snake around my middle. "Our schedules are busier than Walmart on Black Friday." I'm hit with soap and ice as he tugs me even closer. "I want to at least know I get to come home to you at the end of the day."

Is he asking what I think he's asking?

"Will you move in with me?"

Oh-em-gee! He is!

"Are you serious?" My voice rises an octave with each word. I already have the code, but a key to the deadbolt? That proves the place would be mine too.

"As serious as I take my potatoes." He winks again, his eyes swirling green and gold in anticipation of my answer.

I jump him, my arms circling his neck and my legs going around his waist. I taste hints of coffee and tomato sauce as I kiss him long and deep.

"Couldn't have written it better myself," Maddey cheers.

"Am I going to be subjected to this any time I come visit?" my brother grumbles.

"Don't worry, you get used to it," Ryan offers.

"Bullshit, Cap," Becky says. "You still gag whenever Jake loves up on your sister."

"Kissing and hearing about the latest way one of your best friends just dicked down your little sister are two completely different things."

"Can you not use the words *dicked down* and *little sister* together in the same sentence ever again? Please and thank you," Jordan asks.

"Are you sure this is what you want?" I lock eyes with Jase.

"Absolutely." He cups my ass, holding me up like I weigh nothing. God, his strength is one of my biggest turn-ons. "I want to have you in a place all to ourselves."

"All to ourselves?" I arch a brow. "Your place is busier than Grand Central some days."

He nods. "True, but that doesn't change the fact that I want to go to bed with you every night I'm not on the road."

Why does he have to be so swoony?

I bring our foreheads together. "Yes."

His eyes flash the brightest green yet. "Yes?"

"Yes, roomie."

His smile is so wide it rivals any I've ever seen before.

I have a feeling the role of his *roomie* will be my favorite one of all.

Epilogue 3- Justin

While the rest of my friends are distracted by the most recent cohabitation of the group, I step outside onto the back deck, shutting the doors behind me, and make my way onto the beach to avoid being overheard while I handle some business.

I love my sister more than words, but Maddey's stubborn streak is going to get her killed—potentially literally.

For months she hid the fact that she has a stalker from me —and make no mistake, it is a stalker, no matter how much she tries to brush it off—then she goes and rebukes any attempts we make at keeping her safe. It's *infuriating*.

I don't hit women, but I'm *this* close to strangling one.

First, she says nothing.

Then when she does, she downplays the issue entirely.

Every attempt at offering her protection is shot down, no matter where it comes from.

Ryan, the ex-boyfriend turned bestie? Nope.

Sammy, childhood best friend, and his husband Jamie offering up use of one of the rock star's security detail? Declined.

Me, big brother, ex-Navy SEAL turned cop? That would be a big, fat no.

Even our father failed to make her see reason.

Get why I want to strangle her?

The most exasperating part is that she was able to counter any argument we made by throwing the training *I* taught her in my face.

I've only known about it for a month, but to say I epically lost my shit when I found out it has been going on for *eight* months would be like me saying BUD/S was easy.

Maddey tried to mollify me by saying it's only ramped up in the month I've been aware of the situation. Yeah, that went over as well as doing a HALO jump without a chute.

There's only one person she won't be able to charm. He is also one of only a handful of people I can entrust with my sister's life.

The logistics of getting him here and making it possible for him to have the time off will be…complicated.

Good thing there are more than a few brass who owe my family favors.

Time to make some phone calls.

♡

Holy crap! What is going to happen? Find out in June in *Writing Dirty.*

How did Jase and Nate bury the hatchet? Continue reading to find out in the bonus epilogues.

Are you one of the cool people who writes reviews? Puck *Performance can be found on Amazon, Goodreads, and BookBub.*

Bonus Epilogue 1

June, day of the Tony Awards

"Stop being a dumbass and rub the balm on your shoulder *before* you put your tux on." Rocky's gray eyes narrow at me from the television screen.

"Yes, Mom," I drawl.

My bestie's tired face blooms into a smile at my words. They may have been a joke, but as of four days ago, the title became official when my second nephew Ronnie entered the world. She places a kiss to the dark head resting on her shoulder before turning her attention back to me.

"Fine, don't listen to me. It's not like fixing injuries is my job or anything."

"Don't you have more important things to worry about than me?" I point to the sleeping baby.

"I'm both a woman and a Covenette. I can multitask like a pro."

I nod. Damn Coven.

"Look." She levels me with another hard look. "I'm only trying to help. Instead of your night off being used to take it easy, you're going to be doing god knows what as your girlfriend's date. You should be doing whatever you can to make sure you're in top form for tomorrow's game."

Like every other series we've had this playoff season, the Stanley Cup has gone to Game 7. Rocky isn't wrong to be worried. I took one hell of a hit into the boards during the last game and should be resting tonight, but my baby has the biggest night of her life, and I'm not missing it for anything.

My phone rings in the kitchen, and I hold up a finger so Rocky knows I'll be back.

I greet my doorman. "Hey Tobias."

"Hello Mr. Donnelly." I roll my eyes—I've lost count of the number of times I've told him to call me Jase. "I have a Mr. Nate Bishop here to see you."

What is he doing here? Only one way to find out.

"You can send him up."

"Very well." There's a pause. "The limo should be here in half an hour."

"Thank you, Tobias."

"You're welcome, sir."

"Why do you look confused?" Rocky asks as I tap my phone against my thigh.

"Bishop is here."

"Melody's brother?" Rocky sounds as confused as I feel.

I nod. I'm not sure what this means. I figured he'd be with Mels since he's another one of her guests to the Tonys.

I must be more lost in my thoughts than I realize because it feels like no time at all passes before there's a knock on my door. It really is rare that I have a guest who doesn't just let themselves in, and it takes me a second to react.

Moving swiftly to the door, I open it to a sheepish-looking Nate Bishop—not a side of him I'm used to seeing. It's been two and a half weeks since Mels declared herself mine in front of the world—well, anyone tuned in for Game 7 of the Conference Finals—and this is the first time I'm seeing Nate.

"Bishop."

"Donnelly." His hands are stuffed in the pockets of his tuxedo pants. I really do need to finish getting ready.

"Aren't you supposed to be with your sister?"

"Yeah." He drops his gaze, one of his hands lifted to grab the back of his neck. "Um…there's something I…" He clears his throat. "There's something I needed to do first." He shoots his eyes up to look behind me. "Can I come in?"

Respect for my girlfriend has me stepping aside to open the door wider, but there's also a dose of curiosity too.

"Well at least he's dressed for the occasion." I have to bite back a laugh at the way Nate startles hearing Rocky's voice from the speakers in my living room, reminding me I never disconnected our call.

"Goodbye, Balboa." I reach for the remote.

"Don't you dare disconnect this call, Jason Richard," she orders. Ronnie stirs from her raised voice, and she pats his back to soothe him.

"Whoa." I hold my hands up in surrender. "What the hell is with not just the full name but the middle, Raquel Anne?"

She hisses in a breath, not liking having the tables turned.

"Blue," Gage's voice cautions from somewhere off screen. "Let the man go."

"Don't you start, Champ." Rocky's gray eyes continue to bounce between Nate and me, barely paying her husband attention. "If there's a witness, there's less chance of blood-shed. How do you think Jordan would react if she knew I didn't stop her wombmate from ending up in jail?"

Deep male laughter rings out, and Gage steps into view. "You know Jase wouldn't do anything to piss off a Covenette, Blue." He takes his son from his clearly insane wife and drops a kiss to the top of each of their heads before looking my way. "Right?"

I give a mock salute. "Aye-aye, Octopus Man."

Gage shakes his head, muttering, "Asshole."

I smirk.

"Please refrain from doing anything that involves Coven intervention," Gage advises before saying to his wife, "Now say good night to your best friend, Blue."

"Bye, Jase. Love you," Rocky says.

"Bye, Balboa. Love you too."

The screen goes blank as the call disconnects.

Nate's mouth hangs open as his gaze bounces between the television and me. "What?"

"Trust me, you don't want to know," I assure him. "Wanna tell me why you're here?"

Before he can answer, the three beeps signaling my front door unlocking sound and Cali lets himself into my place.

"*Shiiiit*," he drawls when he catches sight of Nate and me. "I shoulda brought my popcorn."

"Rocky?" I have a feeling about his sudden appearance.

"Yup. Not gonna lie, I thought she was messing with me when she called, but looks like tonight's festivities are starting early." He strides inside, making himself at home on one of the stools at the kitchen island.

I want to say something about Rocky calling him to come over, but honestly, I'm more surprised she didn't call JD.

Ring! Ring!

Twin ESP for the win.

I know better than to let the call go unanswered—she'll just keep trying until I pick up. Still, I ignore it in favor of finding out Nate's reason for coming over when I would have seen him anyway in an hour. Unfortunately, Cali isn't of the same mindset and hops over the back of my couch to grab the remote.

I seriously need new friends.

"If it isn't my favorite Donnelly slash Donovan," Cali greets when my sister's face fills the screen, always the suck-up.

"Cali!" She beams at him before looking around for me. "Wow." Her mouth forms an O when she finds me standing next to Nate. "I thought Rock was having a sleep-deprivation-induced hallucination or something."

Unlike when Rocky called, JD's house is packed with the majority of our friends and family. How the hell can Logan be asleep in her arms with the level of noise around him?

"Why aren't you dressed yet?" she scolds.

"I'll be fine." I wave her off. "Unlike you, it doesn't take me hours to get ready."

"Hey!" Her eyes narrow. "I resent that."

"Bro." Jake's face pops into view over her shoulder, placing a quick kiss on her temple before focusing back on me. "If you wanna piss off a Covenette, stick to your own."

My own. I can't help but smile at the fact that yes, yes I do have my own Covenette.

"Cali," Becky calls out, dropping onto the couch.

"Yeah, Beck?"

"Make sure Hemmy puts on the balm Rocky told him about."

"Yes ma'am." He salutes.

"Don't call me *ma'am*."

"Ooo, don't you look handsome," Lyle flirts as he takes in Cali in his tuxedo.

"Why thank you," Cali vamps then tosses a look at me. "At least *someone* can appreciate all this." He waves his hands down his body.

I roll my eyes. *Do not encourage him.*

As if hearing my silent plea, Lyle says, "Well give us a twirl. Let's see the whole thing."

Cali does as asked, and I'm getting the feeling we won't be getting out of here on time and it won't have anything to do with me.

Because this whole thing wasn't enough of a shit-show already, Tucker pops up on the other side of JD, liberating Logan from her arms before pointing to Nate. "Look, if you're adding to the brother husbands, don't you think Vince and I should be there?"

"Yeah, Donnelly, that just hurts," Vince shouts from somewhere in the background.

"Oh bite me, Steele," I retort.

"Oh!" Lyle raises a hand in the air. "Can I volunteer as tribute?"

Jesus. I rub the ridge of my brow. They are in rare form tonight.

"RYAN!" I yell to be heard over the noise. He's the only person—when JD is one of the trouble leaders, at least—who can get them all under control.

"Bro?" He's just in view of the camera inside the kitchen.

"Can you please captain it up in there and control them?"

He snorts. Yeah, yeah, not possible—I know, but I need him to try.

"All right everyone." Ryan pulls out his captain voice. "Say good night to Jase. We'll be watching them on the red carpet soon enough."

A chorus of goodbyes sound and the call blessedly cuts off. If only I could get rid of Cali as easily.

Nate's fish impression from earlier has nothing on the shell-shocked one he's wearing now. Then again, we tend to have that effect on people.

I hold up a hand to cut off any questions before they can form.

"Ryan won't be able to stop them from calling back for long. So, if you wanna have any chance of getting to the reason you're really here, I would save all that"—I circle a finger, gesturing to his *I'm so confused* expression—"until after."

He shakes his head, as if needing to shake himself out of our squad-induced stupor. I know the feeling.

Nate takes a deep breath, his chest rising and falling as if prepping for something. He clears his throat, then does it again before he finally breaks his silence.

"I came here to apologize."

Well that was the last thing I expected him to say.

I fold my arms over my chest. "For what exactly?"

Yes, he's my girlfriend's brother, but I'm not gonna make this easy for him. For years we had beef. He talked shit about me, and more importantly, my wombmate.

Then there was the whole us-not-dating ultimatum he issued Mels...

So yeah, he's not my favorite person.

His Adam's apple bobs as he swallows, looking even more uncomfortable than he did a minute ago.

"For all of it." I arch a brow, not giving him anything. "It was one thing when I made it about us, but I took it too far when I would use Jordan to get under your skin."

Ya think?

Plus, 'under my skin' is an understatement. He's lucky I didn't knock his teeth out.

"I wish I could say *why* I thought it was okay to bring her into this, but I can't." He looks down as if ashamed. "Hell..." He goes to run a hand through his hair but stops at the last second, as if remembering he has it styled for tonight. "I have a sister. I fucking *know* better."

He said it, not me.

"I always assumed you were a player, and I guess when I thought you hooked up with my girlfriend, your sister was the only way I could think to get back at you."

The puzzle is coming together, and I don't miss the piece that is my fault. Looks like Bishop won't be the only one apologizing tonight.

"So...yeah...I'm sorry." He meets my eyes before looking at the blank television then back to me. "If you want to call them back, I'll apologize to Jordan as well, and I guess your brother and Jake too."

I should make him wait, should play with him a little and make him sweat it out, but we don't have time for games. Tonight isn't about us; it's about Mels. Time to squash this so we can finally move on.

"You don't have to," I say.

"Yeah I do."

"No you don't." I shake my head. "I never said anything to them about any of it."

His eyes go wide in disbelief. "Why not?"

I only shrug in response, and he blows out a breath.

"Wow. Shit. Now I really feel like an ass."

My turn. Deep breath.

"It wasn't all your fault." Dark eyes turn my way. "I let you believe we hooked up…we didn't, by the way."

"Mels said she suspected as much."

"You told her?"

"Yeah." Nate nods. "Let's just say she disliked Dana enough that even if you did, she would probably still thank you."

I laugh, the tension gone. "How about a little quid pro quo?"

"What do you mean?"

"I'll never tell my family about the JD stuff if you promise never to bring up how I let you think I hooked up with your girlfriend while I was dating Rocky."

"The one you were talking to when I got here?" He points at the dark screen.

"Yup." I nod. "Even though nothing happened, she would still kick my ass for letting someone assume I could have cheated on her. I'd rather not mess with the MMA Princess."

"Deal." Nate reaches out a hand to shake then starts pacing.

Cali—who has been watching us like an episode of *Keeping Up with the Kardasians*—barks out a laugh, but other than that, he stays quiet.

"This all just makes me feel guiltier for issuing that ultimatum." Nate stops his pacing, closing the distance between us. "If that's the type of guy you are, I'm proud to have you date my sister." He holds out his hand for another shake.

After Melody's *very* public declaration, he came to terms with us dating, even if we would never be besties. But...who knows? After this, maybe that's a possibility.

To joke or not to joke?

"Look," I say, deciding to go with serious, "I love your sister very much. I'm going to do everything in my power to never hurt her again."

"I know." The way he says it, I can tell he means it. "She's happier with you than without. I noticed it even when she was keeping your relationship a secret."

"Bro." I can't help but laugh, the *Girl, same* GIF flashing in my brain. "I know *all* about sisters dating in secret. Remind me to tell you about JD and Jake after I get ready."

We share a bro nod of understanding. I start for my bedroom but pause.

"Look..." It took a lot for him to come here; I recognize that. Time for me to extend an olive branch of my own. "I know all about how much your parents suck—don't even get me started on them not coming tonight—so I want you to know...Mels isn't the only one who gets to be a part of our crazy." I circle a finger in the air. "We'll take you too."

With that I spin on my heel and head off to change into my tux.

"Looks like we are getting another brother husband," I hear Cali call to my back.

Can't really argue with that.

Melody

Bonus Epilogue 2

The Tony Awards

I'm not sure *what* has happened in the few hours since my brother up and left my apartment, but I highly suspect he was abducted by Pod People because the way he and Jase have been acting together is weird.

"Should we be worried they're on drugs?" Zoey links an arm with mine as we make our way down the aisle to our seats inside Radio City Music Hall.

Stopping to watch where Jase, Nate, and Cali are yucking it up, I let the significance of what I'm seeing wash over me. Zoey's question mirrors some of my own thoughts, but this is too special to let any doubts ruin it.

Yes, things have been okay between Nate and myself and civil between Nate and Jase since the day I laid down the law with my brother and went to get my man back. But...if I'm being honest, I haven't been able to shake the feelings of sadness and abandonment I felt during those months Nate and I barely spoke.

I never doubted my conviction to be with Jase, but life would be *so* much easier if the two most important men in my life got along. The longer I watch them, though, the more I think maybe not so much.

"Oh, let them have their fun." Ella also links an arm with me on my other side.

Following Ella's advice, we take our seats as the guys finish taking a selfie and Cali says something about tagging their other brother husbands. Though he has a penchant for stopping by unannounced and interrupting things, he has quickly become one of my favorite people. I still can't believe he's here, but he *insisted* on being included as one of my guests.

"Nervous, Sweet Potato?" Jase's voice rumbles through me when he places a kiss to the soft spot behind my ear.

"Yup." I peek at him out of the corner of my eye, a smile tipping the edges of my lips up. "I'm more excited than anything, though."

Our show will be performing one of our bigger numbers later in the evening, and that is what I am choosing to focus on instead of my nomination. My category is one of the later-presented ones, and I'll be a complete basket case by the time it comes if I think about it now.

Though this is my first time being nominated individually, this isn't my first time at the Tonys. It never gets old, though. There is just something so special about this community, and it's so much fun to celebrate with them all.

We cheer, we laugh, and some of us tear up as we watch the performances and listen to acceptance speeches. Jase fields a few texts from Vince complaining about us not letting him come because Mr. Wolverine himself, Hugh Jackman, is hosting—again. I tried to explain how accomplished of a stage actor the ex-X-Man is, but he didn't want to hear it.

After our show nails our performance, it's finally time.

"And the Tony Award for the Best Performance by a Leading Actress in a Musical goes to"—Jase squeezes my hand and I suck in a breath, the seconds spent waiting for the announcement feeling like years—"Melody Brightly!" Everything else the presenter says turns to static after my name.

I won.

Oh my god, I won.

I won. I really won.

Is this real life?

I'm wrapped in my favorite pair of strong arms and kissed before being passed off for another embrace. In a daze, I accept the hugs from Nate, Zoey, Ella, and Cali before receiving another from Jase.

They said my name, right?

"Baby." Jase's voice breaks into my stupor. "It's time to get your fine ass up on stage." He jerks his chin.

"Don't trip, Broadway," Cali supplies, so not helping.

I know both the audience here and those watching at home are being told how this is my first time being nominated and winning, but I don't hear any of it as I walk up the stairs to the stage and accept the spinning medallion statue that serves as the award for the Tonys.

The lights are bright, my eyes blinking furiously against both them and the tears I will be losing the battle to any second.

There's applause and cheers and more than a few comments from my people that I'm sure aren't usually heard at the Tonys.

My hands clutch my award like a lifeline, one hand supporting the base, the other wrapping around the neck underneath where the medallion spins.

I swallow, looking out into the clapping audience, many of them on their feet, including my fellow nominees.

I'm pretty sure I'm dreaming, but if I am, I'm going to enjoy it until my alarm goes off.

Find your words, Mels. Time to give a speech.

One more time, I scan one of the most iconic performance halls in the city, starting with the seats at the top and finally settling on the group I brought here with me. Ella and Zoey are holding hands, leaning into each other for support over the armrest separating them, tears openly falling down their cheeks. Zoey looks just as happy for me as she did when she accepted her own Tony for Best Choreography.

Cali keeps cupping his hands around his shit-eating-grinning mouth, bellowing in a way more appropriate for one of his hockey games than this awards ceremony.

Finally I look at the two most important men in my life, both watching me with so much love and pride it should be illegal. Even more surprising than the award in my hands is the bromance that seems to be brewing between the two of them. I have no idea what happened when Nate left my apartment earlier, but I'm starting to suspect I may have preferred it when they were rivals.

Speech, Mels.

Oh right.

Okay, I can do this.

Clear the throat. Deep breath.

"I already know I'm going to forget at least one person, so for them I want to say thank you."

Titters of laughter meet my statement.

"Marilyn Monroe was a dream role for me in so many ways." I lock eyes with Nate. "As my dear brother will attest, I have been obsessed with who I refer to as the OG bombshell pretty much my whole life."

I see Nate nod, and I'm sure they are showing it on TV for those watching at home.

"I tortured him with hours of watching her films over and over through the years. But, to be fair, Marilyn was hot, so I *doubt* it was *that* much of a hardship for him."

Another round of laughter.

"Plus I know I more than returned the favor going to so many of his hockey games through the years."

He thumps his chest twice then points to me as if to say, *I got you.*

"I was hit with the acting bug early, and from every teacher I had from kindergarten through high school, I share this award with you for all the things you taught me. Broadway has been a second home to me for more than half my life, and I've been blessed to work with so many amazing people through the years."

I shift my gaze back to Ella and Zoey.

"Two of my best friends have been a part of some of them, and though Zoey, our amazing choreographer, took *great* joy in kicking my ass both across the stage and back at home, it is as much of a dream come true to be able to share this with you as it is to win."

I smile when Zoey buries her face into Ella's neck, but I sober quickly, not wanting them to miss the sincerity of what I say next.

"Zoey, Ella, and Nate." I wait until I have their attention. "Without you, I wouldn't have been able to do this. My support system may not have been large (mentally flipping dear ol' Mom and Dad off), but the three of you were strong enough to carry the load until our cavalry of Covenettes and other crazies found us."

Finally, I shift my gaze to Jase, finding his hazel eyes already locked on me. He mouths, "*I love you*," and I know he caught my reference to him.

"My ah-may-zing boyfriend"—I shoot him a wink, thinking of how I give him crap when he says that word like that—"likes to say my eight weekly shows put his own game schedule to shame, but getting to do the thing I love six days a week never feels like work."

I lift my Tony and use it to point at Jase.

"I won my award. Now it's your turn." Cali wraps his arms around Jase's neck in a headlock. "Besides...we can't drink champagne out of mine like we can the Cup."

All the hometown fans inside Radio City cheer for the Storm as I turn from the microphone, and before I can make it backstage, Jase is there, pulling me into his arms and dipping me back for a kiss worthy of its own Tony.

I grab one of his lapels with my free hand, holding on for dear life, though there's no need because he'll never drop me. As his wicked piercing whirls inside my mouth, I know this right here is the only award I'll ever need.

Randomness For My Readers

Whoop! Welcome to the craziness that makes up my mind.

I hope you enjoyed Jase and Melody's story and hanging out with the BTU Alumni Squad again.

If everyone was new to you, you can see where the group began and learn the story of Jordan's ex in *Power Play*, see what went down with Curtis 'The Cutter' Cutler in Tap Out, and how Jase told Vince to bend the knee in *Sweet Victory*.

So now for a little bullet style fun facts:

* I have the same Marilyn painting as Melody and until I moved in with the Hubs it hung above my bed too.

* *Gentlemen Prefer Blondes* and *How to Marry a Millionaire* are my favorite Marilyn movies.

* The Hubs and I love all the different sports All-Star Skills Challenges. The NHL's is our favorite but our Valentine's Day weekend tradition is to watch the NBA's skills comps.

* The old shootout challenge was my favorite and I can't tell you how many hours of footage I watched on YouTube writing this. Trust me, if you aren't familiar with it, look it up. I dare you to watch it without a smile on your face.

* If this was the first book you've read of mine I can tell

you *Friends* is one of my all time top shows. But like the crew here, *Sons of Anarchy, Saved by the Bell,* and *Full House* are right up there too.

* The Duel is loosely based off of a piano bar in NYC.

* You can meet all the boys from BoP in The Rule Breaker Anthology coming out April 2020. I'm super honored to have Sammy and Jamie's story to be included in a book with some of my author besties.

* Karaoke was a staple of my squad when we were younger. We would go to the bar for it every Wednesday night.

* I too played Peter's sister in a school production. But I was in 2nd grade and that was the end of my acting career lol.

* You know I love to fangirl and give a shoutout in my books to some of my faves so of course I had to go with my girl LJ Shen's Hotholes. I just love all those alpha holes so damn much. Plus she is one of the sweetest people the internet has brought into my life.

* The TV show *SMASH* was a big inspiration for Melody's musical. I was so, so sad when it got cancelled.

* Fun fact. I went to a wedding this past fall and one of my Covenettes used packing tape to secure her boobs. And yes I did warn her I would tell this story lol.

* The Cup Day stories are a real thing. I have a bunch of them pinned on the BTU4 Pinterest board.

*The story about the Garden's mortgage is actually a true story about the NY Rangers.

If my rambling hasn't turned you off and you are like "This chick is my kind of crazy," feel free to reach out!

Lots of Love,

Alley

For A Good Time Call

Did you have fun meeting The Coven? Do you want to stay up-to-date on releases, be the first to see cover reveals, excerpts from upcoming books, deleted scenes, sales, freebies, and all sorts of insider information you can't get anywhere else?

If you're like "Duh! Come on Alley." Make sure you sign up for my newsletter.

Ask yourself this:
 * Are you a Romance Junkie?
 * Do you like book boyfriends and book besties? (yes this is a thing)
 * Is your GIF game strong?
 * Want to get inside the crazy world of Alley Ciz?

If any of your answers are yes, maybe you should join my Facebook reader group, Romance Junkie's Coven

Join The Coven

Stalk Alley
 Join The Coven
 Get the Newsletter

Like Alley on Facebook
Follow Alley on Instagram
Hang with Alley on Goodreads
Follow Alley on Amazon
Follow Alley on BookBub
Subscribe on YouTube for Book Trailers
Follow Alley's inspiration boards on Pinterest
All the Swag
Book Playlists
All Things Alley

Acknowledgments

This is where I get to say thank you, hopefully I don't miss anyone. If I do I'm sorry and I still love you, just you know, mommy brain.

I'll start with the Hubs—who even though he gave me crap **again** that *this* book also isn't dedicated to him he's still the real MVP—he has to deal with my lack of sleep, putting off laundry *because... laundry* and helping to hold the fort down with our three crazy mini royals. You truly are my best friend. Also, I'm sure he would want me to make sure I say thanks for all the hero inspiration, but it is true (even if he has no ink *winking emoji*)

To my Beta Bitches, my OG Coven: Gemma, Jenny, Megan, Caitie, Sarah, Nova, Andi, and Dana. Our real life Coven Conversations give me life.

To Stef and Michele for taking another pass over Jase to make sure he was as perfect as he deserved.

To Jenny (again) my PA, without her I wouldn't be organized enough for any of my releases to happen. Thank you for being the other half of my brain and video chatting all hours, damn our timezones and letting me break your heart over and over with this book. You know I live for your shouty capitals.

For Jess my editor for always pushing me to make the story just that much deeper. Some of those shouty capitals are in your honor lol.

For Caitlin my other editor for entering my crazy and making sure my words sparkle.

To Gemma (again) for going from my proofreader to fangirl and being so invested in my characters stories to threaten my life *lovingly of course* I can't even begin to tell you how entertained I was by all your hockey questions.

To Dawn for giving *Puck Performance* it's final spit shine.

To Mama Dukes for taking me to my first Broadway show and making me fall in love with musical theater from the first time you ever had me watch *The Sound of Music*. All these years later seeing a show with you is still one of my favorite things to do.

To my street team for being the best pimps ever. Seriously, you guys rock my socks.

To my ARC team for giving my books some early love and getting the word out there.

To every blogger and bookstagrammer that takes a chance and reads my words and writes about them.

Thank you to all the authors in the indie community for your continued support. I am so happy to be a part of this amazing group of people.

To my fellow Covenettes for making my reader group one of my happy places. Whenever you guys post things that you know belong there I squeal a little.

And, of course, to you my fabulous reader, for picking up my book and giving me a chance. Without you I wouldn't be able to live my dream of bringing to life the stories the voices in my head tell me.

Lots of Love,
Alley

Also by Alley Ciz

BTU Alumni Series
Power Play (Jake and Jordan)

Musical Mayhem (Sammy and Jamie) BTU Novella

Tap Out (Gage and Rocky)

Sweet Victory (Vince and Holly)

Puck Performance (Jase and Melody)

Writing Dirty (Maddey and Dex)

Scoring Beauty- BTU6 Preorder, Releasing September 2021

#UofJ Series
Cut Above The Rest (Prequel)- Freebie

Looking To Score

Game Changer

Playing For Keeps

Off The Bench- #UofJ4 Preorder, Releasing December 2021

The Royalty Crew (A #UofJ Spin-Off)
Savage Queen- Preorder, Releasing April 2021

Ruthless Noble- Preorder, Releasing June 2021